CHRISTOPHER MATSON

Half Sword

Tapestry – Codex I

BISAC: FIC009100 (Fantasy / Action & Adventure), FIC009030 (Fantasy / Historical), FIC014020 (Historical / Medieval)

Editing by Jessie Campbell - https:// ruffdraft.pub

Cover art by Drazenka Kimpel - https:// creativedust.com

First edition

ISBN: 978-1-7368811-1-8

This book was professionally typeset on Reedsy.
Find out more at reedsy.com

Contents

Author's Note

The Tapestry adventures take place in the turbulent early medieval period when the crypts below Rome were filled with mysteries and sorcerers plied their dark arts in the decaying ruins of the former empire. I've maintained historical accuracy by drawing on period sources dealing with demonology, hermetic philosophy, Zohar, and ceremonial magic. The dialog is peppered with words borrowed from the languages of the time and I tried to keep their meaning clear through context or brief explanation as part of the narrative. A detailed Appendix covering language, characters, and key elements can be found at the end. I have also created some maps that can be found on my website at www.cbmatson.com.

If you enjoy this story, please be sure to leave me a review on Amazon or Goodreads.

Christopher Matson

Anno Domini 1187

Simon walked the rutted path alongside a great rotating wheel of oak staves and iron rim. Drawn by two stoic oxen, the high-sided cart rumbled along. The oxcart moved, the wheel rotated, and at his feet, the path remained as steadfast as ever from time immemorial.

The road had always been part of young Simon's life, or what little of it he remembered. The flower bedecked fields, the profusion of birds, the high puffy clouds, any of these wonders would have fascinated most travelers. Not Simon. No, it was a dirty gray rag tied to one spoke that held his attention. Circling behind him and rising up, up above his head, it plunged to the earth at his feet... and that was the mystery.

Simon dropped two paces behind and watched it again. *I will catch it next time.* The cart lurched forward, the wheel turned, the rag circled to the earth until that briefest of instants when it kissed the solid ground at a dead stop, then up, up, and around again. *How could something move forward by constantly stopping?* Simon looked away, counting—*six, seven, eight*—his eyes flew back to the errant rag. It rested against the ground as if it had never left.

He trotted to the head of the laboring team where an old man guided his animals. "Master, what deviltry is it that allows a wheel to move forward while standing still?"

The old man didn't bother turning. He flicked a slender willow switch at the near ox. "Yesterday, you asked why a bird sings for all to hear but will not allow itself to be seen." Simon began to speak, but his master interrupted him. "And... the day before you wanted to know if there was a place where rain fell upward that it might later descend on our heads."

Simon held his tongue. He understood that he was being rebuked but not why. Master Jacob knew so many things yet explained so little. They rolled on in silence, crossing one boggy meadow after another. The sun broke from behind a bank of clouds as their path climbed from a muddy creek bed and passed beneath the lowering eave of a shadowy forest. Jacob switched the oxen. "Run on ahead, boy, and find us a dry place to rest for the night."

Snatching that scrap of liberty, Simon bounded up the path. His bony knees bobbed like a pair of feeding swallows. Beneath his feet, the slippery clay gave way to pebbles and clumps of grass. He passed a stand of twisted oak and thorny brush. Beyond, more trees bent their boughs overhead and cast a myriad of wavering shadows in the afternoon sun.

Simon estimated that he'd gone a thousand turns of the oxcart's wheel when he found the clearing. No water, but grass for grazing and a dry place to make camp. Downwind from where he knew his master would want the cart, he set a circle of stones and a stack of twigs. Simon used his knife to scrape a dry stick and create a nest of shaving. *Hurry, hurry, the team comes here soon.* He fumbled flint and steel from his cloak. *Light fire, I can do this.* By the time he heard the creak and rumble of wheels and oxen, Simon had a modest fire banked to coals next to a stack of firewood.

Their life on the road had followed the same pattern since leaving the Volga river-port of Tver. Master Jacob guided the oxen and chose the road, while Simon attended to smaller matters such as camp chores. The old man seldom spoke, and Simon usually contented himself with his own private musings. But now, with light fading from the evening sky and their fire little more than glowing coals, he caught his master eyeing him where he sat. Simon touched one of the warm rocks. "Why are there river-washed stones up here in the forest while only mud and weeds grow down in the creeks?"

"Perhaps it's time I asked some questions." His master shifted a little closer. "Why is it that people call you Simon *Prostoi*, Simple Simon?"

"I am not so smart like they are. I don't know much."

"You must know something—you can read, write, and count. You ask questions that would baffle a pack of philosophers."

"I don't want to baffle philosophers. Just sleep now."

"First, tell me who you were before I found you."

Simon poked their fire with a stick and watched the ensuing sparks glitter into the evening air. His chest burned every time the old man asked this question. "Empty. I was hungry and cold and empty."

"You speak Latin like a priest. Your rags were once fine wool. You were somebody."

"I don't know a somebody—I just don't know." Simon dropped the stick and buried his head in his arms. "They emptied me."

"They? Who did this to you, Simon?"

"I don't know." It hurt so much that he couldn't suppress the sob. "Just leave me alone."

In the darkness of his crossed arms, he didn't have to bear his master's gaze, didn't have to think. Simon waited, but no more questions came. He dozed off, huddled in a ball. Shivering awake, the fire gone to white ashes, Simon rummaged through the oxcart for his blankets and made a bed in the shelter of the cart's enormous wheels.

The next day, they rumbled through a sparse forest where the path narrowed, dwindled, and vanished into a maze of stones and dead leaves. Master Jacob let him lead the oxen this time. Simon walked on their left and switched the near ox to let it know he was in charge. *Tumbrel*, Master Jacob had called it—a big word for nothing more than a box on two wheels. "*Tum, tum, tumbrel,*" Simon mumbled as he walked.

On occasion, a row of saplings would bar their way. The tumbrel would creak to a halt, the oxen would snort and stamp their great splayed hooves, and Simon would drag out the rusting stump of a broken sword to hack a path through the new growth.

The first time they stopped, he counted two generations of dead trees, hewn to the ground. Simon vaguely recalled cutting them himself. Later that morning, they eased the team and their heavy cart down a steep hill, only to find the way blocked once more. Simon dragged out the ancient blade and cleared a passage through the brush. "Why is it, Master, that we don't stay on the main road to Krakow? All the other traders go that way."

"And all the other traders pay tolls and suffer the predation of robbers. In centuries past, this was a Roman military route. My father showed me the way long after the others forgot.”

“This takes us to Rome?”

“It would, if we didn’t stop in Vienna.”

“Wolf of Nussdorf,” Simon chanted. “We pay at the river… Oh yes, we always pay the Wolf.”

The old man picked up the willow switch and goaded his oxen forward. Simon marched along behind. “Tum, tum, tumbrel.”

At the bottom of the hill, they forded a shallow stream and climbed the opposite side. Simon pushed, the oxen strained, and slowly the heavy cart ascended a rough cut in the bank. They passed a ruined stone abutment. He remembered it from earlier journeys, but this time Simon recognized it for what it was. “A bridge was here.”

“Indeed, a few timbers remained in my father’s day, but it is nearly gone now.”

“So this *was* a road, but how do you find it every year?”

“Just ahead. I’ll show you.”

“If I was a robber, I would wait right here for us to come.”

“If you were a robber, you would starve waiting. No, they have too many opportunities on the road to waste time in this wilderness.”

Simon trudged on for a while before saying, “What if robbers knew we had ermine and sable from the North?”

“That’s why we never go farther than Vienna. We will pay our ferry tax to cross the Danube at Nussdorf. By the time we reach Vienna, the whole world will know what we carry. I would rather sell it there than chance the river or the road any farther. Now stop a moment, and I’ll show you something.”

Master Jacob indicated a polished white stone half buried in forest debris. “Take a closer look at that.”

Simon knelt and dug away the leaves and rotting sticks. A square marble column emerged—perhaps two hands’ width on a side—it bore markings, numerals. “Forty-eight, Master Jacob. Why does it say forty-eight?”

“Forty-eight Roman miles to the old fort outside of Krakow. We will sleep within the city walls in less than three days.”

"How did you know this was here?"

"The Roman army left a stone for every mile along their road. I knew we would come across one soon."

Simon counted turns of the great wheel as they walked. Over a span in diameter, it ate up eight paces, four long strides, every time the tattered rag spun into the air and flopped against the ground. At two hundred turns, he started watching. By two hundred and fifty, he became anxious. Simon searched the bushes and grassy clumps along the way. He gave up at two hundred and seventy but kept counting.

The great wheel turned five hundred and twenty times before Simon spotted the white crown of another milestone poking through the ground. Almost at his feet, he bent to dig the hard rocks and clay from its face. When Simon looked up, the oxcart had disappeared over a low rise. He abandoned the project and ran to catch up with his master. "Why did the Romans bury their markers?"

"It was time that buried those markers, boy. Time, a thousand years of time and neglect."

The entire next day, Simon played a game of looking for milestones. He saw five before they stopped that evening. The following day he tried *not* to see them. Still, fifteen pale white stones peeked out of the weeds and leaves as he passed. Master Jacob halted them early, and Simon recognized the site as one they had used before. A square marble column stood nearby. He read the inscription: XV. "Only fifteen miles to Krakow. Why do we stop here?"

"Would you prefer arriving at night when the gates are barred? There will be plenty of brigands outside waiting for just such fools."

Simon grinned at his master and stirred a thick gruel of crushed oats and lard. "I rather am inside eating sausages, but I can wait."

The old man smiled back, stood, and returned shortly with a palm-sized block of brown material. "Here, the last of our salted venison—chop it up and stir it in. Tonight, we feast."

Simon built up the fire and added the meat. He had to replenish the wood twice before the hard block of venison cooked down enough to cut. The old man gazed up at the ascending pillar of smoke, shook his head, and grunted about thieves.

They ate as darkness fell, and their fire burned to glittering coals. Master Jacob slept in the oxcart as usual. Simon tried to sleep underneath, but the ground was littered with stones. Instead, he arranged his blankets behind a clump of trees where soft grass and brackens grew thick.

Dark dreams of fire and pain gave way to the sound of soft voices and bellowing oxen. Simon opened his eyes and tossed off the blankets. *Visitors?* He was about to step into the clearing when Master Jacob cried out. Shouts, blows, then a cacophony of smashing and harsh laughter. Simon stood in the darkness—his heart compressed in fear. He should go to his master's aid. He wanted to do something, but his feet wouldn't move. Falling to a crouch, shivering, holding his knees, Simon closed his eyes and let the waves of terror bathe him in shame.

He waited, unable to move. After the clank and rattle of harness, the rumble of wheels, and the laughter faded away, Simon remained frozen, unwilling to see what waited in the clearing, clinging to the fantasy that he was still Master Jacob's helper and not the trembling coward who had let his only friend die. Finally, the awakening birds, the growing light, and his aching muscles drove him to stand, drove him to step from the woods into the clearing.

Stripped naked, Master Jacob lay crumpled in a heap, his face bludgeoned to an unrecognizable mass. One of the intruders had emptied his bowels on the old man's back, and all about, their small possessions had been scattered like trash. Simon couldn't bear to look at the body. He retched on an empty stomach and shook in the gray dawn chill. Shredded blankets and trampled cooking gear, Simon poked about the ruined campsite. What little food remained stank of urine.

Not far from the path, the hilt of Jacob's broken sword poked from beneath a cluster of leaves. Simon dragged it into the morning sunlight. About half the blade remained. Slightly longer than his forearm, fresh blood smeared its jagged stump. He pictured his master swinging it in the darkness, a last futile defense against the marauders.

Marauders, something he almost remembered. Something from long ago stood at the edge of his consciousness, then fled.

The sword made a better shovel than it had a weapon. Simon spent most of that morning digging a shallow grave next to mile post fifteen. He used the blade to lever cobbles and large stones from the hole. Standing almost to his knees, he scraped the dirt into mounds and scooped it out with his hands. When the rusty hilt had finally torn enough skin from his palms, Simon looked up and regarded what remained of his master.

Bony and frail, the battered corpse bore little resemblance to the man he'd once known. Simon climbed from the grave and crept toward Jacob's body. With a scrap of torn blanket, he scraped off the mound of feces and cleaned the blood and filth from his master's wrinkled skin. Face up, Simon dragged him to the grave and buried him beneath a pile of earth and rocks.

I need something—something more. A Latin phrase came unbidden to his lips. "*Requiem aeternam dona eis, Domine.*" Simon couldn't remember where he'd learned it—*Grant him eternal rest Lord*—somehow the words seemed fitting. His world spun, and Simon fell to his knees. Words spilled from his mouth like water from the lips of a drowned man. "*Dies iræ, dies illa, solvet sæclum in favilla...*"

And there was more. Simon clutched his breast and sobbed them out, line after line. He had no idea why he knew these strange phrases and barely understood what they meant. Eventually, the fit passed. The boy, stoic at first, now simply wept for the loss of his friend.

It was the emptiness, the feeling of utter abandonment that finally cut through Simon's grief. That and the emptiness in his belly. He rose from his master's cairn and surveyed the litter strewn about their campsite. He thought of planting the broken sword as a grave marker, but the Roman milestone served just as well. Wheel ruts and disturbed loam provided a clear trail. Simon followed them and didn't look back.

Most of that afternoon, he trudged after the oxcart, fearing he would never catch up while hoping he didn't. Tucked into his belt, the broken sword thumped against his leg. Simon considered tossing it by the wayside, but it remained his one connection with Master Jacob.

As the sun fell below the line of trees, Simon realized that he hadn't seen a milestone in some time. Shadows creeping from under thickets of brush obscured the oxcart's passage. Daylight faded to evening's gloom and Simon found himself blundering through a maze of pine branches and thorn bushes. Halting in confusion, he realized night was coming, and he'd lost the trail.

Master Jacob would know. Simon remembered that he'd buried his master that morning. He thought of calling for help, but his imagination filled the dark woods with bandits and worse. He could sleep, but he had left his bedding back at their old encampment. Simon crouched and hugged his knees. Quiet rustling—small creatures pursued their own business in the leaves. Nightjars flitted between the branches, cooing and churring. He remained still and listened for wolves.

It wasn't wolves but the shouts of men that roused him. The forest had gone dark with only the barest gleam of moonlight shining between the trees. At first, he cowered, afraid of being hunted, afraid of the jeering, shouting band that had murdered his master. Hunger and curiosity warred with fear and eventually won. He crept toward the noises.

Farther away than he thought, the shouts and sounds of fighting echoed through the woods like the cries of a lost phantom. Stumbling down a short slope, Simon brushed pine branches from his face and stopped at a broad clearing. There had been a fire. He could smell it now, though only coals remained. Across the clearing, Master Jacob's ponderous tumbrel stood, limned against the night sky, and surrounded by dancing shadows.

Drawn by the familiar silhouette, Simon took a few steps closer. A blow to his back drove him sprawling, face-first onto the ground. A pair of knees crashed down on his ribs. A knife pressed against his neck, and a voice hissed in his ear, "We kill spies."

A Northern dialect of the Vulgate, Simon barely understood. Spitting out grass and dirt, he responded in Latin, "I am Simon. That is my master's cart."

The knife pressed harder. A rough hand clutched him by the hair and bent his head back. "Where is your master?"

"You know he is dead. You left him, and then I had to bury him. Why did you steal his cart—are you a thief?"

The knife hand relaxed and the weight came off Simon's ribs. "Leave your sword and stand."

"It is only half a sword. The half with a handle on it. It was my master's, and I want to keep it."

A few moments passed before Simon heard the man sigh and felt the knife leave his neck. "Stand then, Halfsword. I'm tired of killing tonight."

"My name is Simon." He pushed himself to his feet. "I came with that cart and I am very hungry."

The shouting and commotion had fallen quiet, and someone had rekindled the fire. Simon felt the other man sizing him up. A grunt and a shove sent him stumbling toward the flickering light. Others had congregated around the makeshift camp. As the two approached, one of the men accosted them. "Is that you, Yohan?"

"Ya, I caught us a spy."

"I am not a spy." Simon found he could understand their dialect, locked away perhaps in the lost halls of his memory.

"He says he is Simon Halfsword, owner of this oxcart."

A shadowy figure approached. Taller than Simon and broad through the shoulders, the man wore a short beard and an iron helmet. "If you owned this oxcart, Halfsword, you would be dead by now. Stand near the fire that I may get a better look at you."

Simon was glad of the warmth and relieved that he wouldn't be killed right away. As he stood under the gaze of the two men, another pair approached, dragging a bloody corpse. Shortly, two more arrived with their own grisly burden. Simon realized that three other bodies lay in a heap nearby. "Are you going to shit on their backs?"

"Ya—What?"

Simon tried to copy their odd dialect. "Will you steal their clothing and foul them like you did my master?"

His captor, the one they called Yohan, grabbed him by the collar. "Do you mock us, boy? We did not kill your master."

The taller man put a hand on Yohan's shoulder. "Easy, friend. I think I know what is happening here." He looked at Simon. "Who was your master?"

"Master Jacob. He was killed and that is his cart."

Four others had gathered while Simon spoke. They didn't gawk or jeer but stood in watchful silence. The tall man said, "Ramon, Luca, secure our horses and gear." He turned to Yohan. "Take Stephan and Carla. Check our perimeter and set a watch for tonight. We ride in the morning."

Yohan gave Simon an appraising glance before disappearing into the shadows. The others departed in silence. Simon waited while they left. "If you didn't kill my master, then why did you kill these men?"

"They were thieves, marauders, a pestilence infesting this land."

"Then you infest this land too? Is that what you do? Infest?"

"No, we cleanse, we..." The tall man paused a moment, pushed his iron helmet to one side, and scratched his head. "By Holy Freyja, perhaps we do. Where are you from, Simon Halfsword? You speak church Latin."

"I came from the woods, where knife man Yohan found me."

"Before that, do you remember?"

Now it was Simon's turn to scratch his head. "We left Tver. Now it is the woods and the cart, only the woods and the cart. I'm hungry—do you have food?"

"When Yohan returns, we will all take a small meal. You should rest."

"I will rest. Oh yes, that will be good. Are you master of the cart now?"

"I am called Cernak of Umbria, leader of this cohort. And yes, perhaps I am master of the cart. Rest, Simon Halfsword... and try not to ask so many questions."

Krakow

Once again alongside the rumbling wheel, Simon noted with satisfaction that the rag he'd attached when they left Tver still circled overhead and flopped to the earth. Simon decided that Cernak would be a fair master and helped where he could in breaking down their camp and harnessing the oxen.

Dawn had barely lit the treetops when they hove in sight of the Krakow city walls. Yohan rode up from behind, and Simon hailed him. "Now we will have sausages."

"What makes you so sure?"

"We always have sausages in Krakow. They are the best, and we eat them."

"And who will buy these sausages, Halfsword?"

Simon halted midstride. "Master Jacob always bought me sausages." It came back to him—his master was dead, buried beneath milepost XV. "I... I cannot have sausages in Krakow anymore."

Yohan had reigned his horse back and stopped a few paces farther away. "Perhaps I will buy you some sausages. What will you give me in return?"

"I have nothing." Simon thought on that for a moment, then ran to overtake Yohan. "Oh yes, the cart. You may choose whatever you wish from the cart."

The man smiled down at him. "Be careful what you promise. We need to speak with Cernak before anyone chooses from that cart."

Simon looked up at the cart in question. Its tall sides jolted and swayed with every bump. They had eased their way down from the hills, intercepting the road only a few miles from Krakow. Yohan had taken two men to patrol behind them. Two others guarded their flank, and Cernak had ridden ahead with dark little Luca the Sicilian. Simon preferred it that way since it left him in charge of the oxen.

The team plodded on, indifferent to guides or guards. Simon knew they would follow the road at their own steady pace, regardless of what he did. Nonetheless, he switched their flanks to prove his authority.

The night before, Cernak had sat with him at the fire and prodded him with simple questions. "Do you know where your master was going?"

Eager at first to show his knowledge, Simon explained that after they rested in Krakow, he and Master Jacob always crossed the mountains into Vienna. "The Wolf of Nussdorf. We have to pay the Wolf."

Cernak had scratched his beard a moment, then smiled. "Of course, the Danube ferrymen—atrocious thieves. So, you were his helper. How old are you?"

That was one of the questions Simon had tried to avoid. "I think I can't be old because I'm new."

"Certainly this is not your first trip. How many times have you gone to Vienna?"

"No. I go *from* Vienna. Vienna to Krakow, Krakow to Kiev, and then north— north to Tver. Many times."

"And Jacob was your father? You were born in Vienna?"

Too many questions. Simon buried his head, rocking forward and back on the log where he sat. Shutting out the cold night air, the campfire, the murmur of men preparing for the evening, Simon squeezed his world down to a muffled cave of damp wool. When he peeked out again, Cernak was gone. Placing a hand on his shoulder, Yohan stood behind him, gesturing toward the shadows. He had found blankets and a place for Simon to sleep beneath the tumbrel and its contested load.

Now, with the morning sun warming his back, Simon thought on Master Cernak's questions. They had been the same questions his old master had asked. The same questions he had asked himself so many times in the past. The days gone by, like turns of the tumbrel's great wheel, faded into the dust behind him. Ahead, Krakow's timber palisade and earthen berm glowed in the morning sun. Lazy columns of smoke drifted in the morning air, and Simon thought only of sausages.

Yohan had continued riding alongside the tumbrel. By daylight, the tall warrior was an intimidating sight. Clad in chainmail and iron helmet, he bore a sword at his side and a scarred oval shield on his back. The man rode in silence as they approached the walls, one hand resting on his sword hilt. Simon rested a hand on his own rusty weapon and looked about for possible bandits. Seeing none, he grinned in satisfaction, switched the uncaring oxen, and followed them through the city gate.

Cernak had insisted on loading the dead marauders and carting them to Krakow. "The *voivode* is the lord of this region. He will need to know we've solved some of his troubles. We will bring the boy to corroborate events."

"Will I have to baffle philosophers?"

Yohan had smiled, and Cernak made a wry face. "I should hope not, at least not this time."

On entering the city, Simon's attention turned to the street vendors, but Yohan shook his head. "Not yet, Halfsword." The man gestured toward a castle that crowned an adjacent hill. "We will deliver these bodies to the voivode first."

Simon gazed up the steep road that climbed the hillside. Never had he dared venture up to the castle, and he doubted the oxen would make the climb. "Can you help push?"

Yohan cocked an eyebrow, looked at the heavy cart, and shook his head. Cernak rode over, and the two spoke for a moment. The oxen stamped and snorted. Simon wondered if he would ever get his sausages.

Standing in the middle of the road, he endured the glare of all who had to walk around his balky cart. Fidgeting, he felt stupid now for wearing the rusty broken sword, for standing, switch in hand next to the motionless team. Merchants spitting curses steered their loads past his stalled cart. Housewives with impossible bundles balanced on their heads filed past, glaring at Simon. And like a faint wraith, seen then gone, a diminutive red-haired girl slipped between the milling throng.

When the waiting became unbearable, a miracle happened. Four stout men converged on the tumbrel and put their shoulders to its frame. Cernak whistled from the back of his horse, Simon switched the near ox, and they all trundled slowly up the hill.

With his willow switch and rusty sword as emblems of authority, Simon raised his head and marched alongside the oxen. It felt right, familiar almost, his oxen, his cart, his willing servants. Like a leaf blown across the corner of his vision, Simon caught the swift memory of something, something gone before it was recognized. He straightened his back and kept walking.

Upon reaching the castle gate, Yohan gave each of the sweating laborers a few copper coins and Simon's retinue fled to the market below. Cernak had preceded the cart and negotiated with the castle guard. As the tumbrel rolled up, they stood back to let it pass. Simon hesitated a moment, then hand on his sword hilt, he followed the others into an open courtyard.

Defended by walls of pounded earth, the voivode's castle was less imposing from the inside than Simon had feared. Across from him stood a red brick church, its three towers crowned with copper domes. To his left, smoke rose from a smithy with its adjoining stable. The voivode's residence itself stood opposite the smithy, two floors of rough brick with a timber third level.

As they approached, a tall figure stepped from the residence. Wearing a sable cloak and matching fur hat, he swept toward them in long strides. Two others struggled to keep up. Before any of them reached his small company, Cernak spread his arms and bent into a deep bow. Simon watched and followed his new master's lead. Ceremonies aside, the voivode addressed them in a language Simon didn't understand. Evidently, neither did Cernak. The man called Stephan stepped forward and spoke with the voivode, gesturing toward Simon and the tumbrel. A moment of confusion, then Stephan said, "Boy, uncover the bodies that our host may see what we have brought him."

Simon bowed again for good measure, then pulled himself up onto the cart. A rough hemp canvas had been stretched over the bed. He peeled it back, revealing six pale corpses, already stiffening in the morning air. If the voivode was startled or repulsed by the grisly load, he didn't show it. Instead, he motioned to Simon and spoke a few words. Grinning, Stephan looked up. "Toss them out. He says he'll take the lot."

One by one, Simon rolled each body from the back of the cart and watched it fall to the earth in a tangle of limbs and bloody rags. Looking down at Stephan, he said, "Now will the voivode shit on their backs?"

Yohan covered his face for a moment. "No, put that out of your head. Nobody is going to…"

Stephan stopped laughing long enough to interrupt. "Even better, young man. He's going to have them hung from the castle gate. Better still, we are to be his guests of honor today."

"And will we have sausages?"

Yohan sighed and nodded. "Ya, ya, I will see to it that we do, even if I have to run to the market and fetch them myself."

The voivode saved Yohan a trip by offering a breakfast of pickled beets, rye bread, and sausages. He led them to a large refectory on the first floor and seated them at a table near the fire. An old woman in white cap and apron glided in, bearing pitchers of foamy gray kvass, a mild brew of fermented bread. Shortly thereafter, she returned with their food. Simon dug in, swabbing his wooden trencher with lumps of dense black bread to soak up every scrap. Yohan sat across the table, talking. Between mouthfuls, Simon responded in monosyllables and grunts.

Stephan, Cernak, and the voivode ate at the far end of the table, where they huddled in private discussion. Occasionally, one of them would glance up at Simon, but they too couldn't compete with the sausages for his attention. Eventually, Cernak came over and sat next to the boy. "Our host is interested in your sword. Do you mind if I show it to him?"

Simon hauled the broken relic from his belt and handed it over. "This belonged to my master, Jacob, and now it belongs to me."

"I'll see that it is treated well."

"Don't worry. I use it to chop trees and dig holes. It is not sharp."

Simon watched his new master deliver the sword to the voivode. Holding it in both hands, the Prince of Krakow examined the blade, then looked up and met Simon's eye. Shaking his head, the voivode turned back to Stephan and Cernak. He said a few words and stood. The others stood with him, and with a glance back at Simon, they filed out.

Luca, the small dark Sicilian, with two others at the table, had watched the proceedings without comment. He swirled the muddy gray kvass in his bowl, tossed it back, and said, "We should know what happened, *sè, cretino?*"

Yohan put a hand on his shoulder. "Easy, brother. Our Simon is not as cretino as you might think."

In response, Luca clenched the two middle fingers of his left hand and peered at Simon between the other two. "I am watching you, *diavulu.*"

Finishing his second trencher of sausages, Simon smiled across the table. "I am eating but you only watch. You should eat."

Luca stood to leave. "I am not hungry." He stopped halfway to the door. "Brothers, you will remember my words. This *liccu*, this sausage glutton, is not one of us."

Simon watched the Sicilian slip out into the morning sunlight. "Who does he mean, *us?*"

Yohan leaned across the table. "I thought Cernak had explained. We are what remains of the ancient *Eprotrofia Dikaiosýnis*, the Fellowship of Justice. Most people know us today as the Knights of Palermo."

Simon wasn't quite sure he understood. "Master Cernak said you infest the land."

One of the other two leaned forward. Short curly hair framed a tall regal face. Simon had to look twice. "You are a girl."

"I have not been called a girl in years, but yes, I squat to piss." She grinned at him. "I am Carla. Perhaps I can explain what we do. Say you have many rats infesting your granary, then you must purchase many cats, no?"

"Oh yes, the cats to eat the rats."

"Good. So now, is it rats that infest or do the cats infest as well?"

Simon thought a moment, then brightened. "You baffle philosophers—but I understand." He waved his arms. "You are many. Everywhere, Knights hunt rats."

"We are few, but yes, we hunt marauders and outlaws. And like cats, my friend Simon, we are seldom seen until we are needed."

As Carla spoke, the door opened and Cernak returned. He gestured to Yohan and the two bent in conversation. Simon noted that his sword had not returned with Cernak. Carla turned. "Is there a problem?"

Cernak joined the group, sitting across from Simon where Yohan had been. "Before I can say, I need Simon to give me some answers." He looked him directly in the eye. "Did you know exactly who this Master Jacob of yours was?"

"Of course, he carried furs. I rode with him…"

"Have you ever heard of Jacob ben Reuben?"

Simon rubbed his nose and thought. Many names he heard, but not this one. He shook his head and hunted for another sausage.

Yohan settled into a bench next to him. "Look at me, Simon. This is important, ya. How many years did you ride with your Master Jacob?"

Simon remembered the cut trees, but there had been earlier trips, he was sure. "Three, maybe four times—winter in Tver, Vienna in spring. I think so."

Carla glanced from Yohan to Cernak. "What does this mean? You think he is son of this devil, ben Reuben?" She spat on the floor.

Stephan returned, carrying Simon's broken sword. "It is as we thought. The markings are clear." He pushed aside bowls, platters, and trenchers to lay the blade in front of Simon. "Was this your master's sword?"

For a long moment, Simon sat speechless. The rust gone, the pitted gray steel clean, the hilt now wrapped in leather, it gleamed on the table before him. A string of graceful letters adorned the blade, he ran a finger over one of them. "I cannot read this."

"It's Aramaic," Cernak said, "a talisman of protection from the Book of Zohar." He put his own hand on the blade. "More than once I've faced this very sword. More than once I barely managed to escape with my life."

Carla looked up from the sword. "This is good news, yes? Jacob ben Reuben has been killed, and *mira*, here is proof."

"It's not so simple." Cernak looked around the room. "Where is Luca?"

Further down the table, another of the Knights sat up. "He is not agreeable with our Simon. Brother Luca is"—he touched his lips—"*phtt*, not here."

"Then find him, Ramon. We have decisions to make, and I want everyone part of it."

Taller than Luca but with corded muscles in his bare arms, Ramon had the same chestnut skin and curly dark hair as the little Sicilian. Simon watched him rise and glide out the door. "Luca is not my friend, Master Cernak."

"Then before he returns, tell us all one thing, Simon. Is Jacob ben Reuben your father?"

Another question about his past. So many, the questions hurt, they burned in his heart. Simon pulled in on himself and withdrew, rocking forward and back. *Simon is lost. Simon is empty. Simon is cold.* "Master Jacob finds lost Simon."

Cernak sat back as Simon continued to rock. Yohan put a hand on the boy's shoulder. "You did well, Simon." He glanced up at the others, then looked back at the boy. "I understand. You are not lost now. Can you trust me?"

Rocking, face down, forward and back, he couldn't meet their gazes. "If Simon tells, it hurts him."

"Look at me, Simon," Yohan said. "What will hurt you?"

Hugging his knees, he made himself safe, pushing the world away. "No-o."

By the time Ramon and Luca returned, Simon felt calm enough to stop rocking. Luca scowled as he came in. He didn't sit but stood behind Cernak and looked down at the table. "*Merda!* That cannot be."

Cernak said, "It is Luca, and you can relax. Jacob is dead."

"And this cretino—this *mafankulo* cretino—he sits with us, drinks with us, eats our food. I first see this *bastardo* and I know him."

Cernak stood. "Easy, brother. Simon may not be Jacob's son. We still don't know who he is."

Luca is not my friend. Simon looked down, hugging himself and rocking once more.

Yohan whispered to him, "Simon, you can have your sword back."

Simon buried himself deeper, rocking, rocking. Cernak stood and raised his voice. "Put the damned sword away."

Simon blinked up at him. "I will. Can we leave now?"

Luca shook his head and stared across the table at Yohan. "He is yours, brother. You find him, you care for him. For me, I want nothing."

Cernak held up a hand. "Sit down, everyone. We have a bigger problem to discuss." He waited until all five of his Knights had found a seat. "I have asked the voivode to award us the tumbrel and its contents in return for protecting his town. He has countered that it was stolen from Simon and should be returned to him."

Luca stood amid the ensuing uproar and yelled, "*Cazzo—*"

Cernak cut him off. "Sit, Luca." He glared at the others. "Quiet, all of you. The voivode has a point. We are not thieves. We are not marauders. We all took an oath to protect those we can and to avenge those we cannot protect."

Simon alone had sat quietly through the uproar. He'd returned the broken sword to his belt and waited for his chance to leave. When none of the men seemed inclined to do likewise, he said, "I could just give you the cart."

In the silence that followed, all eyes were on Simon. "Do you know what is in that cart?" Cernak asked.

"Skins, sable, and ermine skins. Master Jacob paid with gold. He said, 'No foxes.' We don't have foxes in our cart."

"So you know that tumbrel, that cart, is valuable? Why would you just give it to us?"

"It is your reward. You saved me and bought me sausages. You infested this land and killed the rats."

Yohan sighed and slumped. "I understand the problem now." He turned to Simon. "The Knights of Palermo, we do not take payment, ya? We take no reward for what we do. It is against our code. It would make us the same as the mercenaries, the thieves, and the marauders."

Cernak nodded. "We can take help. We can take shelter and food. Sometimes princes like the voivode will give us supplies, but nothing more. We are sworn to poverty and service."

Simon beamed at him. "If I swear to poverty and service, can I be a Knight? Oh yes, I already have a sword."

Chapel Perilous

Sitting alone, a smoking tallow candle his only company, Simon now regretted his impulsive request. Luca, of course, had leapt to his feet, but Cernak quieted him with a fist to the table and a sharp rebuke. Yohan had said nothing but moved back as if to examine him in a new light. It was Stephan who finally nodded and said, "We have all that is needed for his trial: the Chapel Perilous, the Lair of the Beast, and the Waters of Redemption."

Simon had not imagined they would approve, that he would not simply be slapped down again as the prostoi, the fool. Cernak fixed him with a hard stare. "Do you know what you ask? You would wander, owning nothing. Your only friends would be the Fellowship. No woman would marry you, as they might see you once and nevermore."

"Simon wanders and his only friend is dead." Simon ducked his head and blushed. "No woman has me, none."

Yohan stood and announced, "I would stand as Witness for Simon Halfsword if he is willing to take the trial."

Luca crossed himself and said nothing. Ramon flashed a grin at Simon, then turned to the little Sicilian. "Come, friend. With Simon's gift, we can clothe every orphan in your village—we can feed every hungry mouth between here and Palermo. We will journey to St. Peter's Basilica and light a candle for your mother's soul. God knows she needs it."

Luca flew from his seat and launched himself at Ramon. The two grappled on the floor, cursing and punching. Cernak and the others stepped back. Simon stood beside Yohan and asked, "Is this how you become a Knight?"

"No, this is how we settle our differences, hand-to-hand, without weapons."

Simon had favored Ramon, taller than his opponent. But Luca was fast and wiry, dodging Ramon's fists and often landing his own critical blows. As quickly as it had started, the scuffle broke up and both combatants resumed their seats, puffing and bleeding. Ramon laughed, then winced in pain. "Is that all you have, my friend? Is that your best?"

"Mention my mother again, mafankulo, then you will know my best."

Cernak dragged his stool back to the table and sat. "Will there be any other discussion?" He let a moment of silence pass, then continued. "Very well. Simon, are you resolved to undergo the trial? Are you willing to swear our vows, to become a Knight of Palermo and a Sword of Justice?"

"I am ready if Master Cernak says I am ready."

Yohan nudged him in the ribs. "You must choose for yourself, Simon."

"Then I am ready."

Once he had accepted, Simon was surprised to find how quickly events unfolded. Cernak had grasped him by the elbow and hustled him across the courtyard. "Hermanowska Cathedral is the seat of the holy bishop for this region. He will consecrate you for this undertaking."

As Simon's Witness, Yohan followed. After a substantial offering of coin, an acolyte had glided out and returned with a gaunt elderly man in linen robes. The bishop had mumbled something in Latin about confession, and Simon explained that he was still hungry. Yohan had nodded. "Gluttony, Your Holiness."

The old man blinked and waited, but Simon could think of nothing more to say. Yohan poked him and gave him a questioning look. Unsure of what was expected, he shook his head. The bishop had closed his eyes until Yohan finally broke the silence. "I think that is all."

With one hand on Simon's forehead and the other signing the cross, the bishop said, "I have heard your confession and absolve you of your sins." He paused. "Sin. Go and sin no more."

Simon would have explained that he couldn't sin because he had to fast, but Cernak took him once more by the elbow and led him deeper into the gloomy cathedral. Daylight from the western entrance reflected off a marble floor but provided little illumination. Simon craned his head back and gazed up at a constellation of burning tapers that blazed in the twilight universe overhead. Music from a hidden choir echoed through the rafters and seemed to spring from the darkness itself. And like the shadow of a ghost, a phantom of memory gripped his heart in bony claws and then vanished.

"You have been shriven by the bishop himself," Cernak said. "Now you must begin your vigil."

Clutching his chest, Simon followed his master to the foot of an immense altar. Yohan bent and lifted a heavy wooden door set flush in the marble tiles. Rough stone steps led to a dark chamber beneath the floor.

Cernak drew a tapered candle from within his cloak and lit it from one on the altar. "Follow me." He descended the stairs. His wavering shadow danced along the walls. "We descend to the Chapel of St. Gereon, known to some as the ancient Temple of Hermes."

One step, two steps, Simon followed Cernak down a narrow, brick-lined stairwell. The yellow flame smoked, filling the air with the rancid odor of burning tallow. Simon had listened to his master's instructions, hoping to hear something encouraging, but could make little sense of it. He chanted, barely a whisper. "Hermes—Hermanowska, Hermes—Hermanowska..."

Cernak halted. "Yes, yes, there is some hope for you, Halfsword. You will be delighted to know it contains the sarcophagus of St. Simeon, patron saint of wise fools."

Simon had not been delighted to know he would spend the night with a dead man, saint or otherwise. Sitting now in the darkened chapel and gazing at the dusty sarcophagus, Simon also realized he had not been ready, he had replied much too quickly. Cernak had explained that he would have no food until his trial was over. But hunger wasn't the issue. It was the sausages. Wrestling in his gut like ferrets in a rabbit's den, they consumed Simon's attention. He tried to belch. He bent double and held his sides. Still, his bowels heaved and gurgled, bringing tears of pain to his eyes.

Cernak had told him he must keep vigil as long as the candle burned. He held it up. Maybe a finger's width had been consumed. Ten times as much remained. The pain returned and, with it, a new urgency. Frantic, Simon looked about—anything—a jar, a pot. The stern visage of St. Gereon stared down from a mosaic wall, all judgment and scorn but no sympathy.

Simon turned to the carved travertine sarcophagus. A stone image of St. Simeon smiled in silent mirth at the ceiling above. Somehow, it seemed right. They'd done it to his master—he would have to do likewise to the bones of this saint. He put his shoulder to the lid, only meaning to shift it a handbreadth. At first, nothing happened. Then with a grumble, the entire stone box slid back into the wall, revealing a dark pit beneath.

Simon raised his taper and peered into the gloom. More stone steps descended a narrow slot in the floor. Another spasm brought home the urgency of his situation. Simon scrambled down to a smaller chamber hewn into the rock below. A rusty iron bar protruded from one wall. He planted his taper in the dirt floor, dropped his breechclout, hiked up his knee-length tunic, and leaned back against the bar.

Three things happened at once. Simon found relief. The iron bar rotated back. And above, a low grumble marked the return of St. Simeon's cheerful visage to the chamber of St. Gereon. Candle raised high, Simon returned to the stairs. Above, the flickering light revealed only flat stone. He climbed and pushed against the overhead. Nothing moved. Returning to the chamber, he seized the rusty lever and pulled. It resisted a moment, then broke off, sending him stumbling back.

The candle fell over and glowed blue against the dirt floor. Simon snatched it up and watched the tiny flame shrink, then crawl up the wick and reignite. He held the precious light and sat on the lowest step, not sure which smelled worse, the tallow smoke or the remains of his breakfast. As he sat, the smoke began to win out. Only a few fingers' width had burned, and already the fumes had become nauseating.

Simon waited for Master Jacob to come. *No, my old master is dead.* He remembered his friend Yohan in the cathedral above. *If Yohan had eaten sausages, would he come down here and move the sarcophagus?* It seemed unlikely. He stood and looked for a place farther from the smoke.

Behind the steps and against one wall, he found a tiny alcove where the air smelled cleaner. Simon left his candle and bent double to crawl inside. Feeling a slight current of damp air against his cheek, he crawled farther. The light disappeared, the rough stone walls closed in about him, and Simon backed out in a panic.

Repositioning his candle, he tried the alcove, looking for a place he could sit upright. Once more, as he crawled inside, the light dimmed, and the walls seemed to converge around him. Simon finally yielded to the inevitable. He retrieved his smoking taper and pushed it in front of him as he crawled through the narrow passage.

The floor dropped away in a series of long steps. He soon found that he could stand upright. *When Yohan comes, will he follow this far?* Something told Simon that his friend wasn't coming, that his vigil had become a journey.

At the bottom of the passage, Simon reached a wooden door. It had rotted off its hinges and collapsed against the arched brick opening. He pushed it aside and heard it fall into the darkness beyond. Simon wondered if he had somehow returned to the cathedral. "Hallo, Yohan?" His call echoed into silence.

Hearing nothing and seeing nothing, he raised his candle and stepped into the chamber beyond. Left and right, a broad hall disappeared into the darkness. Rising from a smooth stone floor, heavy marble columns marched down both sides. He craned his head upward. Simon could barely see the vaulted ceiling above. Turning around, he peered both directions into the darkness.

He turned again, and then back. Or was it back? Simon looked for the doorway, the broken door. Somehow, he had lost them in the silent shadows. A vague gleam caught his eye from the far end of the hall. It glittered as he approached, reflecting his candlelight from a thousand tiny facets.

Hiding behind the columns, he edged nearer. Every step, Simon felt something tug at his heart. His chest burned like he had been running from wolves. Simon halted and raised his smoking taper. The glittering shadow mocked him from the gloom. He knew that form sleeping in the darkness, *Serpens Crucis*, the crucified serpent. A moth to an evening lamp, Simon approached.

Towering in the shadows, a rough-hewn stone pillar rose from the floor. It supported a horizontal beam high above his head, the tau cross. With a start, he knew it, the ancient symbol of sacrifice and immortality. Hung crucified on the cross's arms, an ebony black serpent fixed him with its jeweled eye. His heart pounded. He struggled with every breath. In desperation, he arched his back and gasped, but the bony claw in his chest only clenched harder.

Wavering, Simon's knees bent. He knelt to set his candle on the floor. A tug at his waist threw him off balance. Jacob's broken sword had lodged against the marble tiles. Simon waved his arms before sprawling face down. Once more, his candle glowed blue, and the crushing darkness closed around him. Struggling with the awkward sword, he tried to rise. He grasped the hilt and drew a deep breath. His arm found new strength and held the candle high. The flame, once barely visible, sprang forth in radiant glory—and Simon remembered.

The evening sojourns into the crypt, the bundled codices, the false monks chanting in darkness—they all flew by like leaves in a whirlwind. He knew the imprecations, the curse he bore, and ultimately his own apostasy. He knew a name as well, *Apostoli Lucis*—his name perhaps, or one he once bore.

Simon drew the sword of Jacob ben Reuben and held it before him. He saw the double serpent entwined about the hilt and knew its meaning. He read the inscription on the blade and felt its protection. And before him, the great dusky idol smiled down on her prodigal child.

Sword in hand, he stepped back and felt something crush beneath his foot. Another step, Simon looked down and saw the withered fragments of dried flesh and crumbling bone scattered beneath the stone cross. He wished he'd never eaten the sausages, never agreed to the trial. *Run, run! Drop everything and flee...*

Step by cautious step, Simon retreated down the hall. The great serpent, once the center of his universe, now shrank to a distant glittering eye, then faded into the shadows. Unsure of where he'd entered, Simon followed the tall columns to the far end of the chamber. A Greek temple adorned the entire rear wall. Complete with portico and faux Doric columns, it towered above his head. Simon's candle illuminated little more than the doorway and lintel, but he could read the inscription above, *Solve et Coagula*.

A whirlwind of vague images, a wrenching memory of betrayal. The skeletal fist gripped his heart and threatened him with death. Simon stood in confused indecision. *Forward into the darkness, or retreat to the safety of the chamber above?* He recalled the noisome mess and stepped through the darkened portico.

Beyond the temple façade, Simon found another rough corridor of dripping limestone. He held the candle high and followed a tortuous path through narrow clefts and low tunnels. Crawling on his belly and pushing the candle before him, Simon took heart in the draft that welled up from somewhere below. He passed through chambers of fallen stone—perhaps fine galleries in days gone by, but now mazes of broken rock and mud.

Scrambling through a collapsed jumble of brick and stone, Simon crawled into a circular room. He held his candle up and gasped—only a hand's width of yellow tallow remained. *Back, back. Go back up.* He recoiled in panic. *Master Jacob will find me.* Once more he remembered his old master was dead. Master Cernak wouldn't come. Yohan wouldn't find him. *The trial then. Surely, this is part of the trial.* He choked down his fear and examined the chamber.

A few paces wide and capped by a dome of cut stonework, the only exit was a black well that opened at his feet. Simon crawled to the edge and peered into the darkness. Brick steps spiraled down its walls. Narrow and steep, they twisted into the pit like a snake descending a tree.

Simon glanced back the way he'd come. A rumble of falling dirt and a few loose bricks tumbled out of the opening. He held his candle to the pit. In the short interim, the wick seemed to have burned even farther into the soft tallow. With no other option, he placed one foot on the first step, then ventured another. Two, three steps down, he placed one hand on the stone lip to steady himself and advanced another step. The chamber floor vanished from view and Simon continued his descent into darkness.

After one complete turn, he reached up to touch the step above. Little wider than his boot, each brick projected from the wall uncomfortably far below its neighbor. Even with his long legs, Simon found it difficult to step down while holding his candle and maintaining his balance. Damp air rose from below and the yellow flame flickered and guttered before him. One hand steadying himself against the wall, he stepped lower.

The next brick shifted beneath his foot. He sprawled forward, grabbing at the rough wall. His knee struck something and plunged him face-first down into the pit. Candle clutched in desperation, he grasped at the steps flying past, slapping one, then grabbing the next. Simon hung a moment, his legs flailing. Gasping, slipping, his feet touched something, then one toe rested on an unseen step. White knuckles on the step above, he kicked with his free leg, trying to find purchase. Nothing beneath his foot, Simon felt his hand slipping. A final desperate kick spun him toward the wall. His foot found a step. Simon let go and lurched forward before clutching another brick.

Molten tallow streamed down the back of his hand. Simon held the candle stub upright, thanking the gods of this place that he hadn't dropped it. He tried another step. It held. Much slower now, he continued down until far below, he saw a tiny light ascending toward him. "Yohan, come. It's me." His voice echoed back up from below.

He called again, but only echoes returned. Forgetting his near disaster, Simon rushed down the steps. Wavering in the shadows below, the wan yellow light rose to meet him. A dim figure held it out, climbing like a silent ghost. *Yohan, he knows the way out.* Simon took one more step and splashed waist-deep in cold water. His climbing reflection scattered into a thousand glittering waves.

Loneliness haunted that deep chamber. Like a leach against his chest, it bled the remaining hope from his heart. Leaning back against the damp wall, Simon shook with sobs, bending double in his despair. No one had told him that hell was a dying candle in a buried lake. He put one hand to the hilt of his broken sword. No new strength answered his touch. He had failed his Master Jacob, and now he would fail Master Cernak. *What will they do with the wagon now that I failed the trial?*

Simon straightened himself and stood. He couldn't leave the wagon. *I still must pay the Wolf of Nussdorf.* He waded into the dark lagoon. Above, the cavern ceiling hung almost to the water. Simon refused to look at his candle stub, refused to see the dying light. He ducked under the rough stone, no longer reinforced with brick or masonry. Not far off, a rocky shore marked the lake's margin. He sloshed through the shallow water and climbed the loose cobbles.

A path wound along the foot of the cavern wall. He followed it to the right, ending at a rotted mass of sticks and tiny bones. Six large eggs huddled in the center, each the size of a man's skull. A glaze of ancient lime welded the mass together. Simon shuddered to think what beast could have left such a nest.

He turned and returned the way he'd come, past where his dripping footprints emerged from the lake. The track ended in a hole, large enough for a full-grown hog to walk through. Simon ducked and crawled along the dirt path until he came to another passage. High and wide enough for a team of oxen to pass, it disappeared into the gloom. In cautious awe, he stepped forward, slipped on a loose stone, and dropped his tiny candle stub.

Lair of the Beast

Yohan followed Simon's gaze up into the rafters of Hermanowska Cathedral. The boy seemed interested, but not overwhelmed. *Has he been here before?* Cernak led the way, trying to explain the holy vigil. Simon nodded and mumbled in response. Most of the time, Yohan found it impossible to imagine what the boy was thinking.

Somewhat surprised at the turn of events, He had discussed it with Cernak. The Old Man, their leader, had been doubtful at first. "He cannot fight, he cannot defend himself. What will he do in a skirmish?"

"He will have to finish his trial first. If he can't do that, then I will agree—Simon should not join the Fellowship."

Cernak had stroked his beard and looked back at the boy, blissfully eating sausages. "Perhaps the voivode would want him as a field hand."

"If Simon goes with us, we can teach him to defend himself. He can certainly learn the elements of *pankration*, hand-to-hand combat."

"You seem to have a stake in the boy's welfare."

"I have a nephew..." Yohan paused a moment. "I *had* a nephew, my sister's son. He was much like Simon. The priests, the superstitious fools of the town, they killed him, ya? The boy died on his tenth birthday."

Struggling to speak around the knot in his throat, Yohan studied the floor, considered his own motives. *Sentiment, pity—both weaknesses that could get a man killed in battle, get a fellow Knight killed as well.* He turned and met Cernak's eye. "But I will leave him here and not look back if he doesn't have the wit or the courage to complete his trial."

The Old Man had nodded and gripped Yohan's shoulder. "I think Simon may surprise all of us."

The bishop had been difficult. Old and traditional, he'd argued against letting a boy like Simon sit vigil in his cathedral. A large offering, and the promise to confine the vigil to St. Gereon's buried chapel, finally convinced him. After Simon's rather perfunctory shriving, the old bishop had fled, leaving them to find their own way to the crypt beneath the altar.

Cernak led. Simon followed. Dressed in full regalia for the occasion, Yohan had little to do but witness the proceedings and attest to the boy's conduct. When they reached the high altar, Yohan stepped up to drag the heavy crypt door from its frame and lower it to the cathedral floor. Cernak took a thick beeswax candle from the altar and lit a yellow taper of his own from the holy flame. Yohan lit a duplicate taper and placed it on a simple iron stand next to the open crypt.

Once Simon's curly head vanished below the cathedral floor, Yohan descended as well. Five hundred years earlier, St. Gereon's chapel may have been the center of Christianity in this region, but to Yohan's view, it was little more than a sanctified grotto. On the wall, the Christian God himself glared through St. Gereon's gilded eyes at a reclining Lucifer in the guise of St. Simeon. The fallen one, heedless of God's judgment, smirked in perpetual ease at the holy sanctuary above.

Regardless of the irony, Simon appeared duly impressed with the proceedings so far. Yohan checked the boy's candle. Its yellow flame burned strong and true. He looked the boy over. "You are certain you are ready for this trial?"

"Oh yes, I am ready. You are my Witness."

Yohan clasped his hand and climbed back to the echoing cathedral apse above. Cernak emerged a moment later. Together, they raised the heavy wooden door and lowered it back flush with the marble tiles. Cernak dusted his hands and nodded at Yohan's tallow candle. "That should burn the rest of today and through the night. Wait until only two fingers' width remain of the stub."

"And if he comes out before?"

"Then we'll know. I explained to him. He cannot sleep and he cannot leave until his candle has burned down."

"And if he remains until dawn?"

"We will go early to the *Smocza Jama*, the Dragon's Den, and prepare for the second phase of his trial. Escort him through the western gate and meet us at the river."

After Cernak left, Yohan found a simple wooden stool behind the altar. The old bishop obviously liked to stand a little taller when he delivered his benediction. Yohan borrowed the stool and set it where he could see the door as well as other activity in the cathedral.

As he waited, a trickle of people arrived, lit candles, and prayed. Yohan watched them pass through the holy stations and wondered if it even mattered what they did. Outside the cathedral they still fought, stole, lied, and fornicated as men and women had been doing since the fall of Eden. *What could it possibly matter that they burned a little wax and left a few coins?*

Yohan stood and paced, annoyed with himself for diving into that quagmire. He'd joined the Fellowship to avoid such doubts. Two older women approached, perhaps mistaking him for a priest. On seeing his chainmail hauberk and sword, they squealed and shuffled off. He granted them absolution anyway. He granted absolution to all the souls wandering Hermanowska Cathedral this evening, to all the souls haunting Wawel Castle, both above and below the ground. He even granted absolution to the six thieves now dangling from the castle gate.

As the evening drew late and daylight faded from the cathedral doorway, Yohan heard the hour of *matins* ring down from the tower above. If he was going to take a little bread, drink some kvass, and relieve himself, it had better be now. With the large yellow altar candle, he ran a heavy bead of wax between the wooden door and the marble tiles. While the wax remained soft, he pressed the carved pommel of his dagger into the bead.

Stepping into the castle courtyard from the smoky cathedral interior, Yohan stretched his back and stared up at the sky. A flock of swifts circled above Wawel Hill, screaming and bleating into the evening air. Cernak touched him on the shoulder. "Birds of heaven, they have no legs, you know."

"How do they alight?"

"Save to nest, and then only on the highest towers, they never do. Swifts live among the clouds, messengers of the gods. You should listen when they speak.”

"You didn't come here to tell me of birds."

"I was on my way to invite you for an evening meal. How is our initiate?”

"Quiet. I've heard nothing from him since he entered the chapel, and the door is sealed. I'll know if he emerges early."

Yohan followed Cernak to the castle refectory. The others had already gathered, talking and finishing off trenchers of mutton stew. Settling for a heavy lump of black bread and a foamy mug of kvass, Yohan sat at the end of the table, watching his comrades. Carla of Andalusia addressed the others. Her regal figure hinted at Norman heritage, but her bronze complexion betrayed Moorish blood as well.

Ramon listened, nodding. Yohan knew him to be the youngest son of a prominent Corsican family. Expected to join the priesthood, Ramon had fled to Sicily and joined the Knights of Palermo instead.

Luca sat between the two, pretending he listened to Carla. Yohan knew him well, fierce in his loyalties, fiercer still in enmity. Right now, Yohan knew the little Sicilian watched him eat. *He weighs the chances I will defend the cretino.*

Cernak and Stephan had left, citing some further negotiation with the voivode. Yohan munched on his bread, trying to ignore Luca's glittering eye. The voivode, Prince of Krakow, would want Simon's tumbrel for himself. *He maneuvers to separate the boy from the Fellowship without losing the Fellowship's protection.* Yohan had worked that out while sitting in the dark cathedral. *Cernak must know. He will be a strong ally for keeping Simon if he can be convinced.*

Stephan too—he'd supported the idea. Yohan suspected that Ramon had only provoked Luca out of capricious rivalry. *Those two will likely oppose Simon's initiation.* Another mug of kvass in hand, Yohan moved down the table. "What is the topic tonight, Carla?”

"It is the voivode who has room for us in his halls, but not in his heart, yes? It is that cart, that golden apple that brings discord to our Fellowship. It is this simpleton, who has us all walking on nails. That is what."

Yohan grinned. "And perhaps it includes the brother Knight who defies all common sense and defends our simpleton, ya?”

Luca wet his finger in Yohan's kvass and drew the sign of the fig. "And perhaps that brother desires a little companionship on the road. Do you tire of women, or has it been so long you've simply forgotten?"

"Is that all you can think of Luca—who will be your next catamite? Aren't you afraid you'll make your friend Ramon jealous?"

Yohan saw it coming, the mug of kvass dashed in his face. He pretended to be blind, staggering back. Luca jumped to the table and sprang at him. Yohan let the man's momentum bring him close enough, then planted a fist just below his sternum. Like a hawk struck from the sky, Luca crashed to the floor. Gasping for air, he stayed down.

Ramon squared off, feet apart, fists at waist level. "You insult me as well, bastardo."

Luca gasped from the floor. "No, that mafankulo is mine. I will kill him—you can have what is left."

Yohan sat on one corner of the table and poured himself another bowl of kvass. "Tomorrow, after the trial is finished, I fight you both. But you lose, you support me at council, ya?"

Luca was still gasping and cursing as Yohan walked out. Carla followed Yohan and said, "You didn't leave any allies back there. I've been trying to convince them to accept Simon all afternoon. Now there's not a prayer of it."

"Never was one, sister."

"But Simon will need a unanimous vote. Without Luca and Ramon, we're just wasting time."

"I never waste time. Be sure that Cernak knows of the challenge. I will meet you at the Smocza Jama tomorrow morning at the hour of lauds."

Stopping a moment at the common latrine, Yohan thought of Simon and remembered they hadn't left him a chamber pot. He hoped there wouldn't be too much mess to clean it up before the bishop returned. In the cathedral, Yohan checked the wax seal and found it intact.

Compline, the evening prayer floated down from a hidden gallery as daylight faded from the cathedral entrance. A team of deacons set about lowering the iron candelabras and snuffing the wicks. New wax candles replaced those on the altar, and Yohan sat alone in his own pool of light. He must have dozed off because the lonely silver chime of *matins* startled him awake. He glanced around the shadowy space. Movement, a slender wraith of diaphanous gown and red hair slid behind a column and disappeared. Yohan shook his head and looked again. Nothing.

At his feet, the smoking tallow candle had burned over two-thirds of its length. Still, he'd heard nothing from Simon entombed in the chapel below. Matins, that darkest hour of the soul. Yohan at once both feared it and sought it. *Do I stand Witness at these vigils to test myself?* He wondered. *Or do I await the ghosts I know must come?*

He took up his candle and once more checked the wax seal. It still bore the imprint of his dagger. The silence bothered Yohan more than if he'd heard the boy calling or singing or doing anything below. He could just as easily raise the wooden door and check on Simon, perhaps reassure him that he wasn't forgotten. *And that is* my *test,* he realized. *If I break this vigil to allay my own fears, have I not broken faith with the boy as well?*

Yohan stood and paced the length of the cathedral apse, returning to his pool of yellow light. He repeated the journey until his candle had indeed burned down half of the remaining wax. Measuring it against his fingers, he counted heartbeats. *How much would it burn in a thousand heartbeats?*

At seven hundred and thirty-one beats, he lost count, lost track of the candle, and dozed where he sat. In the golden dawn, lauds rang him awake in a great thundering peal of bronze bells. Yohan jumped up and nearly fell over. His tallow candle had burned to a stub, no more than two fingers' width above the iron candleholder.

The boy, he should be out by now. He should be hammering at the door. Yohan bent and checked the seal one last time. It had not been disturbed. He dragged the door open and let it fall with a crash to the marble floor. "Simon, it's time." Nothing but a dull echo answered his call.

Flickering stub in hand, he clattered down the steps. Darkness, nothing. Yohan held the candle high enough that the glittering golden eyes of St. Gereon flashed their imprecations back at him. Nothing. No Simon.

He checked around and behind the sarcophagus of St. Simeon but found no sign that the boy had ever been there. No candle stub, no trail of long-held urine, nothing. Could he have crawled inside with the saint's rotting bones? Yohan pushed at the lid. In desperation, he tried levering the stone cover with his sword. It wouldn't move.

Was this the right cathedral? Were there two altars, two identical chapels? Yohan shook off his confusion. *Perhaps the boy had an accomplice who'd restored the seal once he'd left?* Climbing back to the cathedral apse, Yohan knelt and examined the broken wax. It matched the silver raven on his dagger too well to have been restored.

Footfalls behind him. Cernak approached in the dim morning light. "You are late. Where is the boy?"

"Gone."

Yohan showed Cernak the broken seal. He explained about setting it before leaving the cathedral and checking it several times during the night. Cernak descended the stairs and looked around. "He was never here—and yet—I left him here. Smell the air, Yohan. Do you detect any candle smoke other than our own?"

"If anything, it smells of the devil, foul and sulfurous."

"Have you opened the sarcophagus?"

"I couldn't. Perhaps the two of us should try."

Yohan pried and Cernak pushed. Eventually the stone lid yielded, and they managed to shift it a hand's width. Yohan held his candle stub and peered inside. A dusty gray skull smirked back at him. "Bones, nothing more."

Cernak put his shoulder to the lid and slid it back. "Are you certain your seal could not have been duplicated?"

Yohan showed him the dagger. "Someone would have to take this from me to restore the seal. It didn't happen."

Climbing back to the cathedral apse, Yohan closed St. Gereon's chapel and replaced the borrowed stool. Cernak lit a fresh taper and checked around the altar. "Simon found another way out. That's the only possible explanation."

"So where is he now?"

"We will need more information. Perhaps the voivode knows something? Perhaps the bishop? For now, we must tell the others."

Smoke rising from the smithy glowed silver in the morning light, as did smaller plumes from the castle. Yohan followed Cernak west across the courtyard to a grassy common and the outer wall of timber and pounded earth. A square stone tower guarded the western side. They passed through a narrow postern gate and descended—the path weaving back and forth across the face of a steep embankment.

Yohan paused a moment to take in the broad Vistula River. He had once rowed its length to the Baltic Sea. A river pirate in those days, he didn't dwell on the memories. He was a different man now, he had comrades, friends who waited for him at the foot of the path.

They would all be clustered about a large cavern that led back into the heart of Wawel Hill. Yohan had been inside, searching for treasure. Bats clung to the ceiling, and near the entrance, an immense rat's nest occupied one corner of the cave. Nothing else, he had found no sign of its legendary dragon, and certainly no hidden treasure.

Below, Cernak completed another loop of the path. *Better their leader arrives first with the news.* When Yohan finally reached the riverbank, four sets of eyes focused on him. Cernak didn't bother to turn. "They ask how our Witness could have lost his acolyte."

Ramon said, "I've been here all night preparing."

Carla laughed. "Then who was it I saw with the wineskin and the serving girl? You arrived here just before sunup like the rest of us."

"But I have been preparing—I have this." He produced a torch of rags and pine pitch. It had a kitchen-bellows affixed to the shaft. "Do I need to demonstrate on your lovely ass?"

Luca produced a short length of cord with a flat wooden paddle tied at one end. He whirled it over his head making a roar like a charging bull. "It would have been fun, watching the cretino piss down his leg. I think you let him go, told him to hide. I'll save this and use it on you some night."

"You may practice on each other all you wish," Cernak said. "The fact remains that we have no acolyte to test."

Luca tossed his bull-roarer to Ramon. "Yes, but we have matter of honor to settle, don't we, Brother Yohan?"

Cernak cocked his head to one side. "Just a moment, brothers. I thought I heard something."

Yohan listened. He heard it too. Echoing from the cave entrance, a faint voice called, "Yohan... Master Cernak, are you there?"

Luca jumped back, crossing himself. "*Santo cazzo Madre di Cristo!* The devil, he returns."

Yohan spun around. "Simon?"

The boy's curly head ducked through the cave entrance. He blinked in the morning light. "I got lost."

Cernak rushed over and took him by the arm. "Are you..." He looked Simon up and down. "I would ask if you were all right, but it seems so. What in the flaming hell happened?"

Simon paused, still blinking at the men standing around him. He turned to each of them before meeting Yohan's eye. "I went in a passage, then the door closed. I was lost and dropped my candle, and now here I am. Did I complete my trial?"

In that moment when Simon had looked directly at him, Yohan saw something more than a simpleton, a fool. *What little the boy had said was certainly the truth.* Yohan wondered what he held back. Cernak still gripped Simon's arm. He faced the others. "I say that Simon Halfsword has completed his vigil. Does anyone doubt that?"

Ramon stroked his beard. "He was told to stay in the chapel, and clearly, he did not."

"No," Yohan said, "he was told not to come out. No one said he couldn't go farther inside. I would propose that he has completed his second test as well, passing the Lair of the Beast."

Simon turned and looked back at the cave entrance. "There is a beast in there? Wait, is this the Wawel dragon cave?"

Ramon said, "Yes, the dragon's cave, the notorious Smocza Jama. But you have spoiled the test. You were to go in and face the dragon, not come out and confuse all of us."

"Oh yes, I have baffled philosophers."

To Yohan, Simon's grin was one of duplicity rather than innocence. When no one else spoke, he made a suggestion. "Why can't Simon reenter the Lair of the Beast and complete his test?"

"You know the reason," Ramon said. "If he goes back in, how will we know he faces a dragon when there is no—"

"What if I bring out a dragon's egg?" Simon asked. "Can I be a Knight, then?"

Luca stepped up and looked Simon in the face. "If you bring out a mafankulo dragon's egg from that shithole cave, I will kiss your mafankulo ass and make you a Knight myself."

Cernak had not intervened, but Yohan could see that his credulity had been stretched to the limit. "You would stake everything on finding this dragon's egg?"

"If there is a dragon, it must have eggs. I will steal one and bring it out."

Cernak looked at the others. "Do you agree?"

Yohan wasn't sure if Simon was playing with them or if he actually thought he could find a dragon's egg. Either way, it was too much to risk. "I still say finding his way from the Chapel of St. Gereon, all the way to the Smocza Jama, goes far beyond the second test."

Ramon shook his head. "No, I am with Luca. The boy has made a boast—now he must prove it."

Cernak said, "Brother Yohan, this time I agree with Luca as well. Let the boy prove himself and remove any doubt."

Simon beamed at all of them. "I need another candle."

Cernak produced the taper he'd used that morning. "I think Brother Ramon can help you light it. He has an oil lamp going somewhere."

Luca said, "I should follow him to be sure he has no other devil tricks to play."

Cernak shook his head. "No, Simon must face the dragon alone. You certainly would have had it no other way if things had been different."

Yohan watched the boy duck his head and return to the cavern mouth. He seemed so confident. Not the innocent confidence of a fool, nor the bravado of a cheat. Something had happened between St. Gereon's chapel and the Dragon's Den.

Cernak found a seat among the rocks. "Did anyone think to bring some food?

I'm starving."

Yohan sat nearby waiting for the sun to rise above Wawel Hill. "We break our fast after the trial. Simon has one more test. We must bathe him in the Waters of Redemption, then send him to bed."

Luca sat himself between them, shaking his head. "He is fled back to the devils beneath that rock. We will never see him again. Besides, Brother Yohan here has made me a challenge. I will kill him, then eat his food."

"He owes me some blood as well," Ramon said. "Let me fight him first."

Cernak held up his hands. "I thought the challenge was after Simon's trial."

Yohan stood. "I will fight Ramon now and save Luca for later. I want to see him kiss the boy's ass first. No tongue, eh, mafankulo?"

Luca spat on the ground. "You are such a dead man."

Cernak found them a sandy patch near the river. "You fight by the rules of pankration—no gouging, no biting. The fight ends when one of you concedes. Agreed?"

Yohan nodded. "One last thing—if he submits, that means he will support Simon."

Ramon agreed. "If your boy returns with a dragon's egg and if you can take me down, then I will support him. Not much chance of either happening."

Yohan dropped his sword belt and stripped off his mail hauberk. He unfastened the leather gambeson beneath and pulled his tunic over his head. The chill morning air raised the hairs on the back of his arms. He stepped out of his boots and set them with the rest of his clothing on a river-washed log. Clad only in a woven hemp belt and linen breechclout, he waited for Ramon to disrobe.

Yohan dug his toes into the sand, feeling where it yielded and where it held. He watched the morning light play across the river. The sun would soon crest Wawel Hill. He would not want to face that glare with his back to the water. *Ramon may be too eager to notice.* Yohan had seen the man fight, tactical, calculating, but every fighter had his weakness. He called out, "Are you stalling, Ramon?"

"I'm letting you live a little longer."

Yohan bent his knees, left leg forward, hands shoulder high. Ramon came in sparring, striking with fists and feet. Testing him. Yohan ducked, dodged, and deflected the blows. A conversation of fists, he let Ramon do the talking. His right arm, not so fast—the man had probably been born left-handed. Stepping back, Yohan let his guard slip. Ramon stepped in with a left jab to the throat, easily deflected. The right came straight at his body center, an instant late.

Yohan held fast and took the blow, forcing Ramon to overextend. His counter to the face knocked the man back. Yohan stepped in and delivered a kick to the knee. Ramon seized his leg and dragged him down. Hooking an arm beneath his elbow, Yohan tried to twist it behind the man's back, but Ramon countered with a knee to the groin and a handful of sand in Yohan's face. The sand he expected, the knee was unfortunate. Yohan rolled away and lurched to his feet.

Ramon was already on him, raining a series of punishing blows on his abdomen and face. Backing away, defending, warding off the strikes he could and absorbing the ones he couldn't, Yohan watched out of swollen eyes as sunlight dappled the water behind his attacker. *Now.*

Dodging a kick that was meant to cripple, Yohan shrugged off the anguish in his belly, the searing pain in his face, and charged Ramon. A clumsy right deflected, Yohan slammed into the man's midriff, sending him back into the river. The morning sun, once behind the castle walls, now shone directly in Ramon's face.

That momentary blindness was all Yohan needed to grapple him by the legs and upend him in the shallow water. Ramon floundered a moment, but Yohan dropped both knees on the man's chest and forced him beneath the surface. His struggles grew weaker. Yohan let him up to choke and gasp, then plunged him into the river. The third time, Cernak yelled, "Enough!"

Yohan let Ramon up, fists ready. The man choked and flailed. Yohan looked him in his eye. "You want to live, ya?"

Ramon gagged and nodded. "*Cedo.* I yield."

Yohan helped him up and walked him back to the beach. "Well fought, brother."

Still gasping and choking, Ramon clasped him by the wrist. "Brother."

Waters of Redemption

Cernak, Stephan, Carla, and Luca watched from the shore. Behind them, Yohan saw another figure standing unnoticed. "Simon, you're back early. What is it?"

"I have the egg. Does that make me a Knight?"

Luca turned and jumped back. "Merda!" He paused a moment, staring at the skull-sized oblong object in Simon's hands. "It is a rock you hold, cretino, nothing more."

Simon handed the object to Cernak. "You be the judge, Master. Did I return with an egg or not?"

Yohan edged closer for a better look. Elongated like a goose egg but much larger, Simon's object was coated on one side with a crusty white rime.

Cernak hefted it, then shook it. "There's something inside."

The others stepped back. Luca crossed himself, and Simon grinned. "Shall I open it?"

Cernak set the object in the sand. The boy drew his broken sword, flourished it once in the air, and brought it down with a crack. Yohan knelt. Picking through the shards, he gasped and held up a withered claw. Cernak moved a few pieces of shell. There, half-buried in the sand, a small skull bared its lipless teeth at them.

Simon held it high for all to see. "I told you. A dragon's egg."

It took Yohan a few moments to register before he laughed, holding his bruised ribs. "Mother of the gods, Simon, only you could go into that stinking hole and bring out an actual dragon's egg. Brother Luca owes you a kiss."

"Those are the bones of a dog." Luca approached the broken egg fragments.

"Look, legs of a dog, tail of a dog—the cretino plays a trick."

Cernak shook his head. "Not possible. The egg was hollow. A rock wouldn't have broken. Simon would have to be cleverer than the six of us combined to devise such a trick."

"He had help." Luca pointed at Yohan. "You planted that egg. You put the cretino in the cave last night and told him where to find it."

"Give it up, ya." Tired of sparring with the man, Yohan held up his hands. "On my word, I could not have done that. I would not have, even if I could."

"You still owe me satisfaction, mafankulo. I think you should deliver it now."

Still holding the toothy little skull, Simon had watched the exchange. "What about my trial?"

Cernak stepped in. "Let it be, Luca. Simon must first pass the last stage of his trial. Since Yohan and Ramon are dressed for the occasion, I will ask them to administer the test."

Simon held Yohan's eye for a moment, then turned to Ramon. "You have been fighting. Must I fight too?"

Shaking his head, Yohan said, "No, Simon, the final test is easy. You need to bathe in the river."

Simon held up his hands and backed away. "I can't do that."

"You must. To become a Knight of Palermo, you must submit to the bath."

"I'm not strong enough. It will kill me."

"What do you mean? I just saw you descend into the pit of hades itself and return with a dragon's egg."

Simon crossed his arms. "I can't."

Luca marched back and forth, sputtering. "Now I am insane. Our cretino does the impossible, but he will not go in the river. I have wasted a day—no, I have wasted a life waiting for this." He turned, held out his arms, and cried, "Madre di Cristo, must I drag him to the water myself?"

Cernak said, "Again, I agree with Luca. You cannot come this far and refuse. We've prepared the trial. We've fought for you. I have ordered a feast for tonight in your honor. Do this now."

To Yohan, Simon's look of anguish spoke more than his words. He put a hand on the boy's shoulder. "It will kill you?"

"You know?"

"I think you are keeping a secret. You remember more than you are saying—isn't that true?"

Simon ducked his head. "If I hold the sword, sometimes it protects me."

"Then touch the sword if you must, but do this one last thing."

The boy nodded and turned his back to the others. He pushed the broken blade into the sand at his feet, untied his belt, and threw off his tunic. Hand on the pommel of his sword, Simon turned.

Cernak grunted and stepped back. Luca bent his middle fingers and held up a sign against evil. "*Diavulu*. I know it. I know he is the devil's son."

As the others shrank back, Simon clutched the pommel of his sword and bent, gasping, to his knees. "Please—the mark, it is killing me."

Yohan only caught a glimpse of the red scar burned into Simon's chest, but he knew the sigil for what it was. Stepping forward, he draped Simon's tunic over his shoulders. "Turn away, everyone. For God's sake, stop staring at him."

Whether the Sword of Jacob or the tunic helped, Yohan didn't wait to find out. "Ramon, come. We do this now."

One man on each arm, they half carried, half dragged Simon into the water. Waist-deep, Yohan grabbed the boy by his curly hair. "We will hold you under for the count of one hundred. Pray to whatever it is you worship that you don't drown."

Simon gulped in one last breath as the two men plunged him backward into the Vistula River. Counting out loud, Yohan reached fifty before the boy began to struggle. By seventy, it was all they could do to hold him under. Twenty counts later, the struggles weakened, then ceased. When Yohan reached one hundred, he nodded to Ramon.

Between the two, they dragged Simon's limp body back up on the shore. Cernak drew the broken sword from the sand and laid it across the boy's chest. For a moment, his face bore a beatific innocence. Then, twitching, choking, gagging, Simon rolled to his side and vomited a fountain of water back into the river.

Cernak looked down, shaking his head. "It might have been a greater mercy had he never recovered."

Yohan wasn't so sure. "This boy is a key to something. He is an enigma we need to solve."

"He is a curse we need to purge," Luca said. "You saw his mark. No wonder he consorts with dragons. No wonder he cannot long remain in a holy place. When I first see him, I say, 'This is the devil.' Now all can see I am right."

"And I see an acolyte who has completed his trial," Cernak said. "Beyond anything I could imagine, he has passed every test. What do the rest of you say?"

Carla eyed the boy as he tried to sit up. "I thought I knew, but he hid this from us. Can we trust him?"

Stephan had fished Simon's wet tunic from the river, folded it, and handed it to him. "A curse was placed on this boy, a powerful *geas*, that steals his wit. That's what I see."

Ramon had pulled on his own white tunic and began refastening his leather gambeson. "Before this morning I would never have considered accepting one such as him. He has the mind of a child, the wit of a fool. That is what I thought last night. Now, I could change my opinion."

Luca grinned down at Simon, struggling into his wet tunic. "What you say, it is *phtt*, nothing. On this, all must be in accord. I oppose him. That is that."

He turned to walk away, but Yohan stopped him. "You are forgetting something."

"I forget nothing. You will pay for your words last night."

"So you remember your agreement. If you yield..."

"I will kill you before I yield. *That* is our agreement."

Simon had stumbled to his feet, bracing himself with his sword. "Why will you kill Yohan?"

"Because I cannot kill *you*, diavulu. Because you are not a brother, I cannot challenge you."

"Then it is easy, friend Luca. Make me a Knight, one of your brothers. Then you can."

Luca spat on the ground. "I am never friend to the devil. I will kill you anyway."

Yohan broke in. "By the oaths he swore, Luca cannot kill you unless you attack him. He can't kill me, even in a pankration match. Besides, I took Ramon. I can take Luca."

Luca paused, tugged on his short beard, and considered Simon. Yohan didn't like the look on his face, but before he could comment, Cernak interrupted. "We are done here. Simon has completed his trial. Now we hold council."

Yohan bent and picked a smooth white object from the sand. The size of a child's fist, it could have been, as Luca said, a dog's skull, save for the rows of sharp conical teeth. "You should keep this." He handed it to Simon. "You may be the last person alive to have entered a cave and returned with the head of a dragon."

Cernak started back up the path to the west castle gate. Stephan and Ramon followed. Luca gave Simon one last look, then climbed the path behind them. Carla said, "I have a few things to clean up here." She held up the pitch pine torch and bellows, shook her head, and continued. "Go, both of you. Simon must rest while we hold council. I will follow shortly."

Yohan waited while Simon retrieved his sword and tucked the small skull into a purse at his side. They climbed the hill in silence, passing through the postern gate. Simon looked around and said, "I should have told you about my mark."

Lost in thought, Yohan trudged a little farther before stopping. "Something changed last night, ya?"

"I had an encounter down there, and now..." He stared off at the Hermanowska Cathedral for a moment. "Now I remember things."

"Do you remember how you got from St. Gereon's chapel to the Smocza Jama?"

Simon smiled, not his usual foolish grin but a knowing smile. "It is a long and ridiculous tale. Perhaps I can tell it one day if I can overcome this mark on my chest."

"You know that mark, the crucified serpent?"

Simon closed his eyes, his brow wrinkled in pain. "Don't say it again."

"How long do you think you can hide from it? We all know the mark you bear. We know what it means. Are you one of them?"

The boy walked on. Head down, long strides, he wouldn't look at Yohan. "Cernak was right. I must rest, and you must hold your council. But please, I ask one thing. Let me remain Simon the fool for a little while longer."

As Simon's witness, Yohan made sure he had a cot in the castle barracks. Cernak intercepted him on his way to the refectory. "Do you still intend to fight Luca?"

"That is my plan. It's the only way I see to achieve full accord and make Simon a brother."

Cernak stopped before they reached the refectory door. "Hold a moment and talk. Have you considered what could happen if you lose?"

"Luca will beat me bloody. I'm prepared for that."

"And Simon?"

"You must have noticed. Our Simon is not so... cretino as he once seemed. I think if he does not join the Fellowship, Simon will find another way."

"And what if you win? What if we agree to take Simon as a Knight in training? Have you considered the consequences?"

Yohan knew that he hadn't, not fully. "I can't plan for everything. I just know it's for the best. Isn't that enough?"

"Go then, make your case. Let's see what the others decide."

On entering the refectory, Yohan found a table set for six. The brothers sat about, eating pastries of stewed beef and turnips. A seat at the head had been reserved for Cernak. Yohan took the vacant stool at the foot. Ramon, sitting on his right, set a tall pitcher next to him and grinned.

Yohan sniffed the contents, ale bittered with juniper berries. He poured himself a bowl and scooped a pastry from the common platter at the table's center. The brothers ate with fingers and daggers, using lumps of bread for both napkins and utensils. Luca sat on his left, ignoring the others and sucking gravy from his fingers. He glanced up and nodded at the pitcher. Yohan slid it across to him.

Cernak had settled himself in at the head of the table. He rapped three times with the hilt of his dagger, and the conversation died away. "I trust the voivode's food, ale, and lodging are satisfactory?"

Yohan raised his bowl and nodded, knowing that Cernak usually opened the council with light talk and banter. The others followed with compliments, mostly to the ale. Luca had emptied his own bowl and poured himself another, holding the pitcher out for Yohan. He took the peace offering and accepted a refill. Cernak tipped back his ale and continued. "We have a few decisions to make. Foremost is whether to accept Simon as an acolyte Knight in training."

Yohan groaned inwardly. *So much for the light talk and banter.*

Carla stood. "I would like to ask Brother Yohan exactly what happened last night."

Cernak said, "I will go first." He then related sequestering Simon in St. Gereon's chapel. "And no, I saw no way out other than the stairwell at the altar."

Yohan told of waiting until vespers rang, then sealing the door with wax from the altar candle. "Then I met the rest of you here. When Cernak left, Luca and I had our little disagreement."

Luca leaned back in his stool, nearly lost his balance, then smiled. "You are forgiven, brother."

Carla said, "And nothing else happened?"

"I returned to my station and waited until dawn."

"And I want you to swear an oath before all of your brothers that you did not let Simon out of that chapel."

Yohan sighed and stood. *Unlikely they will believe me, whatever I say.* He placed his right fist above his heart and spoke the strongest oath he knew. Looking at each in turn, he resumed his seat and finished his ale. "I can prove nothing. I'd already broken the seal when Cernak arrived."

Carla continued to press her point. "Did you fall asleep while on watch? Could he have crept out then?"

"I dozed, ya, near morning. But he would have made too much noise opening that door." Yohan paused a moment. "And to answer your next question, no, I do not think anyone could have come, let him out, and resealed the door using my knife pommel. Not, not without awakening me."

Stephan, who had been silent the whole time said, "Clearly there is another passage, one that leads to the Smocza Jama."

Cernak nodded to him. "The Temple of Hermes. Simon must have stumbled on a secret entrance. It makes sense. The ancient dragon's lair, the temple, they are connected."

Stephan scooped another pastry from the tray. "The dragon's egg, he knew where to find it. That is how he returned so quickly. I wonder what else he saw?"

Luca raised one finger in the air. "You miss the important point." He belched, poured himself half a bowl of ale, and turned the empty pitcher upside down. "Your cretino, he wears a sign of the diavulu on his heart."

Cernak passed another pitcher to the foot of the table. "We didn't miss that. We just haven't gotten to it yet."

Ramon said, "I had a close look at Simon's chest while Brother Yohan was trying to drown him. The mark is a brand, burned into his flesh by someone. I doubt he did it to himself."

"The Serpens Crucis," Cernak said. "We all know that mark, the badge of Apostoli Lucis, the self-named Apostles of the Light. Is that his connection with Jacob ben Reuben?"

Yohan listened to the exchange—nothing he didn't already know, nothing the others hadn't known. They talked like a potter testing his clay, like a smith, working dross from the metal. *Would it be better if they knew of the change in Simon?* He decided to keep the boy's confidences for now. "Ya, his mark is the tau cross with a Roman letter 'S' draped over it. It might not be the crucified serpent at all. It could be his initials."

Luca rocked on his stool and laughed. "Brother lies like a mafankulo priest, but he knows it is all merda, sè?"

Carla nodded in agreement. "Your argument is weak, Yohan. I'm with Luca on this."

"I've had enough run-ins with the Apostoli to know their sigil," Cernak said. "Simon wears the crucified serpent, but it's sinister, reversed with the head above his heart. That means something."

Luca drained his bowl and poured another. "It means he is cursed. The first day I say that, and I say it today."

Stephan had cut his pastry in four equal pieces. He tasted one of the quarters and looked up. "That doesn't mean we should abandon him. Isn't it our role to help the afflicted?"

Carla had finished one of the meat pastries. She reached for another. "Help, yes. Adopt, accept, train? I'm not sure."

Yohan said, "Yesterday, you favored his joining the Fellowship."

"Yesterday, he had not emerged from a dragon's den with the mark of the serpent on his breast. I think I will cast my lot with Luca, however he chooses."

"Very well," Cernak said. "It's time we decide."

Yohan stood, arms folded. "Not yet. Brother Luca and I still have an issue to settle."

Cernak pointed to the door. "Take it outside. I don't want to abuse the voivode's hospitality any more than we already have."

Luca jumped up and his stool fell over with a clatter. Wobbling a moment, he bent to recover the stool and slipped to the floor, laughing. "Cedo, cedo. I yield to the ale and to my brother's prowess with the bowl."

Yohan hooked an arm under his shoulder and helped Luca to his feet. "You'll have to kill me some other time. But now I must enforce our agreement."

"Where is the boy? I will kiss his mafankulo ass."

"Our agreement last night, Luca. You will side with me in this decision."

Yohan didn't like the smirk on Luca's face. The little Sicilian somehow climbed on the seat of his stool and stood, wobbling over them. "I tell, before sister and all my brothers, before the high holy cazzo bishop, and all the *capos de merda* in this mafankulo*castello*, I will side with whatever my dear Brother Yohan chooses."

With that, the stool flew in one direction, and Luca toppled in the other. Yohan managed to catch him as he fell, tumbling them both to the floor. Luca pushed himself away. "And yours will be the guilt for what happens today."

Council

Simon lay on his cot, listening to the quiet barracks activity of men entering and leaving. The cathedral rang *terce* for midmorning prayer, as it had once before in a time forgotten. His chest tightened; his breath choked down to short gasps. Then as the third strike echoed off the castle wall and faded to silence, the hidden claw relaxed its grip on his heart.

A warning perhaps, but late in coming. Simon had already begun picking through that foreign library of memories that now littered the back of his mind—pigeons and swallows nesting among the bells.

High above a stone courtyard, boys in gray cassocks wielded brooms, cleaning a mess of sticks and feathers from the ancient stonework. They drove flocks of outraged birds into the sky. Half in dream, he recalled flying down, down, down on wings of rope to land with a bounce on the paving below.

Simon lost himself in a vision of hooded monks chanting by midnight candles. He awakened to a single deep toll of the cathedral bell, *none*, the ninth hour, midafternoon prayers. He let himself doze, only to be awakened again by someone shaking his arm. "We have reached a decision. It is time."

Decision? About what? He sat up, then flopped back. *Who reached a decision, and why?* Once more, the shake. "Simon, wake up. It is time, ya?

He opened his eyes. *Yohan. The man's name was Yohan.* Like recalling a night's drunken revelry, Simon pieced together fragments of his recent past. The trial, the river. He touched the scars on his chest and coughed. "I need a moment more."

"I will wait outside." Yohan turned to go, then looked back. "Do not be too long."

Simon elbowed himself up. A narrow gallery of timber and plastered brick stretched fifty paces in both directions. His cot was one of about two dozen that lined the back. Rows of gear hung from the opposite wall—swords, pikes, leather gambesons, and cloaks. *Wawel Castle, Krakow, the barracks*, Simon remembered.

Like a story he'd heard as a child—his time with the Knights of Palermo, his travels with Master Jacob—came back as a vague memory of something once significant and now meaningless. He shook the sleep from his head, rubbed the curly tufts of beard on his chin, and wondered how he'd made it this far. *Knights of Palermo, the trial, he'd asked to join... Yohan waited.* Simon hunted for his boots. His breechclout was still damp from the river, but he found a clean white tunic folded beside his cot. He pulled it over his head and belted it tight. Hanging just above his knees, it was a little short. *They had reached a decision. Yohan waited.*

Stepping from the empty barracks, blinking in the late afternoon sun, Simon nodded in recognition at Yohan. "What decision?"

"Cernak will announce it when we reach the refectory."

Cernak, Master Cernak. Simon recalled a face, broad forehead, reddish beard, straight brown hair gone to gray. Cernak, a wolf among dogs. Simon followed Yohan across the courtyard. The castle refectory stood in the shadow of Hermanowska Cathedral. His gut tightened at the memories. *Only yesterday?* Past the cathedral, almost at the castle residence, Yohan paused at an arched doorway. "Are you ready?"

"You told them?"

"I've told them nothing that they didn't already know."

"Then I am ready."

Within the refectory, Simon found a semicircle of five hooded figures standing about a flaming brazier. Yohan followed him in and guided him to stand before the group. Across the brazier, Cernak's gray-blue eyes glittered in the firelight. He pushed back his hood. "Simon Halfsword, the Knights of Palermo find that you have completed your trial. If you are to join us, we all must agree. Do you understand?"

It was only then that Simon grasped what, in his innocence, he had committed himself to. He touched his chest and felt the claw tighten. He nodded, hesitant to speak.

Yohan whispered behind him. "You must say it out loud."

"I understand."

"Then we will begin," Cernak said. "Brother Stephan, how do you declare?"

The figure to Cernak's right pushed back his hood and stepped to the brazier. He drew a candle from beneath his cloak, lit it, and held it up. "I accept Simon as a Brother Knight."

Cernak took the candle from him and placed it in an iron candelabrum. "Sister Carla?"

Another of the hooded figures revealed herself. The tall Andalusian produced her candle and lit it at the brazier. "I accept Simon as my Brother Knight..." She paused a moment, then continued. "In the hope of learning his true identity."

On Cernak's invitation, Ramon stepped forward. He held the fourth hooded figure long in his gaze before lighting his own candle. "I too accept Simon as a Brother Knight. May God have mercy on us."

Luca didn't wait for Cernak's invitation. He threw back his hood and held up a candle, grinning at the others. "Today, I am asked to kiss the devil's ass." Luca stepped directly in front of Simon. "Do I kiss your ass now, diavulu?"

Simon edged away from the sparkling black eyes and ale-soaked breath, shaking his head. "That is not necessary."

"Not necessary—it is not necessary he says." Luca held his unlit candle high and paraded it around the brazier. "We welcome the devil into our house, but maybe is better that he is inside pissing out than outside pissing in, sè?" Luca lit his candle, bowed, and proffered it to Cernak.

Four tapers burned in the candelabrum. Cernak stepped forward with his own candle, lit it, and said, "I too accept Simon as a fellow Knight of Palermo. Yohan, as his Witness how do you declare?"

Simon heard a low cough. He felt the man's hesitation, the rustle of garments, the shuffling indecision. Then Yohan moved into the light. "I brought him from the woods at knifepoint. I supported him in his trials. I want to think I am both Witness and a friend to Simon." He circled the brazier, looking each of them in the eye. "If we are to accept him into our fellowship, we must do so unconditionally, with open hearts. But I haven't heard that from you tonight."

Simon waited as Yohan circled. Suddenly the prospect of staying in Krakow while the others moved on seemed very real. The sense of loss and abandonment he had felt deep within the Smocza Jama returned with painful intensity. He closed his eyes, recalling the anguish of that abyss.

When Simon opened them again, Yohan stared him in the face. "Ya, I share the doubts of my Sister Carla, the unease of Brother Ramon, and I know Brother Luca has the candor to express what all of us most fear but will not say."

Yohan stepped away from Simon—back beyond his line of vision—and continued. "I know it breaks custom. We have all broken far worse, nor do we stand on the pretty words of kings and prelates. Cernak, I apologize, but before I can light this last candle, I must ask Simon to explain in his own words who he is."

Simon's fingers traced the scar beneath his thin tunic. *So much for keeping confidences.* He looked at the others. Five pairs of eyes glowed in the brazier's yellow light, but it was to Yohan, standing in the darkness behind him, that Simon answered. "I'm not the boy you met in the forest. I'm not the boy who descended beneath the Hermanowska." Simon paused and fidgeted. No one spoke, so he continued. "I do not know who I was before... before I followed Master Jacob."

Luca shuffled his feet and cocked his head to one side. Simon remembered a tale of the condemned witch who sang so sweetly that she was allowed to live for as long as she could sing. Despite the pain in his chest, he continued. "As you have asked, so did Master Jacob ask, night after night, 'Do you remember who you are—where you came from?' And the mark burned my heart as it burns me now, and I could not answer."

Simon remembered how the witch's tale had ended. After singing for ten days without end, the exhausted woman had collapsed and died. He steeled himself and went on. "Now I think perhaps he only tested me. Oh yes, he tested the strength of the curse I bear." Simon clutched his chest and gasped for breath. "Now I think he was not my guardian, but my keeper."

He choked and fell to his knees. "I have no idea why... why I still live."

A corbeled ceiling, heavy timbers—they swam into view along with knees, faces, and a flickering brazier. Simon tried to sit, but a man—Yohan—knelt at his shoulder and held him down. "Easy, not yet."

Cold flagstones beneath his head. A growing lump. Simon reached behind and touched it. Tender, damp with blood, it throbbed with every heartbeat. Calloused fingers lifted his head and pushed a wad of rough fabric beneath his neck.

A murmur of voices, shadows moved against the dark ceiling. *There were candles…Simon remembered, candles and a decision.* A weight on his chest. This time, it wasn't the claw. He reached up and grasped the hilt of his sword. *Had he worn it that evening?* Simon couldn't recall. Once more, he tried to rise. Yohan helped him sit. Cernak stood at his feet, then moved to one side. Six candles burned in an iron candelabrum set before him. *Six candles. That means something.*

Simon managed to roll to his knees and stand. "You have made a decision?"

Yohan put a hand on his shoulder, and Cernak smiled. "Welcome, Brother Simon Halfsword. You are now Knight in training. When we reach Palermo, you may take your vows and join our fellowship."

Luca chewed on his lower lip as Cernak spoke. "And now I challenge you, Brother Cretino."

Before Simon could reply, Yohan said, "I hadn't told you, our Brother Luca will be training you in the art of pankration fighting."

The little Sicilian grinned. "Sè. Now every day I challenge, and you accept. Like it?"

Simon wished his head didn't throb, that his legs didn't wobble beneath him. "I accept. Just not today, I hope."

"No, but maybe go twice tomorrow for lost time. Three times, maybe."

Luca seemed incredibly pleased. Yohan hadn't spoken, but Cernak stepped aside and returned with a rolled bundle. "I had something made for you."

Simon unwrapped it. A broad leather belt, worn in places—it might have been a piece of harness years ago. He fitted it about his waist and fastened the heavy brass buckle. Cernak held out something else. "And this."

A scabbard, shortened to half length, Simon fitted it to his belt. Yohan said,

"No, it hangs on your left side that you may draw it across the body."

"I am left-handed. You hadn't noticed?" By the ensuing silence, Simon realized he had said the wrong thing. "It is not bad, is it?"

Ramon stepped up and helped him adjust the scabbard. "It's not bad. I fight with both hands, and my left is often stronger."

"Good," Yohan said. "You can train him in swordplay."

Swordplay, something he feared. Simon hefted his blade, cleaner than before, polished, and oiled. "Be careful, ya. I've had it sharpened and the point restored."

Still pitted, the steel had been burnished to a silvery sheen. Simon ran his fingers down the black Aramaic letters inlaid into the metal. A simple prayer for defense, he wondered how it was bound to the scar on his chest. As Yohan said, the broken end had been ground to a wedge-shaped point with chisel edges. Simon pushed it into his scabbard and nodded. "Thank you."

Cernak nodded in return. "We have one more tradition, a small celebration. Had you not passed the trial, it would have been a farewell dinner. As it is, we will drink and feast to our newest brother, Simon Halfsword."

Simon found himself at the head of a rectangular table. His head still ached from hitting the floor, but at least the claw in his chest slept for a change. Bits of strained speech punctuated the periods of awkward silence. He so wanted to fit in, but he felt like a rabbit among foxes.

Cernak had poured him a bowl of ale and passed a wooden trencher of roast mutton. Yohan had tried to engage him in conversation as had Stephan, but Simon couldn't think of anything to say. Carla and Ramon had started their own heated argument about the virtues of Damascus steel, and Luca sat chewing on a heel of bread. Somehow, the meal seemed more an obligation than a celebration.

The ale dulled the pounding in his head and eased some of his discomfort. Yohan had poured him a third bowl when Cernak rapped on the table. "We have some business to discuss before too much ale passes our lips. I would ask Brother Simon to tell us about his cart, his tumbrel, where it came from, what it contains, and what he will do with it."

The awkward attempts at conversation suddenly made sense. Simon stood to speak, then realized it was a bad idea and sat back down. "I don't want to do anything with it. I mean..." He belched and took a short sip of ale. "I mean, I said before—before the trial—you can have it." Simon waved a hand in front of his face. "No, we have it now, the Knights, because I am us. Right?"

Cernak nodded, but Simon was pretty sure he didn't understand. "Wait, it's like this. Master Jacob, who maybe wasn't my master, had the cart, but he is dead, and the voivode thinks the cart is mine now. So, Yohan says I cannot give you the cart because that would be payment, and you, no we, Knights cannot take payment. But now I am a Knight. Oh yes, the cart belongs to us."

Once more, Cernak nodded, but this time he spoke. "I understand, Simon. That was the point of your joining our band."

"No, not the point." Simon tipped back his bowl and finished it. "I want to be a Knight, to belong somewhere. That is the point. The cart is just—just a thing..." He forgot for a moment what else he wanted to say. "Could I have some more?"

Yohan smiled at him.

At least someone understands. Simon waited until his bowl was full before taking another sip. Yohan pulled the pitcher back. "Easy, friend. We have a long discussion tonight, and I don't want to carry you back to the barracks."

Simon took a tiny sip. "I usually sleep underneath the cart..." Then he remembered. "Yes, because Jacob slept in the cart. You know, I don't think he was really my master. But he kept money in there in a box under the floor, and he had furs. I have furs—no, we have furs now. They come from Tver in the land of Rus, and he sells them in Vienna." Simon put both hands on the table. "I think I had a lot of ale."

Cernak leaned forward., "That brings up the next question. We were planning to travel north with the onset of summer. Where do we go now?"

Ramon grinned. "Old Jacob sells in Vienna, yes? Maybe we should too. I know a woman who is happy to see us in Vienna." He glanced at Simon and spread his arms. "All of us."

"I suppose this woman has many friends?" Carla said.

"Yes, yes, many friends, and room for all of us."

Stephan looked doubtful. "This year is already past the spring equinox.

Such a diversion would probably keep us there until after the summer solstice. Besides, we can get twice the value if we sell to the Venetians instead."

Simon had heard of Venetians somewhere, something Jacob had said. "I think Venetians robbed us."

Cernak sat up. "Ha, you are right, of course. But you did not have your fellow Knights to defend you. I agree with Stephan. We cannot dally long in Vienna, and we should make the most of Brother Simon's contribution."

Ramon looked hopeful. "Vienna is on the way to Venice, yes? Then we can dally, perhaps a little?"

Stephan shook his head but said nothing. Luca grinned across the table. "In Venice, I have many such friends."

"It's settled then," Cernak said. "We cross the Danube at Nussdorf and head south through the mountains to Venice."

Simon remembered staggering off to the latrine and then stumbling across to the barracks. Yohan and Ramon might have helped him. The morning hour of lauds rang before the sun had more than lightened the horizon. Simon's head felt like a broken chamber pot poorly mended. He managed to sit upright with his face buried in his hands. A tap on his shoulder; he looked up. Luca grinned down at him in the morning light, fully dressed in riding trousers and quilted gambeson. "I come to give lessons in pankration, sè?"

He hadn't forgotten Yohan's words. Simon had only hoped he meant some time other than his present moment of wretchedness. "You can see I am not ready."

"Enemies come any time. You must be ready, always."

Simon looked up at Luca's face and pondered the truth to those words. "I must first make my obeisance at the latrine."

"Hurry. I wait on the common."

Simon lurched to his feet. The room swam, and he stumbled outside to vomit in the grass. Luca followed, chuckling. "Ale is a friend who always betrays. Remember, I wait; I do not betray."

Walking across the courtyard, Simon ached in every corner of his body. He thanked whatever God the bishop worshiped, that the latrine was empty and no one witnessed the ale's final vengeance. *Luca waits.*

He had crossed the common the day before. It was an area for exercising horses and practicing arms. The tumbrel had been parked on the common, against the far wall. The oxen knelt in the grass nearby. Luca was hard to miss, pacing and dancing on the wet lawn. "Do you know I enjoy this, Brother Cretino? Last night, I challenge. Brother Yohan, he says no, I must train the cretino. I think this is maybe more pleasure to train than to challenge. How do you think, Brother Cretino?"

"I think if pankration is fought with the jaw, then I should yield right now."

"No, is like this." Luca stepped forward with a lightning jab to Simon's face. "And this." He followed with a punch to Simon's lower abdomen that knocked him back.

His breath gone, his diaphragm on fire, Simon gasped and fell to his knees. He felt Luca's arm tighten about his neck and a pressure against his back. In his ear, the little Sicilian whispered, "I kill the cazzo diavulu now—if I want. But I will not. No, not today."

Curled on his side, gasping, clutching his gut, Simon heard someone calling to him. The words lost themselves in his roaring head. A kick to his back and again, he heard the voice. *Luca.* "Get up mafankulo. Your lesson only starts."

Simon opened his eyes. His assailant, the little Sicilian demon, jumped back and forth shouting. "Get up, get up, or I change my mind."

Pushing himself to a crouch, Simon wiped the grass and blood from his right eye. He straightened on wobbly legs. Luca stopped dancing and grinned at him. "So is lesson one, sè? Now is lesson two."

Simon couldn't help himself—he stepped back three paces. Luca shook his head and held out his arms. "No, no, idiot, never retreat, always attack. Is like this, legs apart, knees bent, like your mama on her back, sè?"

Luca demonstrated, his elbows cocked, fists at shoulder level. Simon tried to mimic him.

Circling, kicking his feet, Luca said, "You stand like a cow." Luca ended his inspection, arms at his sides, chin out, directly in front of Simon. "Now hit me. Come, try."

Easy shot, Simon aimed for the nose and struck with his left. Luca bobbed his head, and Simon's fist sailed past. He tried again with his other fist. Again,

Luca dodged, laughing. Once more with the left. Luca's hand on his wrist, his arm beneath his shoulder, Simon saw the cathedral turn upside down a moment before he slammed to the ground. Birds circled in a sky the color of lake ice, then a glimpse of Luca's knee coming down and the world turned a frosty gray.

Gasping, blinking, air coming in short painful drags, Simon opened his eyes to Luca's dark whiskery face. "You died again, Brother Cretino. Stand. Is time for lesson three."

Vistula River

On his belly, his arm twisted behind his back, Simon looked up to see Carla and Ramon inspecting the tumbrel. He would yield if he could speak. As it was, the knee on his spine and the hand on his throat had locked him in a world of pain and fog and gradual unconsciousness. When he once more opened his eyes, the oxen had been harnessed and yoked, the great wheels had been unchocked, and the entire rig moved to the castle courtyard. Yohan spoke from somewhere behind his line of vision. "Do you go with us, or will you remain here?"

Almost, almost he considered it. Without moving, Simon cleared his throat and spat blood from his cut lip. "I cannot stand, cannot walk."

"Then you stay?"

"No, but I need to use the latrine and get my sword."

"You have until the sun clears the Cathedral roof."

Simon didn't twitch. Yohan's shadow crossed the lawn and disappeared. The soft grass, still damp with the morning dew, felt like the finest down beneath his belly. He could close his eyes and let the sun warm his aching back. Simon wiggled his fingers, moved his arms. Every bone cried in distress. He rolled to his back, but his shoulders refused to move. Curling, arching, he managed to get his knees under him. Every breath hurt. He staggered to his feet, arms hanging. One foot before the other. *Balance, balance.* The sky lightened above the cathedral.

Upon returning from the latrine, Yohan caught up with him. "I've put your gear in the tumbrel. We are late."

Simon kept walking, fearing that if he ever stopped, he would never find the strength to move again. The oxen cleared the castle gate without him. He caught up as they eased their way down the steep grade. Yohan led on foot, his mount tied behind the cart. He looked different without his chainmail hauberk and steel helmet, older. The big man said nothing as Simon approached. Nodding, Yohan might have smiled as he passed Simon the willow switch.

His oxen once more, the plodding yellow beasts barely rolled an eye when Simon switched them on their flanks. The cart bumped and rattled. Simon trudged along at its side. Yohan untied his horse and rode ahead. *Tumbrel Yohan had called it, a heavy cart not meant to be ridden.* From now on, he would call it a tumbrel as well.

Cernak and Stephan met him at the bottom of the hill. Simon halted the rig long enough for them to load bundles into the back. *Supplies.* He'd never thought much about supplies in the past. Jacob had always looked after their food and clothing.

On leaving Krakow, they followed the Vistula River west, beneath the frowning bluffs of Wawel Hill. Luca and Carla rode ahead. Simon noted that they each carried short horse-bows slung across their shoulders. Above them, a solitary tower looked out over the river. They passed a dark opening, the Smocza Jama. It seemed like an eternity since he'd dropped that candle, seen the faint glow of daylight, and stepped out blinking, to the surprise of Yohan and the others. The tumbrel rattled past the spot where they'd nearly drowned him.

The morning sun stood well above the eastern horizon when Cernak called for a break. Ramon on his dappled gelding rode up from behind. "We have practice swords in the wagon. I will show you a few things while we rest."

Simon found himself in a padded leather coat wielding an awkward wooden blade. He learned how to block edge strikes as well as thrusts. He also learned that being knocked to the ground by a wooden stave was only slightly more painful than being knocked down by a fist. He groaned to his feet when the others returned to their saddles. Once more on the road, Simon focused on keeping the oxen moving, keeping the tumbrel from sliding into the adjacent ditch, and keeping himself upright.

A farmer approached, driving a horse-drawn wagon. Simon jockeyed the tumbrel to one side while the farmer eased around on the soft ground. The wagon tottered. The farmer mumbled and cursed as he whipped his horses to regain the road. Not the first traveler he'd met that day, Simon couldn't help glancing over his shoulder. *Too many people saw him pass.* He wondered about thieves. At their next stop, he cornered Yohan. "We never traveled the main roads. Jacob said they were filled with thieves."

"I don't think six Knights of Palermo and their well-trained acolyte have much to fear from thieves. Perhaps your Jacob has exaggerated the danger somewhat, ya?"

By late afternoon, Simon no longer felt the road beneath his feet, no longer cared whether the oxen pulled true or strayed. His legs ached all the way up to his shoulders, and the road seemed to roll along forever. If Cernak hadn't jumped out of the way, Simon's oxen would have run him down. "Stop here, boy. Stop."

It took him several paces to understand, and several more to regain control of the beasts. Cernak trotted up. "Where were you going?"

"I don't know. Where are we?"

"About twenty yards past our camp. Do those things back up?"

Simon shook his head. He took the near ox by its yoke and led it in a tight circle. The two-wheeled tumbrel followed, reversing in little more than its own width. Cernak pointed out a rutted trail that led north, away from the river. Just over a low rise, Stephan knelt by a well-used firepit, striking a steel loop in his fist against a nodule of flint. Carla and Yohan appeared and began unloading bundles. Cernak pointed off to the north. "You can set your animals to graze over there with the horses."

Grass along the Vistula River grew tall and thick. Simon made sure water was available and hobbled the oxen nearby. Before returning to the camp, he paused to inspect Cernak's tall stallion. It flared its nostrils at him, shying away.

"He knows the diavulu when he sees him." Luca came striding through the grass. "Do you ride, cretino?"

"No, I think I have never ridden a horse."

"Excellent! Then you live long enough, I teach you to ride." He put an arm around Simon's shoulder. "You will find it is not so painful as the pankration, sè?"

"Oh yes, I am sure. With your help, it will be all of that and more."

Luca slapped him on the back and laughed. "We understand each other then."

The little Sicilian followed Simon back to their camp where they were met by Ramon. The two spoke in hushed tones and Simon left them to plot new miseries. At the end of a day's travel, the tumbrel needed his attention.

He checked the yoke first, looking for signs of wear. Jacob had outfitted his animals with a simple harness that looped behind their forelegs and helped hold the yoke in place on downgrades. Padded where they passed beneath the withers, they could chafe if not maintained. Simon looked for excessive hair or other indications of chafing. He then lifted a heavy triangular frame from its place on the tumbrel side and braced it beneath the draw pole, leveling the cart on its two wheels. Finally, he put both feet against the bottom of each wheel and grabbed a spoke above his head, shaking it back and forth to test the hub and axle connection. Satisfied that his rig was fit to travel, Simon joined the others for their evening meal.

Stephan handed him a metal pannier of mutton and barley mash with a lump of hard bread. "We don't eat so well on the road," he said. "But we don't starve."

Simon nodded thanks. He recalled many meals with Jacob that were nowhere near as good. Choosing a log upwind of the fire, he concentrated on his food. Rolled into thick balls and fried in mutton fat, the barley mash smelled delicious. He ate it with his fingers. Yohan sat next to him. "There is some ale left if you're thirsty."

Simon shuddered. "I think I had enough last night. Today has been... painful."

"It won't get better, you know. You'll learn to fight and bear the pain. That's our life."

Simon ate another lump of fried barley mash. "Why do you do it then?"

"Most of us"—Yohan nodded toward Luca and Ramon—"we didn't come easy into this life. Some are deserters from a failed campaign or fugitives from a prince's wrath. The Knights of Palermo include thieves and murderers. Some, perhaps like yourself, are just lost souls searching for a purpose."

"Is that what I am doing, looking for a purpose? Because I don't know who I am anymore, if I ever knew."

"Your night in the caverns?"

"The Temple of Hermes, you mean." Simon clutched his sword hilt. "Oh yes, I can say it now." He paused a moment, staring into the fire. "It's worse. Before... before that night, I didn't know what I didn't know. Now, I've eaten of the fruit. My eyes have been opened. Still, I see nothing."

"Then you have a purpose, Simon Halfsword."

With that, Yohan rose and wandered off to join Luca and Ramon. Simon watched while he finished his meal. They talked and laughed. Feeling like an outsider at a wedding, he scrubbed his pannier out with dirt, wiped it with the hem of his tunic, and returned it to Stephan. The man looked at him in surprise. "No, that's yours, part of your kit. Let me show you."

"I didn't know I had a kit."

Stephan led him to the tumbrel where he pulled out a jute canvas bag. "You do now. Warm clothing for when we hit the mountains, bedding, and this." He held up a short leather jacket. "Padded gambeson. It won't protect you from an arrow or sword thrust, but it will impede a smaller blade and maybe buy you some time."

"Where..."

"We bought it all this morning while you and Luca were practicing."

"Luca was practicing."

Stephan pulled a brief grimace. "You'll get used to it." He rummaged in the bag and pulled out a plain steel dagger in a leather sheath. "Here, wear this."

Simon turned it over in his hands. Longer than the knife he used for eating, it would just fit between his knee and his hip. "For Luca?"

"Not unless you want him to kill you. Ramon will train you in the knife as well as the sword." Stephan turned to leave, then turned back. "You will see far worse than Luca on this trip."

The next morning, Simon would have been hard to convince. He'd made up his bed in the tumbrel, as Jacob would normally do. Dozing off in the quiet security of those wooden walls, he barely stirred until the pale light of dawn dimmed the stars. A soft rustle of clothing, then two hands clutched his ankles and jerked Simon out, throwing him to the ground. Luca fell on Simon's chest. "You are dead, cretino."

The remainder of his lesson passed in a blur of stances, strikes, blocks, and his inevitable impact with the ground. One lucky punch caught Luca in the shoulder. He flopped on his back and flailed his arms and legs, laughing. In the next heartbeat, he sprang to his feet. His fists landed like hail and a kick to the knee sent Simon to the dirt. "Next time, cretino, be ready."

Simon limped most of that day. He tried to hide it when others rode past and silently thanked the oxen for their leisurely gait. Ramon's lesson that afternoon did little to improve things. He pressed Simon hard, always working against his right, his off side. Ramon feinted with a cross-body slash, then struck down at the knee. Simon drew back and lowered his sword, eyes watering in pain.

"You favor your left leg. An opponent will see that. Raise your guard. We go again."

Ramon did not let up, and Simon was forced to fight through the pain. He managed to block most of the blows, but Ramon's wooden sword still inflicted bruises up and down his body. That evening, Simon drank enough water to rouse him before dawn. Awakened in the morning darkness, he rolled off the tumbrel to relieve himself. Stiff, achy, his knee would have to hold up. Wrapped in blankets, he huddled behind a tree to wait.

The birds came first, chiming away in the trees like bells at lauds. Simon stared through the shadowy branches to watch the first gray highlights tint the clouds. Movement. Luca approached, silent as the clouds themselves. Simon awaited his opportunity, then sprang out and locked an elbow about the man's neck, securing it with his other arm.

Luca pushed back, twisting, slamming a fist into Simon's ribs, but it just gave him the impetus to cling tighter. In desperation, Luca kicked back at Simon's knee. Pushing Luca to the ground, he fell on top. Luca struggled and gagged, choking out. "Cedo, cedo. I yield."

"You are dead mafankulo." Simon loosened his choke hold. "You will not attack me while I sleep. Agree?"

Luca said nothing. Simon tightened his grip again. "No? Then you will die."

"Against... against... pankration rules."

"Does your enemy follow pankration rules, Luca?"

The little Sicilian stopped struggling. "Cedo, cedo, *d'accordo.*"

Simon released him and jumped back, waiting for the trick, waiting for the retaliatory blow. Luca only sprawled in the dirt and gasped. Simon wanted to offer help, an arm for support. *Not wise, not with an injured wolf.* He stood back while Luca pushed himself to his feet. "Our lesson is over, sè?"

Simon looked him in the eye. *Was it vengeance he saw, or pride?* "For today, yes."

Their road that morning ran straight while the great Vistula River swung to the south and disappeared among stands of willow and beech. It wasn't until the afternoon that Ramon offered another lesson in swordplay. "Unless you would rather learn the bow. It is not nearly as painful."

Simon drew out his long dagger. He'd taken to wearing it as he walked. "Teach me how I should use this."

Ramon grinned at him. "I heard of your little battle with Luca. Do you think you'll need a knife next time?"

Simon slid the blade back in its sheath. "I think I won't know when I need it until I do. Can you teach me?"

"I don't have a suitable wooden practice blade. We'll have to use sticks." Ramon rummaged the brush for a fallen branch and broke it in half. "You fight the sword with your left hand, so learn the knife with your right."

"What if I only have my knife?"

Ramon shook his head. "Perhaps someday Brother Luca will teach you the *paranza corta,* the short weapon. You must earn his respect first."

Simon picked up his wooden practice sword. Ramon had called it a *waster* but hadn't explained why. He held the broken stick in his right hand. Similarly armed, Ramon fell into a crouch. "Take your stance, knife to the side."

Right foot forward, left foot back, Simon watched Ramon's weapons. He'd already felt the sting of the waster against his ribs. The stick only promised added pain. Ramon straightened. "No, don't look at the sword. Watch me.

Look at my eyes. They will tell you when I strike and where. Always watch your opponent's eyes."

Knowing that the strike would come, knowing that it would likely hit one of his bruises, Simon tried to concentrate on Ramon's eyes. The man weaved back and forth, his waster moving in small circles. "Now, stab me."

Simon lunged forward as he had been taught. Ramon's short stick caught Simon's waster and knocked it to one side. A familiar jolt of pain, Simon's left arm burned where it had been struck. Ramon pushed away. "You looked at my chest when you lunged. I saw your eyes move before your sword arm even twitched. Again."

The session finally ended with Simon having mastered a few rudimentary techniques with his wooden knife. He walked back to the tumbrel feeling like an overripe pear, badly handled. One move, Simon wondered if Ramon had meant him to see it. The man held his knife hidden behind his arm, then spun it out for an upward slash, closing sword to sword, before stabbing Simon in the back.

Once alone, he drew his own dagger, the steel one, and practiced the same move. Simon shuddered. Could he take a life so easily? The narrow blade had a heavy spine and a needle-sharp tip. He slid it back into the sheath at his side and drew it again. Awkward. It pulled too far before clearing its sheath. He tied it lower on his leg. Better, but still awkward. He adjusted his sword to match and tried to draw both weapons.

Blood welled up on his forearm before Simon realized he had cut himself, drawing his own dagger. He rubbed a handful of dirt and moss on the wound to staunch the bleeding and practiced the draw once more, this time slowly. Again, the knife grazed his forearm. He fussed with the sheath, then tried tying it on the right, next to his sword.

He set his feet and drew. The knife slipped into his right hand, hidden behind his wrist and forearm, while the broken sword blade flew out in his left. He repeated the move. It felt almost natural. Simon decided to wear both weapons while traveling.

The following morning, he awoke to the sounds of their camp coming to life. Simon expected to find Luca waiting when he slipped from the tumbrel. His feet touched the ground—dewy grass, campfire smoke, no Luca. A heavy fog had crept up from the distant river and blanketed the land. Glancing behind him, slipping between the trees, Simon approached their campfire. Stephan looked up from an iron pot of boiling water. "Arm yourself, boy. We may have trouble this morning."

Back at the tumbrel, Simon tied his leather gambeson in place before strapping on his sword belt and checking his knife. Stephan remained at the fire when Simon returned. "Where is everyone?"

"We had visitors last night. They stayed hidden, but Luca heard them moving about, and so did Carla."

Simon rested a hand on his sword hilt. "Not cattle or deer?"

"Luca found tracks this morning, human tracks. Eight men, maybe more."

"What..." Simon glanced about and lowered his voice. "What should I do?"

"Guard the tumbrel. I am guarding the camp while the others search the area."

Simon took up a post next to the left wheel. He noted with some satisfaction that his frayed counting rag still clung to one spoke. The fog grew thicker, smothering the morning sky in a formless gray shadow. Small, furtive sounds crept from the surrounding trees. Dripping leaves, the rustle of small birds in the foliage, or perhaps something else. Simon turned at every noise. Bad enough he was alone, worse that he could see nothing farther than a dozen paces off.

Simon remembered his first encounter with marauders. Not so many days earlier, it now seemed a lifetime ago. Vague memories of that night, burying Jacob, of marching to Krakow in the company of Cernak and Yohan. A different fog had enveloped him then. *Had he been aware of anything?* Simon gasped as the silent claw closed within his chest, a subtle reminder of memories best left undisturbed.

A distant shout pulled him from his reverie. Simon checked both sides of the tumbrel. *Where to stand?* An easy target, vulnerable from all directions, he backed away to a copse of small trees. A host of birds fled as he made his way into the thicket. More shouts. They seemed closer. Simon crouched to watch between the branches. A momentary shadow passed behind the far wheel, then another. Cautious, testing, then retreating—intruders, not friends. Simon waited, barely breathing.

One of the shadows leapt to the back of the tumbrel. He jumped off just as quickly, landing with a grunt. *Two, two enemies—how was he supposed to defend their camp alone?* Simon had no idea what he should do. At that moment, he heard Stephan call out, followed by the ring of weapons. It was Master Jacob beset on the Roman road all over, Simon clenched in fear. *Two enemies, once more he would fail.*

Stephan called again, called him by name. Simon had no choice. He leapt from the copse and drew his sword, engaging the closest intruder. The man bore an arming sword, a common foot soldier's weapon. He whipped it from its sheath faster than an eyeblink and crouched, left foot forward, sword leveled at Simon's chest—and paused.

Shortened by half, Simon's broken blade would have been no match for his opponent's sword had the man not balked in confusion at seeing a left-handed opponent. In that heartbeat, Simon lunged forward, batted the intruder's weapon aside, and closed. He brought his blade across the man's neck but found it deflected by a heavy leather collar. The other seized him and tried to throw him to the ground. Simon countered with a knee to the groin. His right hand freed, he drove his hidden knife into the man's side.

Pushing away, Simon raised his sword in time to parry a neck-high slash from the other intruder. Coming unabated, the force of the blow knocked Simon back and he tumbled to the ground. The shortened sword spun from his grip. He tried to roll away, but the sword tip followed him, an inevitable finger of death that never arrived.

The sword fell to the ground. His assailant collapsed, and Simon looked up to see Yohan standing in his place, holding a bloody knife. "Next time, do not lose your weapons."

The Wild Road

Simon saw nothing more of their attackers that morning. Stephan had managed to hold off two of the marauders before Luca and Carla rode to his aid. A wicked slash across Stephan's chest would have been worse had he not been wearing his leather gambeson. Ramon tended to the injury, stitching a poultice of moss into the wound. "It'll give you something to show the ladies when we reach Venice."

"So long as he hadn't rubbed shit on his sword. I don't care to die of someone else's foul humors."

Carla brandished the sword in question. "Shitty steel, but no shit on the blade. I won't say the same of the blade that slew its former owner. Brother Luca, did you have to slash the man in his bowels?"

Ramon laughed. "I think that's as high as he could reach."

"Mafankulo, you will die for that mouth."

Cernak broke in. "Don't kill him yet. He has to finish stitching up Brother Stephan."

Head in his hands, Simon had sat apart from the group, listening to the banter. It wasn't until he looked up that he noticed Yohan sitting nearby.

Still clad in his mail and helmet, the man nodded at him. "You fought well today."

"I killed a man and almost died. It wasn't what I expected."

Yohan ducked out of his helmet and set it on the ground. "Not all glory, is it? We practice; we spar. But battle, real battle, is dirty work, ya? Men bleed—men die."

"Why? Why do you fight? There is plenty of open land here. Why don't you farm?"

"I would ask you the same." Yohan paused, looking out over the misty fields. "You could have stayed in Krakow, bought a farm with that load of furs, found a wife. Why did you want to join the Fellowship?"

Simon returned his head to his hands and examined his feet. His boots were separating at the seams, and his ankles had chafed raw. "This road is all I know. The *wild road*, I think, it is my own special purgatory."

"And, in so many ways, is it the same for the rest of us. I was once *ushkuinik*, a river pirate. Volga, Danube, even the Vistula, I robbed and killed from here to Novgorod. Luca and Ramon were mercenaries, assassins for hire. Cernak? He was a monster. All of us—we eschewed everything to became Knights of Palermo."

"There isn't a third way? A road without conflict?"

"You should have become a mendicant or a monk."

The brand burned on Simon's chest. The claw tightened. Still, he raised his head and grinned. "I fear that is the one road forever closed to me."

Yohan stood. "Then you will learn to fight, Brother Simon. Come, Cernak wants a word with you."

Cernak met them at the tumbrel. He wanted more than a word. "I think it's time we took a closer look at our cargo here." He peered into the high-sided cart. "I hadn't wanted to unpack things in Krakow where everyone could see. Regardless, it seems we've somehow drawn attention to ourselves."

"My master, Jacob—when I was—that is, before I was..."

Cernak interrupted. "Before whatever happened in the Smocza Jama, you mean."

"Like a dream, but yes. Before I awakened in..." Simon clutched his chest and felt the air leave his body. He gagged but could say nothing more.

Yohan continued for him. "Before you awakened in the Temple of Hermes."

Eyes crushed shut, Simon nodded and coughed. "Yes, I'm trying to say that Jacob always feared marauders." He paused to draw a shallow breath. "We took the hidden roads, the old roads abandoned and forgotten."

"And still you were attacked," Yohan said. "How did they find you?"

Simon shook his head. "Maybe someone knew Jacob, knew his habits. Maybe we were expected."

Cernak returned to the back of the tumbrel. Waist-high on a large man, it had footholds on one side. He turned to Simon. "I think if you unload this thing, we may find some answers."

Simon took that as an order and scrambled up the side. Reaching the flat wooden bed, he climbed the mound of cargo and stripped back a rough tarpaulin of woven hemp. Beneath lay bales of fur, each wrapped in oiled doeskin. Simon hefted a bale and passed it down to Yohan.

Five bales later, he stripped off his leather gambeson. By the time the first layer was unloaded, Simon was down to his breechclout. Luca arrived and climbed up to help. "Cazzo *anzianos*. Old men, they talk, talk while we do the work." A smirk lit his face. "Do not think because we had a little dance this morning that I forget I teach you the pankration."

Simon picked up two bales at once and lowered them to Yohan. "I am counting on it."

By the time the sun cleared the treetops and burned off the remaining dew, Simon dragged the last bale from the front of the cart and handed it off the back. No sooner had he done so, then Cernak himself began climbing the side. Luca gave him a hand up. "Come anziano, bend your knees."

Cernak grunted at him. "I hope you live long enough to understand." He eyed Simon's bedroll and kit, then scanned the rest of the tumbrel. "Now where is Jacob's hidden compartment that you mentioned?"

Kneeling on the floor, Simon ran his fingers over the rough wood. One section stood a little higher than its neighbors. "This board here. You will need a knife to pry it up."

Cernak used his dagger to lift the board. In the space beneath rested a yellow leather sack and a small wooden box. Simon sat back on his heels as Cernak removed the sack. He knew what to expect, but the others gasped at the gold he poured out on the bed. "I think Master Jacob intended to stay in Vienna after this trip."

"Merda." Luca bent closer to examine the treasure. "In some cazzo *palazzo* he stays."

"And you?" Cernak said. "What did he intend for you?"

"I don't know." Simon lowered his voice. "I don't know if I was ever meant to reach Vienna."

Cernak picked up the box. "I think the contents will tell us more of Jacob."

Simon shrank back. Not sure if he wanted to know, he flattened himself against the tumbrel's side. Cernak lifted the lid as Luca watched. "Mafankulo diavulu... I know this and I say this." Luca jumped up and shouted at Simon. "You bring only curses. Now we all die."

Cernak stood. "Easy, brother. We don't know what it means."

The tumbrel shook with Luca's wild dance as Simon edged toward the back and lowered himself to the ground. Yohan helped him down and said, "He'll cool off, maybe sometime today."

Ramon joined them. "It sounds like Brother Luca is in good form." He stopped short, seeing the stacks of baled pelts. "I hope you found what you were looking for."

Luca continued to rage, and Simon's gut clenched, thinking about what would inevitably come of it. Ramon poked through the bales. He selected one, cut the binding twine, and peeled back the doeskin wrapper. Yohan whistled at the neat stack of snowy ermine pelts. "Each of these bales is a mercenary's wage for a year." He shook his head at Simon. "You could have been a prince."

"What good is a prince without a name, without a past? Besides, I would be a dead prince by now."

Luca dropped from the tumbrel's deck. He landed in a crouch and leapt at Simon. "You are dead anyway, diavulu. That box, you know what it is inside?"

"Back down," Yohan said. "He wouldn't have shown it to us—he wouldn't have shared the gold—if he had something to hide."

Luca unclenched his fists and walked around Simon. "We dance today, mafankulo. You will not forget."

Ramon walked behind the tumbrel and peered inside. "What gold?"

Cernak had seated himself on the floor, his legs dangling off the back. The heavy leather sack slumped on the boards next to him. "We will count it this morning so everyone knows. Luca, bring Carla and Stephan. They need to be part of this."

Simon had already counted the bales of fur. Fifty-two. They'd filled half the tumbrel nearly to the top.

Stephan arrived. "Carla and Luca are patrolling our campsite. They will return shortly." He stopped to take in the stacked bales, examining the pelts Ramon had opened. "We have too much."

Cernak eased himself to the ground. "What do you mean too much?"

"I mean, if we try to sell this in Venice, it will be like dogmeat—worthless. We fill the doge's wardrobe, clothe a few prelates, then what? Beggars will sleep in ermine by the time we get rid of it all."

Cernak thought for a moment. "We may find a merchant who will take the entire load. Otherwise, we can sell some in Venice and carry the rest to Rome."

Stephan winced. "You remember what happened the last time we were in Rome?"

"Capos de merda, all of them in Rome." Luca ducked through a brushy copse. "Papist bastardos, every one."

Carla followed. "We found nothing, not in the fields or the trees. They're gone."

"Nonetheless," Cernak said. "Keep your weapons handy. They may be back."

Simon toed one of the corpses, still slumped next to the tumbrel's enormous wheel. "How many were there?"

"Two dead here," Stephan said. "Luca killed one at the campfire, but the other fled. I may have wounded him."

"In the field there were more," Yohan said. "We were defending the horses. I couldn't tell how many came at us."

Cernak nodded. "I counted six others, but there were probably more. Say twelve altogether."

Simon couldn't stop staring at the lifeless forms. "Who were they? Marauders?"

"Or mercenaries," Yohan said. "More important is, what did they want?"

"This, for one." Cernak held up a small wooden box. The size of a paving stone, it bore a familiar symbol on its lid—the crucified serpent. He slipped the box beneath his cloak.

Simon breathed once more. He crawled into his discarded clothing and retrieved his sword belt. The reassuring weight hung at his hip. Perhaps he could look at the box now.

Cernak had other plans. "I want you all to know what we guard."

It took both hands to lift the leather sack. Cernak moved it to the middle of the cart and rolled it on its side. A few yellow bars spilled onto the wooden bed. He reached in and dragged out handfuls until the bag was empty. "Golden hryvna. Stephan, will you be so good as to count them?"

Stephan stacked the bars like a merchant and began sorting and counting. Simon knew Jacob kept his money in the secret compartment, but he had never seen more than a glimpse of the bag. He shuddered and watched Stephan count. "That... is a lot of gold."

Yohan gave him a sideways glance. "You knew it was there?"

"Jacob called it traveling money. He never let me see how much."

"Forty-eight sound gold hryvna, twenty-two silver bars, seven bars that have been shaved or clipped, and three that are certainly counterfeit."

Cernak turned his back to them. "Does anybody else see the danger here?"

Carla said, "We six, ah... seven, travel bearing a king's bounty?"

Simon had understood. He'd feared it when they unloaded the bales of ermine. He'd feared it as he watched Ramon's breathless appraisal of the pelts. Shaking his head, he looked at Cernak. "This fortune could destroy our company."

Luca stepped forward. "Nothing destroys our company if you are dead, diavulu."

Cernak remained silent, but Yohan said, "Nothing destroys our company if we are of one mind. This treasure can be a curse, or it can be a boon. We must decide now, together, what it will be."

"We've always used our resources to help the destitute," Stephan said. "That is our calling, our purpose, to share alms with the poor."

"And the papists," Ramon said. "The priests and bishops, they always manage steal it away."

Cernak finally broke his silence. "Stephan reminded us of what happened in Rome. Luca, I know you remember. We've all been there. The city is a cesspool." Cernak paused and looked at each of them. "I think this tumbrel is a gift. Brother Yohan called it a boon. We should use it as such."

Luca tugged on his short beard. "I say we hire mercenaries and burn the Pope's *palazzo*."

Stephan threw up his hands. "Good grace, I hope not."

Cernak didn't quite smile. "Brother Luca should not be taken so literally. What he suggests is that we support the King of Sicily against the incursions of Rome. Am I right, brother?"

"Keep talking."

"We sell a portion of this in Venice and take ship for Brindisi. Once there, we can sell more to traders sailing for Constantinople. The rest we consign to Rome."

Simon had been listening, trying to imagine the journey. "How long?"

"Two months to Venice, minimum. Perhaps another month to Brindisi."

"And the gold, what then? We have a lot of gold, but I don't see how we use it."

"We don't have to. The Fellowship of Justice, our brothers and sisters will find a way. We sail from Brindisi to Castello di Maredolce, our home in Palermo. There, you can be inducted into our order."

"If he lives this long," Luca added.

"If any of us live so long," Yohan said. "We should return our gold to its hiding place and restow these bales."

Cernak held up both hands. "Not until all swear to support this plan, or until I hear a better one."

Each Knight crossed arms against their chest and bowed. When all eyes fell on him, Simon did the same, repeating *d'accordo* as had the others. Cernak twisted his face into another half-smile. "Load up, before this day gets any older."

That afternoon, Simon walked with his oxen, nursing bruised ribs and a swollen eye. Luca's pankration lesson had come at a cost. Ramon too had redoubled his attacks with the wooden knife and sword. He'd cut Simon's waster in half. "If you are determined to fight with that broken blade, then you must practice with it as well."

Cernak marched them late into the evening before calling a halt. "Cold rations tonight. We stand guard in pairs from now on—all of us." He clapped Simon on the shoulder. "You and I will take the first watch, now until nocturn. Ramon, I'll rouse you and Luca, try to stay quiet. Yohan, Carla, take matins and awaken Stephan and me at lauds."

They hadn't lit a campfire that night. Simon shivered in the cool spring air. Small things rustled in the bushes and a nightjar chirred from a nearby copse. He checked the tumbrel to make sure its jack-stand was wedged firmly beneath the drawbar. He dug out his leather gambeson and shrugged it over his shoulders. It wouldn't stop a sword or even an arrow, but he felt better wearing it, warmer too. He buckled his sword belt around the outside and pulled it tight. Still somewhat awkward, he adjusted the scabbard where it wouldn't bang his knee, then checked his knife.

Cernak found him, still at the tumbrel fussing with his gear. "Come, we should walk."

The moon, nearly full, brooded over the eastern hills, painting a band of high clouds silver gray. Simon found that not having stared into a campfire all evening, the pale glow was sufficient light to avoid most of the brambles and fallen branches. He picked his way behind Cernak's shadowy form, watching left and right for... something. "What are we looking for?"

The shadow stopped wading through the deep grass and waited until Simon caught up. "Nothing. We simply need to be seen looking."

"Seen?" Simon turned and peered over his shoulder. "Seen by whom?"

"Nobody, I hope. But if someone is watching our camp, I would rather they thought us too dangerous to attack." He sighed and shrugged. "No one is out here this early anyway. They would wait until just before dawn when the moon has set."

Cernak turned south toward the road. "I mainly wanted a chance to talk while we were away from camp."

They pushed through a hedge of brambles and small trees to step back onto the rutted wagon road from Krakow. A tiny movement caught his eye. Simon spun about. Nothing—nothing but the vague shadow of an elfin face, gone before it was seen.

While Simon caught up with him, Cernak stopped on the road and gazed up at the moon. "There was one topic I managed to avoid this morning."

"The box."

"You know what it contains?"

"My heart. Jacob said that if I look at it, I will die."

Cernak walked back toward their camp. "It is a talisman of sorts. I've never seen another quite like it. What do you know of your Master Jacob?"

"Nothing it seems. All the time I was... *simple*, I thought of him as my benefactor, a fur trader, little more."

"I knew him—this Jacob ben Reuben, the man who bore the blade you carry. He once was a member of the Knights Templar, riding with them on crusade. A ferocious fighter, some say he battled the great Saladin himself."

Simon wasn't sure he knew who Saladin was, but he recalled something about the Crusades. "He never spoke of that. Which Crusade?"

"Second or third, sometime in between. It doesn't matter. Because shortly after, he turned *wærloga*, faithless. Jacob abandoned the oaths given to his Templar brothers and went over to the Saracens."

"I don't understand. He betrayed his brothers—why?"

"Secret knowledge. He was *Apostoli Lucis*, an Apostle first above all else." Cernak gazed out over the river valley. The moon had risen above the fog and painted the scene in shades silver and gray. "Past the gates of Alexander, east of the great desert, devils rule in cities built before the time of Adam. He went there in search of power."

Simon shook his head. "Not possible, not the man I knew. Besides, it is a long way from the eastern deserts to the fur markets of Tver."

"If you follow Mother Volga, she flows all the way to Astrakhan on the Caspian Sea." Cernak paused, glanced about, and lowered his voice. "Consider that your master Jacob carried the wealth of a prince in that two-wheeled farm cart. Do you still call him a simple trader?"

Reference to the treasure made Simon pick up his pace. "We should get back to camp. I'm... I'm still worried about another attack."

"Don't be. While we trudge the fields, Stephan watches from the shadows. When Ramon and Luca go out, I will wait in hiding."

"We are a diversion then."

Cernak clapped him on the shoulder. "Tactics, that's the third lesson you will learn on this journey."

"I hope it is not as painful as the first two."

"Consider that last night's lesson was nearly deadly. Nothing worthwhile is learned without pain."

Simon recalled his descent into the Temple of Hermes and passage through the Smocza Jama. "Then discovering my past will be excruciating."

"Perhaps you should start by discovering something of Jacob's past. Can you remember now how long you knew him?"

The same question he'd been asked before. This time, Simon knew the answer. "Five years, five journeys to Tver. We were returning to Vienna when they killed him."

Cernak walked a few moments in thought. "That would be about right. Lucius III was elected Pope in 1181, just about the time Jacob ben Reuben vanished."

"You tell me Jacob was a fighter, a warrior like you. Now you say he became a fur trader. Are you certain my Jacob is the same man?"

"Your sword is nearly proof enough." Cernak slapped his cloak. "This box makes it a certainty."

"Then why did he take an apprentice and why me?"

"Because, my brother Simon Halfsword, you have more talent than you know. Jacob ben Reuben was many things, but he was no fool. He chose you for a reason."

The Hidden Hand

"Do you know, cazzo diavulu? Yes, I like beating on you. It is religious joy I have, almost a sacrament."

On his belly, damp earth in his face, Simon listened to the little Sicilian gloat. A kick to the knee, and once more he'd sprawled to the ground. No pause, no hesitation, Luca spared him nothing. Simon spat out a mouthful of dirt. "If I say cedo, will you let me stand?"

"Does your enemy let you stand?"

"This time he will because he wants to knock me down again."

Luca laughed and danced back. "*Oborior*, I summon you."

Simon pushed himself to one knee. "Where did you hear that?"

"You know what it means then." He laughed again. "Ah, not so much the cretino now, I think. Did you call a devil to give you that egg?"

Still kneeling, Simon thought a moment. *Egg?* He remembered the Smocza Jama. "No, the egg was there. I saw it the first time on my way out."

"No matter. Stand now. I must finish your lesson."

Once more on his feet, Simon wobbled.

Luca stepped closer. "You are hurt, sè? Your legs, you cannot move quickly, sè? I will show you something. Knock me down."

Confused, Simon hesitated. Luca slapped him in the face. "Do it, cretino."

A hand on the offending wrist, a foot just behind the other's heel, Simon twisted him to the ground. Luca hit, bounced, and spun about, grabbing and kicking like a maddened spider. Simon jumped back, but not before Luca rolled up on one shoulder and landed another kick on his knee.

Simon retreated as the whirling tangle of arms and legs advanced on him.

Nothing to hit, Simon tried a kick to the man's midriff, only to have his other leg seized and yanked from under him. Luca struck him three times before he hit the ground. When the spots and stars cleared, Simon found himself gazing up at his teacher. Luca grinned and nodded. "Is a good lesson. Practice what I show you today."

Simon squeezed his eyes shut. When he looked up again, he found Yohan standing in Luca's place. Extending an arm, he said, "Stand, Simon. We need to get going."

Ramon had already retrieved the oxen. Simon limped back to the tumbrel and hefted the yoke to their shoulders. He fastened the hoops and attached the drawbar. Finally, he tossed his gear in the back and stowed the triangular jack used to keep the tumbrel level when not attached to the team.

He rubbed his left knee. It had swollen to twice its normal size, and even a gentle touch sent a shock of pain up his leg. His latest encounter left a scrape on his right shin as well. It bled down to his ankle. With no time to tend either injury, Simon found his willow switch and led the stoic animals back to the road. As usual, Cernak and Stephan rode some distance in the lead. Almost a verst ahead, Simon saw no sign of them.

Yohan and Ramon loitered at the campsite, waiting for Simon to leave. He knew they would follow at some distance, watching the road behind them. Ramon led two other horses, presumably Carla's and Luca's. Simon didn't ask, but he could imagine them ranging on either side, guarding his flanks.

Well-watered and fed, the two oxen seemed eager to continue west. Simon lurched into a stiff-legged gait to keep up. He cursed the willful beasts, and his leg burned with every step. After a few versts, the pain became a dull ache from his ankles to his hips. He grunted and staggered on. *Stopping means failing. Failing means giving up.* Simon took an extra hop to stay alongside the great rumbling wheel. *Giving up means never discovering who I am or why I have been branded with the serpent's mark.* He watched the road ahead crawl up from the hazy distance to pass clattering beneath the feet of his team. Deep inside, another voice replied, *giving up means never finding your vengeance.*

Piles of fresh manure every few versts attested to Cernak and Stephan riding ahead. On occasion, Yohan rode up to talk or just keep him company. Of Luca and Carla, he saw nothing.

The soft counterpoint of hoofbeats announced Yohan's approach. Simon relaxed his gait and tried to walk naturally. Excruciating, but he maintained an illusion of strength. This was the third such visit. Simon wasn't sure how long he could sustain the deception. Yohan glanced down at him. "Cernak waits for us a thousand paces ahead. Can you keep going that long?"

Simon looked up at him. "Why do you ask?"

The man grinned and raised his voice. "Just that I hope to see you enjoy Luca's cooking."

With that cryptic statement, Yohan kicked his mount into a fast trot and passed on ahead. Shortly Ramon passed as well, two riderless horses following on long leads. Simon mulled over what he'd heard. It made little sense. A thousand paces, then a break. He could do that.

The break included water and a light meal in the shade of an ancient oak. Before Simon could eat, Luca and Ramon appeared from somewhere. Ramon laughed and pushed Luca in the shoulder. The other cursed and glared at Simon. "Brother Ramon comes to help you learn the sword, diavulu. But maybe you are tired, sè?"

Simon stood, perhaps a little more quickly than he had intended. "I am ready when he is."

"Then I say diavulu must have two lessons, Brother Ramon."

Simon stiffened his back. The afternoon would not be easy. He forced a grin back at the little Sicilian and said, "Perhaps you should both attend this lesson."

Luca tilted his head at Ramon and gave an exaggerated shrug.

Simon continued. "Oh yes, Ramon told me you need knife fighting lessons."

Simon wasn't sure if it was a smirk or a grimace that crossed Luca's face. He flashed it at each of them and stroked his beard. "Then I have to kill two lying bastardos today."

Ramon grinned. "He is a clever one, our student. Be careful—he will soon have you cooking his meals."

"More noise from your face, Corsican, and you die first."

Simon held a pointed stick hidden behind his forearm. "Ramon could give you a lesson on how it is done. I'll watch."

Luca rushed at him, fists at ready. Simon waited, arms hanging at his sides. *He strikes in one, two...* Luca aimed a punishing blow at Simon's face, only to have it deflected. The next moment, Luca's shoulder slammed into Simon's midriff and both arms locked around his waist. Together they fell to the ground, and Simon jammed his hidden stick into Luca's ribs. "You are dead, Brother Luca."

The little Sicilian rolled away, roaring, cursing, and clutching his back. Springing to his feet, Luca held up a hand streaked with blood. "Capo de merda, bastardo, you dare stab me?"

Simon revealed his stick. "It is only a wooden practice knife. I think Brother Ramon was right."

Luca would beat him senseless. Simon had resigned himself to that. *It will shorten the lesson*, he rationalized. Like witness to an execution, Ramon stood watching. Simon waited. Gradually, Luca's expression flowed from insane rage, through incredulity, to a calculating smirk. "You wish to dance the paranza corta, the short weapon, with a... a *Sicilianu*? You are not cretino, boy. You are *pazzu*, crazy."

Luca approached slowly. Head down, glaring up beneath his dark furrowed brows. "We do not dance the knives with children's toys." He slapped the bloody stick from Simon's hand. "Show me your weapon."

Simon drew his knife as he'd practiced, holding it behind his arm. He let it drop, caught the blade, and presented the grip to Luca. As Simon's knife slid into view, Ramon scowled. "I never taught you that."

Luca accepted the knife and examined the blade, turning it back and forth. "Yesterday, I wonder how is it my cretino kills a seasoned warrior?" His eyes slid to Ramon. "I think you teach him more than you intend."

Simon held out his arms. "What use is it to any of us if I don't learn what I need to know?"

Luca offered the knife. "I show you then."

Hesitating, watching Luca's eyes, Simon met his steady glare. As soon as he touched the hilt, something flickered behind those dark irises. Simon jumped back as Luca's own blade flashed into view and arced upward between them.

Faster than a hornet's sting, it returned. Simon felt the point press against his sternum.

"Now who is dead, mafankulo?"

Ten heartbeats holding his breath, Simon couldn't move. Imperceptibly, the glare softened, Luca drew back, and his knife vanished like the reflection in a broken mirror. "Bah, you hold it wrong. Look, look." Luca twitched his blade into view. "Like this, in your palm. It is a woman's breast, hard, eager. It is a living thing."

Simon tried. His own knife felt like dead weight. Luca continued to move, dancing back and forth, weaving his blade in the air like a steel serpent. When their eyes met again, Luca stopped. His knife disappeared and he threw his hands in the air. "I cannot—I *cannot*. Look at him, he is a constipated horse. The knife, he holds it like a shovel."

"Just show me how you do that—thing—with your knife."

"This?" The blade glittered in Luca's hand. "Or this?" Once more, his knife vanished.

"Yes, like that."

Luca's eyes flicked over to Ramon. "I should teach this diavulu the secrets of *indraga mano*, the hidden hand?"

"Better that you teach it to him, then he practices it on you."

Luca spun, blade in hand, and pointed it at Ramon. "Better maybe I cut out that annoying tongue?"

As Luca reacted to Ramon, Simon watched. He mimicked the move, his hand flipped upward slipping the blade from its sheath. Awkward, balky, he watched and tried it again. *Better.* Repeating the move, he looked up. Luca still had Ramon at knifepoint, but both stared at him. Ramon grinned. "Your lessons keep improving, Brother Luca."

"Merda, he still holds it wrong. Look, cretino, your knife, she is your lover. You do not grab her like your *minchia*." He clenched his fist and wiggled his hips. "You caress her. Like this, sè?"

Luca held his hand out flat, his knife balanced on the joint of his middle finger, the pommel cradled in his thumb. He spun it, and the blade rested against his forearm. He spun it again and dropped it into the sheath at his side.

"You practice that, sè?"

Stepping closer, Luca lowered his voice. "And ever you stab me again with a mafankulo pointed stick..." His hand flicked. A bright streak of red bloomed across Simon's chest. "...this is your throat."

The burn came moments later as Luca spun and stalked away. Hand to his chest, Simon gasped and stumbled. Ramon at his arm, he tried to sit. The world spun and Simon collapsed on his back, gulping air. Ramon's face passed like a phantom. A fog crept in from the edges and surrounded his world. Simon fought the convulsions as he watched the empty sky dissolve into a gray haze.

A cold weight on his chest, his feet propped up, Simon's stomach rebelled. Trying to roll, faces, steadying hands, he managed to twist to one side and retch up a small lump of bile. Stephan knelt next to him. "Easy, brother. What happened?"

His sword lay beneath one arm where it had fallen when he rolled. Simon patted his chest and drew his hand back tinged pink with blood and perspiration. "I think it tried to kill me."

"Who tried to kill you? Luca?"

Holding the sword, Simon took a careful breath. "Not Luca, not on purpose... look." Simon opened his tunic where it had been slashed. "My sigil, it's been cut."

He tried to sit, propping his elbows behind him. Simon's wound flexed as he moved, burning like a swarm of wasps. He lowered his chin and looked at the fresh line of blood. It wreathed the cross and wandered down the serpent body to collect above his navel. Stephan dabbed his cut with a wet cloth. "The wound is shallow and already beginning to close. I think it was the shock."

Simon wasn't so sure. He'd endured worse just that morning. Staggering to his feet, he braced himself with his sword. "I can walk," he lied.

Camp Followers

Cernak had cut him a walking stick. Simon demurred, *too much like giving in.* But once on the road, the staff helped ease pressure on his leg. The following morning, Luca trained him in more pankration ground moves. "You are injured, the enemy knows. He will attack your weakness. On the ground you do not stumble, you cannot fall. The enemy is confused."

A kick to his injured leg took Simon down. Pain brought clarity, a single-minded need to survive. He slammed an arm into the ground to break his fall. He rolled as Luca had taught him and tried a return kick. His target had jumped back. Simon spun up on one shoulder and tumbled toward Luca. Landing on his swollen knee brought a moment of paralyzing agony. Luca aimed a kick at Simon's midriff that he absorbed, grasping the leg and rolling backward.

Once more, Simon found his face to the earth and gagged out, "Cedo, cedo." He felt Luca's weight shift from his neck. A pair of boots filled his vision. Simon rolled to his side.

Luca's bearded face grinned down at him. "You will learn, diavulu."

Two more days of lessons helped. Simon had learned to avoid the most crippling blows and even return a few. Following his morning lesson, he eased the tumbrel away from their campsite. Crossing a broad ditch, he switched the near ox up the opposite bank, dragging the balky cart onto the road. Cernak and Stephan had ridden on ahead. Luca had disappeared as usual, and Carla followed. Yohan fell back, trailing Ramon and the two horses. Simon glanced behind him. A thin haze of dust followed the riders.

His staff tapped a short counterpoint to the soft footfalls of the oxen. Simon practiced palming and sheathing his dagger as he walked. Not Luca's fluid moves, but effective. Ramon had demonstrated a few two-handed blocks. Sword and dagger, together they could deflect a downward slash. Simon palmed his dagger again. He preferred the indraga mano, the hidden weapon. What was it Cernak had said about tactics? No match for a seasoned fighter, Simon spun his dagger and sheathed it. *Misdirection and surprise*, he nodded as he walked. *My personal tactic—misdirection, obfuscation, and surprise.*

The thought resonated in his jumbled memories. Obfuscation, misdirection, he'd used them before. Sometime before—he clutched his sword hilt— sometime before he wore the serpent on his chest. He forced air into his lungs. *Question the unsaid, question his assumptions. Who had tried to jam that into his head? What were his assumptions now?* Simon tramped along, one hand on his sword hilt, trying to think, to remember.

Jacob—not a friend. His new companions—friends. All assumptions. He thought on how they could have left him in Krakow, taken the cart, and told him to guard the Smocza Jama. *And Jacob, what had he done besides shelter and support him?* Like a fallen cathedral, his memories lay in a heap of debris and broken treasures.

Simon took another deep breath and dragged himself back to the present. The morning breeze hissed through endless fields, empty but for the jackdaws cackling in the grass. No sign of Carla and Luca. He'd assumed they would be out there guarding his flank but never asked. *And if they weren't? If there was another attack? Am I bait?*

He limped along, an injured animal, feeling terribly exposed. In the daylight, archers could wait until he approached, then stand and shoot. Simon fingered his leather gambeson. It wouldn't stop an arrow. He wondered if a mail hauberk like Yohan's would protect him. He considered climbing into the tumbrel and riding behind its wooden walls, but with no one to goad the oxen, they would soon stop.

He imagined archers waiting in the grass on the far side of the road. Six days of hiding, watching, they knew how he walked to the left of his team, how the others deployed ahead and behind. They would have seen him stop to piss, the oxen plodding on for a hundred paces while he refastened his clothing and lurched after them.

Simon craned his neck around. The empty fields rippled in the wind. The unseen birds called from the grass. He saw no threat yet found no reassurance. Obfuscation. Simon slowed to allow the great wheels to rumble past, then crossed behind the cart and lurched along, trying to catch up. His knee throbbed with every step, but better to guide his team from the opposite side today. His oxen snorted their unease. The near animal kept rolling its big yellow eye at him. Never before had they been led from the right.

The rising sun burned off the morning mist and warmed the spring air. Simon hobbled along for what must have been a thousand turns of the tumbrel's wheels. His leather gambeson grew warm, then stifling. His sword belt chafed against his hips, and the oxen kept nudging him closer to the ditch. To Simon, the entire world seemed empty. Even the jackdaws had gone silent, save one, high overhead, chirring in annoyance.

There should be birds. Simon straightened, listening. Nothing, save the creak and rumble of his own passing. He pressed as close to the tumbrel box as he dared without being drawn beneath its wheels. A whisper came from above. "Steady, boy. We see them."

He looked up. Carla rose above the tumbrel side and draw her short bow. She shot twice into the grass as Luca vaulted from the back. Two arrows returned, smacking into the wooden wall. Carla drew and released twice more. Shouts, the pounding of feet. Behind the cart, Simon heard Luca's voice. "Santo cazzo Madre di Cristo, they come!"

Before Simon could move, the long grass parted, and a bear of a man leapt to the road. His mail glittered in the morning sun. Simon drew his short blade and flicked it up to deflect the oncoming sword. Another stroke. Simon twisted to let it pass. Retreating, staring about for other attackers, Simon clutched his knife and tried to get inside the man's defenses. *Not working—not working.* The man wielded his sword like a veteran, forcing Simon back.

Against the tumbrel, now stopped in the road, against the near ox, now snorting and pawing in dismay, Simon felt his leg beginning to buckle, his sword arm dropping. Slashing and thrusting, his assailant stabbed Simon's injured leg. He fell as Luca had taught him, spinning, kicking. It earned him only a moment's reprieve. The next blow came down like a descending axe.

Simon rolled beneath the oxen. The big man knelt, dealing lightning jabs with his sword. Retreating, Simon dodged most of the blows. His assailant followed like a bear on a fox's den. Pinned between the oxen, Simon reached up poked his knife in each of their bellies. The startled animals bellowed in pain.

For a moment, their eyes met, Simon and the florid man, his leering face framed by curly hair and beard. Then the tumbrel with its load of pelts lurched and rolled forward. One great wheel climbed, crushing, shattering, grinding the man's blood and viscera into the unyielding road.

The heavy axle passed a handbreadth over Simon's head, then sunlight and chaos. Luca stood at bay, fending off two assailants. Cursing, slashing, he gave way slowly. A two-handed stroke drove the sword from Luca's grip. The little Sicilian took to the ground, fighting with knife and flailing limbs.

He can't die alone. Struggling to his feet, Simon's leg gave way, and he fell to one knee. He drove his sword against the hard-packed road, pushed himself up, and staggered forward. Ignoring his injured leg, Simon engaged the nearest assailant.

Surprise halted the attack on Luca. Reversing his blade, the man spun, slashing upward. Simon blocked the stroke, but the blow knocked him back. A mustached face, brown from the southern sun; a corded arm, all muscle and standing veins; and a worn leather gauntlet grasping a notched sword all descended on Simon.

Distract him—give Luca some relief. Simon prayed he could hold out until one of the others broke free. It seemed unlikely. His injured leg anchored him like a hobbled ox. His sword, heavy and slow, parried the first thrust but lagged on the counter. Simon let the other's blade slip past his guard, pierce the leather gambeson beneath his arm, and pass through unhindered. Throwing himself at his opponent, he dropped his sword and drove his hidden dagger into the flesh just below the man's ribs.

When Simon pushed away, the fighting had stopped. Carla had found a weak spot in her opponent's mail and Luca had hamstrung the remaining man.

Simon picked up Luca's fallen sword. "Next time, don't lose your weapon."

"Next time, idiota, stay where we see you."

"Then maybe let me in on your plans for once. Did I not complete the trials? Was I not accepted as a brother?"

Luca moved up close and lowered his voice. "Am I brother to the diavulu now?"

Simon nodded. "You always were, *Brother* Luca. You just didn't know it."

Carla put a hand on each of their shoulders. "Enough. We have work to do before Cernak returns. Besides, more could be out there."

Luca grinned up at her. "I think they piss themselves and run."

Thirty paces farther along the road, the oxen and tumbrel had stopped. Simon left Carla bantering with Luca and hobbled up behind them. He took the lead animal by its nose ring and turned the rig about, returning to the scene of the fight.

Carla dragged a well-fletched corpse from the adjacent field and dumped it next to another, similarly decorated. "Four on the road. Two in the weeds. Who are these people?"

Luca knelt, one knee on the chest of a thrashing body. "This mafankulo tells me or I tear out his liver."

Blood pooled beneath the man's legs where Luca had slashed his tendons. Simon knelt beside his head. Groans and vague curses, he made out little more. Carla looked down at them. "What language is that?"

Luca shook his head. "Pazzu—nonsense."

Simon listened more carefully. "It could be Rus. It could be the language of Krakow." By the pallor in his face, the man wouldn't last long. "It doesn't matter. He will die before we learn anything."

Luca rocked back and jammed a dagger into the man's throat. "It is so."

Carla seized Simon by the arm. "Brother, you may die as well."

A heavy streak of blood ran down his leg and stained the ground at his feet. It hadn't hurt—no, he hadn't felt it hurt. A dark trail led back from where he had retrieved the tumbrel. The exhaustion and pain struck like a summer storm. Simon reeled. "I think I should rest."

Staggering, he leaned against a tall wheel. Dust in the distance resolved itself into a galloping horse. A moment later, Yohan swung from the saddle. "What in the devil's wretched hell happened here?"

Busy stripping the bodies, Luca didn't look up. "Cazzo mafankulos try to kill us."

"I count six," Yohan stooped to inspect." He kicked the mangled carcass crushed by the tumbrel. "I stay with six. Were there more?"

"Not here," Luca said. "Otherwise are dead mafankulos."

Yohan cursed and vaulted back to his horse. "I've got to warn Cernak."

He galloped down the road as Ramon rode up with the other horses. Luca waved him over. "Take Carla. There are more of these bastardos you must kill. I will stay with our diavulu."

Before she left, Carla helped Simon drag himself up to the tumbrel's wooden bed. Luca sauntered over. "Bleed on those pelts, and they are worthless."

Flat on his back, watching a white cloud slowly change shape, Simon wondered if he cared. "Help me bandage my leg."

"You think I do nothing then?" Luca held up strips of linen. "Our guests have been generous."

The clouds, the quiet. If I could just rest. Simon flinched when Luca probed his wound. "Mafankulo stick you good, brother. I bind it, but Stephan must sew it."

"I think I was cut on my side too."

"Merda, did you learn nothing?"

"I didn't die." Simon wriggled out of his gambeson. Covered in blood, it peeled half his tunic away when it came off.

Luca cursed and probed the other wound. "Nasty cut is all. You are lucky, bastardo. I would let you bleed, but now is too late."

Dizzy, even lying on his back, Simon felt the tumbrel sway beneath him. Luca worked a strip of linen beneath his chest and tied a thick bandage against his side. Simon surveyed the damage. "Why is it too late?"

"Day two, maybe latest day three, you run away." Luca turned and spat on the road. "I make that bet with Brother Yohan. He says one week, seven days you will stay. He bets his horse, his mafankulo horse."

Simon lay back. The one cloud had almost disappeared, but two others had taken its place, blocking the sun. "Ramon was in on this, then."

"Worthless, ineffective cretino. He does nothing. He laughs at me."

"What did you lose?"

Luca kicked a rock and looked away. "I must cook until we reach Vienna."

Despite his wounds, Simon started to laugh. "Don't... don't make jokes. It hurts too much."

"I do not joke. I must cook until Vienna."

Simon heard them first. "Horses. Is it Cernak?"

Luca stepped out into the road and stared westward. "They come slowly. Someone is hurt."

Helpless, flat on his back, Simon tried to sit. His leg throbbed. Twisting, he propped an elbow against the tumbrel bed. The wound in his chest wrenched open and began to soak the makeshift bandage. Luca glanced over. "No, cretino. Stay down."

"I have to see. Sit me up against the sideboards."

Cursing, glancing back at the road, Luca helped him sit. "You die now, and I cook all the way to Palermo."

Yohan arrived first. Head down, he slid from his horse and said a few words to Luca. The little Sicilian stood a moment, rock still. He then drew his sword and waved it in the air, screaming in Sicilian. Yohan backed away, and his horse shied, ears back, eyes rolling. Luca ignored it and trotted up the road to meet the others.

Yohan wouldn't look up, wouldn't meet Simon's eye. He stroked his horse, calming it. Taking a bag from his saddle, he fed it a handful of oats. The animal snuffled and nibbled from his palm. Finely, Yohan glanced over to the tumbrel. "How are you, Simon?"

"I'll live. Just tell me what happened."

Yohan shook his head and stepped closer. His cheeks wet with tears, Simon's mentor and friend raised his head. "They killed Cernak today."

Firelight

For men used to battle, inured to death, Simon found their grief to be almost overwhelming. Hardest hit was Stephan, who had seen him fall. He could only huddle on the ground, shaking. Cernak had died in an instant, a crossbow bolt through his heart. Stephan had ridden down the attacker and disemboweled the man but not before two others leapt on Cernak's body.

Stephan managed to choke out a few words. "They slashed him where he lay and fled before I could return."

Carla took charge of the marauders' corpses. She tied them behind her horse and dragged them far into the adjacent field for the wolves to find. Yohan scouted out a clear spot less than half a verst beyond where Cernak had died. He led their small band to the site and began lying out a camp.

Once settled, Ramon tended to Simon's wounds. Without banter or even conversation, the clink and rattle of normal activity gave the camp a haunted feel. A few things bothered Simon beyond the shock of losing his friend. *What had the marauders hoped to gain? Why had they attacked such a heavily armed group, and why attack Cernak and Stephan at all?*

Once Ramon left, Simon eased off the back of the cart. He winced, landing on his good leg, and retrieved his staff. *Cernak had given it to me.* He shoved the thought away and went to find Yohan. The search ended ten paces later when he found his quarry unhitching the oxen. Simon endured the expected remonstrance before asking, "Why were we attacked?"

Yohan straightened, one oxbow still in his hand. "Why do marauders attack any band of travelers?"

"But you once said yourself, we are not just any band of travelers."

Setting the first oxbow aside, he knelt and pulled the latch pins from the other bow. "Then if you know something, tell me now."

"I don't know anything, but I think we might learn something from the bodies of our attackers."

"Luca has already searched them. He's very thorough."

"I need boots. Did he happen to keep a pair?"

Yohan's eyes traveled down his legs. Simon waited while he took in the broken soles, the reddened toes poking through the uppers, and the sheer size of his feet. "Let me set the oxen to graze, then we'll go."

Hobbling across camp, he hoped that Ramon didn't see him walking about. Simon found Luca cursing and grumbling at their fire. He didn't look up. "I know you will come. I cannot kill you, so what do you want?"

"What did you find on the bodies?"

Luca straightened and brushed a shock of hair from his eyes. "Nothing of interest to you, diavulu."

"May I see what you found, anyway?"

Grunting, he dragged a pot from the fire, stirred it, and stalked off. Simon followed him to a heap of rags at the edge of camp. "Wear a dead man's clothes. Maybe soon, you are dead too."

Everything had changed in an eyeblink. *He blames me, and I'm not sure he is wrong.* Simon used his staff to scatter the bits of clothing. Coarse wool, most of it. He uncovered two mail shirts, one twisted and caked in blood and viscera. It was huge.

An assortment of weapons lay nearby—swords, knives, bows. Simon didn't see a crossbow. He found four leather gambesons in various conditions. All four clung together like blood-soaked hides in an abattoir. A scrap of white linen peeped from beneath the pile. Simon speared it with his staff and dragged it out. The remains of a tunic but stitched from a better-quality weave than the other rags.

He held it up, and a familiar claw gripped his heart. He forced a few deep breaths. A scattering of memories flashed by like birds flushed from a field— friars, priests, and something else. The claw squeezed harder, and he forced another breath. Simon tried to concentrate. He'd once worn a shirt like this.

Yohan interrupted Simon's reverie. "I thought I would find you here."

"Do you know which attacker wore this?"

"We can ask Luca when we return." Yohan knelt to examine the bandages on Simon's leg. "The bodies are almost two versts north of here. Can you walk that far and return?"

Not sure that he could, Simon nodded anyway. "Oh yes, I have to."

"Then we must go now while it is still daylight."

They waded off across the field until Yohan picked up the trampled swath where bodies had been dragged through the grass. Simon wore his sword for reasons other than protection. By the time they reached the path, it began to grow heavy. Leaning into his walking staff, he tried to take some of the load off his left leg, but the unfamiliar gait only distributed the pain.

Yohan had looked back and slowed twice earlier. The third time, he stopped. "Are you sure you can go on? We can turn back now if you want."

Simon ducked his head and walked past. "If I make it there, then I will make it back."

Pushing through the grass with Yohan behind him, Simon thought of nothing but the next step, then the next one after that. Each one took him closer to the truth. He fought to ignore the pervasive clutch at his heart. Right hand on the sword hilt, left on the staff, step, recover, step. The sweet, damp smell of grass filled the air. Flies and chittering beetles swarmed about his head. Simon's vision filled with hundreds of black specks.

"Crows and ravens have found them already," Yohan said. "You can expect the wolves before nightfall."

Simon broke into a trampled clearing as the sky filled with scolding birds. A crushed torso lay in a tangle of limbs and splintered bones. Simon prodded the corpse with his staff. Two sound boots hung from what remained of its legs. Simon looked back at Yohan. "Could you help me sit? I need to exchange shoes."

He stayed on the ground, scooting from body to body. Their hands told of hard labor. Their arms, crossed with a dozen scars, told of hard fighting. Their torsos, hacked and slashed, told of Luca in his rage, stripping bits of flesh along with ragged clothing. Yohan stood aside, watching. "They look like just what we expected, ya? Common mercenaries descending into thievery."

The sigil burning on his chest told Simon when he found the man he had been looking for. He gripped his sword hilt and rolled the body over onto its back. "I think I knew this one before... before."

Yohan knelt at the dead man's side and lifted the arm, rolling the cold hand up to face the sun. "He wasn't a mercenary. That is certain."

"Nor a farmer, nor a smith..." Simon tried to read the dead man's features. "Nor was he a priest."

"Then what was he?"

"He was the crossbowman. He murdered Cernak from hiding but didn't have the skill or courage to face Stephan." Simon tugged at the man's shoes. "There is something strange here. Have you seen any crucifixes, any amulets, tokens, charms?"

"Nothing." Simon looked over to find Yohan squinting at him. "You have become very perceptive for... for..."

"A half-wit?"

"Cretino, in Luca's words. How is that?"

Simon pulled a shoe open and searched inside. Nothing. "I grow more conscious every day since my trial. Every day I think of something new, remember something more." He reached inside the other shoe and drew out a small cloth bag. "I've found what I was looking for. Let's go back and talk to Luca about a crossbow."

To Simon, the return trudge seemed much easier than his trip out. Perhaps he walked in better boots. Perhaps the simple respect of Yohan eased his way. His leg ached and his side burned. *Nothing worth doing comes without a cost.* Where had he heard that? *Master Jacob?* Simon mused on such trivial things as he walked.

Yohan had made him promise not to bring up the crossbow. "Luca will produce it when it's least expected and most needed."

The crossbow was not Simon's concern. He tried not to think of his next chore, wondering instead what Luca had prepared for their meal. Dusk fell before they reached camp. Simon heard the distant call of wolves in the twilight.

Yohan said, "You don't expect to return to those bodies, ya?"

"I won't need to. We know all they have to tell us."

Luca had made bread filled with cheese and onions. Little was left by the time Simon returned. Yohan cut the remaining loaf into three equal chunks and waved Luca over. "I know you haven't eaten. Come, sit with us."

Simon waited for the tirade. Luca scowled and eyed the bread. "I am hostage now to my own meal?"

"We learned something you should know." Yohan held out the bread. "Take some and go then. We can talk another time."

Simon watched curiosity overcome Luca's anger. He took a lump of the warm bread and sat. Yohan helped Simon to the ground and sat between them. "You fought against those men, Luca. Who were they?"

"Marauders. What is this secret I must know?" Luca's eyes glittered in the firelight.

Simon met his glare. "Not all of them. Not the one who killed Cernak."

"And you know this man?"

"White linen shirt, clean hands, small shoes... no armor. You must have noticed that."

Luca gave the tiniest of nods. "I know him. No coin, no jewelry either. Not one mafankulo who wears even a ring."

"Do you still think they were marauders?"

"Mercenaries then. But they fight like merda."

Yohan said, "What about the men we killed five days ago?"

Luca thought a moment, then nodded. "The same." He caught Simon's eye. "You know something, sè?"

Simon produced a small cloth sack and passed it to Luca. "I cannot look at these, but you should."

He looked away and waited for what he knew would come. A short intake of breath was followed by a string of Sicilian curses. Jostling, Yohan grunted in surprise and put a hand on Simon's shoulder. "I've put them away. How did you know?"

Simon accepted the small parcel back from Yohan. "The only personal item among all of them, and it's hidden in a shoe? Besides, I know what this man was."

"Diavulu, then it is you who bring them here."

"No, something else. Something in the tumbrel."

Yohan stood. "Ya. Then we hold council—now."

Simon stayed by the fire with his injured leg stretched out before him. A man had died, a good man, his friend. As much as he hated to admit it, even to himself, Simon knew he'd had a role in that. Not that he knew what.

One by one, the others arrived. No sound. Simon heard only the fire's soft crackle and the far-off melodious yaps and hoots of feasting wolves. Yohan arrived last, bearing an armload of wood. "I fear this is all of our fuel." He looked around at all of them. "Stephan, I will ask you to lead us tonight."

The others found seats, making themselves as comfortable as possible on the ground. Opposite Simon, Ramon and Luca folded their cloaks and sat. Yohan settled nearby, as did Carla. Once more excluded, Simon tipped his head back to watch a column of sparks ascend into the darkening sky. The evening wasn't about to get easier, and he knew better than to resist the inevitable.

Stephan shuffled, clearly uncomfortable standing before the group, clearly shaken by the day's events. Simon didn't envy him. He kept his head back. The inevitable would come soon. Stephan started off. "We should be drinking ale or mead. We should be feasting our Brother Cernak as he ascends to the Elysian Fields." He paused. Simon imagined him staring at each of his brothers in turn. "And we will. We will feast his memory and his deeds, but not today."

Simon didn't know of Cernak's deeds, but he did respect his memory. Of all including Yohan, Cernak had most believed in him. There would be more. It would start well, but Simon knew where it would end. Stephan began again, a different tack. "I was there. It should have been me. Cernak fell to a crossbow bolt, and there was nothing..." Stephan paused. "Nothing I could have done. The crossbowman is dead. I rode him down and put a sword through his belly."

Simon had seen the body, pink hands, arms free of scars—a noble or a priest. He waited. "There were others. They swarmed our leader's body, still twitching on the ground. When I returned to the road they fled, cowards, leaving our friend slashed and despoiled on the road."

Nothing new here. Nothing that all of them didn't know. Still, Simon felt the pain in Stephan's heart. Stephan who had stood beside Cernak when he died. Yohan broke his reverie. "We will give Cernak the tribute he deserves. We will feast him to the glorious fields of *Fólkvangr*. But first, we must decide what comes next."

Simon sat upright and looked into Stephan's eyes. Clearly lost, the man looked at each of them. "Who will lead us in his place?"

Luca stirred. "Brother Yohan and his diavulu brings us here. Maybe he should lead us out."

Simon waited. He was on the list now. It would only be a matter of time. Stephan, pleased to be off the spot, said, "Yohan, I would nominate you to take Cernak's place as leader of this cohort."

Settling back, Simon waited for Yohan's response. He knew how this would end, as did all the others. Yohan had already assumed leadership.

Luca cleared his throat. "Do you lead us now, brother? Or do I nominate the diavulu to lead us?"

"Ya, if you will have me." Yohan pushed himself to his feet.

Stephan, clearly relieved, looked around the fire. "Opposed?"

On seeing no opposition, Stephan said, "Yohan Kozlov, you are now leader of this Knights of Palermo cohort. I yield the dais."

Yohan stood as Stephan folded his cloak and sat. "That was neatly done, Brother Stephan. I appreciate your faith." Yohan eyed each of them. Simon waited, but there seemed to be more business at hand. "Our Cernak," Yohan said, "would want a Northman's funeral. But this is not the place." A murmur of voices, the first Simon had heard since the others had gathered. "I propose a high pass, west of Nussdorf. Any opposed?"

Simon watched their faces. *Cernak would get his Viking's pyre, all in good time.* Yohan continued. "We will drink and feast in his honor as any Knight of Palermo can expect. Are you with me?"

Simon joined in the unanimous *yeas* that followed. Yohan had allowed the consent to cement his leadership. He continued. "We have another issue at hand. Why these attacks? Why us? Why now?" Yohan paused. "Stephan, you were the first to see Cernak's body. Tell us what happened."

Clearly unready for this question, Stephan drew back. "He was dead. The bolt penetrated his heart."

"But the others," Yohan pressed on, "what did they do?"

"Others?" Stephan seemed lost. "They slashed his body before I got there. Gone, both gone. I didn't see where."

Carla spoke up. "I was there shortly afterward. Cernak..." She paused a moment to collect herself, "our Cernak lay dead, his cloak in tatters. Nothing— there was nothing that Stephan, or I, or Ramon could do. Cernak is dead."

Yohan the interlocutor continued. "What did you find on the body?"

Carla shook her head. "What do you expect? Sword, personal effects, nothing."

Simon didn't wait for the next question. He looked at Carla and said, "What about a wooden box, the size of my hand?" Carla shook her head, and Simon continued. "Stephan, Yohan, one of you must have been through Cernak's personal effects. Did you find such a box?"

In the silence that followed, Luca spoke up. "I see this box. It is a curse on all of us."

"Where is it?" Simon paused and looked each of them in the eye. When he received no response, he continued. "They succeeded then. I thought, hoped even, that Stephan had killed their leader. But no, their leader is too smart to be caught. It was the box that Jacob had secreted within the tumbrel they sought."

Yohan said, "And the men who killed Jacob?"

Simon nodded. "The ones now hanging from Krakow's gates? I don't expect you found much on them either."

Simon took Yohan's silence for a sign to continue. "You have all seen the sigil branded into my chest. Within that box, I believe the same sigil appears on a token. Is that right, Brother Luca?"

The little Sicilian glared at him across the fire. "You know it is, *diavulu*."

"No, I don't know. That is my point. Aside from Cernak, you are the only one who has seen it. This thing was prepared as a *Nemesis*. A bane to kill me on sight. Jacob kept it, perhaps as insurance should I ever have regained my wits."

Closest to Simon, Stephan had sat, listening with his eyes closed. "They killed our friend, our brother, and our leader—only because of you?"

Simon nodded. This was what he had dreaded, the truth he knew he had to admit. "Yes. They killed Cernak, they killed my Master Jacob, God knows how many others they have killed to lay hands on this box, to secure this Nemesis scribed against me."

Simon waited for a count of two before Luca rose to his feet. "Then you are the diavulu as I say from the first day you foul our camp with your presence."

Yohan raised his hand. "Sit down, Luca. Perhaps he is. But let's not judge a man by the actions of others." He addressed Simon directly. "It's time you told us who you really are and who these men that attacked us represent."

"About myself, I know little." He put a hand on the pommel of his broken sword. "I may have been raised to the priesthood. I think I served at St. Peter's Basilica."

A few embers glowed in their fire. Simon watched them dim. He didn't look at the others. "There are factions within Vatican Hill—there are deep chambers, libraries, sacred temples. I remember my training, my initiation, little more."

Yohan stood, a wan ghost in the dying firelight. "And these men?"

The embers drew him into their glowing hearts. Simon knew the fire, knew the spirits that dwelt within each spark. He couldn't explain, but he drew strength from the glowing coals. "They have a name. I can say it now. They are the Apostoli Lucis, Apostles of the Light, and I am one."

Wolf of Nussdorf

Jolting and rolling in the back of the tumbrel made Simon wish he'd been allowed to walk. His only comfort was that Luca, perched atop the load of furs, had to watch the road ahead. He shared the ride with one other, Cernak. His body clad in chainmail, helmet, and cloak, sat in silent watch behind Luca.

Carla had prepared him. Swathed him in rags bound tight, his face beneath the helmet masked in linen. Three days out of Nussdorf, Simon knew the body would begin to decay before they reached the crossing. The high passes were at least five days farther. He hoped to be walking by then.

His admission the night before had cost him, had wrung the life from his heart like a washerwoman wrings water from soiled clothes. Simon had endured. His claw didn't wield the terror it once had. Memories fell into place like soldiers assembling for battle.

The following morning, Ramon switched the oxen and guided them down the road. Simon hobbled alongside for six long versts. After a thousand rotations of the great wheel he yielded to pain and fatigue and climbed back to the jouncing wooden bed. The day after, he made it until their midday break, feigning ease as he joined the others for a light meal. Ramon inspected his wounds that evening and removed the moss from his lacerated leg. "It has drained, and I see no foul humors, but you are an idiot for walking."

Simon couldn't explain. He simply nodded at Ramon's diagnosis. "And the sword cut to my side?"

It had ached all the while, often worse than his leg. Ramon shook his head. "Touch it, feel it burn. If you do not take care, that one will kill you."

By evening, Simon lay on his back, ignoring the bounce and roll of the cart. His entire body itched, his side throbbed, and the fever mounted to his head like Luca's fiery diavulu in fact. Simon tried not to cry out, but sometimes the pain simply overwhelmed his will. Yohan had brought him blankets, but Simon shook with chills that no covering could relieve. Carla plied him with water and wiped his face. Simon watched their fire until he passed into fitful unconsciousness.

Fever dreams of words unspoken, of deeds undone, of impossible tasks and terrible consequences haunted Simon as he slept. Shivering awake, searching for stars in the cold dark sky, he smelled lavender, the briefest whiff before it was gone, and wrapped tighter in his blankets. Awakening later, he inhaled lavender. Eyes closed, his chills finally passed, Simon breathed in the soothing floral scent and passed into a half dream of quiet peace and of a small cool hand pressed against his brow.

A gentle rain greeted Simon when he awoke the next morning. His head throbbed and his joints felt like they had been yanked from their sockets. He wrapped his blankets tighter and sat up, watching a tiny rivulet stream off the coarse fabric and dribble to the ground below. Simon looked closer. A partial footprint, five small toes evenly spaced, collected water beneath his dangling legs.

He slid off the boards to get a closer look. His left foot landed first, sending a shock of pain up through his hips. Simon tried to grab something, slipped, and planted a knee over the small footprint. His staff, he cursed himself for not remembering to use the staff. Clothed and cloaked, he shuffled over to their morning fire. Luca turned a row of starchy biscuits roasting on a stick. They smelled of sage and fennel. Without looking up, he broke one off and passed it to Simon. "So, the lords of *perditio*, the demons, they do not want their diavulu back."

"Good morning to you too, Brother Luca."

The doughy mass had some kind of meat inside. Simon chewed, wondering where Luca had found the filling. *Perhaps it's better I don't know.* Ramon had retrieved their horses along with the two oxen. Hobbled next to the tumbrel, they snorted as Simon approached. Perching the yoke on his shoulder, he hefted it over the wrinkled nape of one ox, then the other. A familiar ritual. They barely moved when he pinned the hoops beneath their necks.

Yohan stopped by and helped him raise the drawbar and shackle it to the yoke. "We should reach Nussdorf tonight. Do you think the ferrymen will recognize you?"

Simon considered that for a moment. "They might. It hardly matters. They will demand a tithe of our cargo to cross us over, plus a silver hryvna for each man and each horse."

"Ya, the Wolf of Nussdorf, they *are* thieves." Yohan tugged on his beard. "Brother Simon, do you scruple at cheating a thief?"

By midafternoon, the road had descended into a swampy fen of ponds and braided streams. The Danube River spread herself across the valley like an old harlot sprawled across a feather bed. Yohan, Carla, Luca, and Ramon had ridden on ahead. Simon guessed that they had reached the main river by now. Stephan paced alongside the oxen, wielding a willow switch. He'd exchanged his gambeson and sword for a plain gray cloak and stout wooden staff.

Simon gawked and shambled at his side, trying to hide his limp and look like the Simon of old. They rolled across several lesser streams. Holding their cloaks waist high to keep them out of the water. Simon understood now why Jacob had chosen the lowly tumbrel for travel. The cart could be turned in its own length and its axle rode well above the deepest stream. After the third such crossing, Stephan said, "And you made this wretched journey every year?"

Simon assumed his earlier persona. "Oh yes, Master Jacob. Every year, our feet are wet, and we pay the Wolf. Always pay the Wolf."

"Well today, maybe we pull his tail. I just hope Yohan knows what he's doing."

Simon had his own doubts. Even as Jacob's simple helper, he'd known the Nussdorf ferrymen to be little more than domesticated river pirates. As they rolled through the weeds and climbed a gravel bank, he caught sight of the collected shanties that marked the northern ferry landing. Nussdorf itself consisted of a timber stockade, a few deteriorating taverns, and a cluster of thatched huts across the river.

Still half a verst out, someone spotted them on the road and waved a white flag. As they approached, the ferry, little more than a timber raft, crawled across the river. An old man awaited them, all withered limbs and rotting teeth. "Hello, Simon," he called out. "Are you going to give me a kiss this year or do you still save it for your master?"

"You are the Wolf, and I will not kiss the Wolf."

The old man giggled to himself and slapped his knee. "No, you pay the Wolf, don't you, Simon? I will see you in Vienna and take my kiss then."

The ferry crunched against the gravel shingle, and two men ran ashore with ropes, securing them to a heavy post. Two other ferrymen stood by with long poles holding the awkward craft against the bank. Stephan goaded the oxen into the river and up onto the plank deck. Behind them, the tumbrel tipped precariously back. Simon joined the two rivermen grunting and heaving at the wheels until the entire load rolled up over the logs and steadied itself on the raft.

The mooring ropes loosened and retrieved, all four men shouted and pushed with their poles. The raft spun halfway, then turned back and began crossing the current crabwise. Near the river's midline, a series of waves slopped over the side and ran off across the deck. Simon parked himself on the downstream side and watched the southern bank grow near. Yohan and the others faced a gang of ferrymen. Simon heard their shouts.

The others on their raft heard it too. They pushed for the shore with renewed effort. Lurching forward, they grounded hard on the gravel beach. Stephan rose up, standing over the load of furs, and yelled, "Stop! Stop, everyone."

Luca screamed a string of Sicilian epithets, holding one man at knifepoint. Yohan stood with a wicked-looking crossbow aimed at another. Swords drawn, Ramon and Carla guarded their flanks. The entire tableau froze at Stephan's words. He clambered down, staff in hand, and marched ashore. Shouting something in Sicilian at Luca, he spun his staff and slammed Yohan's crossbow to the ground.

"What in the name of hell is the meaning of all this?" Stephan glared at each of them.

One of the ferrymen, barrel-chested with bristling black whiskers, stepped forward. "These bastards tried to cheat us."

Yohan drew a sword and met his glare. "Ya, we swim two of our horses, and still they asked for payment."

Stephan nodded in sympathy. "Yes, and you recently lost a friend to the highway marauders." He faced the ferrymen. "I carry his body back to Vienna for them." A sharp whistle, and Simon led the oxen off the raft and up the bank. Stephan continued. "They are upset—you can see that."

Luca muttered further imprecations and pressed his knife closer to the ferryman's neck. Stephan said a few words. Luca growled and withdrew. "See?" Stephan spread his arms. "We can work this out."

While the others watched Luca, the whiskered ferryman peeked into the back of the tumbrel. All turned when he growled and stumbled back, crossing himself, retreating ankle deep into the river. Simon knew. He'd helped strip the wrapping from Cernak's decaying face, he'd helped tie him spread-eagle across the load, crucified like St. Andrew.

Switching the oxen, Simon rolled the tumbrel toward the gathered men, a stupid grin stretched across his face. Stephan stepped toward Yohan, brandishing his staff. "Go now and trouble these men no more."

He gripped a ferryman by the arm. His neck still bled where Luca's knife had grazed his skin. "I'll make good their debt," Stephan said. "What do they still owe?"

The man touched his neck and croaked out, "Two... two hryvna."

Stephan handed the man four stamped silver bars. "Two for their debt and two for the trouble they brought you."

The others flashed looks between Stephan and the gristly load. "Meet us in Vienna," he said, "and we can settle the account for our crossing."

Simon kept switching the oxen, waiting for the shouts of anger and suspicion. None came. Stephan paced alongside. "Don't these beasts have any other speed?"

Simon knew better. Heading slowly toward Vienna seemed the safest tactic. Two versts beyond a bend in the river, Yohan stepped from the underbrush. "This way, quickly."

A narrow path led between two ancient willows. The tumbrel barely cleared their gnarled trunks, bumping over roots and stones. Yohan looked back and whistled. Ramon and Carla sprang out with armloads of leaves to cover the wheel tracks. "This won't fool them for long. We must reach the road before they figure it out."

Carla wielded a camp axe where saplings and brush blocked their path. Simon took over goading the oxen so Stephan could help Yohan scout ahead. A few versts through the forest, across a small stream, and up a broad embankment found them once again on a wagon road. Yohan called a halt. "We are on the Southern Way, about four versts west of Nussdorf and six versts north of Vienna. They wouldn't have waited long before following us south along the river."

Luca laughed. "Big hairy mafankulo sees our Cernak." He muttered something and signed the cross. "Bastardo piss his pants."

"Thank Brother Stephan for that," Yohan said. "And the extra silver, just enough to keep them arguing until we were gone."

Stephan made a low bow. "A brilliant performance by all. I hope you recovered Luca's crossbow."

Yohan nodded toward Luca. "Ya, it is safe."

Simon's leg ached from ankle to hip. His wounded side had reopened, weeping foul humors into his breechclout. He turned to look back toward Nussdorf. "How long before they catch up?"

"That depends," Yohan said, "on whether they followed us all the way to Vienna and how long before they realize we never entered the city."

Ramon closed his eyes. "I see them now. All of them have gone to Vienna, fearful that they will be cheated by the others. They have questioned the merchants who buy Jacob's furs. They have searched the guest houses, the inns. They stand now in the commons, arguing."

"Merda, Brother Ramon. You are not *fatturaone*. You have no sight."

Yohan held up one hand. "Say he does. Say they stand there right now, knowing they have been tricked. How long do we have?"

"We are eight versts, say five Roman miles by road from Vienna," Stephan said. "They could be here with a sizable force by sundown."

Swinging up on his horse, Yohan said, "We move. Now."

Ramon took one look at Simon. "You ride. I'll take the oxen."

Thanking him, Simon clambered up onto the rough wooden tumbrel bed and wrapped himself in cloak and blankets. One glance up at Cernak's baleful visage was enough to roll him back toward the road. No question, the Wolf would pursue its quarry. Alone on the wild road, away from the ferry, they would kill without hesitation and take the entire load. He watched the wheel tracks disappear behind them, waiting to see riders, waiting to hear shouts.

The sun dipped behind a band of clouds, and the open fields and spotty patches of forest faded into a gray haze. Simon dozed as they rolled along. Voices roused him. The sun had vanished and Yohan had called another halt. Above the fields, a yellow twilight painted everything in ghostly shadows. Simon grabbed his stick, pressed it against the ground, and lowered himself to the road. His oxen would need water soon. He hobbled up to the front and checked their mouths. Dry and frothy. *Yes, soon.* Yohan had dismounted. He bent backward, stretching. On seeing Simon, he said, "We need you to guide the animals. You can walk, ya?"

Simon didn't think it was a question. He nodded and took the switch from Ramon. Yohan continued, addressing the others. "We perform a retreat echelon tonight. Luca, you will start. Stay here, stay hidden, and count a thousand heartbeats. If you see nothing, ride to the tumbrel and report."

"And if all cazzo diavuli in hell arrive?"

"Then wait in hiding and follow when they pass."

"Carla, you are next. Ride with us for a thousand heartbeats, then hide. Count a thousand more. Luca should ride past in a few hundred. If not, be cautious, stay hidden. After a thousand, return and report."

Carla nodded. "I understand, but Luca will wait no matter what. I know him."

"He can't." Yohan directed his gaze at the little Sicilian. "You can't, Luca, not this time."

Luca crossed his arms and bowed. "D'accordo."

Turning his gaze to Ramon, Yohan said, "You are third. Wait a thousand heartbeats after Carla rejoins us, then take to the bushes. Be aware. If your brothers ride past, we are safe. If they do not, trouble follows."

Simon wished he were staying, watching. Better he knew what kind of trouble they would find, than ride until it found him.

Yohan continued. "You know the tactic. When I stop seeing riders, then I'll know our pursuers are near. Follow, attack from behind. We'll crush them between us."

As Luca secreted himself a reasonable distance from the road, Simon turned his attention to the oxen. They had drawn the cart all day, crossed stream, river, forest, and glen without stopping. He switched them into motion. The near animal snuffled the ground for a moment then began plodding up the road. As much as he would like to urge them to more speed, Simon thought of what would happen if they balked. He watched the big wheel turn and with it a tiny scrap of rag still clinging to a spoke.

He counted as he walked in the growing darkness. He knew from years of travel with Jacob that fifty turns would be about a thousand heartbeats. After the big wheel turned over seventy rotations he began looking back. At a hundred rotations, Yohan began to look back, muttering to himself. At a hundred twenty rotations of the great wheel, Carla galloped up. "I haven't seen Luca, is he here?"

Yohan cursed and turned to Stephan. "Wait here. Take Luca's place." He looked down at Simon. "Keep that half-sword limber and your knife close. I fear our Sicilian has gone looking for trouble."

Shortly after, Ramon galloped up. "Luca?"

Yohan shook his head. "Start counting, brother—this is about to get interesting."

Another fifty turns of the wheel and Carla dropped off into the shadows. Night had fallen across the land and the road had faded to a vague strip of gray soil. Simon walked along the left edge to keep his bearings in the darkness. As he watched the wheel, his toe hit something, and Simon sprawled on his face. Pushing himself to his feet, he looked down. A smooth square marble stone pushed up through the packed earth, a Roman mile marker. He glanced back then scrambled after his team.

Ramon had just faded into the misty fields when Stephan galloped up. He'd said nothing before a second set of pounding hoofbeats followed. Luca, his horse sweating and blown, nearly rode Yohan down. Catching his breath, he let fly a string of curses. "We are cazzo dead mafankulos, brother. They come with a hundred bastardos. One hundred. We are dead."

Yohan halted. "What did you do, Luca?"

"I ride back. Yes, you say do not wait, and I agree. So I ride back to see what kind of capos de merda come for us." Luca pointed down the road, the way he'd come. "Cazzo soldiers they bring. So I ride. Over fields and woods, I ride. I come to die with my brothers." He glared at Simon and the tumbrel. "And die with this diavulu and his cursed animal cart."

Something, anything. Simon tried to think. How could they vanish? "How far, Luca? How far back?"

"It matters nothing."

"It matters, Luca. How far?"

"Maybe two versts, maybe three. They come fast."

Yohan had said nothing. Simon watched him consider their options, but he knew. *One option, just one.* Standing beneath Yohan's stirrup, Simon looked up. "Half a verst back, we crossed the old Roman road. If we turn around here and go back, we can follow it west."

"They will know," Yohan said.

"I'll lead the oxen back in their exact tracks. We can leave the road, and no one will know."

"Cretino..."

"It's a plan, Luca. Do you have a better?"

Glaring back down the road, Luca cursed the darkness but said little else. Before anyone spoke. Simon reversed the tumbrel, turning practically in its own length, and began retracing their exact track. He shuffled along the road's edge, searching. The big wheels rotated. Nothing. Darkness fell like a black felt cloak thrown across the land. Half a verst from where they turned, Ramon emerged from hiding and shrugged at Yohan. Luca trailed behind, mumbling quietly to himself.

Simon shuffled his feet, tapped with his staff, searching for the marker, so easily missed in the darkness. He was almost lost to despair when he tripped. The same marble stone poked through the worn roadbed, not nearly as big as he had remembered. "Here, here. We should head west across that field.

Jacob followed a road like this. He said it goes all the way to Rome."

As Simon turned the rig, he heard hoofbeats once more.

Carla nearly cantered into all of them.

Yohan answered her unspoken questions. "Help Luca erase our wheel marks. We leave the road here."

Beneath the grass, Simon found a flattened track, barely wider than his tumbrel. He relied on his feet to tell him where it headed. Stephan walked on ahead, prodding the grass with his staff, then fell back alongside Simon. "It runs straight and true as a razor cut. How did you know?"

"A Roman mile marker, I hadn't seen one since we left Krakow. Jacob followed them to avoid being found."

Yohan had ridden up from behind. "It was a lucky guess. We could be up to the axle in a bog by now." He turned to look back into the darkness. "Of course, we could be facing the spears of a hundred soldiers by now as well."

"You know it's only thirty."

Glancing back again, Yohan said, "It wouldn't matter—dead is dead. When Luca and the others catch up, have them stay with the team. I will ride ahead and look for a place to water the animals."

Simon counted almost two hundred rotations of the wheel before he heard Carla and Ramon arguing with Stephan in the darkness. Anxious to hear their news, he allowed the cart to roll on ahead. A few snippets were all he needed. Luca had hung back, waiting to see if his "army" passed without noticing.

Five more versts rumbled and bumped beneath the tumbrel's wheels before they came upon Yohan, sitting like a statue on his horse. "He stayed, didn't he?"

Carla's voice shot back through the darkness. "Good news, Captain. He is not yet galloping up."

"The bad news is," Yohan answered, "he is, right now, holding his crossbow, wondering which one to shoot."

Ramon dismounted and led his horse forward. "We won't know until he gets here. Did you find water?"

Simon knew the answer to that. His oxen stamped and snorted in anticipation. Yohan waved them off to the right. "A spring and a stone basin. We rest here until Luca arrives."

The horses went first, two at a time. Simon had finished watering his oxen when he heard the regular hoofbeat of a trotting horse. Luca swung down from his saddle. "Bastardos ride like they chase the wind. May their horses strangle on dust. Where is Yohan?"

"Ya, I am right behind you."

"Merda! I think I ride with ghosts."

"Not yet. But we will have to ride all night."

"Where is it we ride? To hell, with the diavulu himself?"

Stephan spoke from the darkness. "Ancient Salzburg, city of salt. It was prized by the Romans as much as a city of gold."

"Salzburg to Venice, that would be a hard road through the mountains. I wonder if the Romans even went that way."

"A fig on the mafankulo Roman bastardos. We are cazzo Knights of Palermo. We go where we want. It is almost summer, sè? The mountains, they are beautiful. We go."

As Luca spoke, the clouds parted in the east, revealing a bright quarter-moon rising above a sea of mist. They all stood in silence for a moment.

Then Ramon said, "I think Brother Luca has a woman in Salzburg."

Yohan laughed. "Either way, I would rather cross the mountains to Salzburg than deal with the Wolf of Nussdorf again."

The Road Less Traveled

Simon rode in the tumbrel the rest of that night. The rising moon provided enough light that Stephan and Yohan had little trouble keeping them to the ancient Roman track. Toward dawn, he managed to sleep in snatches, jounced awake when the balky cart rolled over one obstruction after another.

By sunup, he'd had enough of the bruising ride to slide off the back and follow on foot. He caught up with Stephan, half asleep as he walked beside the oxen. The others looked little better. Carla slumped in her saddle, falling slowly behind. Ramon as well.

His stiff legs complaining at every step, Simon forced himself to push past the cart in search of Yohan. After another verst, he picked out a riderless horse in the distance. Striding ahead of the cart he found Luca, sitting on the ground, head between his knees. His horse snorted a greeting and Luca raised his head. "Merda. You all died?"

"All but me, it seems. Where is Yohan?"

"He finds us a place to rest." Luca stared back at the approaching tumbrel and scrambled to his feet. "Come, this procession can lead itself. Today, you learn to ride."

"Why now? Are you looking for another way to torment me?"

"If you are a Knight of Palermo, you ride." Luca put a hand on the saddle and explained the stirrups, broad cantle at the back, and high pommel in the front. "Reins to guide, but horse is smarter than you. He knows where to go."

Luca rubbed his horse on the muzzle, then hauled himself up behind his saddle and perched on its hip. The animal grunted and shuffled. Luca reached down. "Put your foot in the stirrup. Quick now."

Despite his injured leg, Simon jammed his left foot into Luca's iron stirrup. A surprisingly strong pull from Luca swung him into the saddle. Still holding his staff, Simon clung to the pommel while the horse danced and snorted beneath him. Luca bent forward, drawing back on the reins. Simon held on for life as the animal bucked and spun, reaching back to snap at their legs. Luca kicked it in the nose and the horse lowered its head and laid its ears back.

While Simon did his best to hold on, Luca managed to regain control and direct the animal west. Bumping worse than the tumbrel, Simon judged riding a horse only slightly preferable to being dragged by one.

They caught up with Yohan before the sun had climbed much higher. Simon swung to the ground. He dodged a hoof and backed away. Luca looked down at him. "You don't thank me for the ride?"

"Perhaps later, when I have recovered."

Yohan sat by another stone cistern, this one fed by a stream that trickled across the road in a bed of loose stones. "We can stop and water the animals here. If there is trouble coming, we need to be rested before it arrives."

The others dragged in one at a time. Luca helped Carla with the horses, setting them out to graze. Simon took charge of the oxen, freeing them from their yoke and leading them to the water. Checking their legs for sores and their hooves for splits, he hobbled the animals in a meadow near the creek.

The yoke and neck hoops, smooth beneath his hand, showed wear, but no splitting or chafing. He worked his way down the drawbar inspecting it for cracks. Finding no obvious issues, Simon turned his attention to the high, spoked wheels. Yohan joined him. "Afraid of what you find?"

"The axles. I should have greased them before we left Krakow." He put a hand on the hub. "They're warm, but not hot. Next town, we will need to pull the wheels and apply more grease."

Yohan's look made Simon fidget. "Jacob tried to teach me about all of this, the animals, the cart, even the ferrymen. I just couldn't understand, could barely remember."

"But you remember now?"

"More today than yesterday, but still only pieces."

. Circling behind the tumbrel, Yohan stopped and looked up at Cernak, strung across the load like an ancient martyr. "You did well, old friend. Soon now, very soon."

Simon looked up. "Shouldn't we cover him, wrap him?"

Yohan closed his eyes and nodded. "You bring him down and I'll help you bind the shroud."

Cernak's body slid down the stacked bales and collapsed in a jumble of mailed limbs and torso. Heavier than he'd expected, Simon tried to arrange the corpse with some dignity, but the arms dislocated from their shoulders, and Cernak's head only lolled from one side to the other. Yohan produced a gray wool blanket and large iron needle. "You work this under him, while I stitch it tight."

Stephan appeared from the other side carrying a worn leather scabbard. "He should have his sword."

Luca followed close behind, crossing himself. "Charon is one cazzo ferryman not to be cheated." He fished a small gold coin from the purse at his belt and dropped it into Cernak's flaccid mouth. "*Vade cum Deo.* Go with God my friend."

Laying the sword and scabbard across Cernak's chest, Stephan crossed the arms and Luca tied them over the sword. They helped roll the body to one side and the other, while Simon pulled the blanket underneath. Doubling it over, Yohan began a spiral stitch at Cernak's feet.

Stephan watched him pull a stout hemp cord through the coarse fabric. "A travel blanket is a fitting shroud for a man whose life has been spent on the road."

Yohan looked up from his work. "Stephan, get some sleep. Halfsword, Luca, you too."

In the shade of the tumbrel, next to the trickling creek, Simon curled up in his cloak and dozed. He jolted awake to the stamp and snort of horses. Hand on his knife, he craned his neck about. Only Luca and Stephan adjusting saddles. Only Carla and Ramon collecting gear. He eased himself to his feet and stretched. The wound pulled at his side as he moved, aching worse than his leg. *Bearable as long as I don't have to ride Luca's wretched beast.*

After some searching, Simon found his oxen resting in the deep grass, their forelegs folded beneath them. He goaded them to their feet and yoked them to the tumbrel. The sun had crossed the meridian and Simon's shadow pointed back toward Nussdorf. He stared in that direction for a long time. Nothing moved. His oxen stamped and snuffled the ground. Yohan set out west, and Simon followed.

Their road began climbing before much of the afternoon had passed. Simon watched the thick marshy grasslands give way to shrubs and rolling hills. Here, the ancient Roman track cut telltale notches in the earth, so similar to the route he and Jacob had once followed from Tver. Mile markers too, Simon picked them out along the roadside as he walked.

By the time Simon's evening shadow danced long and spindly down the road behind him, his head had begun to drop, and his stomach growled. Luca and Carla had formed a rear guard while Yohan and the others scouted ahead. The road they followed no longer ran arrow-straight over hill and valley but now wound between the steeper slopes and climbed over low passes. Simon slowed his team, watching for the road's edge. The gathering shadows seemed to eat the ground itself and leave only a vague sense of misdirection.

Luca rode up from behind. "You know where we go?"

Stopping the team, Simon walked a dozen paces ahead. A shadow among shadows, he bent to look. A familiar notch marked the hillside. "Here." He pointed at the ground. "The road once went through here."

Behind Luca, Carla rode up, trailing Cernak's horse. "I hope Yohan saw this as well."

Ahead, the sky glowed bright blue with gold bands crossing from north to south. Simon tried to make out a sign of movement in the hills ahead but saw nothing. "It will only get darker," he said. "We must continue."

Luca spurred his horse ahead, riding toward the hilltop. Carla hung back, waiting, while Simon goaded the oxen forward. The way steepened, and as they approached the crest, Simon was sure they'd left the road. Luca waited while the oxen struggled to haul the heavy cart up the final slope. He pointed to the valley on the other side. Tucked into a cleft between the hills, a small fire flickered in the shadows.

Stephan rode up from below. Ramon followed. "I feared we had lost our camp cook and all our supplies."

"And I fear we will lose this load halfway down," Stephan said. "Why didn't you go around the hill?"

Luca turned from cursing at Ramon. "Cazzo cretino here says, 'Go this way.' I go."

Simon had stopped listening. He searched among the trees and underbrush until he found a sapling thick as his arm and twice his height. With a camp axe from the tumbrel, Simon cut and limbed the sapling. Carla helped, and together, they jammed it through the spokes of the two great wheels.

Snorting and grunting, the oxen dragged their load down the hillside, sliding it over rocks and fallen leaves. Simon removed the brake when they reached the bottom. He checked the animals and their harness once more before driving them into camp.

A small creek trickled out of the adjacent hills, and a field of stunted grass filled most of the valley. Yohan had started a porridge of cracked wheat and dried meat. Simon could have eaten it just as it was, but Luca sniffed and muttered a few words. He dredged a handful of herbs from his pack and stirred them in. Wisely retreating, Yohan pulled Simon away. "Let's get the oxen settled while Brother Luca works his magic."

Magic. Simon thought about that as he dropped the hoops from the animals' necks. He shouldered the yoke and set it aside while Yohan braced the jack beneath the drawbar. Simon's hand fell to the soft leather purse hanging at his side. Sorcery, conjuration—things he needed to face, sooner or later. *Things best faced in the daylight.*

Simon waited for Yohan to finish securing the jack before wandering back to the fire. Luca had seasoned the porridge with wild garlic and fried lumps in rendered bacon fat. Simon picked one out and blew on it. "Do you know how happy I am that you lost your wager?"

Luca tossed another scoop of porridge into the sizzling grease. "I spit on those, bastardo, just for you."

"I'm so hungry, I don't care."

Yohan picked up one of the hot lumps and held it between his fingers. "Did you spit on mine too?"

"All of you mafankulos. You know nothing about food. Eat like pigs in a trough." Luca waved a wooden spoon over his head. "Here, I can fry horse turds, and you will eat."

Simon took another bite. "Best horse turds in... Where are we, anyway?"

Yohan chewed for a moment and wiped his mouth. "Moravia? Bohemia? I've never been through here." He gestured off to his side. "Mountains that way—we have to cross them. That's all I know."

"Cretinos all of you." Luca muttered something while he dropped more porridge lumps in the fat. "I was here. Yes, cazzo mountains are here. And more—forests so dark you think night lives in them. Diavuli here too, devils in the woods. Every tree with eyes that watch. Better maybe we fight mafankulo ferrymen."

"The fight we avoid is the fight we win." Yohan glanced back at the tumbrel. "Brother Cernak taught me that."

The pile of fried porridge lumps grew higher as Luca fished them from the grease and tapped them into a steel pannikin. Simon reached for another and caught a rap from Luca's spoon for his troubles. "You eat tomorrow's food liccu, glutton."

Yohan said, "We should all get some sleep. Luca, wake me when you finish here. I'll take second watch. The moon rises sometime in the early morning, after matins. We leave then."

Curled beneath the tumbrel, a kick to his shoulder brought Simon clear awake. "Get up, lazy diavulu bastardo. We go to visit your cousins."

A thin quarter moon rode just above the eastern hills, painting the scene in shades of gray. Shaking the sleep from his head, Simon relieved himself in the nearby bushes, then stumbled down to the creek to wash his face. He wandered through the motion of yoking the oxen and securing his belongings. Much of their supplies had been packed in with his own small bundle. Tightening the bindings, Simon made sure nothing rolled out.

Yohan rode up, looking as if he had slept a whole night in a feather bed. "There was a Roman watering trough here at one time, but all I could find yesterday were its scattered remains." He pointed west along the valley floor.

"I found the next mile marker that direction. You should start with the team while we erase any sign of our encampment."

"Do you think they would have followed this far?"

"I won't take that chance. Luca can go with you. We will catch up."

Pushing the oxen to their usual plodding gait, Simon didn't wait for Luca to join him. He walked a few paces ahead of the animals, inspecting the ground for signs of a road. The faint moonlight was little better than the evening sky had been the night before. He tried to stay on the firmest ground, tried to keep the wheels from slipping into the rocky creek bed, tried to stay awake.

Luca rode up before Simon found the next mile marker. He laughed, swung from his saddle, and slid to the ground. "You walk like grandfather looking for his teeth."

"Did you know your grandfather?" Simon kept searching the ground.

Luca fell silent for a moment. Simon could almost feel him building up to a tirade. Then the little Sicilian let out a short sigh. "You mean that nice, sè? You mean does he live?"

"Yes... No disrespect." Simon realized his mistake. "Was he alive when you were young?"

"My family is old, very old. I know grandfather. He is like a... maybe a god. No, that is blasphemy." Luca crossed himself. "He is, he was a Caesar."

They walked in silence until Luca continued. "Do you think what it is for a boy to live in Caesar's palazzo, sè? He is nobody. He runs away, becomes mercenary, learns paranza corta." Luca grinned and punched Simon's shoulder. "It is good, sè? You learn the short weapon too, the hidden hand."

"And now I walk like a grandfather for it."

"You walk. Your enemies die."

"My enemies still live. They may have sent our attackers, but they are too cautious to come themselves."

"You know them, these enemies? You see them?"

Simon fell back a few paces to prod the near ox. Satisfied that they followed the road, he caught up with Luca. "I think I was one of them—once. Maybe an acolyte. I don't remember."

A shadow in the pale moonlight, Luca led his horse in silence. He stumbled and stopped. "There, you look for that, sè?"

Simon dropped to a knee and brushed away a tangle of leaves and weeds. "Roman mile marker. At least we're still on the road."

Luca looked back the way they'd come. Simon followed his gaze. Silver-gray hillsides, inky shadows, nothing moved. "I hope the others follow as well."

"They follow. Yohan, he is careful. Carla and Ramon, right now they ride back on our trail. They watch for bastardo ferrymen. I know his mind, diavulu. He fears pursuit, looks for danger, never sleeps."

Switching the oxen back in motion, Simon continued along the valley floor. "Did you consider what might have happened if we had stopped to pay the Wolf?"

"Maybe we ride away. Is not a problem."

"I think we would offer them ten bales of ermine, and they would demand we unload the entire tumbrel for inspection. Once we did that, your hundred bastardos would come riding out of the stockade."

"Maybe only fifty, sè?"

"Fifty, it doesn't matter. They were waiting for us."

"Is maybe your enemies, these?"

"No, but someone told them we were coming."

In the darkness, Simon couldn't read Luca's face, but he could imagine the thoughts spinning in the man's head. He waited, while the tumbrel continued climbing west, up the valley floor. Finally, Luca said, "So what is it these enemies want?"

"I thought maybe the box they stole from Cernak. Now, I don't know."

"They want you, diavulu. They lose you—they find you."

"Impossible. I am nothing. I know nothing. They could have found me years ago if they had wanted to."

"Instead, they find your Jacob. They find our Cernak. Why is that?"

Walking in silence, Simon considered the question. Aside from an occasional bird calling from the bushes, the susurration of hoof-falls and rumble of wheels were all he could hear. The road ran straight, a band of grass only visible in contrast with the brambles and small trees growing alongside. He watched for movement on the hills or near the road—nothing.

Luca paced at his side, uncharacteristically quiet. Another verst passed beneath the cart before he finally spoke. "That box they stole, you call it Nemesis?"

The claw tightened. Simon's hand dropped to the comfort of his sword hilt. "A curse—linked to me. Did you see the other side?"

"Only the mafankulo serpent. There is more?"

"A talisman." Simon caught his breath, forced himself to keep walking. "It is a seal, a conjurer's tool."

"It carries a demon, then."

"No, the seal is bound to a powerful entity—perhaps a demon, perhaps an angel."

Luca clenched his left hand, raising two fingers before Simon, warding off the evil eye. "Only now you speak of these things, diavulu. Why is that?"

"Memories. They crush my chest, choke my heart. Even now..." Simon gagged for a moment, forcing the breath that didn't want to come. "Even now, talking is hard. But I've learned that I can take more pain than I ever thought possible."

Simon trudged on, summoning other things to his mind, other things to push back the ceremonies, the invocations, the dark chamber of hooded figures. He turned his face skyward. Pink cloud fingers hovered above the eastern hills. Daylight, it would come soon. The animals would need rest and water. Without a word, Luca swung to his saddle and trotted up the valley. Strangely talkative, almost friendly, Simon wasn't quite sure what to make of him.

At least a thousand rotations of the wheel passed before Simon picked out another mile marker. This one stood above the grass and weeds, a slender rectangular column, any inscription it once bore long weathered away. The sky paled to cream with gray cloud tendrils streaming from the eastern horizon. Walking beside his team, he could have been the only living person on earth.

A hundred more turns of the wheel gave lie to that illusion. The rising sun revealed Luca approaching from the west. He reined in and turned his horse when they met. "Keep walking, diavulu—is five versts maybe to water. I go to find Yohan. We meet you there."

Once more alone with his oxen, Simon watched his gangly shadow dance before him among the weeds. The road had grown smoother, more distinct in the growing daylight. Simon glanced behind him. The feeling of isolation that had accompanied him all morning fled with Luca's arrival and had not returned. He cast furtive glances at the trees and rocks as they passed. Nothing, no sign of another creature ever having come this way, not even deer or badgers scattering into the brush.

Half asleep, he would have plodded right past the Roman water trough had the oxen not grunted and bellowed as they approached. A spring bubbled up from the roadside, splashed across a series of flat stones, and trickled into the marble basin.

Simon hobbled the animals and removed their yoke. Left to themselves, he knew they would drink before grazing in the meadow below. Shoes off, he sat dangling his feet in the cool water. Birds called from the nearby trees. A morning breeze hissed through the short grass and waved leafy shadows over his face. Simon nodded, dozing in the warm sunlight.

Cold legs, head down, he awoke. In the still water between his knees, a long face gazed back at him, sandy hair drawn back and tied, tunic open at the throat, Simon recognized his own image. The pond rippled and glittering sunlight danced over his reflection. Pale, round, framed in a mass of orange hair, another face hovered over his shoulder.

Jumping up, feet sliding beneath him, Simon fell backward into the cool water. A sputtering thing of blundering arms and legs, he rose dripping from the trough and stared about in panic. Birds scolded from the bushes. One ox raised its head. It stared at him in bovine dismay then resumed grazing. Nothing else moved.

Simon searched the ground for footprints, searched the tumbrel for anything amiss. He circled the marble trough looking for something to explain that momentary vision. It could have been the moon he saw, still riding high and wan in the morning sky, the moon in a smear of ochre hair with eyes of clover.

It could have been a dream. He'd had them before, usually when the night was at its darkest or when he'd fallen asleep in exhaustion or fever. More likely, he thought, something in the water had poisoned his mind. He searched for mandrake root or perhaps a graven curse on the water trough itself. Simon checked the tumbrel again, but nothing moved save the legion of flies buzzing about Cernak's corpse.

He'd hung his tunic over the drawbar to dry and wrung what water he could from his breechclout. Before Simon could finish dressing, Luca and the others arrived. Yohan rode in the lead, a bandaged arm resting on his saddle. Carla too, had been wounded—a bloodied shirt wrapped her chest. "Dirty bastard tried to stab me in the tits."

In answer to Simon's unspoken question, Yohan said, "Ya, ten of them, riding up our trail as if we left signposts."

Ramon helped Yohan from his saddle. "Carla and I rode two versts back and waited. When they dismounted to check our campsite, we attacked."

Luca said, "Greedy liccu bastardos kill them all and leave me nothing."

Half afraid of the answer, Simon asked, "Where is Stephan?"

"He took charge of their horses," Ramon said. "We'll see him soon."

Yohan eyed Simon's wet tunic. "I'm glad you finally took another bath. You were starting to draw more flies than your oxen." He pulled a small cloth pouch from beneath his cloak. "I took this off one of our adversaries. We need to talk."

Crossroad

Carla had taken a sword cut like Simon's, slicing through little more than skin and tunic. She gritted her teeth while Ramon stitched and bound her wound. Yohan's injury was more critical. A broken arrow shaft protruded from his upper arm. He seemed unconcerned, as if arrow wounds were normal. "Simon, you should watch Ramon. He will teach you the right way to pull an arrow."

Ramon examined the arm and shook his head. "It is lodged against the bone. I will have to drive it through and pull it out the back. This may hurt, my friend."

Yohan nodded. "Ya, give me a stick, then do it quick."

Simon gave him a short piece of kindling to bite on while Yohan rested his arm on a nearby log. Ramon drew his dagger. "Hold his arm."

Simon put a knee against Yohan's wrist and wrapped an arm around his shoulder. "Ready."

Ramon seized the broken arrow shaft and twisted it free of the bone. Yohan didn't move. Reversing the dagger, Ramon smacked its hilt into the broken end of the shaft. The next instant, Simon tumbled to the ground. Waving and growling, Yohan stood over him like an enraged bear. Ramon stood. "Now just hold still a moment while I pull it out."

They packed Yohan's arm with moss to help it drain and bound it tight with strips of linen. Stephan arrived shortly after, leading a string of horses. Luca produced a bag of woven jute and passed out lumps of fried porridge from the night before. Simon gnawed on his, glad that Luca had the foresight to save an easy meal. Checking on his oxen, he circled their party following the road west.

A hundred paces past the watering trough, he struck another path winding down from the hills in the south and disappearing north into the trees.

A shout from across the meadow caught his attention. Stephan stood in the tumbrel waving his arms. Cutting through the grassy field and its grazing herd of livestock, Simon returned to the group.

Yohan sat on the tumbrel drawbar, his arm in a sling. "When I said we need to talk, I meant we need to talk *now*." He lowered his voice as Simon approached. "Luca told me of your conversation. I agree—we were set up at Nussdorf."

Yohan waited until the others arrived before standing. "We were lucky this morning. Our pursuers were overconfident and careless. Still, they only came with a tithe of their strength and, even then, nearly outmatched us."

Simon waited for the question that should come next. Instead, Yohan held up the small linen purse he'd taken off one of the bodies. "Since you know what this is, Brother Simon, I would ask you to take charge of it as you have the others."

"Others?" Stephan and Ramon spoke almost in unison.

"Talismans." Simon took the bag from Yohan, a single heavy disk inside. "Conjurers' tokens. They are used in sorcery." He pulled a matching bag from his belt. "These we took from the group that attacked us outside of Krakow. I feared to look at them, but now I must."

He opened the most recent bag first and squeezed a single gold disk into the palm of his hand. A coin, pounded flat and polished to remove any former inscription, bore a series of lines and indentions roughly scribed across its face. At the center, a single name had been engraved, *Araton*. Luca leaned closer. "You do not look at it, diavulu. Do it now. See what deviltry you hold."

Simon had looked, a flicker of his eyes as the talisman emerged. The others leaned closer—their gazes fastened on the golden object. Simon glanced down once more and turned the disk over. Its backside held a crude engraving of the crucified serpent, the same emblem branded into his chest. He held it up. "It is the *Serpens Crucis Sinister*, facing left as mine does." Simon dropped the talisman back in its bag and drew a deep breath. "It was badly made, but I think its purpose was to lead them to me."

"And the others?" Yohan said.

Simon opened the second bag and poured three smaller disks into his hand, two of tarnished silver and one of dark iron. He'd hardened himself to the pain, the choking grip. These were easier to look at. He held a silver piece. "I think this will summon a creature to do your bidding. I don't think any of us want to see it." He examined the other silver talisman. "This one is for healing. Oh yes, they are not all evil you know."

Yohan shook his head. "I have fought your Apostles many times, ya, as did our leader, Cernak. Everything they touch is evil."

Without argument, Simon held up the last disk, the one of iron. Blackened by fire, he suspected it had been infused with the female attribute of *antimonium*. "This is perhaps the most dangerous of the talismans I carry. It summons the *salmandre ardente,* a fiery creature that will tell you the location of any lost object. Should you not treat with it properly, it will eat your soul."

The others pressed in even closer. Surprised at their fascination with such dangerous objects, Simon dropped all three tokens back in their purse and returned it to his belt.

Luca was first to speak, with almost awe in his voice. "You dare carry these, diavulu? I should not have walked so close."

"You carry a knife and sword," Simon countered. "You walk with men who have been trained to kill. You worship a God who slaughtered the innocent women and children of Jericho in their tens of thousands. Why can't you walk with me?"

Luca crossed himself and backed away.

Yohan said, "The last one, the black one, is that what led them to us?"

"Three times, it led them to the hidden Nemesis. Once to Jacob before we reached Krakow and again to me after we had left. The third time, the same talisman that led them to Jacob also led them to Cernak."

"It should have been you who dies, diavulu." Luca spoke from behind the others.

"It should have been." Simon nodded, still feeling the pain of their loss, still feeling the guilt. "Recall, we had more than a few to deal with ourselves."

Tugging on his beard, Yohan said, "Then the Nemesis Jacob carried must have been lost by someone?"

Simon hadn't considered that implication. "Stolen, more likely. I don't know why Jacob would steal the thing."

"Jacob ben Reuben was Apostoli Lucis. We have come against him many times," Yohan said. "He is *wærloga,* apostate to the Templars. He could have easily turned outlaw on the Apostles as well."

"Having lost their talisman for finding, they had to wait until they could make that last one, directed at me. It carries the sign of Araton, fallen angel and earthly spirit of Saturn. Tonight, that planet will again be ascendent and they will likely make another."

"That means they will still come for you," Yohan said.

Luca pulled a face. "We nail him to a tree and let them come."

"Not quite so hasty, Brother Luca." Yohan slid from the drawbar and stood, flexing his left hand. "We are a little short on sword arms, ya? Injured as he is, we still need him."

Carla had held back, leaning against the tumbrel wheel, and nursing her wounded side. She pushed herself upright. "Do I understand that our Brother Simon knows how to use these devilish things?"

"As a boy, I was an acolyte. Perhaps an assistant is more accurate. I never made a talisman, but when they were used, I attended."

"So you could call this salamander demon and ask it to find the man who carries your Nemesis?"

"Even if I could, I wouldn't."

"Could you use the one for healing?"

"Even if he could," Yohan said, "I will not permit it. Not while he is a member of the Fellowship."

Invoking a talisman, perilous even for an adept, Simon shuddered at the thought and didn't respond.

Stephan said, "Do we even know if they have enough strength left to pursue us?"

"Fifty bastardos I count yesterday, cazzo ferrymen and guards."

"Not all," Yohan said. "We faced only six guards from Nussdorf this morning. Three others looked like a mixed group of hired brigands. The last, the one hanging back until Ramon cut him down, he was an Apostle."

Stephan nodded. "Every encounter, we've thinned their ranks. Do you think Ramon killed the last one?"

Simon shook his head. "Not likely. Apostoli Lucis is not structured that way. They are *in camerae*, in chambers like Roman cohorts. If one fails, another takes its place. You will never see their true leader. He directs from hiding."

Yohan said, "Then it may take them some time to regroup, to mount a new attack."

Simon read the look on the other faces. Unending days of travel, they all felt it; Stephan said it. "We should rest here then. We have grazing for the animals and our own wounds to tend."

Mumbles of agreement, Carla looked relieved and even Yohan nodded. Luca spoke up. "Our diavulu does not look pleased. Perhaps he wishes another lesson in the pankration."

Simon had to smile despite himself. "As much as I've enjoyed my morning beatings, I have another issue. We have come to a crossroads. Certain, um... entities dwell at a crossroad—I may have seen one this morning."

Yohan squinted and said, "I should see this crossroads. Luca, you come with us." He looked at Stephan and the others. "Get ready to ride. We may have to leave this paradise."

Simon led them west of the watering trough to a bare patch of paving stones laid in a rectangle. Yohan glanced north and south at the meandering track that crossed their path, then fixed his eyes on Simon. "What was this entity you say visited you this morning?"

"A face, it could have been a rusalka—it could have been a dream, a vision."

"Ya, an illusion then." Yohan turned to Luca. "And you, no more about your devils. These attacks, the Apostles, all of that, the less we speak about any of it, the better."

Simon glanced down at the track he'd found that morning, less of a road than a game trail. "I guess this isn't much of a crossroads."

"It's enough of one, now that you brought it up. The last thing I need is for Carla or Ramon to start seeing devils in the weeds. We have to move on."

Yohan called them all back together when he returned to the watering trough.

"As Brother Simon discovered, we have indeed stopped at a crossroads. And I agree, we shouldn't stay here—for many reasons other than his...*entities.*"

Luca left to help Carla retrieve their horses. Ramon had already yoked the oxen. Feeling more than a little sheepish, Simon helped Stephan load equipment. So much clothing, helmets, and gear, they had to move Cernak's body several times while piling it all in. To Simon, it seemed they'd looted an entire army. He gave it all a dubious glance. Stephan explained, "This time, they came with horses and supplies. We will want all of it when crossing the mountains."

Luca stepped forward, grinning at Yohan. "I think my Brother Simon now learns to ride. We have horses enough, sè?"

Yohan smiled. "Excellent idea. You, of course, have volunteered to mind the oxen in his place."

Still grinning, Luca disappeared, returning moments later with a tall horse. Cloudy black and gray, powerful legs, perhaps not built for speed, the beast looked capable of climbing mountains. Luca slung a saddle across its back and said, "Yohan wishes you to have Cernak's horse. He is called Perun, god of thunder."

Unsure of who had the worse of that exchange, Simon quickly found himself boosted to the saddle of Cernak's mount. "Perun followed you all the way from Krakow," Stephan said. "He knows your scent."

Perun had clearly not been consulted in the matter. Although Yohan held the reins and tried to calm the animal, it laid its ears back and bucked. Grabbing at the saddle, Simon felt the world spin—trees, clouds, the ground, then darkness, pain, and flashing lights. Opening his eyes, he looked up at Stephan, kneeling beside him. "Don't move. You may have broken something."

Rolling to his knees, Simon pushed himself up. "Nothing broken, not yet."

Snorting, rearing, fighting the reins, Cernak's horse dragged both Yohan and Luca from the road. Simon felt for injuries as he watched the animal struggle. His right shoulder ached and two of his ribs burned when he touched them. Stephan said, "Maybe we can find a gentler animal for you."

Simon didn't answer, preferring to watch Perun thrashing and jerking at the two men. With only one good arm, Yohan finally had to let go. The horse reared, pulling Luca off his feet, and swinging him around. Stephan started to go help. Simon held his arm. "Wait, I think I'm enjoying this. Which one do you think will win?"

"Perun is strong, but Luca would rather die than yield. My money would be on our brother."

As Stephan spoke, Luca dodged a kick and vaulted into the saddle. Perun bucked and spun until exhausted. He stopped and flicked his ears. Luca gave the horse a moment to recover, then kicked him in the flank and rode back to Simon. "I give your first lesson, free of charge."

Flecks of foam clinging to his lips, Perun snorted and shied away. With his dark coat, long legs, and straight back, Simon could see why Cernak the warrior would choose an animal such as this one. He stepped closer. Perun lowered his ears and snorted. "Get off and give me the reins. I'm going to ride him."

Luca grinned and slid from the saddle. "You do miss your morning beating. I now trust you to my worthy assistant."

Simon took the reins. Perun shied away but put little real effort into it. The horse sidestepped and launched a halfhearted kick as Simon approached. Left hand on the pommel, right hand on the cantle, he vaulted into the saddle and waited for the explosion. With the dexterity of a snake, Perun whipped his head around and bit Simon's leg. He punched the animal between the eyes. It squealed before bursting into a spinning flurry of bucks and kicks. Clinging to the reins, he rose from the horse's back before slamming down on the saddle. Legs splayed, injured ribs burning, he held on until Perun exhausted himself. Yohan stood watching. He nodded as Simon swung from the saddle. "Water your horse before we leave."

The company resumed their westward trek. After a minor struggle remounting, Simon lurched and bounced on Perun's back. His leg had swollen and turned purple, but the row of narrow lacerations hadn't bled as much as he expected. On occasion, Simon had to haul on the reins and kick his horse in the flank to keep them to the road. By the time Yohan called a halt, both Simon and Perun were glad to part company.

As before, they set watches for the night. Stephan argued with Yohan, finally saying, "I don't want to see two of my brothers ride the cart in shrouds. Sleep. I'll wake you if we need you."

Simon drew second watch after Ramon. Prodded awake, he prowled in the cool darkness while frogs chattered in the nearby marsh. Above, a celestial profusion wheeled through the zodiac. He waited until the bright star in Cygnus broke the horizon, then roused Carla to take his place.

Riding out the next morning, Simon passed Luca guiding the oxen. Astride Perun, it seemed that he towered over his Sicilian brother. Luca shot him a look intended to maim, but Simon had become immune. Carla hung back, trailing the tumbrel. Simon could tell her injured side still gave her pain, but she rode without complaining. Ramon stayed with her, as companion and guard.

With Stephan at his side, Yohan rode in the lead. Simon trailed closely behind them. Stephan talked, but Yohan didn't seem to be listening. Instead, he slumped in the saddle, clutching his cloak about his shoulders. Simon matched their slow pace, staying just ahead of Luca.

The road climbed now, following a river of spring snowmelt. They broke for a midday meal in a small meadow surrounded by beech trees and rocky hills. Camp bread and dried meat, to Simon, it seemed a feast, but Yohan barely touched his before the time came to move on.

That night, they all wrapped themselves in extra blankets, and Simon donned a pair of bloodstained wool leggings, simply glad of their warmth. He took first watch, helping Luca clean their cookware and bank the fire. A skein of clouds moved in that evening, darkening the sky, and promising more rain before morning. As he stood his lonely watch, Simon judged the passage of time by the slow dwindling of the coals. When the last visible sparks winked out, he went to rouse Yohan, only to find the man huddled, shivering in his blankets. Simon touched his forehead and felt the heat.

He shook Ramon awake. "Brother Yohan burns with fever. Can you help him?"

Wrapped in his cloak, Ramon knelt at Yohan's side and removed the bandage. Simon kicked the earth from their banked fire and blew new life into the remaining coals. In the flickering light, Ramon unwound the bandage and shook his head. "An evil spirit has entered his arm. You can see its foul excrement oozing from the wound."

Yohan's arm had swollen twice its normal size and a yellow smear ran down to his elbow. He'd only grunted when Ramon used his knife to open the wound and press out a lumpy mass of blood and fluid. Sitting up, Yohan inspected the injury. "I've suffered worse."

Ramon said, "We have to keep you warm and keep your wound clean."

Bucket in hand, Simon stumbled down to the stream for fresh water. On returning, he found Stephan at the fire with an armload of wood. Yohan insisted that all he needed was some rest and warmth. Stephan took the next watch, feeding wood into the fire.

Simon made his bed beneath the tumbrel and woke to a light spattering of rain. The eastern horizon glowed beneath the clouds. Luca puttered and cursed as he prepared their morning meal. Simon checked on Yohan and found him huddled beneath a makeshift tent.

Ramon stood nearby. The look on his face told a story Simon didn't want to hear. "It's not good, is it?"

"Worse this morning but he won't admit it."

Yohan insisted they move on. "I can ride. I will recover in a few days. We need to reach high ground where we can give our Brother Cernak the pyre he deserves."

Ramon muttered something about two pyres, but daybreak saw them all headed westward into the mountains. Simon gave Luca a reprieve, tending the oxen that day as the morning drizzle developed into a spring shower. He needed to think.

His sword cuts had nearly healed, and his injured knee felt almost normal. Simon pressed against his side. Less than two days since his fall from Perun, and the pain had left his ribs. He considered Stephan. Injured two weeks ago, Ramon hadn't cut his stitches out until that morning. Then there was Carla—injured and still mending.

He patted the bag of talismans at his side. The silver one for healing, he hadn't invoked it, but just bumping along at his belt it seemed to convey some protective virtue.

Stephan called a halt early that day. Simon watered his stock in the icy stream and let them graze while the others rested. Scattered logs and a ring of blackened rocks showed this to be the site of many previous visitors, though not lately. Yohan sat slumped on a log and said nothing.

After taking a light meal, they pushed on, climbing ever westward into the hills. By midafternoon, the rain gave way to sleet and then large clumps of wet snow. They camped that evening in the lee of a boulder-strewn hill. Ramon rigged a tarp from one side of the tumbrel. They all spent the night huddled beneath it.

By the following day, the clouds had scattered and fled before a crisp north wind. Yohan set out on horseback that morning. Walking behind, Simon watched him waver in the saddle. The sun had barely cleared the surrounding mountains before Stephan had to catch him before he fell. Luca helped lower Yohan to the ground and lift him into the back of the tumbrel.

Simon rearranged things—blankets, arms, food, spare clothing. Hardest was Cernak's corpse. It gave him thought. His attackers would return, no question there. Apostoli Lucis would never give up. He selected a few small items and stowed them separately. Retying the load, Simon managed to make a narrow bed for Yohan. Knowing how the cart would jounce on this stony road, he took Stephan aside. "I've ridden back there. It's hell. We have to go slow for Yohan's sake."

Stephan ducked his head. "We are going to lose some time. But we must get over these mountains before we face another force like the last one."

"Worse, I think." Simon glanced over his shoulder. "If I know the Apostles, they will send an army next time."

"Then we ride. Yohan is tougher than you think—we all are."

Simon remained with the tumbrel the rest of that day, checking on Yohan as they went. Carla seemed improved. She and Ramon followed, leading their string of captured horses. At their midday break, Perun allowed Simon to approach. Well into the spring shedding season, all the horses wore a patchwork of winter and summer coats. Luca had shown him how to remove the loose hair with a coarse brush. Simon tied the horse to a stunted juniper and tried brushing. Perun lowered his ears and jerked at the lead, snapping and kicking. Simon backed off. Taming this animal would require both caution and persistence.

The Roman road climbed toward a distant pass. All about, the mountains rose like enormous loaves of bread, crusty near the base and topped with floury white snow. Their way had dwindled from a broad, hard road to a chisel thin track. Simon fought to keep the oxen in line and keep at least one wheel on the path. They camped at a wide spot, a broad col hanging from the mountainside like a balcony.

Perun allowed Simon to water him and hobble him for the night. Ramon tended Yohan that evening, and Simon spent half the night with him. The man could barely move on his own. He lasted until daylight, mumbling and thrashing in his sleep.

At dawn, Ramon changed his bandages and repacked the wound. Simon washed Yohan's injured arm and cleaned up the yellow discharge and blood that soaked through his blankets onto the tumbrel bed. In answer to Simon's unspoken question, Ramon jerked his head toward the front of the cart.

Stephan sat on the drawbar with the same question in his eyes. Ramon glanced back. "He surprises me. The man should be dead."

So much of the strength had gone out of Yohan that to Simon, it seemed he had already died. He eyed Stephan. "Why can't we stay here for a day and let him rest?"

"We should reach a pass sometime this morning," Stephan said. "We will rest then, but not before."

Luca and Carla rode ahead to scout their way. Simon followed with the oxen and Yohan. Not long after the sun cleared the eastern mountaintops, Carla returned. "Three versts farther," she announced. "Luca thinks he knows where we are."

Simon found the remaining trail in better condition than what they'd climbed on the previous day. Bumping and rumbling, they arrived at an enormous saddle between two mountains. A broad stone road climbed from a valley to the south and continued up a gentle slope to the north. Luca sat astride a square stone monument. "I come this way, sè?" He gestured south. "There is my Venice. She is *bedda*, beautiful."

Stephan looked the other direction. "This is the road to Salzburg, then?"

"Sè, the road to mafankulo town of thieves."

While Stephan and Luca discussed the road, Simon joined Ramon at the rear of the tumbrel. Yohan gasped and shuddered beneath his blankets. Ramon held a pewter cup of water. "He drank nothing today. We should prepare two pyres."

"Here?" Simon glanced back at Stephan and Luca. "Another crossroad?"

"It is more a junction. This road ends, the other continues."

They all needed a break. Simon knew that. He marched past the stone monument and looked down into a tangled forest of old birches and drooping rowan trees. If ever a road had descended into that dark wood, no trace remained. Luca turned and stood next to him. "You look there for your cousins, diavulu?"

"I look there for firewood. I think it is time we say goodbye to our Brother Cernak."

Stephan agreed, but said, "Cut only birch. I don't want to disturb whatever else may live among the sacred rowans."

Wielding camp axes, Simon and Luca cut trees while Carla harnessed the oxen and dragged them to the road. A few dozen paces into the forest, the sunlight dimmed to an arboreal twilight and the sounds of Stephan and Ramon setting out their camp faded to a distant murmur.

Simon notched out the base of a small tree, then cut it from the other side. Luca pulled it toward the road while Simon finished his cut, jumping back when it cracked and fell. He rolled up the sleeves of his tunic and cut another. The work felt good, quelling the anger and remorse in his heart. When the fourth tree swooshed to the ground, Luca called back, "Is enough, sè?"

Simon shouldered his axe and nodded. "Enough."

Luca slung a rope around the last two trees and started climbing. Simon stopped him. "Wait a moment. Tell me what you meant by *cousins*."

"Diavuli, forest demons. This wood, it crawls with them. You say, maybe is *leshi*, no?"

"Jacob spoke of *leshia*, shapeshifters. He had laughed and called them children's tales. But then..." Simon paused a moment, "...then I was like a child.”

“Cretino, sè.” Luca shoved him on the shoulder. “You are still.”

“Perhaps so. Perhaps I always will be. Perhaps I belong in this forest with the leshia and the diavuli. Just remember that.”

Luca stroked his short beard. “I think it is you who knows something.”

“What happens when we leave here?”

“Then we have the comfort of my Venice. Maybe I introduce you to a woman who is not afraid of the leshi?”

“That will be weeks from now. What happens before we reach Venice?”

Luca clutched his axe. “It is true. Cazzo bastardo Apostles wait for us.”

“Because I am with you and for no other reason. Just remember that as well.” Simon started back up the hill. “Carla will expect some help cutting this wood.”

North of where they had stopped, a rounded knoll jutted from the mountainside. Climbing from the dark wood into the midday sun, Simon blinked at Stephan and Ramon toting birch logs to the top. By late afternoon, a pyramid of wood and brush crowned the knoll.

Yohan lolled against the Roman monument, barely conscious. Simon had checked on him throughout the day, but his condition continued to deteriorate. With Cernak’s pyre finished, Simon sat on the ground next to his friend. “I will stay here with you. The others can send his spirit to Elysium when the sun sets.”

Yohan twitched his head and mumbled something. Simon leaned closer. “What can I get you?”

Yohan coughed. His mouth half open, he barely whispered the words. “Fólkvangr. Cernak was Norse.”

Ramon knelt next to Yohan and once more offered him water, but after speaking those last few words, he had lapsed into a silent daze. Simon touched Yohan’s forehead. His friend still burned with fever but no longer trembled. Far worse in Simon’s eyes that he slumped corpse-like on the ground than before, when he still huddled and shook. Ramon said nothing and walked away.

Darkness came quickly in the mountains. Carla had prepared crude torches of birch branches and resin-soaked rags. As the sun's final rays lit Cernak's pyre in shades of gold, Stephan led four of them up to make one last farewell to their brother.

Simon remained with Yohan. As twilight faded, he leaned back and watched ten thousand stars blaze above the mountain tops. Something he had to do, something best accomplished unseen, something to end Yohan's pain. Simon waited until the others left, until the fire atop that far-off knoll blazed bright and high. He then reached to his side and drew his blade.

Perun

The suffering had ended before any of the others returned from Cernak's pyre. Still clutching his sword, Simon gasped and retched, but the crushing pressure in his chest had subsided with every breath. Yohan looked so peaceful now laying there on his bed of blankets. Sheathing his sword, Simon sat next to him and watched the parade of torches stream down the hillside. Stephan arrived first. He knelt at Yohan's side. "Is he...?"

"His fever broke. I think the worst has passed."

Ramon put a hand on Yohan's forehead and an ear to his chest. "This is not possible. It is a holy miracle."

"A miracle, sè." Luca shot Simon a glare. "I think it is maybe not so holy."

Beyond exhaustion, Simon remained next to Yohan, waiting for the question, the accusation, but Luca said nothing more and Ramon was too overjoyed to ask.

Stephan stood. "We rest here until our leader is well and then feast to the memory of Brother Cernak."

Too tired to move, Simon wrapped himself in his cloak for the night. Three times, Yohan stirred awake, and three times Simon brought him water. At dawn, the man tried to stand. A sapling beside an oak, Simon helped him stagger to the edge of camp and relieve himself. Yohan growled and farted as he stood, then refastened his codpiece. "I could eat something now."

Luca had preceded them. Up before the sun, he crouched by an open fire, roasting lumps of bread on skewers. A pot of salt-pork gravy lay next to the coals. Simon brought a pannikin of bread and gravy to Yohan. Doling out his own portion, he sat on a length of birch log. Ramon hovered nearby, watching

Yohan eat. He left when it looked like the man was not about to vomit and die. Simon waited.

Yohan belched and picked a piece of gristle from his mouth. He inspected it, grunted, then ate it. Simon mopped his pannikin clean with his last bit of bread. Yohan did likewise, stretched his legs, and said, "I know what you did."

"I had no choice. Cernak's memory haunts me daily. I couldn't just let you die."

"Do any of the others know?"

"Luca suspects." Simon paused. "Not just suspect—he knows."

"The Knights of Palermo stand against sorcery. We are at war with Apostoli Lucis. You knew that, and still you used that infernal talisman. Why?"

Simon hung his head. There would be consequences. He knew. Invoking the silver amulet ended any chance he had of becoming a Knight. "I should leave the Fellowship. Luca was right all along. I am a curse." He raised his head and looked Yohan in the eye. "Still, I would do it again. If it meant saving even one life in this company, I would use the talisman for healing and be damned for it."

Yohan nodded. "So be it. My weapon is my sword, but yours has always been your art. Stay with us for now. We can let the Masters of Palermo decide your future."

Carla walked by, grinned, and slapped Yohan on the shoulder. Simon watched the others. Only Luca refused to look at him, not that it mattered. He'd become an ally of sorts, almost a friend. Now, Simon wasn't sure.

Heaving himself to his feet, Yohan wobbled a moment, then left to confer with Stephan. Simon watched him go—he had other matters to attend. First the oxen. He walked down the road and found them grazing a short distance away. Satisfied that they had water and sufficient forage, he went looking for the horses. Their small herd had scattered across the opposite hillside. He spotted Carla standing with the brown mare she usually rode.

Simon worked his way up the hill. Carla waved him over. "Amazing our Yohan, yes?"

"He had always insisted that he would recover."

"Still, it is like magic—a final blessing from Brother Cernak maybe."

Simon looked up at the knoll where Cernak's pyre still smoked. "Perhaps so. I expect we will be leaving tomorrow. How do our horses look?"

"They all need shedding." Carla displayed a wooden block studded with heavy bristles. "I've almost finished my Falcata here. She is beautiful, yes?"

"She lets you do this?"

"She delights in the attention. All horses do."

Simon glanced up the hill. Perun had watched him approach the herd. He stood apart from the others, head up, ears erect. "Maybe some of them do."

Carla followed his gaze and laughed. "Cernak's horse, maybe your horse now, he is a stallion, but you have seen that."

In the confusion, Simon hadn't thought of anything except Perun trying to dismember him. Looking up at the animal now, it began to make sense. "He thinks he's king of the herd. Why would Yohan give me that... that monster to ride?"

Grinning, Carla said, "It is the man's way. He tries to kill you. If that fails, he tries something else. If you survive, he lets you stay. Think, who is it that made Luca your pankration teacher?"

Perun snorted and tossed his head. Simon thought about their first encounter. He remembered the lightning-fast teeth. "How can I care for the animal if he won't even let me near him?"

"Did you bring food?"

Simon had two doughy lumps meant for a late morning snack. He took one from his cloak. "Do horses eat bread?"

"You can try. Hold it in the palm of your hand and mind your fingers. He will be curious. Get close but make him come to you. Did you bring a halter? No? Then here, use mine."

Carla slid a double loop of leather and rope from Falcata's nose. Simon wasn't sure he knew how to use such a thing. He tried putting it back on the mare. She snuffled and blinked at his attempts. Third try, he slipped it over her nose and pulled a strap behind her ears. He patted her head, slipped it back off, and started up the hill. Carla followed.

Two spans away, far too close for Simon's comfort, he stopped. He'd made sure to stand upwind and to climb high enough that the animal didn't tower over him. Simon tore the lump of bread in half and placed a chunk in the center of his palm. Perun didn't move, but his nostrils twitched. A moment later, he extended his neck and took a step. With his next step, he accepted the offering. Simon felt those teeth graze the palm of his hand.

He offered the other half. When Perun took it, Simon looped the halter around his nose and behind his ears. The anticipated explosion of hooves and teeth never came. The animal simply nudged his cloak. Simon took out the other lump of bread, bit off half for himself, and offered the last piece to Perun. Carla stepped up and hooked a short rope lead to the halter. "He has his little tempers, but it's mostly bluster."

Simon let Carla hold the lead. "Someone else can risk getting kicked or bitten if they like, but that is as close to either end of this beast as I want to get."

"If you detest the horse, why do you come up here?"

"Everyone rides but me. I need to learn."

"And you need to prove something to Yohan, yes? You need to ride the devil's horse."

Simon had to grin at Carla's insight. "That could have a little to do with it. Can you show me?"

"If I must be Yohan, then you will ride this horse without a saddle."

"Is that possible?"

"It is the first step. Ride without a saddle, and you will learn more quickly."

Simon thought of himself as tall, but Perun's back came almost to his shoulders. He probably could muster a jump that would put him up there, but for how long? "He's not going to like it."

"Do you dare this thing?"

Simon vaulted onto the horse's back and wriggled upright. One heartbeat, two heartbeats, Perun shook his head. Three heartbeats, he squealed and reared. Perun slammed down on his forelegs and nearly threw Simon over his head. He clung to the horse as it danced and snorted, but the tantrum ended as quickly as it started.

Carla had stood well back but stepped up to pass the lead rope to Simon. "Bravo, now do it again. This time, hold the lead. The animal must know who is *el jefe*, the boss."

He slid off and jumped away, almost dropping the rope. Perun jerked and shied. Simon watched his ears. They seemed the best indication of the horse's mood. A second leap to his back brought on less reaction. After a few moments of dancing and kicking, Perun dropped his head and began munching on the sparse grass.

"Now..." Carla said, "Now you must convince him to carry you back to our camp."

The rope in his hand didn't seem of much use. Simon gave it a shake. Nothing happened. He tried hauling the animal's head up. Perun turned, snapped at his leg, then resumed tearing at the grass and weeds. Carla laughed. "He thinks you are a fly."

"I need my willow switch. Then I'll show him what a fly feels like."

"Try this. Move back a little, lean forward, and kick him with your heels."

The reaction wasn't quite what Simon expected. In one smooth motion, Perun raised his head and broke into a full gallop. Careening down the hillside, Simon clung in desperation, fully expecting to be dashed to bloody rags on the rocks below. They thundered past the oxen, leapt a narrow ditch, and flew up the road. Roaring through the camp like a tornado, Simon glimpsed Stephan jumping for his life and Luca's cookware exploding in a cacophony of tin pots and wooden trenchers.

They crossed the road to Salzburg as if it wasn't there and plunged over the opposite bank into a maze of birch and rowan trees. Once in the shadow of the woods, Perun seemed to regain some sense of self-preservation. He leapt over a stand of bushes and slowed to a bouncing run, scraping the trees left and right. Simon clung to his neck, ducking low at every branch they passed.

Inevitably, the soft earth and brush knocked Perun's feet from beneath him and they both went down in a tangle of flying limbs and screaming horse. Simon found himself in a copse of thorny shrubs.

He picked himself out of the branches and staggered to his feet. His tunic hung in tatters. Fearing what he would find, Simon approached the downed horse. Wedged against a tree, it rested on its back with all four legs thrashing the air. He knelt next to the animal. It stopped kicking, twisted its neck, and rolled one eye at him.

Despite his aches, Simon had to laugh. "I should leave you here for the crows."

The horse seemed otherwise intact. Simon inspected each leg. Bracing his feet against a weathered block of marble he dragged on the halter. With some effort, he managed to roll Perun away from the tree. The horse thrashed his legs and twisted until he pushed himself to his feet.

Shouts from the hilltop echoed down through the trees. *The others, they must think I'm dead.* Simon wondered what Yohan would say and recalled Carla's words. He boosted himself up on Perun's back and gave him a light tap on the flanks.

Cautious, like an old man carrying a bowl of gruel, Perun picked his way out of the forest. They met Luca and Ramon trudging down between the trees. Luca only muttered and cursed, but Ramon stared up in wonder. "You still live, both of you?"

Simon wasn't quite as sure. "If Luca doesn't murder me for ruining his supper."

"Pazzu cretino bastardo! Kill yourself if you want. I care nothing."

"He means you scared the crap out of us all. What were you trying to do?"

Simon shook the lead, and Perun resumed climbing. What *was* he trying to do? "We were coming to terms." He straightened and resolved to maintain the fiction. "I wanted to know whether he would obey his rider."

"Merda, the horse tries to kill you." Luca turned and spat into the leaves.

Simon shrugged. "We've reached an agreement."

He leaned forward and clutched Perun about the neck as the horse scrambled up the final embankment to their campsite. Carla waited there, astride her mare. Yohan and Stephan stood beside her. Simon heaved a leg over and slid to the ground. "Next time, I would like to ride him with reins and a saddle."

Yohan shook his head and walked away. Stephan tugged at Simon's shredded tunic. "I think you were in a fight, and I'm not sure who won."

"I'm not sure either, but I rode him back. That should count."

Carla leapt down from her horse. "It counts. I will mind the horses and find our gear if you want to change your shirt. We have plenty now, some without blood."

Simon nodded. Sometimes, things worked out. He'd already inventoried their supplies, choosing clothes that fit and spare blankets that weren't too filthy. Standing behind the tumbrel, he dropped his belt and slipped out of his ragged tunic. Simon pulled a brown linen shirt over his head. Woven from rough-spun fiber, it itched his back. He added the leggings he'd worn earlier and fitted a codpiece over his breechclout. Scanning the camp, he spotted Carla talking with Stephan. They wouldn't expect him to finish for a little longer.

From their food stores, he selected a block of lard, a joint of salted meat, and a sack of rolled oats. He wrapped these with his pannikin and a water skin, then tied them together with his bedding and clothes. Flint and striking steel he slid into a pocket in his cloak. One more item he'd almost forgotten. Stuffed in a corner of the tumbrel, Simon found a small linen purse. He shook the dragon's skull out onto the wooden floorboards. A special token, he could feel the link it formed between Simon Prostoi, the simpleton, and Simon Halfsword, the erstwhile Knight of Palermo. He returned it to its purse and tied it to his belt next to the clinking talismans.

"Are you ready to ride?"

He spun around.

Carla stood behind him. "First you must learn how a saddle is fastened, how a bridal is attached."

Simon glanced back at his supply bundle. *How much had Carla seen?* He realized it probably didn't matter. "And how not to be bitten in the process?"

"He will kick you as well—or trample your foot. Always watch those hooves."

Carla had tied Perun to the tumbrel drawbar. A stack of gear lay nearby. "We start with the saddle. You put it on. He knows you will ride."

Simon wasn't sure. "I would rather he not know until it's too late."

"Horses don't like surprises. If he knows you ride, he lets you. If you surprise him, he bolts."

Carla showed Simon where to stand, how to position the pad to a horse's back, and finally how to heave the saddle over the ridge of its spine and secure the cinch beneath its belly. "Watch." She rubbed Perun's stomach. "He is tight like a pregnant mare. He thinks to fool you." Carla punched the horse below its ribs. Perun grunted as Carla pulled two more notches in the cinch.

"He likes it loose so maybe he can shake you off. You prefer it tight, so you stay on." Carla checked the buckle. "Now the bridle. With this, you control him."

She showed him how the bridle straps fastened around a horse's ears and under its chin. "Next time, you don't disturb Brother Luca's cooking, yes?"

Simon nodded. The next time he rode would be for practice. After that, he hoped to disturb no one. "Ride with me then. I want to explore the road."

Carla had already saddled Falcata. "Ramon is scouting the southern route. We should go the other direction."

Cutting around the camp, they hit a line of earth and gravel packed so hard that only low weeds grew on its surface. The road climbed to the north, skirting the mountain and heading for an unseen pass somewhere above. Simon looked up at the knoll where Cernak's bones lay among the ashes and wondered what he would say if he were here. Climbing higher, they crossed a broad ravine and paused to let their horses drink from the snow-fed creek. Simon pointed up at a crumbling stone foundation. "The Romans had a bridge here once, fallen long ago, I'm sure."

"Still," Carla said, "this road gets used, salt traders maybe."

The road, little more than a track at this point, climbed out of the ravine, passed through a dense copse of birch trees, and broadened again when they reached the other side. Simon picked out a Roman mile marker among the weeds, the fifth he'd seen since they left camp. Carla stood in her stirrups, trying to look beyond a curve. "How much farther do we go?"

"I want to reach the pass if we can."

"Then these lazy horses should trot for a while. You too—it will be good to learn."

Perun didn't want to trot. Simon managed to kick him into a kind of lunging lope that ate ground but pummeled him against the saddle. Carla had told him to move with the horse, but riding this way seemed little better than being beaten with a stick. Simon stayed with it, wondering which of them would quit first. After three Roman mile markers passed, he reined Perun back to a walk. Carla caught up with him shortly after. "Do you still want to continue?"

"Not really, but I want to reach the top." Simon pointed up the road to a notch between the mountains. "There, another two versts, maybe three."

It was more like five. The broad road of packed earth had eroded to a narrow trail that clung to one side of the mountain. Simon passed a tumbled ruin of a broken wagon-frame and rimless spokes. Further up, their horses danced single file along the crumbling trail above a debris-strewn hillside. Rounding the mountain's shoulder, they crested the pass. Simon stopped and gazed across a broad valley on the other side. Glittering in the distance, a river wound beneath a sky of tiny white clouds. Carla stopped behind him. "Down there somewhere is Salzburg."

Simon turned his horse. "I would hate to do this at night."

"You won't have to. We travel south in the morning, yes?"

"The tumbrel wouldn't make this journey anyway. I've seen enough. Let's go back."

Simon waited while Carla turned and started down. He hadn't quite seen enough, not yet. He tried not to think about the treacherous footing or Perun's mercurial disposition as they picked their way back around the mountainside. As Simon rode, a new vista opened before him. Tree by tree, grove by misty grove, a great forest of birch and rowan appeared from the valley below. As far as his eye could see, it sank into a deep fold in the mountains, an uncharted ocean of trees.

Up ahead, he watched Carla taking in the same panorama. Luca had called it a place of demons. Simon wondered what the woman thought. Falcata ambled to a halt. Carla sat, mouth open, and said, "*Madre de Dios, la sylva perditia.*" She glanced back at Simon. "It is a forest of lost souls."

River's End

After the singing, after the feast of meat pies and onions, after the cups of sweet red wine, Simon helped Luca clean his cookware. They exchanged few words until Simon had stowed their pots and set out wood for the morning's fire. As he readied to take the first watch, Luca caught him by the elbow. "I know what you do, diavulu."

"I had to. Otherwise, Yohan would be dead."

"It is not that. God will forgive what you do last night." Luca pulled him closer and lowered his voice. "It is for tonight, sè? You are gone."

"You know I have to do that as well. They will kill you all if I don't."

Seizing him by the shoulders, Luca kissed Simon on the cheeks. "Go then, my brother. The Holy Virgin watches you until we meet again."

With that, Luca walked away, leaving Simon to do what he must. The wine and food, together with long days on the road, felled the others before evening crept into darkness. Simon gathered his supplies and bedding. By the light of a single candle, he saddled Perun and lashed his gear behind the cantle. One last round of the camp satisfied him that the snores were both loud and genuine.

He returned to the tumbrel, stroked its weathered side, and touched the tiny scrap of rag still clinging to the left wheel. For years it had been his home. No, not his. It had been the home of Simon Prostoi, the simpleton, the cretino. He laid his hand on the leather sheath at his side. This too had been a part of Simon Prostoi and now of Simon Halfsword. He drew the blade and held it for a moment, feeling the strength, the confidence it gave. He knew it was also the strength of a crutch. He left both sword and sheath lying on the back of the tumbrel.

It wasn't hard to find where Perun had blasted over the bank that morning. By wan candlelight, he led his horse down the same slope. One more set of hoofprints would be indistinguishable, should anyone suspect he'd gone that direction. In the darkness, their passage through the brush and leaves sounded to Simon like a herd of cattle. Every so many steps, he stopped and looked back, half expecting to see a row of figures highlighted against the evening sky.

It wasn't long before Simon reached the tree that had stopped their headlong flight. Searching by candlelight, he found the stone block, a weathered Roman mile marker. He'd recognized it that morning when he helped Perun regain his feet. Simon pressed on. *A Roman road always leads somewhere.*

Half the candle burned before he felt comfortable stopping for the night. Simon hobbled Perun before wrapping himself in his cloak and blowing out the light. A curtain of darkness swept everything from his sight. Simon curled up tighter, pretending not to hear the night sounds grunting and chirring all about.

He might have slept. One arm ached and tingled beneath him. Simon rolled over, keeping his eyes pinched shut. Nothing out there to see, nothing he wanted to see. Perun whickered nearby and stamped his foot. Simon listened. The horse snorted and whickered again, then all went quiet. It registered a moment later, the night sounds had ceased.

Eyes open, he stared up at a sky milky white with stars. The forest below still cloaked itself in darkness. Simon pushed himself to his feet and faced a maze of shadows. White birches loomed nearby, gray in the starlight. No sign of Perun. He called, whistled, clicked his tongue. No response. Somewhere in the darkness, the sound of soft footfalls. Simon worked his way toward them, stumbling over brush and fallen branches. How far could a hobbled horse wander, especially if he had just heard it?

Turning around, Simon had no idea where he'd left his saddle and gear. A twinge of panic. He waited. Again, footfalls, then a low whicker. It came from somewhere to his right. He knocked his shin against a log, scrambled over, and dropped a half span into a creek. Shoes soaked, he climbed the other side and listened. A shuffling sound like something heavy dragged through the leaves drew closer as he stood. Not daring to move, to breathe, he watched an enormous shadow form between the trees and grow until it towered over him.

Perun whinnied like a stroke of thunder and pawed the ground. Simon jumped back, slipped, and slid once more into the creek bed. Scrambling out, he reached up and touched his horse. Perun shivered and flicked his tail. Four long steps, he descended to the creek and began slurping up water. Something Carla hadn't taught him, Simon realized, was how much forage, how much water, a horse needed. He sat on the edge and waited for daylight.

The moon appeared first. Rising later every night, it now glowed between the trees, thin and pale, a sliver soon to be eaten by the sun. The birds came next, a few at a time, then more until the forest rang with their calls. Simon made out individual trees, bushes, branches. Perun stood a few paces downstream, cropping the rough grass that grew along the banks.

It didn't take long for Simon to find his gear. Somehow, everything looked different in the morning light. He didn't remember unrolling his bedding or unwrapping his supplies. He repacked the pot, the pannikin, and the food. A loaf of bread and block of hard cheese lay beneath his cookware. Simon held one in each hand, bewildered. *I didn't pack these. Luca must have slipped them in while I rode with Carla.*

He gathered up his bridle and reins, collected Perun from the streambed, and saddled him. Except for a few exploratory kicks, he cooperated. Simon hefted the roll of bedding and clothes, preparing to lash it behind his saddle. Shoulder high, he stopped and sniffed. A floral scent, something, something beneath the rich aroma of rough wool and unwashed traveler. He sniffed again, trying to recall.

Perun stamped and snorted. Simon shrugged and finished loading his supplies. He would try to follow the road this morning, and if not, then follow the creek. He swung into the saddle. Wary at first, Simon couldn't quite trust Perun not to bolt. The horse seemed to have recovered from his fall, but Simon's legs and back still ached.

By midmorning they reached a level clearing. Although they'd passed no mile markers, a few rough stones stacked together betrayed the wall of a ruined building. Simon hobbled Perun to graze and dug out the bread and cheese.

With the dusky forest all about, this one island of daylight seemed an oasis. *Stay here?*

Simon hadn't planned much beyond leaving the company and disappearing. He hoped that Carla would assume he'd returned to the north road and made for Salzburg. It really hadn't been a choice. Going north, the Apostles would be on him before he reached the first town. Luca would have figured that out—Simon hoped he kept it to himself.

Sitting on a rock and nibbling the cheese, he thanked what luck there was that the tumbrel couldn't manage the north road. His friends would head south while his enemies converged on the forest. Wishing that in fact his art was his weapon, Simon felt as helpless against the conjurers as he did against the mercenaries.

He counted five days since the Apostles' attack, enough time for their *Sethiarch*, their Grand Master, to bind another talisman to the figure on his chest. How much longer, Simon wondered, until another sortie of armed mercenaries stood at this very clearing? How much longer before he heard them baying like dogs on his trail? Unwilling to find out, he saddled Perun and continued west.

By late afternoon, he discovered another mile marker among the fallen branches and leaves. Whatever road this was, the Romans had built it with the same precision they had applied to their other works, then abandoned it to the elements. Simon pressed on until shadows gathered between the trees and obscured the road ahead. He found a level spot near the creek and once more hobbled his horse for the night.

As he'd done so many times for Jacob, Simon struck a fire with his flint and steel. It was the one art where he felt perfectly adept. He boiled a thin handful of dried meat, dropped in oats with a lump of lard, and let them all simmer next to his fire. He counted on his rations lasting until the Apostles found him or until he managed to contrive an escape. He missed Luca's cooking and the evening camaraderie. Most of all, Simon missed having a destination, a goal.

Darkness fell like a summer downpour. Nearby an owl called out. Somewhere off in the forest, another responded. Simon wrapped himself in blankets and a cloak, resolving not to go chasing noises that night. The stream hissed and clattered, carrying him off to a dreamless sleep.

At daybreak, Simon broke his fast on the gelid gray remains of his evening's meal, scraping the pot out and returning it to his pack. It wasn't until midmorning he discovered the second loaf. Pausing where the road crossed the stream, he dug through his supplies for the remaining bread and cheese, only to find that Luca must have slipped two loaves in with his gear. Glad of the extra food, he once more traveled until dusk and found a sheltered spot for the night.

The creek had picked up tributaries along the way. It now flowed broad and fast along a bed of rounded stones. That night, he could hear little more than its rushing growl among the rocks. The best Simon could tell, it bore due west, chasing the setting sun. The forest itself had slowly descended into a wide valley between the mountains.

Simon continued the next morning, dismounting and leading Perun around places where the rushing stream had undercut its bank and dragged portions of the road into its rocky bed. With some regret, he finished his cheese that day and broached the second loaf of bread. The stream led somewhere—hopefully, somewhere he could find food. It had occurred to him that he'd left without money. A few other things would be nice as well, such as a tarp for wet nights. He counted the days and wondered if it mattered, if the Apostles weren't right behind him.

As the afternoon progressed, the stream slowed to a meandering slough, winding through a valley of bogs and rushes. Simon's road, what traces of it he could find, held its course well above the marshy ground. He found himself once more pushing through dense stands of birch and rowan, hugging the hillsides, and searching for markers.

The sun burned red in the west before Simon reached the edge of the woods and gazed out at the valley below. Like a great cauldron of fire, a silent lake caught the blazing sunset and reflected shades of crimson and gold. Far across the lake, a ruined fortress rose into the evening sky, casting shadows over the water like the fingers of a skeletal hand. The ancient Roman road angled down the hillside before him and circled the lake. It ended at the shadowy fortress gate.

Shuddering, Simon drew back into the trees and made camp on the only level spot he could find. One more night in the open beat venturing into those dark halls after sundown. A fallen log made a place to sit and cook his meal. In the waning light, he sorted through his kit. He'd packed the bow drill he'd used for years to repair parts of the tumbrel and oxen harness. From a pouch at his side, he found another small object and turned it beside the fire to find just the right spot. Satisfied, he strung the bow, wrapped the iron drill, and began his work.

When it became too dark to see, he set aside his little project, laid his bedding beside the log, and tried to sleep. Simon awoke to a cold westerly wind that rattled the leaves and rubbed creaking branches one against the other. Nothing showed in the sky, neither stars nor moon. He wondered how long he'd slept, how long he would have to sit here in the darkness awaiting the dawn. Perun snorted nearby. Simon huddled behind his log and contemplated the vast empty void his life had become. It came to him in a rush, like a flood, the void.

He may have missed the first far-off flashes, white flickers on the invisible horizon, but his horse didn't. Grunting, whinnying his displeasure, Perun woke Simon from a confused dream of battling phantoms. Moments later, the sky flashed a swirling mass of silver before vanishing once more. Suddenly the old fortress seemed a better refuge than this cold hillside.

Gathering his belongings, Simon belted his cloak tight and went to harness Perun. Little grass grew on the rocky hillside, so he'd tied his horse off to prevent it from wandering in search of food. Perun stamped and jerked at the lead. Saddling the animal, Simon managed to secure the cinch strap and tie his roll of belongings behind the cantle.

A light spatter of raindrops peppered his face as Simon led his horse down the hillside. Feeling for every step, he followed the old road north around the lake. Bursts of lightning lit a scene of wind-whipped water and chaotic sky. The rain slacked off at times, then returned in double measure. Simon pushed on, back bowed, head down, dragging his reluctant horse behind him.

As the storm bore down on them, Simon could hear distant reports of thunder echoing through the mountains. He redoubled his efforts. A bright flash—snakes of flame shooting across the churning sky—outlined the ancient ruin not half a verst distant. The road, a silvery band, beckoned them to its gaping entrance.

Perun balked and reared, backing away, yanking at the lead. The rain poured from the sky, a deluge of icy water. A blinding flash of lightning struck the fortress wall. The explosion of thunder almost knocked Simon off his feet. Screaming, Perun broke free and galloped off.

Simon stood in shock, watching his horse, his blankets, and his provisions vanish into the darkness. Another flash struck the hillside above. He turned and dashed for whatever shelter the abandoned fortress might offer.

Lavender

Its fallen roof a jumble of decaying timbers and broken tiles, the fortress still retained an aura of strength and even menace. Simon found a tiny doorless chamber sheltered from the weather. It cast him back to that doubtful vigil he spent in St. Gereon's Chapel—a lifetime ago, yet less than a month had passed. Outside, the storm continued shrieking between the broken stones, swirling through the open roof, and throwing debris about like an angry child.

Cold and wet, he crouched in his tiny alcove and watched the water pool around the fallen roof and rise with every lightning flash. He thought of Perun, trapped in the marsh or fallen from some cliff. His friends, Simon prayed they had escaped to the south or found a better refuge than he had.

Water lapped around his feet by the time Simon noticed the sky had lightened. He hoped dawn would bring an end to the storm, but the rain only grew worse. Falling in a sheet of gray, it blotted out everything else. With the rain, he felt a new sensation, a trembling, deep, almost imperceptible. It thrummed beneath his hand. It vibrated through the soles of his feet. The entire fortress shivered as if in fear.

Wondering what new evil had come for him, Simon crept to the entrance of his alcove and peered outside. A brief pause in the rain showed him a ghostly figure wading through the fortress's broken doorway. It barely took a step before a blinding explosion of light blasted Simon back into his refuge. Picking himself up, he looked out on a scene of flaming timbers, hissing and smoking in the deluge. Nothing else moved.

Simon argued with himself. It had been a phantom, an animal. Armageddon

"

had arrived, and he'd witnessed another lost soul rising to the final battle. Unable to contain his curiosity, Simon ventured into the pounding rain. Wading through a sea of floating wrack, he spied a body slumped against one wall—a girl, a young woman. She weighed almost nothing when he picked her up and carried her back to the shelter of his chamber.

Soaking wet, she hung lifeless in his arms. He put an ear to her chest, listening for a heartbeat. It was then that he realized she wore only a thin gauzy robe that clung to her body in wet folds. Closing his eyes and stumbling back, he almost dropped her. He felt her against his arms, warm—her skin, soft. He bent again to her chest, no heartbeat, no breath, nothing but the pervasive scent of lavender.

Simon fumbled at his belt and drew out a silver disk. *No time, there is no time.* But he needed fire to make this work. Leaning the girl against one wall, he dashed outside. Rain had quenched the flaming timbers to a few pockets of guttering coals. He climbed a rotted beam and wrenched a piece of burning rafter from its side. Sliding, half falling into the water, Simon twisted his ankle. Ignoring the pain, he hurried back to the girl.

With the silver talisman perched on the fading speck of coal, he drew his knife and pricked the girl's finger, squeezing blood onto the hot metal. He pricked his own and added it to the bubbling mass. Simon wasted no time reciting the invocation. He'd been taught the words, the motions one must make. As they came back to him now, so did the claw gripping his chest. Without his sword for protection, the pain spread from his hips to his neck. Still, Simon gasped and croaked out the words.

Crushing the life from his heart, the claw only gripped harder. When he could no longer speak, he mouthed the words and continued. His vision faded behind a speckled gray curtain. He fell to his knees. Consciousness fled.

Simon awoke to a rumbling that shook bits of stone and mortar from overhead. Every joint ached like he had been beaten with a cudgel. *The girl.* He listened again to her heart. This time, he heard it thump within her chest and felt her breath on the back of his neck. Simon recovered his talisman and secreted it in the pouch at his side.

Peering out through the entrance, he saw sheets of water covering the ruined floor. A harsh west wind continued to whistle through the broken battlements, and rain fell unabated from the sky. Outside, the ceaseless rumble had built to a low roar that filled the air like ten thousand wagons crossing a wooden bridge.

The remains of a stair still climbed the western wall. Once leading to an upper level, it ended in a broken mass of stonework. Anxious to see whatever monster rumbled and roared in the valley beyond, Simon crept up the steps, clinging to the wall. The wind tore at his cloak and rainwater poured down in a miniature cataract. The top tread ended in broken stonework and crumbling mortar. Simon crawled along the wall's naked edge, the wind constantly threatening to fling him off. Gray sheets of rain hid everything else.

He clung, waiting. Then, like a stage curtain, the rain cleared. Below, a vast chasm, a cliff towering hundreds of feet, dropped from the face of the wall to a swirling abyss of mists and shadows. Where the meandering creek had flowed, a vomiting torrent of mud and broken trees cascaded from the hills. The lake below, once so placid, had filled the valley with a churning sea of logs and brush.

Overbrimming its edge, the rising water now poured over the cliff like an ocean at the edge of the world. Muddy streams of water swirled about the ancient walls before roaring off into oblivion. As Simon watched, a large mass of stonework leaned, broke free, and toppled into the thundering chasm. Shaking, backing down the wall, he reached the stairs. Body aches, twisted ankle, all forgotten, Simon scrambled from his high perch.

The girl is gone. No, she is still here. Plastered against one wall, almost invisible, Simon looked again. Far from invisible, she practically glowed. Frozen with longing and desire, he stood and stared. A stone fell from above and glanced off Simon's shoulder. The spell broken, he pointed toward the entrance. "Go. We must go."

Her eyes, large and round, stared at him from beneath a crown of matted hair. "Go," he repeated, pointing to the entrance.

She didn't respond. Simon felt the stone paving shudder beneath his feet. Without another word, he peeled her away from the wall and dragged her toward the door. Crying and fighting, she tried to back away. In desperation, he grabbed her about the waist, hoisted her kicking screaming to his shoulder, and bolted for the entrance. The water, now covering the road, dragged at his legs. Once outside, he tried to run but fell before he made a dozen paces.

Kicking, thrashing, the girl broke free. She took two steps back toward the fortress before Simon caught her by the ankle. Down again, he wrestled her from the water and slung her over his shoulder. Hoping his feet stayed on the road, hoping he could somehow get through to the girl, he splashed along the shore and made for the hills he had fled the night before.

It was his ankle that betrayed him. He stepped in a submerged hole and it dropped him to a knee. Simon's unwilling passenger slid from his shoulder and staggered to her feet. She didn't run, she didn't scream, she just stood and looked back. Simon turned as the ground beneath him began to heave.

The fortress, once a bastion at the end of the world, crumbled into the chasm. With it, the entire cliff gave way. The lake itself, like an upturned basin, rushed toward the abyss. The girl staggered as a surge of water swept around them. Again, the land shook, and a gaping cleft opened across the lake bottom. Big as a city, a slab of mountainside sheared off and tumbled into the gorge below. This time, the girl needed no urging to go. She hiked her robe to her hips preparing to run, then stopped and took Simon's arm. Together, they hobbled and splashed through the cascade of floating branches and tree trunks.

In an eyeblink, the world shifted. Simon found himself on all fours scrambling up a cliff of earth and broken rock. Water, filled with sticks and broken branches, gushed down its face. *The girl?* He spun around. She hung, clinging to a twisted clump of brush. Simon slid back to her and reached out his hand. Grasping, slipping, he gripped her wrist and pulled her to him. A gigantic tree, all roots and thrashing branches, plunged toward them like a battering ram.

Simon threw the girl against the muddy bank. Clinging to the wet earth, he pressed himself over her as the tangle of broken roots flew past their heads. An instant later, a cascade of leaves and branches buried them both. Wedged against something below, the tree stood nearly upright against the wall of broken earth.

Scrambling up, they gained a foothold among the limbs. Simon favored his twisted ankle, dragging it as he climbed. The girl reached the trunk, then turned and helped Simon haul himself up the smooth bark. He nodded and gestured to the top. The tree took them almost to the cliff's edge. A trailing mass of roots dangled from above. Simon pulled himself up and reached down to help the girl crawl over the edge.

Forest debris littered what remained of the shore. The water had dropped so quickly that it left a maze of storm wrack and mud behind. Simon broke their way through, not pausing until they reached the hill and began to climb. Below was chaos. The stream, now a river of mud and rock, plunged in a roaring cascade down the broken jumble of naked boulders, each the size of a cathedral.

They both paused and gazed out at the pandemonium that had once been a peaceful mountain lake. Simon couldn't help glancing once, then again, at the young woman at his side. Covered in mud and leaves, she still left him breathless. "What," he said, "what do I call you?"

She pulled her robe tight and crossed her arms, but never looked down. Simon tried again. He put a hand on his chest and spoke his own name. She only huddled tighter and shivered. Simon felt it also, the wind had fallen but turned cold. He peeled the cloak from his back, wrung it out as well as he could, and draped it about her shoulders. She gaped back at him like he'd done something amazing.

Now Simon shivered. He thought of shelter, of a fire. They had to do something before nightfall, or the cold would finish what the storm had failed to do. He took her arm and led her uphill. She followed, stepping lightly as a dryad among the wet leaves. At the top, Simon found nothing of his earlier camp, save a drenched ring of stones and cold ashes.

He balked. Of course, his flint and steel were in his cloak... which now hung about the young woman's shoulders. If he tried to retrieve them, Simon wasn't sure how she would react, even how he would go about it. They would die of cold... because he couldn't touch her? He dared defy the entire Apostoli Lucis, yet... He shook his head. "I need to make..."

She kept staring at him.

"I'm sorry. We need a fire." He took her about the waist and reached beneath the cloak.

The woman—and of course he saw now she was a woman, not just a girl—she moved closer, took his hand, and pressed it to her breast.

Simon jerked back. "What? No... not that."

She followed, put an arm about his shoulders, and touched his hand.

Simon shook it free and grabbed the pack of flint and steel. "This." He held it up. "This we need."

She looked at him with her round eyes, her crown of tangled hair now an orange halo in the daylight. The aroma of lavender enveloped him. He nearly dropped the striking steel. Something new gripped his heart, not the familiar pain but a feeling as if it would burst from his chest. He felt it other places too. Simon crossed his legs as he knelt, fishing about the wet coals for a bit of unburnt wood.

He found the stub end of a charred stick. Not daring to look up, not daring anything beyond the task before him, he used his knife to split the wood and raise a nest of fine shavings. He tried to concentrate. Steel against flint, the first few strikes sputtered but wouldn't spark. He kept trying. A tiny speck glowed among the shavings. He blew softly, willing it to life. Cut splinters from the charred wood fed his tiny flame.

He looked up, not sure what to expect. The young woman had vanished. It didn't matter. He needed a fire. She would return if she wanted to. Simon hunted about for more fuel. A hint of lavender. He turned around. She stood behind him, holding a bundle of sticks. He split a few pieces and laid them in the fire. They smoked, then charred and caught. He set the rest nearby to dry.

They'd need more wood. Simon regretted abandoning his sword for a moment. With it, he had cut trees. Without it? Without the sword, he hoped to overcome the curse branded into his chest. And the girl? She'd disappeared again, collecting wood—he hoped. Small, she barely came to his shoulder. And not a girl, certainly much more. His head spun, something she did. He thought of the talismans, the Apostles, daring the claw to seize his heart and crush his chest. A lavender scent surrounded him and vanquished his claw. She had returned.

Woman of the Woods

They had taken turns scavenging for wood and feeding the fire. Despite his injured ankle, Simon managed to drag a birch sapling up from the former lakeshore. Its roots had been sheared off as if by some massive scythe. He laid it across the fire and let the heat char the white bark away and ignite the wood. At first, the intermittent showers undid most of their work. As the afternoon drifted into evening, the clouds cleared, and the blustery west wind shifted to the south. Simon's stomach knotted and growled—he wondered whether the girl had eaten recently.

She'd hung his cloak on a branch to dry and sat, with her back to the warmth, rubbing her arms and shivering. Simon had doffed his tunic and leggings. Although he wouldn't look at the girl, he felt her presence like a second fire in the forest. He didn't have a name for her, didn't know if she could speak or simply couldn't understand. He threw another bundle of sticks on the fire. It was going to be a long night.

Darkness fell with Simon still watching slender ribbons of flame dance among the coals. He felt her move next to him, facing the fire, leaning against his arm. The girl no longer shivered. *Something, I have to say something.* Putting a hand to his chest, Simon tried again.

The girl took his hand, put it to her own chest, and said, "Amala."

He'd let the hand linger a moment too long. Silently, Simon recited a conjuration—it hardly made him twinge. *Amala, her name is Amala, and she is running a finger over the scar on my chest.* It should have crippled him. In a way, it did, but not as he'd expected. Simon crossed his arms at his waist and closed his eyes.

Eventually, they'd compromised... in a way. The ground between the fire and their log had dried enough that they could lie there, wrapped in Simon's cloak. He faced the log, and Amala plastered herself against his back. One arm around his waist, her hand wandered. Simon held it and pressed it to his chest.

He awoke to a cacophony of birds as the first streaks of daylight crossed the sky. Amala was gone. Her scent, her warmth, vanished. Simon sat up and pulled on his tunic and leggings. Nothing showed that she'd ever been there. He hung the cloak on a branch and walked some way from the fire to do his morning business.

Retying his breechclout, Simon heard shrieks from somewhere below. He ran, sliding down the hillside, and stopped at the forest edge to gaze out at the devastated valley. No less of a shock in the morning light, the utter collapse of the mountain lake was like a hole in the world, a place where something should be but wasn't.

A flock of crows circled in the sky above the devastation. Nothing moved below. Simon heard it again, a shriek and a high-pitched animal squeal somewhere in the forest. He dodged between the trees, jumping over rocks and branches. Something white flashed by, then something else, large, dark. *An animal?* He couldn't make it out. Again, the white figure, running. It had to be Amala. Simon drew closer. She seemed to be laughing. Moments later, he recognized the animal. Perun.

It turned to him and whickered. Amala reached up and patted its head. "*Seimon*, look." Enormous, towering over the girl, Perun nudged her in the back. She laughed again and rubbed its nose. "Is yours, yes?"

Simon started to answer, then stopped. She had spoken. Latin of a sort. Still, he understood. He stared at the horse, and then at the girl. Words wouldn't come. Finally, all he could think to say was, "You caught him?"

Amala cocked her head. "He finds me."

Approaching Perun, the animal snorted at Simon but didn't shy away. He reached up and touched the bridle. One rein had torn from the bit. The other hung in a twisted knot. Perun still wore his saddle, but the roll of bedding and supplies was gone. Various scrapes and cuts on his legs and flanks spoke of a rough gallop through the trees and underbrush. Simon inspected his hooves and fetlocks. The animal seemed to be otherwise sound. Without looking up, he said, "Perun likes you."

"He play, yes?"

"Oh yes, he plays. We play all the time."

Again, head to one side, green eyes beneath a cloud of orange hair, she looked at him. Simon's wits fled like a man who's had too much ale. When he said nothing more, Amala tried to repeat his words. "...pla'll thatim?"

"Where did you learn Latin?"

"*Lateen?*"

"To speak?" Simon put a hand to his mouth. "Laa-tin."

She nodded as if understanding but said nothing more. Simon led Perun by one rein as they walked back to their campsite. He couldn't help watching Amala glide through the forest. She didn't seem uncomfortably cold, despite the chill morning air. Simon remembered how she felt, warm and soft, pressed against his back. When they reached the cold firepit, he hung his cloak about her shoulders.

Amala smiled and kissed him. Pointing east, she said, "Lateen."

At a loss for a better idea, Simon nodded and pointed east. "We will find your lateen."

Vaulting into the saddle, Simon reached a hand down to Amala and hoisted her up. She sat before him and seemed comfortable, even familiar riding a horse. Simon wondered where she came from and why she followed him. Certainly, it was Amala he had seen reflected in the watering trough. The floral scent—lavender—he remembered it from earlier. The girl slid back against his hips as he rode. It played havoc on his concentration.

Simon had intended to give them a rest once the sun cleared the treetops, but after only a few versts, Amala patted Simon's hip and pointed up. "Lateen."

Before Perun had come to a stop, she swung a leg over his neck and slid to the ground. Simon dismounted and followed her to a large rowan tree. She untied a length of cord and lowered a bulging satchel. A cache, it suddenly made sense. She'd followed, holding her distance until the storm broke. The girl couldn't have seen him, couldn't have known. Simon let that sink in.

Before he managed to make sense of his thoughts, Amala had rummaged a loaf of bread from her satchel, broke it, and offered half to Simon. "Lateen, eat."

Starved, he could have eaten two of them. It didn't matter that she must have stolen it from Luca. He bit off a large chunk and chewed on the crust. The girl watched, then laughed. "Little, little." She broke off tiny fragments and nibbled on them.

Simon tried, but it seemed like drinking ale from a nutshell. He tore off another chunk and jammed it into his mouth. Amala dug out a second loaf and offered it to him. Simon held up his hands and gulped down the last piece. "No, thank you, no. We should save some."

She sat on the ground in one fluid motion like a bird alighting on its nest. Simon crouched next to her, arms around his knees. "Where," he gestured about, speaking slowly, "where do you come from?"

Amala smiled at him and patted the ground. "Here my home is."

Simon steepled his fingers above his head. "House?"

"Sisters' house. You will see. Yes?"

Simon wasn't sure what he would see. Alone, with him, in a forgotten corner of a forgotten woods, the girl seemed entirely unconcerned. *How I once was.* He shook his head. *No, how I should have been. How I should become.* He'd resisted the urge to open Amala's satchel, inventory its contents, estimate days of food, travel time. Instead, he sat back, crossed his legs, and took her hand.

Riding again, they continued east. Simon had repaired the broken rein with a piece of Amala's cord. When he asked, she'd smiled and said, "It is ours."

He mused on that for a while. Owning things had been a leap. He couldn't quite remember owning anything before Jacob had been killed. How was he different now? He put a hand on Perun's mane. "Ours?"

Amala turned and smiled at him. "Ours, yes."

Something in the way she said it, he didn't quite understand. Before he could ask, they reached a place where the road ended. The stream had poured across, gouging the hillside and swallowing most of the valley. Simon dismounted and led Perun into the forest. Amala still clung to his saddle. They followed a faint game trail up the brushy hillside until they crested a low ridge.

Below, the forest had been trampled flat, as if by Titans. The stream, once a devouring monster, had retreated to a maze of channels that wound like braids through the devastation. Amala pointed south across the valley. "House of sisters."

Simon nodded. It made sense. They would cross the valley of death in search of her lost family. The thought triggered an old memory. "Have you brought the golden bough?"

The girl's mouth dropped open. "No, sisters would forbid. We need it?"

Simon wondered for a moment if he had survived the storm, if this wasn't some cruel bit of mummery before judgment and perdition. He looked up at Amala sitting wide-eyed astride Perun. "No, I think if we are careful, we can cross over without it."

Once they had descended again to the valley, Simon began to doubt his own words. His feet met a tangle of stones and branches that gave beneath him. He ventured out ahead, scouting for firmer ground and hoping Perun did not break through some hidden cavity. From her vantage on the horse's back, Amala pointed out possible openings in the mountains of roots and broken trunks. Simon explored, doubled back, and tried a different route. Every step forward met an obstacle.

By early evening, they hadn't made it halfway across. Simon pushed through a maze of fallen branches and jumped back when the ground caved beneath his feet. The stream, three spans below, hissed and growled along its gravelly bed. Simon backed away and signed to Amala. She and Perun met him in a sandy clearing between the upended roots of two enormous rowan trees. "We camp here tonight. Tomorrow, we try farther upstream."

Amala dismounted. She had to see the problem for herself. Simon stood back and pulled her away as the bank caved even more beneath her feet. "We'll never get the horse down there before dark."

While Simon cared for Perun and built a fire, Amala explored up and down the stream embankment. The light had faded toward dusk before she returned. "All is worse."

"We'll find a way in the morning. You wouldn't happen to have a joint of mutton in that satchel, would you?"

"Bread, cheese, you like?"

Simon nodded. He'd lived on worse. Amala broke another loaf in half and handed him a lump of cheese. It smelled the same, tasted the same. "You put the bread and cheese into my pack."

Head down, face obscured by her frizzy nest of orange hair, Amala said, "You are hungry."

"I had food."

"You do not know the forest."

Simon sat on a broken log to eat. The girl perched next to him and wrapped the cloak over both of their shoulders. "Ours," she said.

There was no good reply. Had the girl never come, even without the storm, he would likely have wandered until he starved. They watched the fire together as evening settled in and the clattering stream filled the night with its music. Amala's head settled against Simon's chest. He put his arm around her and inhaled her subtle aroma. This night, he would turn beneath their cloak. He would let her guide his hand. He would—*what else would we do?* His face burning, he brushed his lips against hers. She pulled away and shook her head. *The void again.* He felt it come rushing back. *Prostoi, cretino.* Nothing he could do.

The first drop struck Simon on the cheek. He looked up into the starless night. Amala huddled closer as a spatter of cold rain blew in from the west. Perun snorted at something. Far-off downstream, the sky flickered white. Simon rose from the log and faced the west wind. The next flash came soon after. The echoing rumble that followed sent Perun into a fit of thrashing and squealing.

Amala stood. "It returns."

"I am cursed. I am damned." Simon clenched his fists. Another flash, much nearer. He threw the saddle on Perun's back, tightened the cinch, and untied him. "Get your bag. We must go. Now."

"Where?"

The wind rose to a howl. The spattering of raindrops grew to a blinding deluge. Simon had to shout his response. "Between the trees and down the bank. It's the only way."

He wasn't sure if she understood. No time to explain, he pulled their horse back toward the crumbling embankment. Before he made two steps, a bolt of lightning struck just downstream, sending Perun into another frenzy. Simon hung on, trying to calm the animal. In a single fluid leap, Amala jumped to the saddle. "Go," she yelled. "I ride."

Perun bucked and pawed but at length settled back to dancing and snorting. Simon passed the reins to Amala. Arguing would waste precious minutes, and he wasn't sure who would win. Disoriented by the downpour and sudden darkness, he glanced around in confusion. Locating their fire, he dashed past its glowing remains to a tangle of downed limbs.

Simon eased his way in. The edge, it would be right at his feet. He felt the ground shift and leapt back. Perun's nose caught him between the shoulders and shoved. In a wave of collapsing sand, he tumbled down the bank. Perun's screams of dismay followed. Simon let the momentum carry him into the icy stream, the horse grunting and splashing just behind him.

Most of the bank had come down with them, giving Simon visions of the day before. Nothing so dramatic, Perun stood and shook himself. The next lightning flash highlighted Amala still on his back. Simon waded forward, picking between mounds of churned-up brush and broken limbs.

They crossed gravelly bars and fast-flowing channels. Driving rain and rising water pushed them on. In the dark, Simon was never sure if he had crossed the streambed or not, but eventually they climbed a low rise and waded into a swampy forest. He'd given up ever finding high ground when Amala called, "Here, come."

Simon followed through a mass of brush to the base of a steep hill. He caught a glimpse of her in the next flash, leading Perun up the slope. Climbing in the driving rain, he caught up with them on the crest of a flattened knoll. All around, birch trees bent and shook before the wind's onslaught. They found shelter behind a fallen log, victim perhaps of the earlier storm. Amala had blindfolded Perun with a cloth from her bag and tied him nearby.

For most of the night, lightning stabbed the hills, and rain sheeted from the sky. Simon awoke, still sitting upright. Amala huddled in his lap, fast asleep. The rain and wind had vanished, replaced by a familiar growl. The stream in full flood wandered like a hungry predator somewhere below. He eased himself from under the girl, propping her gently against the log.

There would be no moon this night, nor the next few after that. Simon did what he could to find a broken branch thick enough to split with his knife and dry enough to raise a nest of shavings. It seemed like ages before he could strike any kind of spark. By the time he'd generated a tiny yellow flame, Amala had awakened and gone in search of more fuel.

The wood they found was too wet to do much more than hiss and smolder. Simon and Amala stood back-to-back in a pall of stinking smoke to capture what warmth they could from the tiny flames. While they stood shivering, the sky lightened to a gray tent of clouds hanging just above the trees. Amala said, "It is more."

"I don't want to wait here and find out." Simon pushed an armload of brush into their fire, willing it to burn. "As soon as we can see the way, we leave this cursed place."

"Place is cursed, or is it you?"

Simon stopped abruptly. He remembered his own words of the previous night. "I am cursed." He looked at her in a new light. "You knew. You have been following—how long?"

She wouldn't face him. "Long."

"How long, Amala?" He took her by the chin and forced her to meet his eyes. "How long have you followed me?"

She held his gaze. "All my life." Shaking free, she turned her back.

"Did they send you? The Apostoli Lucis, is that how they found me?"

Amala crouched, sobbing. "No, no, no..."

Simon wouldn't wait to hear more. He saddled the horse, ignoring the fire, ignoring the weeping girl. He had been an idiot, a fool, still the cretino. He thought of her touching him. Lavender, a witch's snare. He'd slept the last two nights with a serpent at his back.

He decided to continue south, not that there were many options. She might follow. He couldn't stop her. Simon climbed into the wet saddle, wondering how much damage it had taken. He didn't really care. In a few days, he would have to butcher the horse and eat it.

With every passing breeze, a cold shower rained from the leaves above. Simon shivered, wishing he'd taken his cloak back. How reckless. *What made me think a girl appears from nowhere and means anything but trouble?* He picked his way down the hill. Perun waded through a brown swamp studded with trees. On the far side, the land rose again. Simon kept his shadow angling to the right, hoping he could keep a reasonably straight course.

By midmorning, enough sunlight glittered down beneath the dripping trees to warm his back. It didn't fill his stomach. It didn't salve the ache of betrayal. Simon rode without stopping. If he could only find an end to this forest of the damned. They climbed higher into the hills. He watched his shadow reappear on the left, lengthening with every verst.

Simon eventually gave Perun the lead, letting the horse find its own way through the forest and up the shallow valleys. It didn't really matter where they went—the Apostles would know. Contouring up a rocky hillside, the game trail they followed ended at a sheltered vale. Simon dismounted and set Perun to graze. Finally yielding to temptation, he looked back along the way they had come. Deep between the trees, a mist drifted through the slanting sunbeams. Nothing else moved. No sign of the girl.

He scanned the vale. Grass, trees all around, a tiny rivulet trickled through its center. Nothing else. He envied Perun, champing at the tall grass. His stomach growled. As much to take his mind off food as anything else, Simon collected wood and set a fire ring. A few strikes and he had a glowing nest of tinder. He cupped it in his hands, crouched, and blew it to a flickering yellow glow.

A few tiny sticks, the fire crackled in its bed of stones. Simon warmed his hands and looked up. Amala stood, looking back at him. She held out his cloak, dry as the day he'd first put it on. "You want?"

Her face, framed in a nimbus of orange hair. Her tiny, child-like nose. Her green eyes, so expressive, now expressed nothing but emptiness. She seemed so much older, almost eternal like the trees surrounding them. Simon slowly rose to his feet. "Why do you follow me?"

No change of stance, no change of expression, a specter, she repeated, "You want?"

He closed his eyes and thought. Of all he had learned in his life with the Church, the Apostles, Jacob, and even the Knights, nothing had remotely prepared him for this. *I am still the cretino.* Simon gave a slow shake of his head. "No, it is yours."

"Ours, or nobody's."

Simon opened his eyes and met her gaze. *Cazzo*, all he could think of were Luca's endless curses—applied to himself. She was right. Without her, he was nobody. He took the cloak and wrapped it about her shoulders. "Ours."

Amala didn't smile, didn't speak. She had abandoned her girlish manner from the day before. Simon returned to tending his fire. The new Amala suited his mood. She made more sense this way, not as a waif but a young woman. He stirred the coals with a stick. "They will kill us both when they catch us, you know."

She left without a word, returning with an armload of downed branches. "They not catch us."

They split another loaf of bread that evening. Amala broke a lump of hard cheese and gave Simon half. He suspected they had just about eaten everything, but the girl seemed unperturbed. Small deliberate bites, he watched her eat. She caught him at it. "Why watch, so?"

"You never explained who you are or why you followed me. If you can follow, why can't Apostoli Lucis do the same?"

"I am a Weaver. My sisters will tell."

He could get nothing else from her that evening. They sat in silence next to the fire where the ground had dried. Amala produced a blanket from her seemingly bottomless satchel. They folded it beneath them and huddled together under Simon's cloak. There was no lavender when they lay together. She nestled her head against his shoulders and wrapped an arm around his chest. "Sleep, *Seimon*."

Sometime in the night, Simon awoke. He had rolled onto his back. Amala lay beside him, her head on his chest and one leg hooked over his own. He'd been dreaming of her, of them. Further sleep out of the question, he watched the stars blazing above. Amala wiggled her hips and kissed his chin. "You are very awake."

"I can't sleep."

She placed her hand between his legs. "Ours."

He rolled to face her and put an arm around her waist. Warm, soft skin, she'd somehow wriggled out of her robe without his knowing. He kissed her lips, her neck. She guided his hand. Simon inhaled the fragrance of lavender and followed his dreams.

Spin, Weave, Cut

nitiation, or simply a rite of passage, Simon wasn't sure which he had just passed. He did know that something had changed between them on that mountainside. Amala had ridden with him again, pointing out the way. She seemed more open, more confident. In particular, she spoke more. As he had suspected, they had finished the last of her bread and cheese. Simon asked if she had another cache somewhere. Amala shook her head. "Sisters' house. You will see."

Their trail descended along the south side of the mountain into a broad valley. Birch and rowan gave way to meadows studded with pines and scrub juniper. Well before evening, Amala dropped off Perun's back and beckoned Simon to do the same. Before he could comment, she cupped a hand over his mouth. "Go quiet."

Without another word, she disappeared between two large pines. Both curious and confused, Simon followed with Perun on a lead. The narrow trail climbed through a brushy copse before cutting west along the valley wall. He tried to see past the trees, but only caught occasional glimpses of Amala farther up. After about a thousand paces, almost a verst, he lost sight of her completely.

The trail dwindled beneath Simon's feet until he ducked between the trees in the general direction they had been going. Another verst took him to a small clearing. Hopelessly lost, he paused. Nothing moved, no birds, no small creatures rustling in the bushes. Perun cropped the grass at his feet, reminding Simon of how hungry he was. He looked back but couldn't see the way they had come. Turning again, Amala stood next to Perun, stroking his mane and watching him eat. She put a hand over her mouth, shook her head, and disappeared.

Dumbstruck for a moment, Simon spun around, craning his head. She had vanished into the grass. He almost remembered her stepping to one side, or maybe moving behind the horse. It all seemed vague, like an old memory. He unsaddled Perun to let him graze. Simon searched the clearing for any sign of a path or break in the trees. Like a penned animal, he saw no way out.

To pass the time, he sat in a patch of soft grass and worked his bow drill a little more. The hole he'd started days earlier finally broke through. Holding his project up to the light, he cleaned and smoothed the rough edges with his knife. Satisfied, Simon returned everything to the pouch at his side and settled back on his elbows. He might have dozed in the late afternoon sun. When he next looked up, Amala sat beside him. "You are seen."

Jumping up, he stared about. He didn't notice Amala rise, but she stood next to him. "It is good. Come we have lateen, yes?"

"We? Who is *we*?"

"The sisters. They wait."

Simon couldn't see where Amala had appeared from, nor did he have any idea where these *sisters* might be, yet he followed her across the meadow. Perun didn't even look up. Upon reaching the far side, Amala walked through a tree. Simon approached, his hand out. The tree was there. A clever illusion, it stood two paces back from the others. Simon walked around and Amala met him on the other side. "We climb now."

She set her foot to a well-used trail that wound back and forth across the mountainside. The path grew steeper. Simon's chest pumped like blacksmith's bellows as he followed her lithe form gliding just ahead. Soon the pathway became a staircase of cut rock that buried itself in a narrow cleft. Higher still, the stairs ended, and they entered a hidden valley.

Simon stopped to catch his breath. He hadn't expected a village, much less the clusters of half-timbered walls and tiny windows that clung to the rock on both sides of the valley. An older woman approached. Amala drew the cloak about her shoulders and waved. "Sisters here."

One woman—save for her, the village appeared deserted. Simon straightened and stood closer to Amala. Tall, older, the *Sister* walked like royalty. Clad in a curious garb of brown skirt and yellow vest, the woman wore her hair in a single long braid, twisted and knotted almost to her waist. Her skin the color of chestnut wood, her eyes of black pebbles, Simon had never seen nor imagined anyone like her.

Close up, she was hale and trim, with only a scattering of wrinkles about her eyes and mouth that betrayed her age. The woman halted, looking only at Amala. "You have taken a cloak."

Her words were clear and well pronounced. Vulgate, the common tongue of traders and travelers across half the world. Amala dashed a glance at Simon and took his hand. "Ours."

Only then did the woman look at him. He felt her gaze pass right through him. *She saw what I did with Amala last night. She saw Cernak die because of me. She saw me desecrate St. Simeon's tomb. Those eyes even saw me cower in hiding while they butchered Master Jacob.* All this rushed through Simon's mind moments before the woman spoke. "I am Huna'alu Aluná. You should call me Mother Aluná."

Her thin smile seemed genuine. Simon bowed. "I am…"

"I know who you are Simon deVia, Simon of the road. I knew your father. I know of your time with Apostoli Lucis. It was I who carried news of your mother's death to their deep chambers beneath the basilica."

Aluná tilted her head. Simon drew a breath. *She watches my reaction.* He calmed his face, squeezed Amala's hand, and dared the claw in his chest. "Then you know more of me than I know of myself."

"Do I, Simon deVia?" Her smile crept a little wider. "The Simon I knew would be paralyzed on the ground by the sound of his true name. Do I even have the right Simon?"

Amala pulled him closer. "He is the *Seimon*."

"Then come, Amala. Bring your man. We have much to discuss."

Simon found that discussing meant low conversation between Amala and Aluná in a language he did not recognize. *It hardly mattered.* They'd entered one of the small dwellings. He'd blinked twice at the size of the interior. Hewn from the mountainside, it extended back at least twenty paces. A long table flanked by chairs ran down the center. Simon peeked into an adjoining chamber. Several women bent over a row of looms. He could hear the clatter of their shuttles. None looked up, but he felt their curiosity ooze out like a warm breeze.

On the table before him, he found plates of dried fruit and bowls of stewed vegetables. Aluná caught him staring. "Please, help yourself. You must be hungry."

Simon didn't let the absence of meat deter him. He ate slowly, not wanting to look as desperate as he felt. Both women would glance at him occasionally. Like a prize rabbit awaiting the pot, he feigned inattention and tried to listen to their words.

Amala spoke a language akin to that of the Rus he had heard in his travels with Master Jacob. He picked out a few words. Dvoch *might mean girl,* malch *could mean boy, and* ploch *would be a word for evil.* The rest flowed past him like the murmur of a mountain stream. Simon contented himself with a slice of honeyed pear. He would hear it all soon enough.

A stout woman, her gray hair pinned in a bun, brought in a tray of warm bread. Amala paused in her conversation to take a loaf, break it, and hand half to Simon. "Lateen is good, yes?"

He would have to work out their language issues before he left. Simon offered a bowl of vegetables. Amala declined and nibbled on her bread. And, he would have to leave. As comfortable as this sister's house was, Simon couldn't bear the idea of bringing the Apostles' wrath down on all of them. *At least,* he thought, *Amala will be safe here.*

He was on his second bowl of vegetable stew when the older woman turned to him. "Do you know anything?"

Simon chewed on what tasted like a small turnip, swallowed, and said, "I know that you have been talking about me—and about curses." He shoved another lump of bread in his mouth.

If Mother Aluná was surprised at his answer, she didn't show it. Instead, she leaned closer. "What do you know about this girl you married?"

Half chewed, halfway down, the bread stuck in his throat. At that moment, he wished for a bowl of ale to hide his confusion. With none at hand, he swallowed the dry lump of bread. "I'm not sure…"

Aluná interrupted him. "No, you are just ignorant. Did you realize that in her culture, exchanging a garment means betrothal? That intercourse consummates a marriage?"

"She was wet and shivering with cold. What else I could do?"

"And you had to take her, like that? In the woods like an animal?"

Simon thought about it, about how she had stayed with him, despite his doubts. "To survive, we shared blankets. Besides, she was not unwilling." Simon took a deep breath. Something else he realized, something else that needed saying. "Even if I knew her… her culture, even then, I would have done the same."

The woman stood and spoke with Amala. She nodded and smiled at Simon. "I go to Perun, yes?"

"Please. He needs water too."

Aluná waited a moment after the girl left, then twitched her head toward the Weavers at their looms. "We should discuss this outside."

Simon led the way, blinking in the bright sunlight. A few paths led between cottage entrances. Dark furrows crossed the valley floor bearing a tartan of green sprouts. Aluná showed him to a bench. "She is one of the last, you know, the old ones, the *Álfar* as they were called."

"Then I am bewitched, and it matters nothing to me. You must know that I am also cursed. If I don't leave soon, you'll have a cohort of mercenaries and conjurers climbing those stairs. That should matter to all of you."

"I know of your mark, and I certainly know of the Apostles. There once was a time when they were a symbol of hope, guardians of knowledge. Did you know that your father was one of them?"

He heard her speak but could not draw breath, could not respond. *Amala, she should be here.* Squeezing his eyes shut, he willed the pain in his chest to cease. Simon gasped. "Another time."

Aluná said nothing. Simon could feel her eyes on him. *Did the woman test him?* He tried to relax and let the painful spasms subside. After a while he opened his eyes. "Tell me more of Amala. You are not her sister nor her mother. So, who is she to you?"

"The *Álfar*, Amala's people, remain within the hidden valleys and high meadows of the wild lands. They were here before Rome was built, and I'm sure some of them will be here long after Rome is dust."

"I understand a few of her words."

"She speaks a number of languages—Rus, Germanic, Greek, but very little Latin. Amala understands more than she speaks. Eventually, she will learn words from you and make them her own. I know some Rus and a little of her Álfarish. We get by."

"But you are not one of her people, and these women..." Simon gestured about, although he saw no one. "These women are not her people. Why is she here? Why am I here?"

"To know that, you would need to know who we are, what we do. I don't think I'm ready to share our entire story, but I can tell a part of it. Have you heard of the Weavers?"

Simon worked it over in his head, but finally he admitted he couldn't recall. Aluná continued, "The Weavers are an ancient tradition. There are those who call us the *Moirai*, the Fates. We are not that, but our roles can be similar. Many of the sisters are known as Travelers, some are Dwellers, and some few of us are Cutters. Amala is a Traveler—most Weavers start out that way."

"She left her people to become this... Traveler?"

"Amala left her people because we needed her."

Simon leaned back, his hands behind his head. A small voice kept insisting that he had died in a lightning flash or been swept away in a flood. Everything that followed was then just his own demented road to perdition. He listened for a while before deciding that it was another of those things that didn't matter. "You needed her? Why?"

"We needed her to watch after you."

Unbidden, images of cloisters and bells, of ancient stone and smoking tapers passed through Simon's mind. "How long has she been watching?"

"Six years. You were an eleven-year-old acolyte of St. Peter's Basilica, already training with Apostoli Lucis. A most precocious boy you were, young Simon."

"Ha." He sat upright. "You say that you sent a child, a little girl, to watch after me?"

"Amala had just turned twelve summers when she began her training as a Weaver, sixteen when your father disappeared. In the spring of her seventeenth year, your Master Jacob risked his life to spirit you from beneath the nose of the Apostles. That summer, she set out from this very haven to follow you. How old do you think she is?"

"Not as old as you say—it's not possible."

"How old do you think I am?"

Simon stared at her and shook his head. "I don't know. But Amala cannot be... what, twenty-two?"

"She will turn twenty-three on midsummer's eve, just four days from now."

Aluná sighed and gazed off across the valley. "Weavers face many hazards, many hardships. Even the Dwellers who keep these havens cannot always rely on secrecy. However, we enjoy one boon, given to those of the sisterhood. We age slowly."

Simon followed her eyes and saw Amala climbing toward them. *My wife.* He watched her move. Like a hot coal, her hair blazed in the setting sun, but for the rest, she drifted like a wraith. "Why her? Why one of the Álfar people? Master Jacob told me of them, but his tales were stories for children."

"The Álfar are masters of stealth. They can become almost invisible at will. In your six years with Jacob, did either of you ever once notice her?"

"Maybe in dreams, or just in that moment before sleep. But no, I still can't believe she followed us all that time while we wandered between Tver and Vienna."

"She did. Of course, she had help from the Dwellers along the way—and I visited her on occasion."

Amala glided up and sat between them. "Perun happy. Simon happy?"

"The saddle?" He took her hand, "*Our* saddle?"

"Covered, hidden. Not *creeteeno*, yes?"

He sighed and made a bow. "I am beginning to believe."

Sensing he would get little more from Aluná that evening, Simon leaned back to think on what he'd heard. Holding tight to Amala's hand, he tried to sort out his past. *Master Jacob was not my father—not Jacob ben Reuben.* He still felt the claw, but somehow her presence shielded his heart. *She strengthens me.*

Amala bent close to the woman's ear. *Whispering secrets, I'm sure.* Simon caught her peeking back at him and smiled. Peaceful, quiet, he could just stay and work their fields. *But I can't.* Little chance he could disappear like he had with Yohan and the others. *I will need supplies, clothing, bedding.* He added it up—Amala, his wife, would follow regardless of what he said.

Lights flickered in windows across the valley when Aluná stood and said, "It gets cool here in the evenings, and Simon needs a new cloak."

With that, she returned to the cottage. Amala followed, beckoning to Simon. He did feel the chill, and perhaps a little hunger as well. More women had gathered inside, sitting about the long table where he and Amala had eaten. They ignored him, making Simon feel like a stray dog at a banquet.

At the far end of the table, Aluná spoke with three others. A full head above the tallest, she seemed aptly called *Mother*. Simon watched the interplay. Little question of who their leader was, he just couldn't understand their purpose.

Aluná looked up from her conversation, raised a hand, and said, "I think we are all here—sit, everybody."

Simon pulled up a stool for Amala, but before he found one for himself, Aluná shook her head. "No, not you two. I need you up here."

Shooting a quick glance back at the door, he led the girl—*my wife*—to the head of the table. *Here is where they perform some obscene ritual, and I die in agony.* All eyes followed him as he walked the length of the room. Aluná didn't smile, but Simon noted that she wasn't carrying a knife either. The woman pulled out a chair and murmured a few words. Smiling, blushing, Amala climbed to the seat and stood, only slightly higher than Aluná.

The woman took one of Amala's hands and held it up. "I would like to welcome the return of our Traveler and announce that she has chosen a husband."

Simon forced a polite smile, but none of the women were looking at him. They slapped the table, and a few made suggestive gestures. Amala shouted something back that brought laughter, then grinned down at him. "They like, yes?"

Feeling more now like a side of veal hanging in a market stall, Simon tried to return the grin. He looked down the table of smirking women and wished he had a talisman for invisibility. Aluná stepped in front of him and proclaimed, "In the eyes of the Weavers' Sisterhood, I declare you wed."

Simon gulped. It was so fast. *But more than I'd ever dreamt.* He took Amala's hand, held it up, and stared back at the women. "She found me when I was lost, saved me when I would have died, and stayed with me when I doubted even myself." He looked up into her eyes. "I will always..." Simon choked and tried again. "I will always love you, Amala."

Aluná pursed her lips. "We have more business tonight, so I invite our sister to choose bedding and clothing for both of you and show her husband to the guest quarters."

Amala hopped down from the chair and took Simon's arm. "Come, come."

He was never more relieved than when she led him through an opening at the back and down a long hallway. *Married—he was married. What would Yohan say? Luca? Luca would go into shock.* Doors lined the hall on both sides. Simon had to stop at a junction and stare back the way they'd come. "Caverns, this village is one big cavern."

Amala nodded. "*Jama...* caverns. No *smocza.* Yes?" She grinned at him. "Here, in, in."

Simon pulled open a door and retreated to a room filled with folded linens. Once safely inside he pointed back the way they'd come. "All smoc... smocz-*ina.* Dragons all of them."

Amala bent double and laughed like a brook trickling into a deep pond. Once again, Simon fell under her spell of lavender and sunlit hair. Hearing her laughter, he forgave her rowdy sisters. She straightened and touched his mouth. "*Smocziniaya,* all."

A moment later, she pushed him against a pile of blankets and began tugging at his breechclout. He pushed back. *This isn't the place.* He tried protesting. "Someone might come. No, no, Amala..."

She grinned even wider, grabbed him by the ears, and kissed him on the mouth. Simon relaxed and realized that although she knew the word for *dragon,* she did not understand the word *no.*

Midsummer

On the third day, they left the Weavers' haven. The sisters had presented Amala with a mare, Epona. Small and spirited, Simon felt it was a good match for his wife's temperament. Perun reacted as expected, trying to mount the mare as soon as they were introduced. Epona spurned his advances, and after a day, he gave up.

On departing, they followed the same broad valley that had brought them to Aluná's refuge. Amala chose the route, skirting just within the forest lining the valley floor. On occasion, they would pass a goatherd's hut or tiny cluster of farms. Otherwise, the valley looked unchanged since the day of creation.

He'd had further opportunities to speak with Aluná. She had dismissed his fear of the Apostles invading their refuge. "They are cowards," she'd said. "They hide behind their talismans and send others to do their fighting."

"They send mercenary soldiers, not the kind of men you would invite into your home."

"You have been both Apostle and soldier, yet we invited you." Aluná paused a moment. "That was unkind. You are the chosen husband of our sister and will always be welcomed at our havens."

When he didn't answer, Aluná touched his chest. "Your scar, may I see it?"

Simon pulled his tunic a little closer. "Only with my wife present."

"I didn't suggest..."

Simon shook his head. "It's not that. It is my curse, my Nemesis."

Aluná stood. "Now I *must* see it. I'll fetch the girl."

She shouted to someone in another room and hustled off. Feeling again like goods in a market, Simon waited. Aluná returned shortly, followed by three other chattering women and finally Amala. They all fell silent and looked at his wife. She took his hand. "Please, *Seimon*..."

"No." He stood and pushed his way to the door. "No, some other time maybe. We can have a show—I'll stand on a chair. But not today."

Amala followed. "*Seimon*..."

Totally disoriented, he barged down a series of corridors until he found an open window. Crawling through, he landed in a plowed garden and trampled his way across. Upon reaching a gravel path, he stopped. Amala caught up with him. "*Seimon*, no."

He gazed down the valley where he knew a stairway would lead to a path that led to his horse... and freedom. "Am I a prisoner here or a guest?"

Aluná had approached from another direction. "We don't have many guests, and few of them are men."

"I can see why."

"You are the first Apostle we've had here in over two hundred years. I apologize for my sisters' rude manner. Forgive them their curiosity."

Simon put an arm around his wife. "You were all thrice forgiven last evening, but I am nobody's show."

"I still must see your mark."

He untied his tunic and pulled it over his head. Taking Amala's hand, he said, "You may touch it."

Mother Aluná stiffened when she saw the symbol. "A Serpens Crucis Sinister, please tell me you have the talisman that controls this thing."

"It was stolen from us twenty days ago."

She closed her eyes and bowed her head. "Then may the Great Mother have mercy on you both. You are indeed cursed, and I see no hope for your situation."

"The storms?"

"They never touched this village."

"Even a master of the art could not have reached me so soon."

"He didn't need to. Someone among your Apostle brotherhood has pronounced Anathema on you. They need do little else. Instead of mercenaries, they have sent elementals and earth spirits. Run, Simon deVia. You may enjoy a few more days of life, but a Nemesis haunts your soul and Anathema treads your heels." She turned to leave, and then turned back. "I hear from Amala that you have used a talisman lately. Use it again, and the Apostles will know."

Daybreak the following morning, Simon and Amala saddled their horses. He'd double-checked their supplies. Dried fruit, walnuts, and bread joined a block of hard cheese and a large sack of crushed barley. He'd also lashed a bag of salt to his saddle. Jacob had long ago taught him that it was a better currency than gold in these wild parts.

Aluná met them on the trail. "I have a wedding gift for Simon." She handed him a folded bundle of gray cloth. "It is a Traveler's cloak. You may find it useful."

Simon bowed and thanked her, saying, "And I have a gift for my wife, a token of our bond." He held up the tiny dragon's skull he'd carried all the way from Krakow. It hung from a leather thong threaded through the hole he had drilled.

Simon wore his new cloak as he rode in silent thought. The outer shell of tightly woven wool would shed water for hours. The quilted lining bore pockets on both sides. He had filled them with necessities like tinder, flint, and steel. He also transferred his bag of talismans and other tokens to the cloak's innermost pockets.

As they rode off, the long valley seemed endless, but Aluná had warned them that it only led higher into the snow-capped mountains. *The mountains might be a refuge, yes, but they would be a prison as well.* He considered other options—rejoining the Knights or returning to Krakow. *Only to bring disaster with me.* Then too, he had Amala now.

Evening came all in a rush. The sky darkened, and shadows sprang up as if from the ground. Simon found a shallow swale where they built a small fire and sat in its glow. For the hundredth time, he mused on his wanderings. *How many nights,* he wondered, *had Amala spent without even the comfort of a fire?* She leaned against him. "Who is hate you?"

Simon chewed on his modest supper. *Who does hate me and why?* It made little sense. "If only I knew."

When the fire burned down and stars filled the sky, they slept huddled together under blankets and cloaks, as much for the comfort as for the warmth. Simon lay on his back, watching stars fall from the sky. It seemed like moments before he awoke to the pale glow of dawn and the raucous music of ten thousand birds. In the clear light of morning, it seemed obvious. *If I am ever to know, I must go to the Apostles and ask.*

Amala had already slipped from under his arm. Simon took care of his morning business and set a fire among the ashes from the night before. Amala returned shortly, bearing an armload of sticks. Once the coals burnt down, Simon prepared a pot of stiff barley gruel with currants and dried pears. Amala said nothing as they squatted by the fire and fished gobs of breakfast from the pot with wooden spoons. Horses saddled, bedding packed away, cookware clean, Amala stood at Epona's side and said, "Where, *Seimon?*"

"We go to Rome. If the Apostles intend to kill me, I want to know why."

Amala nodded and swung into the saddle. Simon wondered if she understood and didn't care, or if she simply trusted him. He climbed on Perun's back and let the horse buck and snort for a moment. It seemed to be a morning ritual. Simon was glad it no longer included kicking and biting.

They crossed the valley at midday and forded the shallow river that ran down its center. After resting their horses and taking a light meal, they set out west again. By late afternoon, a small creek crossed their path. Simon was all for continuing, but Amala dismounted and went to investigate a dead tree at the confluence of the two streams. She returned carrying a braided cord. "Travelers say here is south."

Simon took the cord from her. It didn't say anything to him except that someone must have been excessively bored. Amala added a few knots and ran back to the tree. "I say we go."

Here is south? Simon wondered how she knew where to find the cord and what else it might have told her. Amala said nothing more. Swinging back in the saddle, she let Epona pick her way up the rocky creek bed. They followed a faint trail, and it occurred to Simon that her horse, at least, had come this way before.

By dusk they went on foot, leading their mounts up the hillside and around a series of waterfalls. Simon remembered the last time he had followed a creek.

The void he had experienced that night came creeping back. Amala pushed it away with a giggle and a kiss on the cheek. She prodded him to keep climbing for one more verst. Finally, as the light faded and the evening shadows crept down from the hills, she stopped. "Is here."

Simon tried to pick out details, to find something special that made this particular place *here*. Some distance from the creek he spotted a cluster of fallen logs. On closer examination, it proved to be a rude cabin neatly hidden beneath a canopy of brush. He tied the horses off and removed their saddles while Amala carried their bedding inside. She grinned at him when he asked how she knew. "Traveler string."

Simon prepared a frugal supper, hoping that Amala's Traveler string would guide them to more supplies. That night, after the fire burned low, Amala brought out a small parcel wrapped in leaves. She unwrapped a flat cake and broke it in half.

Accepting one piece, Simon tasted it. Honey, flour, he detected a faint musky odor. When Amala ate hers, he followed, wrinkling his nose at the gummy texture and odd flavor. "Mushroom?"

She laughed and kissed him. "Sweet dream."

Amala rebuffed his advances that night. Simon lay on his back, unsure of what he'd done wrong. He didn't dwell on it long. The chattering brook and day of hard riding conspired to close his eyes and carry him off. Tumultuous dreams followed. Hurtling through the forest on the wings of an owl, drowning in a sea of leaves, borne aloft once more on the upraised arms of a hundred naked dryads, he spied the sea, glittering in the distance. Just a glimpse before the world turned black and he fell like a condemned soul.

Simon awoke in a sweat and reached for Amala. Her blankets were cold and empty. He tightened his breechclout, pulled on a thin tunic, and ventured out. The moon had not yet risen, yet all about, the forest seemed to shine with its own internal light. Each leaf, its own color, each trunk a glowing column. Simon turned about, gaping in wonder. Fireflies, like dancing angels, whirled and spun about his head. He followed as they filed off into the woods, a procession of supplicants to the halls of Dionysus.

And music, he heard it now in the dancing grass beneath his feet, in the swirling rainbow air itself. The frogs, the crickets, the nightjars that flocked to the branches above, they all sang in fervent chorus to something... something deeper in the wild forest. Simon glided, floated, almost flew between the trees. The fleeting angels raised their tiny lanterns and drew him on, painting the leaves in starlight, a clear path among the glowing trunks.

Ahead, the file of lanterns entered a clearing of golden light. Simon followed, his heart thundering in his chest. At the edge of the clearing, he paused in wonder. Amala danced. Naked as the dawn, glittering in her own perspiration and burning with internal flames, she writhed to the music of the night. While Simon watched, she dug her hands deep into the earth and raised them to the stars. In glorious abandon, she stamped to the rhythm of his heartbeat. Amala shook her tangled crown of orange hair and turned to meet his gaze—her eyes ten thousand years old.

She beckoned and he approached. Beneath a rain of flower petals, they coupled in the dirt until morning lit the sky. Simon clung to Amala, shivering. She kissed him on the lips and whispered, "Midsummer."

Simon didn't speak as they trudged back to the creek, a much longer trek than he recalled from the night before. He never found his tunic, discarded somewhere along the way. His feet burned, cut and bruised from walking barefoot through the woods. Still, he couldn't help grinning all the way back. Amala's shapely form twitched and wiggled as she threaded her way between the trees. Simon let her lead.

No words were necessary while breaking camp nor on the trail. Epona knew the way. Perun let her lead. They climbed past a boggy meadow that fed the creek and continued into the hills beyond. Camp that night was a simple affair, nestled in the lee of a brushy copse. Wrapped beneath his cloak, Simon fell at once into a dreamless slumber.

Starting early the next day, they climbed that morning to a high pass. Craggy peaks loomed on either side, still clothed in their mantles of winter snow. Amala and Simon both walked, leading their horses up a steep trail strewn with broken rock. He kept watch on the peaks as they climbed. A blizzard, a rockslide, even a host of manticores coming to devour their livers would not have surprised him. The sky remained cloudless, cold, and clear.

No manticores came. They rested only a moment at the top, their breath comingling in a silent wraith that drifted down the trail ahead.

It wasn't until the third day that either of them spoke. Back to lower elevations, they traversed a wooded hillside and picked up a well-used trail leading down from the pass they had just crossed. It followed a broad river flowing south. Early that third morning, Amala pulled to a halt. "Traveler string," she said, and dashed off to a pile of loose stones.

She returned carrying a decayed tangle that looked like nothing more than a mass of dead roots. Simon dismounted and helped her straighten it out. Blackened and disintegrating, she had to piece it together across the palm of his hand. Amala fished a new length of cord from her scrip and whisked it into a knotted braid. Dusting the crumbled bits of old string from her hands, she replaced it with the fresh one.

Simon remounted and waited. Upon returning, she looked up at him and said, "Two days."

He didn't reply. Knowing her, she could have meant anything. Simon thought of midsummer and wasn't quite sure if he was ready for another such night. On the second day, they reached a narrow footpath leading away from the river. Amala dismounted and held up her hand. "Wait, yes?"

Not sure if it mattered what he said, he nodded and took Epona's reins while Amala followed the path and disappeared into a grove of trees. The horses munched and whisked their tails at flies. With the girl away, Simon thought on his friends, his one-time fellowship with Yohan, Luca, and the others. Likely in Venice already, they were gone now, possibly forever. Once more the great emptiness swooped down on him. The void, hiding somewhere since midsummer, again darkened his thoughts. Simon pushed it back, tried to banish it. Startled by a fly biting his neck, he slapped and found blood on his hand.

Another landed on his arm. He swatted it away only to have two land on his face. Epona fidgeted and jumped. Flies swarmed about Perun. He backed away and whickered. Simon smacked flies with both hands as his horse squealed and reared, throwing him to the ground. Both animals bucked and ran off.

Staggering up, Simon waved his arms. Large black flies swarmed like angry bees. They covered his neck, his legs, his face. Simon crushed them by the hundreds. Still, thousands came, crawling in his ears, biting every exposed scrap of flesh. He opened his mouth to scream, and scores of the creatures crawled past his lips and crept into his nose, all the time biting, biting.

Driven to the ground, Simon pulled his cloak over his head and covered his legs. Still the swarm buzzed between the folds, crawled beneath his clothing, and drank blood from his back, his belly, and his loins. *I am suffocating.* Panic seized him. Every impulse cried out to stand, to run. Then Amala screamed his name.

He spat the flies from his mouth, swallowing half of them, and forced himself to think. Amala once again howled in pain and fear. He couldn't run. He had no art, no weapon against the swarming madness. *Fire, my art is fire.* Fumbling beneath his cloak, he found his flint, steel, and tinder. Dropped them. Hands swollen and stiff, he groped through the grass. Flint and steel in his fingers again, he struck a spark, then another. *Tinder, it must be here.* He struck a third spark that remained glowing in his nest of shaving.

He fed dry grass to the tiny flame. It flared, and Simon stood, throwing open his cloak. "Here, here," he called. "To me, to me."

Spinning, looking, he found her not five spans away, huddled on the ground, a crawling black mass of wings and legs. "Amala!"

Simon dashed to her side and snatched her from the ground. He carried her back and stood in the flames and smoke. Unable to wipe the myriad of legs and hairy bodies from her face, he stood and clutched Amala to his chest.

The fire spread, slowly at first. Simon felt it scorch his legs, driving the swarm back. Amala wriggled free. "I stand. I stand."

Bending, he tore up handfuls of dry grass and fed them to the fire. A small clump of dead weeds smoked and caught. Simon grabbed it by the roots and held it above his head. Swarming about, a few flies hissed and popped in the fire. Then, with a roar, the flames leapt from wing to wing, climbing the swirling mass that darkened the sky above them.

Simon recoiled, his hair singed and smoking. Amala had fallen into the fire and jumped up, swatting her clothes. A moment later, the swarm disbursed, gone as quickly as it had come.

Gaunt, spectral, a strange woman in black glided toward them. Amala bent double, weeping and vomiting. He stepped between them, ready for whatever new curse the Apostles might have sent. Simon slipped his dagger from its sheath and held it behind his arm, indraga mano.

The woman stopped just short and held up a hand. "Peace, Simon deVia. I come to help."

On hearing her voice, Amala straightened. "Is friend, is Dweller, *Seimon*."

She staggered to her feet. The strange woman helped her stand. Simon finished extinguishing the fire, all the while trying to watch this... *Dweller*... through blurry eyes. *She looks like a witch.* He wondered if she hadn't called the flies herself.

The horses. Simon turned and searched. He barely saw more than a haze of smoking grass and gray sky. He raised a hand to his brow and found his arm swollen, red and tight like an overcooked sausage. The stench of burnt flies, the smoke, he retched and gagged up a mouthful of wings and legs. Hands on his knees, the earth turned beneath his feet. He lifted his head and gazed at the sky. Then it too spun and faded.

Venice

Ramon and Carla argued whether Simon had truly gone to Salzburg or had ridden ahead to Venice. Yohan tried to ignore them. *On their second pitcher of ale, it likely amounts to nothing new.* He had enjoyed his time as Cernak's lieutenant, doing the needful and leaving the decisions to others. Now, he had to forego the ale, the dice, and the exotic Venetian women that Luca always seemed to find. *Someone must maintain a clear head. Someone must make the decisions.*

His first decision had been the hardest, to continue south after Simon had disappeared. Carla had insisted the boy headed for Salzburg. "I've seen him ride. I've seen him fight. Simon can take care of himself. We should follow this road to Venice as we always intended. He will either meet us there, or he won't."

Stephan had agreed with Carla, as had the others. With some reluctance, Yohan turned his back on Cernak's pyre and led them south. Luca had spoken the truth about his contacts in Venice. Upon arriving, he had set them up in a *locanda* on the *Terraferma*, the mainland side of Venice Lagoon. Yohan had inspected the premises. "Locanda, that is how you say 'brothel' in Venetian, ya?"

Luca had just grinned and disappeared out a side door. True to form, he'd provided them with other indulgences as well. Yohan didn't argue but didn't partake. For the first time, thirty-two years felt old.

As he sat considering options, Stephan entered the common room, pulled up a bench, and sat next to him. "I've negotiated to sell our entire cargo to the Vendini *collegantia*. They have twelve wealthy partners and a galley that departs for Smyrna in a few days."

Yohan watched him smile and nod as he spoke. Ten heartbeats passed. "But?"

"But they want us to take a letter of credit"—Stephan poured himself a cup of red Piedmont wine and drank—"on a Roman bank."

"It is worthless then."

"They offered double the face value."

"Ya, two times nothing is still nothing."

"And they will send their factor to vouch for it."

Yohan allowed himself a cup of wine. Sweeter and stronger than the northern vintages, it matched the heady Venetian lifestyle surrounding them. "Have you met him?"

Stephan nodded but said nothing. Yohan took another sip. "And?"

"Her. Their factor is a woman."

Finishing his cup, Yohan poured himself another. The prospect of leaving the tumbrel and plodding oxen in Venice tempted him. The prospect of entering Rome again, even for twice the value of their furs, was not so attractive. "Say nothing to the others until I've had a chance to talk to this factor."

"Luca knows."

"What doesn't Luca know? Tell him to hold his mouth—no, even better, tell him to join me for the negotiation. The two of us will work out the terms. I will present them, and..."

Carla jumped up and knocked over her stool. Shouting at Ramon in her native Andalusian, she waved her arms and stalked out.

"And we can all agree whether we accept or no. Ya?"

Yohan had a private apartment within the establishment that Luca had engaged for them. On the Terraferma side, a little gold went a long way. Carla had spent some coin, made some friends, and been invited to stay with the resident women of the hostel. The others commandeered a large room on the second floor to stow their gear and snore away the nights.

Yohan's apartment boasted a washstand, a pallet on a wooden frame, and a balcony overlooking the canal. He could piss directly into the water or dump his chamber pot without leaving the room. Choosing to do neither at the time, he simply stood and watched the sun setting over a steamy maze of mudflats and channels that made up most of the Terraferma. A flock of gulls swept by. Heading south, they were little more than a pack of flapping shadows against the sun's glare.

His door opened. Yohan didn't turn. "Come in, Luca."

"We go tomorrow and visit the mafankulos *grande*, sè?"

"Don't call them that." Yohan stepped back into the room. "Our meeting is with the Vendini *famiglia* and their business partners. We may have an opportunity here."

"Cazzo Venetian bastardos. They see opportunity—we get..." Luca made a sign with his fist.

"Perhaps... and perhaps we are their last best chance to salvage a bad debt."

"Explain, *monsignore*."

"They offer a note on a Roman bank in return for all of our furs."

"Bastardos, they cheat us."

"At twice the value, sight unseen."

"I still don't trust them."

"Ya, that is why I want you with me. Just try not to get us both killed."

Stephan joined them the following morning at the canal side. He had hired a six-oared launch to ferry them to the islands. "They will take you to Palazzo Vendini, just north of San Marco Basilica."

Yohan looked down at the launch. Broad of beam with three rowers on each side, he'd piloted worse. The steersman stood in the stern and beckoned them down. Luca eyed Stephan. "Mafankulo, you stay and drink ale while we bargain with Venetian bastardos?"

"He has arrangements to make and work to do. We will all be busy today."

A stone stairway led down the quay wall to a lower landing. Yohan followed Luca, hoping he would stay silent long enough to complete their negotiations. They found seats near the bow. Luca picked his way over the side, nearly tripping on a coil of rope before he settled behind the tall prow. Yohan stepped directly on the gunwale, walked halfway across on a bench, and sat facing Luca. "Are you good, brother?"

"We do this quick, and I come back quick. Then we are good."

A nod to the steersman, the rowers pushed away from the landing, and moments later, they sped toward the open lagoon. Wavelets slapped against the bow. A morning breeze blew through Yohan's hair and he lost himself in thought. *How might I plunder Venice if piracy were still my trade?* For centuries, force had failed against the Venetian navy. *Stealth then. Appeal to their avarice and vanish before they know what they've lost.*

Once in the lagoon, the launch bobbed and rolled in the short chop. Perhaps four versts of open water, Yohan grinned at Luca. He glared back. "If I am sick, it will be on your feet, *monsignore.*"

"You'll make it. I need you healthy when we talk to this factor of theirs."

"We are stupid. We meet on their territory, their schedule." He spat over the side. "We have no *maschio*, no strength to bring."

"We have our wits. No mention of the gold hryvna now. I expect they know something of it—let's see if it whets their interest, ya?" A cluster of islands drew near. "As long as the tumbrel with all its treasure stays on our side of the lagoon, we have strength. Eventually, they must come to us. Besides, I would rather they thought us stupid."

Once in the lee of the islands, the wind chop died and the launch settled into a slow lunging roll. Ahead, an orange curtain of haze resolved itself into a mosaic of tile roofs and whitewashed stucco. Yohan expected the Grand Canal to be somewhat grander than the winding corridor of stained walls and rotting doorways that rose before him.

A variety of craft passed, some narrow launches with one or two rowers, and some beamy cargo barges with banks of oars. Yohan glanced up the side canals as they passed, interesting but uninviting. He knew Rialto Island was on their right and that they approached San Marcos Island on the left, but the rest was a bewildering maze of canals, streets, and buildings that jostled for what little land the islands offered.

Ahead, a narrow bridge crossed the canal. Their steersman called an order. The oars began a complicated dance, turning the launch in the middle of the canal. Yohan watched a side canal swing into view. Another order, and they glided past a row of windows and slid into the shadows of the smaller canal.

The creak and splash of oars in their tholepins echoed in the narrow canyon of walls. Yohan looked up at a slot of sunlight. Another launch approached. Both craft raised their oars as they glided past. Luca watched every passing doorway. "Is Charon that guides us. Is hades we enter."

"Ya, steady friend, almost there."

A series of landings passed on their left. They looked to Yohan like backdoors—anonymous, confidential, the sort of place one could enter or leave without notice. They passed beneath a bridge and the steersman barked a quick order. Oars up, their launch drifted across the canal and thumped against one of the landings. Indistinguishable from its neighbors, Yohan wondered how they had found it in the maze of canals that crisscrossed Venice. Stepping off, he took a line from one of the rowers and looped it around a bollard. Luca followed. "They take us back, sè?"

"I only hope. Otherwise, it's a long swim."

A short flight of steps led up to a nondescript white door, painted to match the adjacent wall. Yohan looked behind him, taking in the surroundings. Nothing threatening. Still, nothing looked reassuring either. He pushed on the door—it opened inward. One last glance at the canal, and he stepped through.

A narrow hall led to an open atrium. Flowers, shrubs, a bubbling fountain. Yohan stayed in the shadows surveying the interior. Nothing moved. *Stephan would have entered from the street.* He felt like an intruder.

"Ushkuinik, so it's true. You live."

A blonde woman of medium build and indeterminate age approached from across the atrium. Yohan stepped out from the wall, wincing inside. "Ruslana Ursupova, why am I not surprised? What mischief do you have in store for the Vendinis?"

"No mischief, ushkuinik, certainly no more than your own. I am their factor in this... transaction, or didn't Stephan tell you?"

"He wouldn't have known, and let me be clear, I gave up piracy long ago."

Luca appeared from behind a pruned juniper bush. "I am clear too, *madonna*. Is only negotiation, no transaction."

Ruslana didn't seem startled. She didn't even look at him. "Is that true, Yohan? Your Brother Stephan seemed quite eager to accept our offer."

"Stephan may be several things, but he is seldom eager. You must have misread him.”

"So, they sent you in his place." She glanced back at Luca. "You and your little Sicilian friend here. Tell him he can put his knife away now."

Luca flicked the blade from behind his left arm. It spun, glittering in his hand before vanishing, only to reappear in his right. The blade turned once, then evaporated like a morning sunbeam. Luca raised both hands and grinned. "For you, madonna I obey."

"I like a man that can handle his weapon. Perhaps we should talk later."

Yohan let her smirk and toy with Luca. His hurt had passed, scarred over, left in the bottom of a sleek river *ushk*, with a goodly amount of his blood and a few tears. He wondered how she remembered it, if she even did. It no longer mattered. It wasn't Ruslana he had come to see. "When do we get to meet these Vendini and their collegantia?"

"Now you are the eager one. You don't want to catch up on a few memories?"

"I have no memories worth discussing. The Vendini?"

"Very well. They are not here."

"Merda." Luca sucked in his breath.

"Signor Vendini felt you would be uncomfortable meeting in his own palazzo. He has taken a room for us at Locanda San Marco. We will meet him there."

All in, or all out? Yohan looked back toward the canal. *Ushkuiniki do not win by retreating.* "Lead us to him."

Yohan doubted he could retrace the tortuous path Ruslana chose. For a while, he feared that she was lost. Then he began to suspect she tried to confuse them. Twice they crossed the same canal by different bridges. Luca followed, muttering at every dark alley they passed. "Is there no longer way to this cazzo locanda?"

"We could have taken the canals, but that barge you arrived in would never have fit."

Ruslana brought them through a series of narrow passages to a wider street fronting an imposing brick structure. "In here. They're waiting."

Two men in baggy red uniforms stood on either side of a massive pair of wooden doors. Yohan approached. They pulled open the doors and Ruslana followed him in. Turning to Luca, she said, "Go. You should enter before me."

Yohan looked back. Luca grinned, bowed, and waved his hand. "*Pi favuri*, madonna. I insist."

Scowling and shaking her head, Ruslana marched behind Yohan. "Go on in, but if your dog gets lost, don't blame me."

A short vestibule brought Yohan to an open dining hall. Dimly lit by candelabra hanging beneath the high ceiling, it felt more like a cathedral than a public establishment. Another uniformed figure, this one resplendent in cape and sash, met him. "This way, monsignore."

Four men sat at a long table on the far side of the hall. Silent as a midnight chapel, those four were its only other occupants. His guide beckoned Yohan to go first. One of the men stood. Tall, he wore a black surcoat and breeches in the eastern style. As Yohan drew closer, he saw a strong face with mustache and bearded chin. The man bowed. "Welcome, Yohan of Palermo. I am Sebastian. These are my brothers, Paulo, Adolfo, and Christián." The man paused and looked past Yohan's shoulder. "And please, tell your friend that the kitchen and corridors are safe."

Yohan bowed in return and took the proffered seat. "You must excuse Luca's caution. We encountered a few difficulties on our recent journey."

Seven chairs. The Vendinis knew in advance how many would come. Yohan noted their seating positions. Sebastian, clearly the padrone, sat on the long side of the table, facing him. Paulo on his right and Adolfo on his left, both nodded as Yohan sat. Christián, wiry, fidgety, perched on a chair at the end of the table, ignoring the others.

Ruslana pulled out a chair at the opposite end and prepared to sit. At that moment, Luca stepped from the shadows. "Allow me, madonna."

Surprise and anger, the look crossed her face faster than any but Yohan saw. She smiled back at him. "Thank you, and please, sit with us."

Yohan wondered if Luca's prowling was for show, for provocation, or for actual caution. *A little of all three*, he concluded. After bowing to the others, Luca took the chair between Yohan and Christián. "Apologies. I am Luca."

Yohan repeated the introductions while Sebastian waved to the uniformed attendant. "You must all be hungry. Shall we have some food?"

Food meant a heavy meal with meat and bread—wine too. Before Luca or

Ruslana could answer, Yohan said, "Thank you, but not until we have discussed business." He smiled at Sebastian and slapped Luca on the shoulder. "Perhaps if my friend here gets hungry enough, he will push me to conclude a deal, ya?"

Sebastian crossed his arms and sat back. "Ruslana warned me about you. Very well, talk first—eat later. I'm sure you understand our *proposta*, yes?"

"Not really. How can you make an offer on merchandise you haven't seen?"

Sebastian looked at Paulo. "Explain, brother."

Paulo nodded and examined his fingers. "This is the tumbrel Jacob of Tver brings south every winter." He glared at Yohan. "Do not deny it. We have our sources."

"I don't deny it."

"You don't deny stealing it? You don't deny murdering the guards in Krakow and in Nussdorf?"

One hand on Luca's shoulder, Yohan smiled at Sebastian. "Please tell your brother that his sources are mistaken."

A few words passed between brothers. Their Venetian dialect of the local vulgate, peppered with foreign terms, flew by too quickly for him to catch. Yohan had half expected a ploy like this when Ruslana addressed him as ushkuinik, pirate. He let them talk. Adolfo joined in with a few words, but Christián sat in silence, his eyes flickering between Luca and Ruslana.

A moment of silence, a nod from Sebastian, and Paulo said, "You have proof?"

"I have a letter from the Voivode of Krakow attesting to our ownership of the tumbrel and its cargo."

Paulo leaned forward and looked down the table at Ruslana. "You have seen this letter?"

Yohan shook his head. "She has not. Nor will anybody see it until they come to the Terraferma and inspect our cargo."

Adolfo had been making notes on a sheet of parchment as they spoke. He set his pen on a blotter. "I spoke with your Stephan yesterday. He told of Jacob and the boy... Simon. Where is he? Why isn't he addressing us?"

An odd expression crossed Ruslana's face. Yohan wasn't quite sure whether he was meant to see it or not. "Simon is a member of our company. He inherited the tumbrel when Jacob was murdered and contributed it to the Knights of Palermo when he joined. The voivode has attested to all of this in his letter."

"You didn't explain why the boy isn't here."

"He left on a mission of his own. We expect to meet again in Palermo."

Sebastian held out both hands, palms up. "You understand we must have assurance that this cargo is lawfully yours to sell."

Yohan nodded. "Assume it is. Let's talk of your offer to buy."

"It's simple. We have a valuable letter of credit that we will exchange for the... for *your* tumbrel and its contents."

Luca snorted. "Paper. Is worthless."

Adolfo looked up from his notes. "I thought we had explained that to your representative. It will be honored."

"In cazzo City of Diavulu. Or maybe no."

Again, Yohan put a hand on Luca's shoulder. "We have all day to say no. I want to see this bank letter they offer."

Sebastian smiled and turned to his right. "Paulo, the letter."

Without looking down, Paulo reached beneath the table and pulled up a thick portfolio of heavy leather. He set it in front of Yohan and sat back. "You will require a key to open the cover. If the binding or lock is damaged, the letter becomes void."

Adolfo leaned forward, a complex bronze pin in his hand. "Allow me..."

Yohan opened the portfolio and laid it flat. "Of course," Sebastian said, "it is written in Greek."

A circumstance Yohan had not considered, he flipped through a few pages. The letter had been penned by a steady hand, its rows of Greek characters straight and evenly spaced. He fingered the parchment. *Certainly document grade.* Yohan suppressed a sigh. *Work for scribes and clerics, not an aging ushkuinik.*

Luca bent over his shoulder. "Back, back... I see something not right."

Leafing back through the sheets, Yohan tried not to show his surprise. Luca stopped him. "There, look. *Banko Grigorio tis Constantinoupo-lis*—Constantinople, not Rome."

Paulo nodded. "They are a Templar bank with houses in Cyprus, Rome, and Malta. You will have no trouble redeeming this letter."

"Constantinople," Yohan looked up from the document. "They do not love Venetians."

"Nor does Rome love the house of Vendini," Sebastian said. "Believe me, if we could convert this letter, I would not be wasting my time today with a known river pirate."

Yohan squeezed out a smile. "*Reformed* river pirate, but I fully understand... and appreciate your honesty." He pushed the letter of credit over to Luca. "My colleague will review the document. Why don't we go for a walk? Ruslana, you may come with us, if you wish."

Stepping out into the sunlight felt like stripping off a suit of filthy clothes. Yohan inhaled the morning air with all its smells of cooking, sweating, and shitting, tempered by a sweet saltwater breeze from the south. As he stood in the sunlight, the bells of San Marco pealed out the hour of sext, midday. Sebastian followed him out. Yohan stretched his arms above his head as a flight of pigeons glided by. "How long has it been, Sebastian, since you stood, bare feet on the deck, and watched the oars churn beneath you?"

The man laughed. "Am I that easy to read?"

"We are not so different, you know. You plundered in your way, and I plundered in mine."

"And now let me guess, monsignore ushkuinik. You lead an honorable collegantia but long for the open water?"

"Sometimes I do, then sometimes I'm glad to be needed rather than feared."

Sebastian nodded. "I think we should get drunk and tell stories."

"Let's walk first. Will your factor be joining us?"

"She begged a moment to wash. We can go now if you wish."

"Now or later, Ruslana can always find me."

As he spoke, the woman in question caught up with them. "Nothing bad, I hope?"

Sebastian took her by the arm. "We only talk of ships and days long past."

Yohan set off in the direction of the bells. "I would like to see the *piazza* while I'm here."

Ruslana gave him a bright innocent smile. "And you didn't see it the last time?"

"It was dark. Other business... I had to leave quickly."

Sebastian said, "Then we must visit Piazza San Marco. But come. This way will be faster."

He led them diagonally up a narrow street and then down a wider cross street that opened on a broad stone-cobbled plaza. At one end, San Marco Basilica rose from the pavement in a panoply of marble spires and gilded domes.

Yohan stared a moment. "It is magnificent."

"Then you must go inside. I know the priest. Together we take communion, yes?"

Ruslana grinned at Yohan. "Our ushkuinik kneels to other gods, I think."

In response to Sebastian's look, Yohan said, "I have taken sacrament from rabbis, imams, druids, and bishops. None have harmed me, and some may have helped. We should go now and see this priest of yours."

San Marco Basilica by far outshone the Hermanowska Cathedral, or any other he had seen, including even St. Peter's on Vatican Hill. Yohan ate the bread, drank the wine, and lit a candle. He also dropped a large handful of silver coins in the alms box on his way out. Sebastian noticed, as did the priest. He kept his eyes on the ground in thoughtful meditation. *The negotiations start now.*

Once outside, Sebastian spread his arms. "Beautiful, no?"

"It has made my entire trip worthwhile."

"But not complete, my friend. Not complete."

Yohan walked with him in silence. *Stealth, the only way to take Venice.* Sebastian walked at his side, and Ruslana followed—both waiting. As they left the piazza, the trader took him by the elbow. "This exchange, it will benefit you. It benefits me. *Capisci?* We take this letter in payment for Egyptian sugar delivered to Sicily. That week... no, no, that *day*, Rome tells me Venetian trade agreements are not honored. With the furs, I have a chance to make whole, yes?"

Yohan nodded. "I must wait to hear what my colleague says."

"Forty thousand gold bezants. Your man will like it."

He almost stumbled. Head down, Yohan made a few calculations. Even with a heavy discount, forty thousand bezants could finance a significant campaign. He said nothing more until they reached the locanda.

Yohan found Luca exactly where he'd left him, head bent, bowed over the open document. Paulo and Christián had left, but Adolfo remained, sitting motionless on the other side of the table. That alone told Yohan that the Vendini collegantia had more at stake than Sebastian had revealed.

While Adolfo and Sebastian conferred in low voices, Luca peered up at Yohan. "We talk, brother, sè?"

Jerking his head toward the door, Yohan said. "Outside." He looked back at Ruslana who had followed them in. "Why don't you take charge of this letter while Luca gets some air?"

Luca bowed to the doormen as he left. Yohan led him across a narrow path to a stone balustrade along the canal. "I didn't know you read Greek."

"It is language of thieves."

Glancing back at the doormen, Yohan said, "We should probably move a little farther down."

Luca followed. "This letter. It is filled with merda. It has legs like a scorpion, all with sting. It is written by diavuli for entrapment of souls."

"Is it genuine?"

"Sè." Luca squinted. "Does Vendini tell is forty thousand cazzo bezants?"

"The weight of a large man, yes. That's a lot of gold, brother."

"Is entire army for a year. Navy too."

"So, you will say no, Luca. I will argue, but you must remain strong."

"You see this Christián mafankulo? He has paranza corta knife just for me."

"Are you worried?"

Luca spat in the canal. "Dead mafankulo. But why is no?"

"We can refuse as often as we want, but we can only say yes once. Besides, I want to see how desperate they are."

"It is dead Cernak who talks with your mouth."

Yohan laughed and clapped Luca on the shoulder. "Maybe it is. I learned a lot from him."

Fair Trade

Flopped across a canvas tarp just forward of the rowers' bench, Yohan opened his eyes to a pink morning sky filled with puffy gray clouds. *Rain. It would rain.* His head throbbed with every stroke of the oars. A shadow blocked the light. A face with blond hair. It spoke. "Do you live, my ushkuinik?"

"You were to come with the others."

"No, that will be your Sicilian friend. I was elected to hold your hand and wipe your ass."

Yohan slung an arm over his face. "You mean he couldn't stand up."

"If it's any consolation, neither could Sebastian."

The real consolation is Luca vomiting all over someone else's boat. Yohan felt the roll and heard the slap of waves against their sides. "Weather coming in from the west."

The boat pitched up. Yohan heard the clatter of oars, then the bow dropped, and a sheet of water flew over the forward rail. Drenched, he sat up. "Did they do that on purpose?"

"Time to wake up, ushkuinik. You have gold to collect."

Yohan had bargained hard into the evening, all the while Luca muttered and cursed. He refused food or drink until a deal could be reached. Sebastian had finally agreed to a five percent advance payment to be returned when his letter of credit was redeemed. Then food came. And wine. A necessary part of sealing the bargain, of building trust, it lasted most of the night. *Now one last bit of charade.* Yohan and Ruslana watched the Terraferma come into view.

With a bump and a clatter of oars, the boat made fast alongside a low quay landing. Yohan tossed a line to Ramon. Carla took a line from the stern and secured it to a wooden bollard. Stephan met Yohan as he stepped from the boat. "I see you've brought our factor, but where is Luca?"

"I sold him for two thousand pieces of gold."

Carla made a face. "Impossible. I would have given as much to get rid of him."

Ruslana danced across the thwart, over the gunwale, and hopped to the quay. She looked Carla up and down and scowled. "If one of you strong *men* would get my scrip, I'll show you Luca's ransom."

Carla bared her teeth at Ramon. "I think the woman talks to you."

Yohan winced and shook his head. "Quietly, people, and not here. The courtyard."

Their hostel had a small stable with an enclosed yard. Stephan led them up the steps and along the top of the quay to a narrow postern gate. He waved the two women through. The others followed.

Parked in its center, the two-wheeled tumbrel dominated the yard. Ruslana walked around, looking up at the tall wheels, the backboard, the drawbar, and the yoke lying beneath it. Yohan let her poke about. It would be some time before the second boat arrived. She grabbed one wheel by the spokes and shook it, looked at the high sides, and said, "A farmer's cart."

"Would you care to inspect the cargo?"

"Later, when the others arrive. Why don't you show your comrades what two thousand bezants looks like?"

Ramon heaved the leather scrip up on the tumbrel's backboard. "It's heavy enough."

Ruslana emptied twenty bulging linen bags onto the wooden platform. Yohan nodded to Stephan. "Pick four at random and count them."

Smaller than the hryvna that Jacob had carried, the bezants in each bag formed a glittering heap of yellow gold. Stephan pinched one between his canine teeth and inspected the mark. "They look genuine, early mintage and not debased." He finished counting the first bag. "One hundred, exactly."

Ruslana snorted. "Adolfo counted them himself. Of course, they are exact."

Three more bags each yielded the same results. Yohan said, "I never doubted them, but I needed all of us to see."

Carla flicked a glance at the other woman. "So, what is their offer?"

"Our offer?" Ruslana pointed at Yohan. "He agreed to our terms last night."

Shaking his head, Yohan produced a folded sheet of parchment. "The agreement is pending your acceptance of the cargo and the full concurrence of our company. You were there when Paulo drew it up."

Ramon and Stephan were replacing the linen sacks in the scrip. Yohan waved them over. "Brother Luca is not here, but he knows what is offered and he concurs." He handed the parchment to Ruslana. "Perhaps you should explain the terms."

When she'd finished reading aloud, Yohan looked each of them in the eye. "We must be unanimous and of one heart in this decision, ya? The tumbrel, oxen, and furs stay here. We take our horses and all our other possessions and go to Rome, where we will attempt to cash this letter of credit."

"And if we can't cash the letter?" Ramon asked.

"Then we have two thousand gold bezants and Vendini's factor. We could probably get another thousand for her at the Roman brothels. Any more questions?" Yohan paused a moment. "Then how do you say?"

Each in their turn repeated *d'accordo*, although Ramon thought on it for a little longer than the others. "I will support this," he said, "but I will not accept new conditions after the inspection."

"Ya, neither will I. Now, can we get some breakfast while we await the Vendini collegantia?"

Yohan had just finished a pastry filled with meat and started on a bowl of small beer when word came that a second boat was in sight of the hostel. Outside, he found that a light rain had started to fall. Stephan followed him out. As they descended to the landing he said, "I've taken care of everything. Carla and Ramon are ready."

Oars up, the second boat approached. Luca stood in the bow, looking defiant. Yohan wondered how he felt. Five others sat behind him. With a bit of a start, Yohan identified one as Christián Vendini. The man stared off across the canal. The other four wore light helmets and carried swords on their hips. Guards, mercenaries—Yohan wasn't sure which.

They remained on the quay as the boat approached. Two men jumped off and took lines. A moment later, all four stormed up the steps, brushed past, and filed through the postern gate. Luca shrugged and stepped ashore, followed close behind by Christián. Yohan didn't wait for them. "Let's see what those four are doing."

Ruslana met him on the way in. "Ushkuinik, is this how you show trust?"

Carla and Ramon sat on the courtyard wall, holding crossbows. Yohan waved up at them. "Ya, since when do you need swords to inspect cargo?"

"Since we make deals with pirates."

"You make deals with the Knights of Palermo. Now inspect your cargo before this rain gets worse."

"And tell mafankulo Vendini to put away knife or is dead man." Luca approached Ruslana. "Does bastardo even talk?"

The woman exchanged words with Christián, and the man stepped a few paces back. "He doesn't speak Latin or the vulgate, only the Venetian dialect."

"Why then does he come?"

Ruslana smiled at him. "To protect me, of course."

Glancing at the sky, Yohan said, "We waste time. You need to inspect this cargo now, before the rain starts in earnest."

A few words between Ruslana and the men, a furtive glance or two at the wall, and they climbed into the back of the tumbrel. With the tarp rolled up, she instructed them to drag bales from the middle of the load. Ten lay on the ground amid the growing puddles. Ruslana signaled a halt and pulled a few pelts from each bale.

"Sable and ermine," Yohan said. "Simon told us sable and ermine, no foxes."

She looked up at him and nodded. "We go inside and sign then."

Christián followed them in, Luca right behind him. Sitting at a bare wooden table, Yohan gestured for Ruslana to do the same. Carla came in and shook like a wet dog. "Ramon is keeping an eye on the stables. I'll bring him some food."

"Stay a moment and witness the signing." Yohan nodded toward Christián. "I presume he has your copy of the agreement?"

Stephan produced pens, blotters, and ink. Agreements changed hands.

Signed, they passed back across the table. Examined, countersigned, blotted, and sealed, each document was returned to its respective owner. Christián swept the Vendini copy from the table and left.

Ruslana looked around the empty common room. "You hired the entire hostel?"

"Only through tonight," Yohan said. "Your men are welcome to stay here until the weather improves."

"And where will you stay?"

"We are packed and ready to leave. Nothing keeps us here. You are packed too?"

"Shouldn't we stay, celebrate, and leave tomorrow when it's dry?"

"You are a Weaver. You travel on a moment's notice, or no notice at all. You sleep in the wild, you ride in any weather. We leave this morning, and you will come with us."

The room fell silent. Carla had started to stand but froze, half bent above her bench. "This woman is a Weaver?"

Ruslana stared at them. Yohan was glad she sat across the table. "I know it's true," he continued. "What I don't know is where the Weavers' interest lies in this transaction."

"You had intended all along to agree."

Yohan stood. "And you are bound to come with us. The Weavers never break trust, not even on threat of death. We have spare horses. Ramon waits." He headed for the door and looked back. "Stephan, help our guest choose a mount. Carla, Luca, let's go."

In the courtyard, Yohan noted that the Vendini rowers had begun transferring cargo from the tumbrel. Christián and his guards supervised. Stephan watched for a few moments and said, "We have maybe until midafternoon."

"Then we need to ride hard."

Ramon had sorted their supplies in advance. He rode out, leading four spare horses packed with gear. Ruslana had chosen a tall brown mare for herself. She leaned down and said something to Christián as they rode past. If the man was surprised, Yohan couldn't tell.

He left last, right behind Carla. She turned as he caught up. "They'll probably burn the tumbrel tonight to roast the oxen. They may roast the horse too, for all I know."

"We left a horse?"

She nodded. "The lame one. It won't make ten versts before going down."

"Not even with a determined rider? Vendini will be furious when he finds the compartment empty."

Carla grinned at him. "I'm counting on it. When the animal founders, he'll have to walk back."

Yohan didn't share her confidence. *I don't want to provoke the Venetians any more than I must.* He kicked his horse into a ground-eating trot and caught up with Ramon. "Where is our factor?"

"She rides ahead—says she meets us at midday."

Pulling his hood down against the rain, Yohan said, "Hell's harpies, I don't trust her."

"Luca says this factor woman is a Weaver. What is Weaver? A spider demon?"

"She's human, mostly. Like the Apostles perhaps... mostly." Yohan considered it for a moment. "No, Weavers are more dangerous. Where the Apostles traffic with their little infernal entities, Weavers traffic in ideas. Information is their weapon. Where the Apostles have their secret cabals, the Weavers live among us, an invisible nation within nations. They entangle themselves in the workings of men to build cities or destroy empires."

Ramon rode in silence for half a verst. "You didn't sleep well last night."

"No, not at all. But I'm telling you the truth. By tonight, perhaps already, she knows we have the gold hryvna. She knows too that we did not break our word. We sold the Vendini collegantia exactly what we had agreed to."

"How would she know about the gold? How could she even know about Simon's tumbrel?"

"I repeat, the Weavers traffic in information. The more important question is how did the Vendini collegantia know about our gold?"

"Weavers?"

"Ya, I would not be surprised if this letter of credit issue was contrived by the Weavers. This Vendini galley, conveniently bound for Smyrna, was likely delayed by the Weavers. Delayed for our sake. My next question is... why?"

"You see faces in the clouds, Brother Yohan. Rest today and we talk tomorrow."

Head down, water dripping from the mantle of his cloak, Yohan didn't rest—he brooded. *It's been years, so why does Ruslana devil me now?* He listened to Carla and Luca bickering behind him. *At least some things are normal.* He tried to anticipate the next event, the next little twist the Weavers had planned for him. *They want us to do something. They expect us to do something—what?* He hunched over the saddle, mulling on the issue.

Deep in thought, Yohan didn't notice the rider that pulled up beside him. "Regret leaving that nice dry hostel?"

Of course. He turned to Ruslana. "We will find shelter in Padova when we arrive. Do you regret playing Vendini's factor?"

"I have a purpose in my life. What about you, ushkuinik? Do you have a purpose, or do you simply wander the earth, picking up bits and pieces without understanding their greater meaning?"

"You know I ride for the Knights of Palermo. We serve in our own way, preventing injustice when we can, restoring order where it is needed. And yes, I pick up bits and pieces, as did Cernak before me, the lost, the condemned, as I once was."

Ruslana smiled at him, not her usual smirk. "My ushkuinik has acquired wisdom with age. I almost do not know him."

"But I know you, Weaver. What purpose do you have for us, whether we like it or not?"

"I am to see that you get paid in Rome for the letter you carry, nothing more."

Yohan thought on her words. Weavers seldom answered a direct question, prevaricating, stalling, anything to avoid revealing their secrets. *Still, Weavers don't lie. Not often anyway.* He held out a hand—the rain had let up. Spurring his horse past the string of spares, Yohan caught Ramon's attention. "We rest here."

Rest meant a light meal, grazing for the horses, and a chance to stretch their legs. Yohan wanted to see what else might play out. Luca had remained their camp cook. Carla pestered him about the food. Ruslana had cornered Stephan. Yohan tried to listen in but gave up after she kept eyeing him. *He can take care of himself.*

Once more on the road, Yohan pushed up their pace. He sent Stephan ahead to secure lodging in Padova. Ruslana insisted on following. Carla cantered up and said, "You trust her?"

"Not in the least, but for now, we share common interests."

"And what does the woman get out of this? Whose gold buys her?"

"Vendini for one, but think, she has likely spied out Venice. If I know anything, she will have learned what the doge himself is planning. Someone in Rome will pay her for that knowledge. When she leaves, she will have spoken with cardinals, the Pope even. Who knows? She may travel next to Saxony and lay all of this at the feet of the Emperor Fredrick, the Barbarossa."

"And she calls *you* pirate."

"In return I would call her *spy*, but she betrays no one. Her only allegiance is to the Weavers, and they have no country."

Carla stayed with him for the rest of the afternoon, riding in silence. Glad for her company and glad for the silence, Yohan considered their next moves. Christián Vendini might have followed on the lame horse. More likely he would have returned to the family palazzo and vented to Sebastian. Yohan smiled inwardly. *The older brother will appreciate our subtle misdirection, but the younger will want vengeance.* He played a few scenarios in his mind. *Sebastian will content himself with profit on the furs, as will the collegantia.* Yohan hoped it would be enough.

He heard the bells of Padova ring vespers before he saw the town. As they topped a low rise, Stephan met them on the road. "Considering the circumstances, we have decent rooms for the night and stable space for the horses, a blessing of Signore Vendini's bezants."

"What circumstances?"

"Why, midsummer, of course. Tonight is midsummer's eve, and the town is preparing for the fair. But we must hurry; the city gates close when the monks ring compline."

Yohan let Ramon and the others ride past before following with Stephan.

"Where is our factor? You didn't lose her, did you?"

Stephan rolled his eyes. "Still at the stable. She's very persistent."

"You have no idea, brother."

"The woman is most interested in our plans for this journey. She asked why we didn't take a galley from Venice to Brindisi, south of Rome, and ride from there."

"And?"

"And I told her I didn't know. That's somewhat the truth, yes?"

"It is the entire truth because I'm not really sure myself, and I have no idea where we go next."

With the sun still well above the horizon, Yohan followed Stephan through the city gate and entered Padova. They passed through a market, where people milled about, erecting stalls, buying food. Stephan turned down a narrow way between warehouses and granaries. At the far end, a low shed adjoined a stable and small paddock. "Not quite Vendini's palazzo," Yohan said, "but better than the lee side of a hedgerow."

Ramon and Carla took charge of their mounts. "Our factor is inside," Stephan said, "guarding the premises."

Yohan started toward the door, but Stephan stopped him. "She said she didn't want to be disturbed."

"Nothing she's got I haven't seen." He pushed through the door.

Ruslana sat cross-legged on the floor. Muttering, her eyes closed, she blinked and looked up. "You—out. Can I have no peace?"

"We need to bring our gear inside. Get your saddle and pack. Your peace can wait."

As Yohan spoke, it seemed that she pulled herself back from some other place. Ruslana rose to her feet. She caught Stephan staring in through the open door. "All of you," she turned to Yohan, "I know what you've done, and I warn you, the Vendinis do not easily forget."

Luca came in, lugging a saddle. "What is it Vendini not forget, madonna?"

"He broke trust." Ruslana pointed at Yohan. "He took something from the tumbrel before leaving Venice."

"Our agreement was for the cart, the furs, and the oxen. You were there when I discussed removing our supplies and personal items."

Stephan, Ramon, and Carla entered behind Luca. Ruslana glared at each of them as they came in. "Thirty gold hryvna were supposed to be among the furs. Who took it?"

"Your information is bad," Yohan said. "It wasn't thirty. It was sixty, mostly sound bars. That is twice the weight in bezants that Sebastian gave us. Is that why he agreed so quickly?"

"I don't know why he agreed on anything with you, ushkuinik. I just know that he expected gold among the furs, and it wasn't there."

"Màgaru..." Luca put a hand on his belt knife. "*Maldicaru*, witchcraft! How you know this?"

Yohan stepped between them. "Easy, Brother Luca. She's a Weaver. They have their ways."

"Cazzo màgaru she is." Clenching his middle fingers, he raised the other two. "She puts eye of *diavulu* on all of us, and we rot from our minchia."

Carla said, "Well, I'm not worried."

Ruslana crossed her arms. "You could have told me."

"And you could have told us what the collegantia expected," Yohan said. "Trust goes both ways."

Ramon said, "We have the Vendinis, the Apostles, and maybe the Weavers after us. What now?"

"You forget papist mafankulo," Luca said.

"One problem at a time, ya? Ruslana, go to the market and buy yourself some travel gear. Tomorrow we leave early."

She sniffed and headed for the door. "Don't wait up."

Yohan slept on a pallet across the doorway. He awoke several times, listening to his companions' snores and wondering if Ruslana had found other company for the night. In the gray light before dawn, he slipped out to perform his morning ablutions. When he returned, he found her in the stable, brushing her horse. "Did you sleep?"

"Does it matter? I'm here, ready to leave. Where is your brave band of pirates, ushkuinik?"

"Peace, woman. We have a long road together."

Stephan entered, lugging a pair of heavy leather scrips. He caught Yohan's eye. "No trouble here?"

"None. We were just planning today's journey."

A moment later, Carla followed. "Why is it a man thinks he can just piss anywhere?"

Yohan let that one pass. He spotted Ruslana glancing at the scrips. "Yes, that's our treasury, hryvna and bezants. Keep watch on it for us while we bring the rest of our gear over."

Carla said, "I'll stay."

"No, Ruslana already has her kit here. She can watch it."

He met Luca coming around from behind the shed. Ramon was inside, rolling up his bedding. "Any sign of our factor?"

Carla snorted, but Yohan said, "She watches our treasury for us. Let's get loaded up before the woman rides off with it."

High in the cathedral tower, the bells struck lauds. Somewhere far off, Yohan heard a choir of monks intone the dawn prayer. As the city gates opened, he led his band out into the misty cool morning. Ruslana rode beside him, saying nothing. Daylight found them fording a shallow stream. "Do you eat?" she asked.

"We can take a morning meal here. The horses will need water anyway."

Luca seemed less enthusiastic. "Màgaru expects a feast, sè?"

"I think you can manage a hot porridge while the horses rest." Yohan slid out of his saddle. "Put extra sausage in the pot, and we'll eat it midday as well. Maybe our Weaver can help you find some wood."

"Better still," Ruslana said, "I can start our fire while your Sicilian boy assembles his pots."

Squinting at her, Luca said, "I hear màgaru make to me a challenge. I say this: slowest fire cooks."

"I take that challenge." Ruslana grinned at him. "Slowest fire cooks all the way to Rome."

Ramon eased up next to them. "I am witness. Gather your tinder but do not start until I say."

Luca prepared a stack of tiny sticks and leaves around a nest of dry shavings.

Ruslana knelt next to him. He drew flint and striking steel from a pouch at his side, paused, and looked at her. "Màgaru concedes?"

"No, I just wait for your friend to give the signal."

Ramon nodded. "Go then."

Luca struck twice. Both blows generated a shower of sparks, but no flame. Ruslana produced a steel cylinder from within her cloak. Inserting a brass pin, she slammed it down on a rock. The pin dropped out, its end flickering. She held it under Luca's pile of sticks. "Fire. He cooks."

Luca jumped up, crossing himself. "Santo cazzo Madre di Cristo, it is a maldicaru. It is a witchcraft she uses."

Kneeling next to Ruslana, Stephan held out a hand. "May I see that?"

She gave him the pin and steel cylinder. "A fire starter. They use them east of the eastern sea. Be careful—it's hot."

Curious, Yohan knelt beside them. A tiny wad of burnt fiber projected from one end of the brass pin. Stephan fitted the pin into a hole in the cylinder and pressed. It only went in halfway. Taking the fire starter back, Ruslana said, "A balance is achieved between the active and the passive principles. By upsetting the balance, fire is invoked from the air."

Yohan stood. "You learned that from the Apostoli Lucis, didn't you?"

"If there are Apostles in the land of Malabar, then possibly so. But it is a lore that my Weaver sisters have had for years—some of us, at least."

Drawn by curiosity, Luca squatted next to the small blaze. "Simon had also a way with fire."

"Good," Yohan said. "She can take his place, setting the fire and gathering fuel. I'm sure our guest won't mind helping with camp chores." Before Ruslana could object, he continued. "And we all should be glad you lost that bet, Brother Luca. She's the worst cook anywhere from here to Kiev. I am witness to that."

Yohan led them west from Padova, refusing to name a destination. He'd considered crossing the mountains and moving them south along the western coast. He sized up his cohort. *Five seasoned fighters and one clever woman— almost enough.* Brigand armies haunted the mountains of Tuscany—Yohan knew that. As he rode along, he imagined how they would defend against an unknown enemy on unmeasured ground. Not for the first time, he thought on Simon as well. *What I wouldn't give to know he was safe.*

Stephan rode up beside him. "Share your thoughts, brother."

"Do you think the ferrymen of Nussdorf still pursue us?"

A perplexed look, then Stephan laughed. "That bad, is it?"

"I'm serious. Since Krakow, we have done nothing but gain enemies. We are so busy defending ourselves, we've lost sight of our goal."

"Remind me," Stephan said, "what is our goal anyway?"

It took Yohan a while to collect his thoughts. "We accomplished some of it. The furs have been sold without carrying them all the way to Rome." He scratched his beard and thought a little longer. "But our purpose was to return with our treasure and aid our fellow Knights of Palermo."

Stephan nodded. "Which we can't do without stopping first in Rome."

"Yes, and that's what bothers me. Our original plan was to take ship for Brindisi once we reached Venice. We no longer have that choice and must travel over land instead."

"They say there are many roads that lead to Rome."

"Roads overrun with marauding armies and Tuscan brigands. Let me think on this some more. There are wheels turning within wheels here, and I wonder if we choose our own path—or if someone else is choosing for us."

Riding late into the evening, Yohan took advantage of the long daylight to take them as far from Vienna as he could. Nightfall found them camped at the foot of a low hill. Yohan chose a log where he could sit and watch Luca grumble while he cooked. Ruslana fed the fire until it burned down to a bed of orange coals. Yohan waited for what he knew would come next. It didn't take long for the woman to dust her hands, turn, and sit next to him.

"There was a time," she said, "that we shared everything."

"I barely remember."

"You can't go on blaming me for what happened, ushkuinik. You went where you wished and did what you wanted. I was like your boat, a convenient asset at best, an encumbrance at worst."

He turned and faced her. "No, I was the convenience, a means of travel and a source of information for a damned Weaver—nothing more. When I no longer served your purposes, you vanished."

"So, your Knights of Palermo were so important. You're not a knight—you're a vagabond, a refugee. And now, you don't even know where you are going."

He stood and bowed. "Nicely done. A Weaver, heart and soul. All you want from me is our route and our next destination. Well, patience, my love. We'll take an evening meal together, enjoy the fellowship of our company, and then I will tell you."

Dweller

The witch called herself Baba Jezinka. That much Simon learned the first day in her tiny cottage. He lay, propped against one wall with Amala curled at his side. The girl wept softly, thumb in her mouth like an infant. They both wore plasters of bog mud, stinging nettles, and honey—nothing else. Simon had thought the fly bites torture enough, but the plaster roasted him alive. His only solace was knowing that Amala had not suffered nearly as much.

For her part, Baba Jezinka did what she could, brewing them hot herbal infusions and helping them stagger to the ditch outside when needed. She had assured them that the horses were safe and their travel kit well stowed. At least he thought that was what she said. Simon barely understood her vulgate, buried under layers of Slavic dialect.

He spent another sleepless night listening to their horses whicker in the darkness. Sometime before dawn, he pushed himself to his feet. Baba Jezinka snored softly on her pallet of straw and rags. Simon crept to the door, loath to wake her or Amala. The drying plaster cracked and itched as he moved but the burn had subsided to a dull warmth.

Once outside the smoky hut, he inhaled the cool mountain air and waded off into a sea of tall grass. Above, Venus and Jupiter plunged toward the western horizon while a straw-yellow glow lit the far mountains to the east. A hundred paces brought him to the river. Simon felt the icy water and rounded gravel at his feet. He kept walking.

The fast-moving stream climbed his legs to the knees. Simon stopped and crouched in the water, splashing it over his shoulders and cupping it to his face. He heard movement behind him and turned to face Amala. She sat, the water surging over her breasts. "I do your back, *Seimon*."

Racing back through the grass in the chilly dawn, Simon and Amala slipped inside the darkened cottage and pulled blankets about themselves. Baba Jezinka knelt by her firepit coaxing flames from last night's coals. Amala exchanged a few words with her in a language he didn't recognize. When the old woman turned to him, Simon realized something he hadn't noticed before. "You, Amala... you are both Álfar."

Baba Jezinka nodded. "She is granddaughter."

Once he could see past the wrinkles and the cropped gray hair, the resem-blance became obvious. "And you are also a Weaver?"

"Dweller. I stay, that others may travel."

"And those cords, those knots, the messages, they are yours?"

The old woman turned a sharp glance at Amala and hissed out a few words. Returning her attention to Simon, she said, "You should not know, should not see."

"Amala is my wife—she knows what I am. We have no secrets."

"Yes, Apostle, we know. I would choose otherwise." The old woman sighed and closed her eyes. "The choice is not mine."

"I will take care of her. I promise you that."

"She dies for you, Apostle."

Simon shook his head. Amala took him by the arm and faced her *baba*, her grandmother. "*Seimon* not die. I not die."

Turning back to the fire, Baba Jezinka said, "Take food before you leave."

She served them bowls of hot goat's milk and a thick porridge of crushed buckwheat. The old woman left them to eat and busied herself outside. Simon found that he was starving and was glad to see Amala eating as well. Her skin still bore blotchy red patches, but she seemed to move without pain. The girl caught him looking at her. "You are well, *Seimon*? Not hurt?"

He held up an arm. Swollen, speckled in red welts, his skin wept clear fluid. "It looks worse than it feels. Your baba is a skilled healer. Is she also a witch?"

Amala glanced toward the empty doorway. "Healer, yes. Baba Jezinka sees, knows. She is baba of my people. That is... witch?"

A woman with the far-sight, a woman who steals thoughts—and Weaver at that. Simon didn't nod or smile. "She is a wise woman," he said. "Maybe that's a witch. Tell me, if we came back here in a month, would we still find Baba Jezinka's hut? Would she still be here?"

Amala pinched her lips together and shook her head. Simon sensed rather than saw the old woman enter. "You have eaten?" Without waiting for an answer, she continued. "You are well. You have food. Now you must leave."

Behind the hut, Simon found Perun and Epona, brushed, fed, and harnessed. While Amala spoke with her baba, he saddled both horses. His bedding and scrip lay next to Amala's satchel and their other supplies. He loaded it all behind the high cantles and lashed it tight.

Perhaps not quite a goddess, Simon thought, *but Baba Jezinka is due a small offering.* He measured out a generous portion of their salt and tied it up in a scrap of cloth. Once back inside, he found Amala and the old woman deep in conversation. Simon left the salt on the hut's lone table and collected a few remaining bits of clothing. Amala took him by the elbow and handed him a bulky package. "Food for travel."

Double-checking their mounts, their saddles, and their gear, Simon brought the horses around. Baba Jezinka stood before him, the morning sun at her back. She seemed taller now, straight and stern. The light played through her mane of gray hair. She stepped closer and placed a hand on Simon's chest. "Amala holds my aegis, my shield of protection. Abandon her, your curse returns."

With that, the old woman stepped back, faded. She almost seemed to wither. Amala glided from the hut, her hair bound with a wreath of flowers. "Quickly, *Seimon*, we go."

He needed no further encouragement. Amala swung into the saddle and turned Epona south. Simon did the same, glancing back toward the hut. Baba Jezinka had disappeared and the cottage itself seemed to blend in with the surrounding trees and grass. He nudged Perun in the flanks and was rewarded with his morning tantrum of kicking and bucking. Amala rode on ahead and didn't look back.

She didn't speak when they took their midday break. She said nothing when evening came, and Simon found them a sheltered copse to make their camp. She held him close that night, tangled in their nest of blankets. Simon awoke as the moon, nearly full, sailed through a sky of broken clouds. Her back to him, Amala wept into the night. He drew close, put an arm over her, held her tight. The girl shook but said nothing.

By morning light her mood had passed. Simon awoke to find Amala tending a small fire. When he returned from his morning ablutions, she kissed him and offered a steaming lump of bread. "You like?"

Juggling the hot loaf on his fingertips, Simon let her know he liked it very much. Amala had a loaf of her own wedged into a forked stick. She let it roast a little longer, then turned it to brown the top. Simon tried to imagine this girl, now his wife, quietly following him for years. He nibbled one end of the crusty bread. Smoke, herbs, hazelnuts—he took a bigger bite and hot cheese burned his tongue. He puffed out around the hot mouthful, blowing steam in the cool morning air. "Ho... hot. But good."

Amala retrieved her own bread from the fire. She broke it in half to let the steam rise from the brown loaf. *More at home here on the road*, he thought, *than any voivode in his own castle.* She caught him watching her eat and smiled. To Simon, it seemed a sad smile. *But mornings can be like that.* He took another bite. "My skin feels stiff like old leather but better than yesterday." He broke a piece of crust off and ate it. "And you, are you well? Do you hurt?"

"I am well. Better than yesterday. Just..." She leaned up against him. "Just do not ever leave me, yes?"

"Never."

Following the same stream that passed Baba Jezinka's hut, they descended into a long valley between tree-covered mountains. By late afternoon, they had both dismounted, leading their horses through a steep forested gorge. Simon called a halt just above a broad river valley. Off in the distance smoke rose from a handful of tiny settlements. Amala peered over his shoulder. "Baba Jezinka say they rob us."

"The Wolf of Nussdorf, yes... same problem." Simon rubbed his chin. "So, when I followed Master Jacob, how did you get across? The Danube River, I mean."

"I ride in cart. Many times I ride and you do not know."

Simon turned back to the problem at hand. *We won't be riding a cart this time.* "I don't like the idea of crossing in the dark, but I see no other way."

The river, flowing west to east, ran deep and swift through the lower parts of the valley. Simon shaded his eyes and looked further upstream. "We have to cross where it's shallow and the horses can wade."

Afternoon sunlight sparkled on a patch of water almost out of view. "We stay in the shadows until we find a shallow stretch." He pointed west. "There. It looks wider there."

Simon led them through the forest's edge, looping around a rude hut of sticks and turfs. A dog barked as they passed. Shouts, yelps, it whined and quieted. Simon kept going. When they reached the clear valley once more, the river was much closer. About two versts distant he saw what he'd hoped to find, a broad marshy area of shallow braided streams. "We cross here. As soon as it gets dark, we go."

Simon looked downstream. Already a pale smudge of moon hovered above the eastern horizon. Amala kept staring at the river. "I don't swim, *Seimon.*"

He put an arm around her shoulder. "You won't have to. Tonight you ride across, and we sleep on the other side."

The horses stamped and whickered as darkness crept down the valley. A few stars glittered in the cobalt sky, barely visible in the moonlight. Simon nodded. "Let's go."

He led them out into the deep grass. There would be goats or sheep in the valley; he'd heard their bells. Simon thought of dogs. *That would be trouble, herders too.* Even in the moonlight, walking was hard. Holes, unseen brush, and branches. Simon fell over a large rock and peeled some skin from his knee. Amala squeaked when he fell but Simon shushed her. "I'm good. We have to go quickly."

They reached the river, blundering into a fast-moving stream before they knew it. Far off, a dog barked. Another answered, much nearer. Simon wasn't sure which side of the river it came from. He told Amala to ride across. "I'll lead the horses. You watch for trouble."

As he'd hoped, the river had spread into a maze of shallow channels. Just downstream he heard the hiss and grumble of cascading water. Almost halfway across, the barking started again. This time, Simon was sure it came from behind them. He pushed himself faster. Another step and he plunged into a deep pool. Gripping the reins with both hands he managed to pull himself back.

Turning upstream, Simon pushed his way through waist-deep water. Loose rocks tumbling beneath his feet, he managed to reach the other side and climb the bank. Dogs barked. Simon smelled the smoke before he saw the torches flickering as they moved through the grass. He tossed Epona's reins to Amala and remounted Perun. "Let's go."

The dogs reached them first. Perun dispatched their leader with a swift kick to the head. The others hung back, barking like devils. The men with torches ran faster than Simon dared push his horse in the dark. "We're not going to make it. Ride for the trees—we'll face them there."

Closer than he thought, the trees sheltered them from the moon's cold light. Simon was tempted to keep riding but knew the dogs could follow wherever they went. Staying just beyond reach of Perun's hooves, three shadows jumped and snarled in the darkness. Dismounting, he signaled Amala to do the same. Before she could move, an arrow came whistling out of the field. The girl cried as she fell.

A second arrow struck Epona, sending the horse into a screaming frenzy, running and bucking. Two of the dogs gave chase, but the third lunged at Amala. It descended on her fallen body just as Simon's knife opened its throat. The torches approached, three in all, two from the west and one rushing up from the east. Another arrow hissed past Simon's ear. He dropped to the ground.

Perun shied back snorting and grunting. Two more arrows flew. The horse shrieked and reared. A third arrow caught him full in the chest. Perun fell like a collapsing tower.

Knife sheathed, Simon crawled toward the approaching torches. At least three, probably more. Six? It didn't matter. They drew within five spans. Simon lay flat against the ground, motionless, knife in hand. Footfalls, heavy breathing, a pair of boots churned through the deep grass. Simon rose from the shadows and jammed his knife into the man's knee. A slash across the throat quieted his screams.

A torch appeared. Simon dropped and spun away from a short axe that struck the ground. Next spin, he knocked the legs from beneath the man and jammed his dagger into his heart. Springing to his feet, torch in one hand, axe in the other, he faced a bowman drawing on him from ten paces off.

Simon threw the torch as the arrow hissed past his ear. He rushed the bowman and buried his axe in the man's neck. Snatching up the torch, he slammed it across his opponent's face. Others came. It didn't take long. Two more ran up, weapons in hand, only to fall to Simon's knife.

A third raised his bow, but one glimpse of Simon's looming figure sent him fleeing. Simon caught him within a few paces. He sheathed his knife and threw the man to the ground before beating him to a lifeless rag. *One more torch, somewhere.* Simon wiped the splattered blood from his eyes and stared about.

He spied it off toward the woods, guttering as it waved above the grass. *Amala... the devil.* Simon ran, heedless of brush and rocks. He tripped, rolled, and kept running. *Close, too close to where she lay.* He howled in frustration.

The torch stopped moving. Simon redoubled his speed. A dark figure turned to face him, torch in hand. The light glittered off a weapon. Simon didn't care. He ran up, deflecting the sword strike with his dagger and following through with a blow to the throat.

Simon ducked too late to avoid the swinging torch. He went down, his face in agony. The sword returned, pinning his cloak to the ground. He let the boot descend on his right shoulder. Something cracked. Ignoring the pain, Simon whipped his dagger around and slashed the exposed tendon.

Cursing, the man dropped his torch, stumbled, and fell. Simon pulled free of his cloak and jammed his dagger into the man's ribs. Standing, panting, he swung about. *More, there had to be more.* Nothing moved. *Huts. Burn everyone— slash every throat.* Simon pulled the sword from his cloak and swung it back and forth. *Every throat, man, woman, infant. They all die tonight.*

A soft voice in the darkness cried, "*Seimon.*"

Like a wet garment, the battle rage fell away. In its place, pain, fatigue, and sudden fear. He snatched up the torch and staggered to the forest's edge. Perun lay in a heap where he had died. Only an arm's length away, Simon found Amala shivering on the ground. Guttering, nearly extinguished, the torch shed just enough light to see the arrow shaft protruding from her cloak. He leaned closer. The arrow had embedded itself just above her right breast.

Rapid breaths, almost panting, Amala rolled her eyes up at him. "I die now."

He touched her face. "No. Not tonight—I won't let you."

Simon cut her cloak from around the arrow and peeled it back. Beneath, she wore a vest and light blouse. He cut those away as well and bared her white chest to the moon. An arm's length of shaft protruded from a bloody gash in her breast. He bent low and put his face next to hers. "I need to roll you on your side. You must be strong for me... for us."

Simon didn't wait for her nod. He took her arm and hip. Ignoring her cries, he couldn't ignore the screaming pain in his shoulder. He rolled her up on her left side and ran a hand over her back. Nothing. *Oh God help me, I need Ramon. I need Aluná.* The point had not gone through, but it was so deeply embedded, Simon knew it would kill her to pull it out.

I can't do this. Simon rolled Amala back and rubbed his face. *I can't do it.* He imagined carrying her, sprinting across the mountains, back to Baba Jezinka. The thought of healers somewhere in the scatter of lighted huts taunted him. But as the torch flickered and burned down, he could only hold her hand and cry.

They would come soon, armed men looking for their comrades. A horse whinnied in the darkness. Simon listened for footsteps, voices. The horse whickered, almost at his back. Simon jumped up and reached for the discarded sword. A shadow loomed against the sky. Epona—he recognized her profile and harness.

She shied back when he took her dangling reins. Simon led the horse away from Perun's massive body and tied her to a bush. Crouching at Amala's side, he kissed her and said, "Epona came back for you."

She gasped and nodded. "Ride, *Seimon*."

Simon took her hand. "I cannot because I love you. Now, watch the moon. Watch the moon carefully and... and... Oh God, girl, forgive me."

With that, he grasped the arrow shaft in both hands and pushed down. Amala screamed and twisted. Simon pushed harder, pinning her to the ground. With a soft crunch, the shaft moved, then broke off just above her chest. He lurched forward and caught himself. *Don't think, just do.* He turned her over. Glistening in the moonlight, the rough iron point protruded from Amala's back. Simon bent, gripped it with his teeth, and drew it out.

Blood, so much blood, the wound itself bubbled and hissed as the girl struggled to breathe. Simon cut her shirt into rags and tied them around her. Amala seemed dazed, listless. Her wounds still bubbled and bled. *Her pneuma, her vital essence escapes.* Simon tried holding his hand over the hole. It stopped the bubbling but only for as long as he knelt there. *Flesh to cover flesh.* He needed something to imprison the life force within her chest.

An arrow through his heart, Perun lay nearby. Simon drew his dagger and cut two patches of skin from his neck. Flesh against flesh, he pressed them to Amala's wounds and tied them tight with strips of cloth. She gasped and coughed. Simon held her down. "Lie still, rest." He stretched out next to her and touched her lips. "It is done. The worst is over, but we must leave soon."

She touched his lips in return. "Your face."

"It was burned in the fight, but I will heal. You must..." Simon broke down for a moment, then opened his eyes. "You must live. I could not go on if you die."

Epona's return meant the dogs must have given up and wandered home. Simon pictured what came next, the search, the chase. *How many did I kill? Six? Seven?* Even if he took Amala and fled, the bodies and the blood, there would come outrage and pursuit. In daylight, the hunter's bows would cut them both down.

If they dared to follow. Simon retrieved the sword and turned to its fallen owner. It took him three blows to sever the neck and detach the head. He jammed his blade into the ground and mounted the head on its pommel.

The moon had crossed half the sky before Simon drew the arrow from Epona's hip and transferred all his gear from Perun's saddle. Once more he knelt at Amala's side. "You must stand now—take my arm."

She straightened, wobbling. Simon closed her vest and draped both cloaks over her back. When she demurred, he shook his head. "Wear them. You must stay warm. It was the ague that nearly killed my friend Yohan." He led her to Epona. "Now, you must ride as well. I know you can do this, my wife. I will help you up."

Simon led them into the forest, contouring along the southern hillside. He didn't look back, didn't strain for the sound of baying dogs. All they could do was flee and hope their pursuers wouldn't risk more losses.

Divine Madness

The trail behind him had already filled with evening shadows, but standing in the gap between two looming peaks, Simon gazed out on a sunlit plain, sparkling with rivers. *So close. So damnably close.* He returned his attention to Amala. She lay swaddled in blankets and robes; a fire crackled nearby. Still, the girl shivered.

They'd fled through the forest all that first night. Amala clung to the saddle while Simon led Epona, blundering between trees and bushes. Daylight found them climbing a narrow valley. He had been overjoyed to see that they'd stumbled upon the same southern path they had been following from Baba Jezinka's cottage. Three days they'd climbed. For three days, Amala grew weaker with every verst.

Simon had rebandaged her every morning and every evening. He'd washed the foul humors that wept from the hole in her back. Even though the precious pneuma no longer bubbled from her chest, the girl's life force slowly crept away. Topping the pass, she'd looked up, then swayed in the saddle and fell. Simon had barely caught her in time, his right shoulder screaming in protest.

Kneeling at his wife's side, he waited for that dark hour between vespers and matins when the sun has gone and the moon, past full, hasn't yet risen. Such hours, Simon knew, were propitious to the art, his art, *goëtia*, conjuration. *Yohan said it*, Simon thought. *The sword was never my weapon. I walk the edge of darkness, the hidden hand, the esoteric path.* He watched the sun fade.

Simon held his silver talisman for healing. *Invocation won't be enough. Amala needs a summoning.* His chest ached at the thought. The claw still lived in his heart. *What entity has bound this token?* He tried to recall the basic steps of a summoning—invocation, purification, invitation, offering, and abjuration. Years earlier, a lifetime it seemed, he remembered watching, assisting. The beatings when he missed a word or reversed a sequence, he remembered those as well.

The claw, ever present in his chest, crushed his heart, throttled his breath. Simon knew now that it had no real power other than fear. He bore the pain of a broken shoulder and burned face. He endured the ultimate fear of losing Amala. "Mafankulo," he cursed beneath his breath. *Oh yes, only another foe to overcome.*

The sun having set, he chanted a few lines. The Latin of the High Church, the Latin of Rome, they formed a simple invocation. He recognized most of the words. Purification normally took days, but Simon knew a simple shortcut. He placed his silver token in the fire for a moment, then flipped it into his right palm. Crushing his eyes shut, he shuddered and gasped until the smell of burning flesh no longer rose from his hand.

Simon invited the entity, not knowing what he would see. *Something, something he'd forgotten.* It hardly mattered, time was short. From behind him, he heard it speak. "Simon deVia, you dare summon me without a protective circle?"

Perfect Latin. Simon didn't turn. *Of course, I should have girded myself in symbols and incense.* He realized if it was going to kill him, it would have done so already. He focused on the talisman. "I come to you unguarded because I am asking your help."

A disgusting toad that walked on a woman's legs appeared before him. "One in your position should be more cautious."

More than he expected, less than he had feared, it stood just within his circle of firelight. Simon examined the creature. "You are not a demon nor an angel. Who has bound this talisman?"

It laughed, a high musical sound totally at odds with the creature's appearance. "Simon deVia, Simon Prostoi, Simon the *fool*, you've summoned a goddess without knowing first who would come?"

"I have called the entity who chose to bind this talisman for healing. I trust you are such."

The image slowly transformed. "It is said that men must worship the gods of this earth, but none know whom the gods themselves must worship."

In the flickering circle of firelight, the thing took on the aspect of an old woman. Naked, hanging dugs, a tangled nest of gray hair on her head and between her legs, she leered at him. "I will tell you a secret—the gods worship fools such as yourself. You have summoned Febris to your fire, goddess of disease and decay."

"Can you heal my wife?"

The old hag grew twice her size and loomed over him. "You are the most naive fool of all the fools ever to call on me. Why should I not just fill you both with pestilence before I depart?"

"How would that serve you?"

"Serve me? Healing is temporary, only death is eternal, only decay serves me."

"Then give her healing now. You will get her death in good time."

Febris straightened and diminished. "I could heal your precious wife, but I must have something in return, Simon the fool. I offer her life for yours. Are you prepared to make such a pact?"

He thought a moment. Always there had been a negotiation. Simon didn't know what to give. *Anything? No, his death would leave Amala alone, deserted.* He shook his head. "Make a better offer."

Febris, goddess of disease, laughed in his face. Her breath smelled of septic wounds and open graves. "Very well, fool, I offer this: give me ten years from the end of your life in return for healing her tonight." Simon started to respond, but Febris continued. "Think long and hard, Simon deVia. You might die this instant. You might die full of health, cradling your newborn son, but you will die ten years before your time."

Simon held up his hand and shook his head. "No more discussion. I accept your terms. The moon will rise soon, goddess. Heal her now and be gone before it does."

Febris smiled at him. "It is done. She lives. Let me give you one more gift, *fool.* You will die on the evening of your greatest triumph, in the arms of your beloved. Carry that knowledge with you always... and fear me."

With that, Febris stepped back from the fire and faded. The silver talisman in Simon's hand crumbled to ash. He stared at it a moment, then turned and lifted Amala from the ground. She awoke with a start and gasped, twisting in his arms. "I breathe. I breathe. How?"

"You live. That's all that matters."

"Your face?" She ran a gentle hand across his cheek.

Simon realized that he held her cradled in both arms. He lowered her feet to the ground and shook out his right shoulder. Minor pain, nothing else. He touched his cheek where she had stroked it. A scab flaked off under his fingertips, the skin beneath smooth and dry. Febris had indeed given him a gift. "I had to use a talisman." He touched his cheek again. "It worked."

They talked that evening, as the moon crept above the trees. Amala barely remembered recent days, climbing the pass, swaying in the saddle, dying. "I am cold. So always cold, and now, no."

"It is the ague that kills, not the wound."

"The talisman, it heals?"

Simon described Febris, how he had called her, how she had destroyed the talisman when she left. "The Apostoli Lucis will know I am here. Using that talisman was like raising a pillar of fire for all to see. Even if your Baba Jezinka protected us from Anathema, the Apostles will be looking for me."

Simon didn't speak of the bargain he had made nor of the red scar on his palm that marked it. Amala fell asleep on his shoulder, but Simon spent most of that night awake, wondering what they would do next. By morning, she had curled up against his lap, and he had failed his vigil by falling asleep slumped over his knees.

Birds awakened them, as did the restless snuffling of Epona. Simon stirred their fire back to life while Amala patted lard and crushed oats into flattened cakes. She roasted them on the fire and smeared them with honey from Baba Jezinka's supplies. Simon stood to eat his, watching sunlight creep across the valley below. Amala joined him. "We go?"

"Do you know where we are? Can you find those strings or something?"

She shook her head. "None here."

Simon pointed at a tiny glint of silver in the distance. "If that is a river, it will lead us to people, to the sea even. We go there."

By the time they picked their way down from the pass and crossed several smaller streams, "there" turned out to be three days distant. They followed a narrow path that wound back and forth across the mountain's face, never once meeting another traveler. Farther down, flocks of sheep decorated the hillsides, but Simon avoided the small huts and cottages they passed.

By the second day, their path had become a well-used track. On the afternoon of the third day, Simon heard a far-off church bell ring vespers. They reached the town gate just as it was closing. Amala searched for signs of a Dweller living among the modest houses and shops, but Simon finally had to barter a portion of salt for stable space and accommodations in the loft above.

The stable master's vulgate bore a strong local accent, but Simon managed to negotiate meals for themselves and board for Epona. That evening, fed and washed, they lay together on a bed of straw and listened to the horses champ and snort. "This town, no visitors," Amala said.

"I think we are the first in a long time to cross that valley and live." Simon paused and laughed. "Even the stable master doesn't know where this town is. Tomorrow, I'll try asking their priest."

Amala smiled at him, and for the first time since midsummer, he smelled lavender. "Tomorrow can wait."

True to habit, Amala rose early and went to tend their horse. Simon spoke again with the stable master and learned that the town and church were both named Ponteventi. "Bridge of the Winds," Simon told Amala. "I didn't ask if the bridge itself still stands or if only the town remains."

"You visit priest," she said, "and I find bridge."

"I don't like it, you wandering about in a strange town."

She took his hand and kissed his cheek. "I wander strange towns six years for you, *Seimon.*"

The whole idea of separating made him uncomfortable. "I don't want you wandering now, my love." A chill ran down his back. "I almost lost you once."

Amala smiled, stepped into a shadow, and vanished for a moment. "I am not lost, yes? I am just hard to see."

Simon shook his head, but he kissed her cheek and left to find Ponteventi's priest. He discovered an old man in a cassock, cross, and stole puttering in a garden behind the church. Simon had to speak twice before the priest responded. Back bent almost double, he straightened before answering.

When he finally understood Simon's question, the old priest croaked out that he wasn't terribly sure where they were. A little prompting revealed that Venice was a two-day ride to the south. He bent forward like an inquisitive turtle and looked Simon up and down. "You speak the Church's Latin. Are you a priest?" He gave Simon's ragged cloak a brief glance, then ventured, "A pilgrim perhaps?"

"A pilgrim of sorts, Father."

"Your clothing speaks of a difficult journey. Perhaps you could use a few days of rest. Can you sing the Mass for me?"

His question took Simon aback. The claw in his heart had not surrendered. It now clutched and strangled. Thinking about Amala, he said, "I... It... It has been years since..." Simon gagged and blinked. The words were there but imprisoned. "Since I was acolyte to the basilica."

"I sense a story in you, perhaps a confession even. You should call me Father Giallo." He waved an arm at the modest apse and bell tower. "Come, pilgrim. We should break bread and talk."

Bread included wine and a side of cold lamb shoulder. Simon was ready for something besides oat gruel and cheese. They ate beneath a grape arbor on a small stone *terrazza*. As Father Giallo poured them each a generous cup of wine, two boys marched by to ring the morning prayers. Simon watched them pass. "I'm sure they have much better voices than mine. Why don't you have one of your own acolytes sing the Mass?"

The old priest shook his head. "Not one of them speaks a word of High Latin."

Simon looked down. Could he? The barbs in his heart... *Only another foe to overcome.* He examined the stains on his tunic. "When?"

"Tomorrow morning after terce."

Simon met Amala while returning to their loft. She had found the bridge, and yes, there was a market in the town. She asked about his visit with the priest. "I don't know why," he told her, "but I agreed to sing Mass tomorrow morning."

Amala nodded and smiled. Simon wasn't sure she understood. They spent the day cleaning and mending their clothing. Amala sorted their supplies. "We have food for two days," she said.

Bent over his cloak, needle in hand, Simon nodded. "I'll see if the priest can give us some bread and cheese tomorrow."

They spent a little of their salt that day buying fresh tunics. Simon replaced Amala's bloodied vest with a green kirtle and bought her two new chemises. She insisted on wearing leggings like his. "We match, yes?"

Simon shook his head. "Something not proper, you in a man's garb. But I suppose it is more practical for travel." She opened her arms and bowed. Simon scratched his chin. "It's too warm to wear our cloaks, but I think we should have hats."

They picked out two round burlets with jaunty crowns that draped to one side. Amala tucked most of her orange nimbus beneath the rolled fabric ring and turned to show it off. "You like?"

"I think we look like a pair of mummers come for a festival. Maybe in Venice, we will fit in."

Simon returned to Ponteventi Church and borrowed a psalter to practice for the next morning. Kyrie, Gloria, Credo, Sanctus, Benedictus, and Agnus Dei, each verse had been annotated with letters and rough scribbles. They might have been notes. He tried to remember how they went. As he read, his life as an acolyte of the ancient St. Peter's Basilica came back to Simon in waves of memory and pain.

Singing a few lines, the claw in his chest clamped down, crushing the breath from him. Simon tried again, tried to wrap himself in the beauty of the music. A line, then another, like breathing fire, the words burned in his throat. He completed nine repetitions of Kyrie and moved on to Gloria, shouting against the pain.

Finishing Gloria, he stopped. Sweat ran from his brow. He gasped and trembled. A creak of floorboards made him turn. Amala. She stood by the empty altar table, mouth half open. "So beautiful. But why?"

"It is a battle, my love. A war I must fight. A foe I must defeat before it destroys me." He put a hand to his chest. "This I can overcome but not without pain."

Amala drifted back. A shadow in the sunlit doorway, she paused. "Be careful, *Seimon*."

He turned once more to the psalter. Credo, Simon read it aloud, gagging at the words. He moved on, not singing, just speaking. Finally reaching Agnes Dei, he finished with "...*dona nobis pacem*."

Panting, dragging air into his chest, Simon chanted the verses, forcing his way through them. Once more, he repeated the process, singing this time. He looked up from the psalter to see Father Giallo standing at the front of the nave. The old man nodded. "You have a strong voice, but I sense something troubles you, constrains you." He approached Simon. "We have a little time before evening vespers. If I take your confession, it may free you from these doubts."

"Vespers?" Simon glanced out the church door. Shadows had already crossed the street outside. "I didn't know it was that late. Maybe after Mass tomorrow." He bolted for the door. "Tomorrow. I will be here... promise." Simon fled.

Once outside, breathing felt somehow easier. *Why in the nine levels of hell did I ever agree to that?* He hustled back to the stable.

Wearing only her tunic and leggings, Amala stood in the stable yard brushing Epona. Simon watched for a moment. She didn't turn around but said, "You like?"

"Me and half the town if they saw you here. Don't be too comfortable—it's dangerous, and we can't stay."

She backed away from the horse and turned. "You defeat foe?"

"Maybe for today. I don't know. There is something wrong, either the church or the priest. Maybe I'm just too close to my past. We leave tomorrow, right after Mass."

"At market I get cheese. You like meat, yes? I get some. *Muka* too."

"Muka?" Simon cocked his head.

"Look, look..." Amala led him back to the stable where they had cached their gear. "Muka." She displayed a bag of coarse brown flour. "For lateen, yes?"

"Yes, well, no." Simon tried to resolve the confusion. It was one word he hadn't been able to explain. Amala grinned at him. He tried again, then stopped. "You're teasing me. You've been teasing me all along."

"My lateen is better now." She laughed and darted for the ladder.

Simon followed her to the loft. Empty. He spun about and looked up. A pair of pigeons eyed him a moment before bursting out through a window in a flurry of rattling wings and stray feathers. A soft giggle from behind. Simon turned and saw the bedding move. That's when he smelled the lavender.

When morning broke, Simon clad himself in new breechclout, tunic, and leggings. He rolled his knife belt and the rest of his gear in his cloak. Amala had packed their food and bedding. Epona waited nearby, fed and bridled. Simon heaved the saddle on her back. "We pack everything," he said. "I want to leave as soon as Mass is over."

Amala wore her tunic and vest. Simon still wasn't sure about her leggings. He helped lash their supplies behind the saddle and tie their rolls of bedding and clothing on top. "We've spent half our salt. I hope we find another of your Dwellers soon."

She finished tying their bundles on her side of the horse. "Where?"

"I don't know. Look for strings or something. We'll cross the river here and follow it south." Simon checked around for any forgotten items. "I feel like we've stayed in one place too long."

Nearby, the church bell began its clangorous call to Mass. Simon looked at Epona and then at Amala. "I don't like leaving her here like this."

Amala took the reins. "I stay with horse outside. You defeat foe. We leave."

Father Giallo met Simon at the side of the church. He didn't seem to notice Amala loitering at the main entrance. Out of breath, the old man wheezed. "I feared you wouldn't come."

Simon followed him through a narrow priest's entrance. "I gave my word."

Nodding, muttering to himself, Father Giallo kept glancing into the shadows behind the altar. Satisfied with something, he scowled out at the gathering congregation. "Look at them," he said. "Come to bow and be shriven. They drag their own iniquities in like mud on their boots. No amount of bread and wine will ever wash them clean."

To Simon, the crowd looked no worse than any others. The old priest muttered something to himself then tugged his arm. "I'm sorry now I talked you into this. Leave if you want to." When Simon refused, he continued. "Very well. I will perform the convocation. You will then chant Kyrie while I swing the censer. We have a visiting priest and his acolytes who will read the psalms."

Simon nodded. "Afterward, I will sing Gloria. I remember the rest of the litany."

As he spoke, the bell pealed once more from the tower above. People had filled the nave, and some stood just beyond the wide double doors, waiting to get in. Simon looked out past their heads and caught a brief glimpse of a pale face beneath a large round burlet.

Muttering and shuffling, the crowd quieted as Father Giallo climbed to the pulpit. Little more than a wooden box fastened to one wall, it stood a full span above the chancel floor, requiring the old man to struggle up a flight of steps. While the priest began his invocation prayer, Simon tried to remain in the shadows. He listened to the old man's hoarse voice. Even in the small church, his words died without echo among the rafters above.

As the convocation rite ended, Simon waited in the hissing silence as Father Giallo lurched down the steps and appeared with a smoking censer. Swinging it on a silver chain, the old man paced out past the chancel into the nave. Simon fell in behind him and began to chant. *"Kyrie eleison, Christe eleison..."*

Nine repetitions, he counted the steps. When Father Giallo turned, Simon spun about and counted steps back to the apse. Even as the priest completed his rites, Simon saw a hooded figure step to a lectern below the pulpit. A moment of silence, shuffling, then a different voice picked up the morning psalm. A strong baritone, it filled the nave with resonant verses. Dark robe, deep hood, something about the man seemed familiar. Simon listened to the crisp, clear Latin words, wondering why he had even been asked to sing.

Once more in his pulpit, the priest stammered out a prayer of forgiveness. A question and response thing spoken in the local dialect. Simon barely understood any of it. He waited for the final mea culpa, allowed time for silence once more to fill the church, then stepped forward and sang. *"Gloria in excelsis Deo..."*

The barbs in his chest, the hidden claw, so absent for Kyrie, clamped down with a vengeance. He forced another breath. "...*Et in terra pax hominibus bonae voluntatis.*" The hooded man stepped from behind the lectern. Simon choked out another line. "*Laudamus... te.*"

Drawing a flat wooden box from his robe the man raised it above his head. Simon dropped to his knees, gagging and retching. The serpent brand on his chest felt like a knife flensing the skin from his ribs. Two other robed figures stepped forward and seized him by the arms. Hood back, head bald as an adder's skull, the man stretched his mouth into a lipless smile. "Simon deVia, long we have awaited this day."

Genoa

The third galley Yohan inspected looked no better than the first two—its oars notched by wear against the tholepins, its rigging frayed and bleached by the sun. Yohan stepped from thwart to wale, then crossed a narrow plank to the quay. He tried to recall the galley master's name. The man approached, heavy arms, black beard. *Paolu Niru, that was it.* He wore a knit skullcap and a short jacket of Genoa blue linen. Yohan knew the type and approved.

"So, my *Bedda*, she is beautiful, no?"

Yohan ran his eye over the galley's lines. Ballasted down and flooded with water to keep her planks and oakum wet, she wallowed in the long swell entering the harbor. On the positive side, he noted the large afterdeck extending out past the stern. Yohan came right to the point. "I have six bound for Palermo. What do you charge?"

Master Paolu shrugged. "We talk conditions—maybe over ale?"

"The place on Via Damiano? You may know it." Yohan nodded toward a narrow street. "The brewer there has passable meat pies. It's early, but perhaps you are hungry."

Yohan led the way. As he had invited, so would he pay. *All for the good.* They entered an ancient structure, smelling of yeast and must. It huddled against the old city wall, just west of the port. The proprietor bowed and led them both to a shaded terrazza behind the building. Yohan gestured for Paolu to sit and found a bench of his own behind a small round table.

The proprietor returned bearing a pitcher, two bowls, and a board of sliced pastry. Paolu looked down at the table, then up at the proprietor's retreating back. "*Sc'chiatta*. How you know this place?"

"We are bound for Palermo, home of the best sc'chiatta in Sicily. I believe you are going that direction as well." Yohan poured them each some ale and raised his bowl. "To safe voyaging."

Paolu tasted the meat pie and took a sip of his ale. "You are not Sicilian. How you know sc'chiatta?"

"Palermo is now my home. Our company of six would travel there on your ship. When can you leave, and what do you charge?"

Finishing his bowl, Paolu poured himself another. He looked up, ticked off a few things on his fingers, and said, "Liccu glutton rowers eat too much, cost too much. Factor pays nothing for cargo." He took another drink. "Nothing. How I hire rowers for nothing?"

Yohan let him talk. Paolu would tire of complaining soon and name a ridiculous price. The shipmaster ate another piece of sc'chiatta and went on about port fees and the cost of sailcloth. "I am a fool," he said, "but for ten gold genovino, I take each."

"Thirty gold bezants for all of us, half in advance."

Paolu jumped up, spilling his ale. "Is you who are pazzu, crazy. It cost me that to feed such gluttons."

"We bring our own food and bedding, but we must have space on the afterdeck."

"You are the Pope now, too good you eat with honest men, too poor you pay honest cost." Paolu spat on the ground. "I charge you more even to row on benches."

Yohan remained seated. He poured himself another bowl of ale. "Thirty bezants is more gold than you will earn the entire rest of your voyage. Think about it while I talk with the other shipmasters."

"Forty then, twenty in advance. We leave tomorrow at dawn."

Yohan put five gold coins on the table. "These now, fifteen at the dock, the rest on arrival in Palermo."

Master Paolu returned to his seat and poured the remaining ale into his bowl. "We make this very profitable trip, sè? Forty barrels of good Piedmont wine and one hundred bolts of best Genoa linen." He rubbed the coarse material of his jacket. "You know they call this? Is famous Genoa blue. Maybe you want to buy into my voyage. Make you rich."

Yohan shook his head. "Maybe I buy us another pitcher of ale and some more food... sè?"

He spent a little more time with Master Paolu, bought him a third pitcher of ale, and took his leave. *His galley should have little trouble reaching Palermo in one piece. Beyond that would be its master's problem.* Yohan was more concerned with his companions' reactions when he revealed his entire plan.

That first evening out of Padova, Ruslana had pressured him to name their destination. Ramon and Carla had backed her up, saying, "If something happens, we all need to know where we are going."

Yohan had answered that their destination was still Rome, but that put no one off. "Very well," he'd said. "I'm not sure myself, so I will ask you. We could journey south and cross the central mountains west into Rome."

Ruslana objected. "The thieves and bands of marauders would cut you down before you reached the fields of Avezzano."

"But not you?"

"I would travel west, up the Po River and cross the mountains south into Genoa."

"I know Genoa," Luca said. "Maybe have friends, sè?"

With the discussion going the way he'd hoped, Yohan held his mouth. Nodding in agreement, Ramon said, "I have family from there. It is safe, and the Genoese, they do not love the Venetians."

Stephan had raised the only objection. "That road will take twice as long. Can our Weaver not spirit us through the mountains somehow?"

Yohan had expected sarcasm from Ruslana. Instead, she lowered her eyes. "Time was, we could expect help from our brothers, the Apostoli Lucis—but that was long ago. Since then, they have turned their backs on knowledge, seeking only power in its place."

"Cazzo Apostles." Luca gestured with his fist. "We visit Genoa instead, sè?"

Their ride through the Po valley had taken twice as long as Yohan expected. They had to travel west as far as the walled city of Cremona before crossing the river. Another full moon had come and gone before the riders wound their way down through the mountains into the port city of Genoa.

Yohan thought out their next moves while walking back from Genoa's waterfront. He followed a narrow alley on the next street that led to their hostel. Ramon had negotiated a large room on the second floor. The only two other rooms had been vacant. Yohan found the privacy an unexpected bonus.

Ruslana will be a problem, as will Luca. He walked through the conversation in his mind. *Or maybe not.* Yohan continued down the alley and stopped at a whitewashed door. The old proprietor bowed as he entered. Climbing a steep flight of steps, he ducked through a low doorway only to be confronted by Carla. "Your factor must think she's royalty."

"You mean she doesn't like sleeping with us."

"Or eating, or talking…"

Ramon laughed from the far side of the room. "Or farting. You fart like a goat, Carla. I almost slept in the hall last night."

"I wish you had. You stink like a pig, Corsican. You shit your breechclout and wash it once a year." Carla spun and pointed at Luca. "And him, he plays with himself all night. Don't you ever sleep?"

"I dream of you, sweet rabbit." He flicked a dagger across the room. Yohan heard it thump into the door behind Carla.

Ramon said, "It isn't me that stinks. It's that dung hole of a latrine at the end of the hall. It hasn't been emptied since antiquity."

Yohan held up both hands. "Enough. I may have some good news." He paused until the bickering quieted. "We leave tomorrow."

"Cazzo rabbit leaves today. Maybe we catch up, maybe no."

Stephan chose that moment to duck into the room. "We leave? Excellent, I've fed and watered our horses. I'll get my gear."

Carla pulled the knife from the door and stuck it in the floorboards between Luca's feet. "Tomorrow, the man says, if we haven't killed each other first."

"What did I miss?"

"Our next decision," Yohan looked out the door, then closed it. "We have some choices about how we ride south."

Carla said, "We ride now, and without our prissy little factor."

Yohan nodded. "That's one choice. Brother Luca would like that, back to just one witch in the company."

Carla didn't take the bait, so he continued. "I think Ruslana would prefer it that way as well, but we need her with us to cash that letter."

"I think our leader has something else in mind," Stephan said. "Out with it. Why tomorrow? Why not yesterday?"

"We take a galley south…"

"Merda! No. Not mafankulo boat."

"…to Palermo."

Luca had been spinning his dagger and slipping it from hand to hand. He stopped. The dagger disappeared into its sheath. He squinted at Ramon and Carla. "Maybe annoys màgaru factor, sè?"

Yohan nodded. "That's what I fear. She won't agree."

"She doesn't have to agree," Carla said. "Just follow. I assume we go to Rome eventually?"

"After we secure our gold in Palermo, we can journey to Rome and cash our…"

The door burst open, and Ruslana stormed in. "You bastard. You treacherous lying pirate bastard."

"Ya, we were just talking about you."

She glared around the room. "He's hired a galley. Did he tell you?"

Stephan nodded. "Well, yes. In a way, yes… and we agreed."

"You too, Luca? You agreed? I wouldn't say you enjoyed that last boat ride."

"I live on island—I ride boat, no?"

"And Rome?" She turned to Yohan. "You told me you were going to Rome."

"And we are, after Palermo. I never said we wouldn't stop first."

Ruslana stepped closer and pushed a finger into Yohan's chest. "If I didn't know you were just a big *ushkuinik* lout, I would say you'd planned this." She turned to the others. "Understand, this river pirate has manipulated all of you."

Stephan shrugged. "Yohan is our leader. That's what he does."

Ruslana swung about the room, looking for support. Finding none, she snorted and left. Ramon shut the door behind her. "Now I can truly look forward to this trip."

Yohan gave Carla and Stephan the task of selling their horses. "Saddles, tack, everything. We can hire a wagon to take our gear to the docks." He set Luca to buying their supplies. "Food for ten days, and water. No, make that small beer instead, nothing stronger. Ramon will stay here and guard our treasury."

"And *reghi*, king pirate, what he does? Sleep?"

"I intend to discover what our factor is about while she is away."

Yohan waited until the others scattered. He nodded to Ramon, then slipped out behind them. *Perhaps a futile effort. The woman could become invisible if she wished.* He played with a few thoughts. *She is nearby.* She must have followed him to the docks. *Invisible until she wants to be seen.*

Waiting at the foot of the stairs, he watched Luca's form disappear down the alley. *She can't watch all of us. What would I do in her place?* Yohan waved to their proprietor and stepped out the door. He looked up and down the alley. Nothing moved. *She could damage the galley.*

He didn't think that likely. *Too overt for a Weaver.* Yohan followed Luca toward the central merchant district. *She might hire someone to do it.* That seemed more her style. *But in a city of seafarers, who would dare attack another's boat?* He'd wandered almost two versts before it struck him.

Cursing, Yohan turned and dashed back. *The gold.* He slapped his side, knowing he'd left his weapons with Ramon. Racing through the city, he brushed past outraged pedestrians and leapt over gutters running with filth. Rounding the corner, he sprinted up the alley and stopped at the open door.

Just inside, blood pooled beneath the proprietor's body. Yohan took the stairs two at a time. In their room he heard arguing, punctuated by the crash of upturned furniture. The door opened with a push. Five men turned to face him. Yohan pulled it shut and stepped back. The door flew open and a figure stepped out. Mailed vest, black leather gambeson, sword, Yohan charged from the hall and flung him down the stairs.

Another came right behind. Dodging the sword thrust, Yohan ducked low, caught the man by the crotch, and threw him over the handrail. Sword leveled, a third intruder eased out into the hall. Given no choice, Yohan retreated down the steps. He glanced over his shoulder. A dark figure struggled to its feet and climbed toward him.

The man above held his sword at ready and didn't move. *Their leader. His subordinate will do the dirty work.* Something bothered him. *Why still here?* Yohan looked over the handrail. *Too far to jump.* He glanced up. *Why wreck the furniture?* Understanding came in a flash. Yohan spread his arms. "Kill me, and you will never see that gold."

Counting to ten, he waited. A nod. The leader grunted and stepped back. Hands open, palms bared, Yohan climbed. He reached the top before a blow from behind knocked him to his knees. Vomiting cheap wine and sc'chiatta, Yohan was dragged into the room. A rope around his ankle bent his leg back and ended in a noose about his neck.

Laying on his side, his calf cramped. The room blurred. He arched his back, but the noose stayed tight. A voice in his ear. "You killed my man. I will break your knees."

Choking, Yohan said, "Have to walk. Have to show."

"The gold, yes. Just tell us, and I kill you quickly."

"In the lobby. Have to show."

Voices. Yohan may have passed out for a time. He awoke to a knife against his throat. "You lie. Nothing in the lobby but two dead men."

They will kill me now—nothing I can do. Yohan had no idea where Ramon might have hidden the gold. He would be dead anyway. Waiting, leg cramping, an eternity passed until the noose tightened, then fell away. "You go to the lobby now. I see gold, or you shit blood until you die."

Yanked up by his arms, Yohan staggered into the hall and turned. His captor pointed toward the stairs. "Walk."

Reaching the top, Yohan looked down. The proprietor and the dead intruder sprawled on the floor below. A shove to the back sent Yohan plunging after them. Tumbling, grabbing, he struck his head and rolled to the bottom.

Draped across the proprietor's corpse, pressure against his thigh, a sword. He looked up at a tall figure, broad shoulders, long sandy hair tied behind his head. "Move before I cut off your dick."

Two others followed down the stairs, clumping as they came. A fourth remained on the landing. *Just tell him now. Get it over with.* Yohan wondered how far he could string them along.

He raised up on his elbows. "I'll show you. Then do it... quickly."

The tall man twitched his sword. "Up."

Yohan eased back. The sword followed him as he stood. *Where? Someplace plausible...* As Yohan regained his balance, he heard a commotion on the stairs—a scream of pain and a falling body. That moment of distraction was all he needed to bat the sword away and hurl himself at the tall intruder. Gouging was not allowed in pankration. It didn't stop Yohan from blinding his opponent. Coming up with sword in hand, Yohan slashed the man's throat and charged the stairs. A clash of weapons echoed down from the landing. *Ramon still lived.*

Scrambling over a lifeless corpse, Yohan didn't hesitate to jam his sword into the back of the nearest fighter. When the other turned, Ramon slashed his hamstring. Yohan finished the job. For a moment, they stared at each other across the bloody corpses. Gasping, Ramon settled to his knees. "I thought I was dead."

Still dizzy and nauseated, Yohan steadied himself against the wall. "I thought you were too, brother. Your timing was good—they almost had me."

"I heard them arguing with our host. Is he...?"

"Dead, ya."

From the entrance, they heard, "*Santo cazzo Madre di Cristo!*"

Ramon nodded. "Luca is back."

Yohan left him to start cleaning up and met Luca at the foot of the stairs. "We had visitors."

"Bastardos. All dead?"

"All dead. Ramon is unhurt, but our proprietor was killed."

"And you, like merda you look."

"I will live. We have to get these bodies out of here."

Yohan looked down at their former host. *Never even knew his name.* He and Luca dragged the man back to his modest apartment. The other four, they hauled up the stairs and dumped in their room. Ramon helped pile the bodies. "We can't stay here."

Cutting a rag from one of the intruder's bloody tunics, Yohan wiped the hall floor. "Do you think we can clean this up?"

Ramon took over that job while Yohan and Luca did what they could to clean the entry way. Luca cursed to himself as he worked. "Cazzo housemaid."

Yohan said, "Forget it." He ducked through the door and gathered a handful of dirt from the road. "Spread this on the worst spots. As soon as we are all together, we go."

By the time Carla returned, they had covered most of the blood. She gave them a questioning look. Yohan said, "We had a little trouble."

"You look like shit."

Stephan stepped inside. He glanced around, then dashed up the stairs. Carla's eyes followed him up. "Anybody we know?"

"No, and maybe yes. Upstairs—we should talk."

Yohan latched the door and followed them up.

Although their room occupied nearly half the second floor, it felt crowded with six dead bodies stacked against the wall. Ramon had cleared some of the broken furniture. Yohan eyed their scattered gear. "One question. Our gold, where did you hide it?"

Ramon put his hands behind his back and danced from foot to foot. "You don't want to know."

Carla sniffed the air. "I would ask, where did you hide yourself?"

"You don't want to know that either."

"*Santa merda*, is not true?"

Carla shut her eyes. "Tell me our gold isn't in the latrine."

"If you need to go, use the hole on the left."

Strokes

Three spans wide and five long, the afterdeck covered almost a third of their galley and hung a span off the stern. From his position at the back, the shipmaster trimmed his steering oar and scanned the far horizon. Yohan sat on a bundle of gear, watching the shore crawl by. He pretended inattention but kept an eye on Ruslana. Their factor leaned against the opposite rail and looked everywhere but at her traveling companions.

A few more bezants had persuaded Master Paolu to wait that morning until Ruslana appeared. Luca was convinced that she had sent the intruders. "Cazzo màgaru works for Vendini bastardos."

"At first, I thought so too," Yohan said. "But our visitors weren't her style."

Carla had leaned in. "And what *is* her style, ushkuinik?"

"Mummers, sneak thieves, she would send a woman with a sick child to distract Ramon while an accomplice slipped in through the window."

"She was the only one who knew..."—Carla looked around and lowered her voice—"...knew about the gold."

"Besides us, you mean. There have been other ears than hers on the road. One of us might have said something at the wrong time."

Carla had shaken her head but didn't argue. They waited while the galley bumped against the quay, its master fidgeted, and the rowers sat mumbling at their benches. Ruslana didn't arrive until after the sun had cleared the eastern hills. Yohan managed to convince the others not to confront her. Luca had said nothing but spent all morning scowling and mumbling. Ramon and Carla avoided her. Polite but terse, Stephan helped load her travel kit on the afterdeck.

Ruslana cornered Yohan as they boarded. "Why the cold treatment?"

"You're late. You cost the master daylight, and you cost us some gold."

"If you had stayed longer at the hostel, you would have been late too. I couldn't get near for all the soldiers. They held me there until morning when I slipped away."

"We had some trouble. You should have stayed with us."

"I stayed with a friend, a sister who was glad to see me. Not this pack of squabbling children I am condemned to follow."

"You've never tried to be a member of our company, only an expensive guest."

"And you've never treated me like anything more than baggage. When did you once include me in your decisions, ushkuinik?"

"When would you have ever followed our lead if we had? Seven men died last night, one of them was our host. The others were armed marauders, thieves looking for our gold."

Ruslana stared down at the water. "So now you blame me. You think I sent them, is that it?"

"Well did you, Weaver?"

"You think I didn't."

"I think you tried something... something more subtle, but the others arrived first and pissed in your ale pot. You were late because you had to clean up some mess of your own devising. That's what I think."

She'd said nothing in response and turned away, finding a place on the opposite rail. Yohan had watched the mooring ropes snake in from the quay, the oars run out, and the lines of rowers bend to their work. Master Paolu had shouted invectives from the helm in Sicilian so heavily accented that Yohan understood none of it. He was only glad that, stroke by stroke, Genoa harbor, the soldiers, the marauders, the Vendinis, and a long road from Krakow vanished in their wake.

Three days out, the island of Elba passed low and cloudy on the horizon. Their galley rounded a rocky headland, and its master swung his steering oar to port. They slewed east, headed into a large cove. Their small square sail rattled against the mast while Yohan and Ramon helped the crew bring it down and secure it along the center aisle.

One of the rowers took the helm while Master Paolu leaned over the side, watching the sea. "It is shallow, then deep," he said. "We watch for sand."

With a grunt, he swung down from the afterdeck and scrambled forward. Gestures, shouts, the galley swung north, then east again. Master Paolu leaned over the bow, straightened, and pointed at the beach. They headed straight in. Yohan clung to the rail as the galley rose on a low wave and grounded against the sand. Four men dropped from the bow, splashed ashore, and strung lines to a cluster of rocks high above the waves.

The master worked his way back to the stern. "This the only chance my men get to stand, to walk, sè? Seven days tomorrow, they row."

Ruslana said, "I will go ashore as well."

"Is not so safe, madonna…"

Yohan interrupted. "I will go with her."

"Your choice, ushkuinik. Just don't get in my way."

He'd stowed his leggings and cloak when they boarded the galley. Yohan had only to don a belt and knife sheath before they left. Ruslana seemed to prefer traveling in a knee-length kirtle. She rolled it up and tucked it into her belt. Luca ignored her, but she caught Yohan's eye. "What are you looking at?"

"Nothing I haven't seen before, Weaver." He waved toward the beach. "Shall we go?"

Ruslana traipsed along the rowers' benches, drawing stares and low comments from the men. Hand on the hilt of his dagger, Yohan grinned at them as he passed. Cargo had been stowed below the afterdeck and forward, behind the bow. Ruslana climbed on the barrel heads, scrambled over the forward bulwark, and dropped a half span to the surging water. Yohan followed.

A small contingent of rowers had already made it ashore. The woman stopped to watch them prowl the beach. "I hope your Master Paolu expects his crew to return."

"They get hungry enough, they'll return. Besides, if they don't complete the voyage, they don't get paid."

"And you, oh Knight of Palermo, when do you get paid?"

"Every day I draw breath in the company of free men and women. Every day I use my sword to protect others. I get paid every day, Weaver, when I can sit for an honest meal with friends who call me brother."

"And all that gold, it means nothing to you?"

Yohan waded up on the beach and pointed eastward, along the curving shore. "Let's walk."

Ruslana left her kirtle rolled up and splashed at the water's edge. "There was a time, you know, that you would have taken that money yourself."

"There was, and I did. About the third time I escaped hanging or worse, I realized that it wasn't the gold I wanted—it was the passion for life it gave me."

She took his arm. "We can still be friends. I might have betrayed you once… or twice in the past, but I won't betray you now."

Yohan kept silent on that. Weavers had loyalty only to themselves. "So what would you do with the gold?"

"Do you mean the scrips we carry to Palermo or the bullion we will receive in Rome?"

"Either. What would the Weavers do with it?"

Ruslana thought on her answer. "That's two different questions. If it were just me, I might buy a vineyard somewhere, become a Dweller."

"You couldn't have both. To become a Dweller, you would have to remain a Weaver. In that case, it wouldn't be just you."

"The sisters might support me on that."

"If they didn't need the money to buy a favor or if they didn't prefer that you remain a Traveler. Besides, I can picture you tied to a winery maybe for, what, two months? No, we're both creatures of the road."

She tightened her hold on his arm. "Here we go, arguing again. Can we just be honest with each other, at least for the afternoon?"

"Very well, Weaver. You go first. What is it you really want?"

"Your side trip to Palermo has upset quite a few plans. Can we just go to Rome first?"

"No. Already marauders have killed for what little gold we have. Jacob, Cernak, both dead. I nearly died, Ramon too. Over two dozen brigands and thieves lay scattered between here and Krakow. In Palermo, we will place the gold in safekeeping and strengthen our company."

"And you know that your friend Simon is not dead as well?"

Yohan lowered his eyes and shook his head. "I don't know. I pray he is well. I pray he is free of his curse."

"Well, he won't be, unless I can get to Rome in time."

Yohan shook his arm free and backed away. "You know something? Out with it, Weaver."

"All I know, the last any of us heard, is that he passed over the mountains on his way to Rome."

"And he's safe? Tell me he is safe."

"His Apostoli Lucis brothers tread close on his heels. It all hangs in a precarious balance."

"What balance could possibly be so precarious that one boy wandering the wilderness matters to either the Weavers or the Apostles?"

Ruslana looked over her shoulder and seized Yohan's arm. "Keep walking. I've already said too much."

He looked back as well. A few others had wandered their direction. She scowled and walked another hundred paces. Glancing back again, she said, "I don't think it will hurt..." Ruslana paused, eyes to the sand. "It won't hurt for you to know that Simon's Master Jacob was not ben Reuben. He was just what he claimed, a fur trader. Jacob of Tver, as he was called, once traded as far south as Rome. I don't know how he found Simon, whether he rescued him or kidnapped him, but he kept him safe and never returned south of Vienna."

Yohan walked at her side, listening. Like some enormous crumbling edifice, the pattern was there, but major pieces were missing. "Tell me more of Simon."

"I cannot. You know I've broken my oath already. I must trust you with what I've given you."

Looking back at the western horizon, Yohan said, "We've walked far enough tonight. It's getting late. We should return, ya?"

"And Rome?"

"You trusted me, now I'll trust you. In two days, we reach Trajan's harbor at the mouth of the Tiber River. From there, I will see that you make it to Rome."

"Then I'll share one more confidence, ushkuinik. Jacob ben Reuben was Simon's father. He is in Rome even now, as we speak."

Returning to the beached galley, Yohan found Luca feeding sticks to a small fire. He looked up from the tiny flame. "Does cazzo màgaru bring firewood?"

Ruslana answered back in a rapid burst of Sicilian that Yohan didn't follow. She spat in the sand next to him. "I hear your filthy mouth, sè?"

Luca jumped up, but Yohan stepped between them. "Luca, you asked for that. Ruslana, we need more firewood."

Luca signed against the evil eye and sat. Ruslana clenched a thumb between her fingers and held up a fist. Yohan nodded to her. "Welcome to the Fellowship, sister."

The following morning, they left. Dragging the galley from the beach with kedge anchors set the day before, the rowers backed oars and let each succeeding wave lift them off the sand. Yohan and the others helped draw on the anchor ropes while Master Paolu shouted down to the rowers. They stowed the kedges on the aft rail just as the sun cleared the eastern hills.

Canvas rattled against the mast. Yohan turned to watch the sail rise from the deck, tighten, then pivot to catch the morning breeze. Luca handed out loaves he'd baked the night before, filled with soft cheese and dried meat. Ruslana sat, her back against the rail, not quite aloof, not quite fitting in. Yohan watched her and the others for a while. *It's the best I'm likely to get.*

The sun stood well above the horizon by the time they'd cleared the cove and once again turned south. Yohan waved Ruslana over and gathered the others at the forward end of the deck. He started without preamble. "We have a change of plans." Luca muttered something and Carla raised one eyebrow. Yohan continued. "Our factor must debark at the mouth of the Tiber and travel ahead of us to Rome."

Carla said, "And we'll never see her again."

Ramon nudged her shoulder. "That will upset you?"

"If we come all the way back to stinking Rome with that worthless letter and she's disappeared, damned right I'll be upset."

"That won't happen," Yohan said, "because I am going with her."

Ruslana snapped around. "You are not. I never agreed to that."

"I never asked, and I'm not asking now. You will go as our factor, and I will carry the letter of credit. For a small fee, Banko Grigorio will agree to store our gold until Stephan and the others return with reinforcements."

"Cazzo bastardos cut your throat and keep gold."

"That's why I'm taking you with us, Luca. I know how much you love Rome."

Carla snorted, then apologized. Ramon shook his head. "I still don't like it. We shouldn't divide our strength."

"It's the only way." Yohan put a hand on Stephan's shoulder. "You lead the cohort from here. Offer our master Paolu more gold if he can return you all in less than fourteen days."

It required another five bezants before Yohan could convince the shipmaster to make a call at the Trajan's harbor. "Is nest of pirates," he complained. "They eat us like sugar cakes."

Yohan had listened to the tirade, then offered the bezants. *Gold, the language of traders everywhere.* Two days later, he, Ruslana, and Luca stood on a quay of crumbling marl and watched the little galley back oars and pivot toward the sea. Yohan wore his sword and mail under his cloak but left his helmet with the others. Luca was similarly attired, but Ruslana wore only her kirtle and cloak. She turned to Yohan. "I can travel in secret, but you two draw trouble like old meat draws flies."

"Never fear, Weaver. I will find a way to get us into Rome without drawing too much attention. First, we need to find a place for the night."

She pinched her lips and glared at Luca. "I have a place, but I'm not sure it's suitable." She turned and poked Yohan in the chest. "You will be responsible for his behavior and your own."

"We are both honorable Knights, dear woman. If you know of a refuge in this dismal place, then please, lead us to it."

Yohan remembered Trajan's harbor and the decaying port city of Ostia from earlier visits, not all of them friendly. Ruslana led them through an abandoned warehouse and paused at a brick alcove. Yohan signed for Luca to watch their backs while Ruslana pawed through a mound of knotted cords. "Our luck holds," she said. "My friend is here."

Darting through a back entrance, she disappeared down a narrow, over-grown path. Large trees leaned between the tumbled stones and bricks of an ancient city. Vines hung from broken walls and waved like curtains across vacant windows. Yohan hustled to catch up. "Where in all this ruin are you taking us?"

"Old Ostia is less than a verst from here. My friend maintains a house near the river."

Yohan followed without comment. He didn't really care where they stayed, and anywhere near the river port suited his plans. Luca caught up with them. "Cazzo bugs." He swatted his arms. "Worse than mafankulo thieves."

Ruslana stopped him. "Quiet, we're almost there. Remember, this is a house of peace and tranquility, so watch your mouth."

Yohan pushed through a hedge and followed the woman down a rutted street. She led him past a gate and stopped before a white marble doorway. Well kept, clean, the entrance had been swept. Ruslana turned and gave them each a warning glare before knocking. The door opened a crack. She spoke with someone in low tones. Yohan couldn't hear the conversation. *Luca's damned bugs or no*, he thought. *We could have just stayed in the warehouse.* He surveyed the area, looked for places a man could hide, looked for exit routes. He gazed up at the lintel above the massive wooden door. Scribed in the smooth gray marble, he read, "*Templum Veneris.*"

He nudged Luca when Ruslana turned and beckoned them in. Passing through the doorway, Yohan came face to face with an older woman. Long gray hair woven and knotted into a crown on her head, diaphanous white robe, short blue vest trimmed in gold, "Welcome to the Temple of Venus," she said.

Luca entered last. He checked the doorway behind them, poked around a pair of marble statues, and said, "*Meràculu*, is bordello, sè?"

The woman ignored Luca and addressed Ruslana. "You did not explain my establishment to your attendants?"

Yohan stepped up. "This woman is in my employ as factor in a certain negotiation. Beyond that"—he glanced back—"she has explained very little."

Ruslana put a hand on his arm. "Perhaps Sister Aurissa can show you around. She is a member of my order—we have no secrets."

Their tour was short. The Temple of Venus consisted mostly of small apartments, a dining hall, and an enormous bathhouse. "We have a meditation garden out behind," the woman said. "Many of our patrons are there now."

Yohan saw some of her patrons, mostly women of various ages. He passed a few men as well, all quite young. Well-muscled, they could have been soldiers. Catching Aurissa watching, he said, "Not a bordello, but not a convent either."

She nodded. "This temple is a safe place where women of Rome come to relax."

Luca glanced at the bathhouse. "And men?"

"A select few—only by invitation."

"Bastardos lucky, sè?"

"Until today, there have been no Sicilians."

"Or ushkuiniki either," Ruslana said. "Especially stinking filthy ones."

Yohan ignored her jibe. "We are few but not very select." He nodded toward Ruslana. "None of us. But we could use a rest if you can accommodate us."

Aurissa showed him to a small apartment with two pallets and a washstand. "I would ask you to use our bathhouse before you do anything else. Leave your clothing at the entrance, and I'll have it washed."

Relaxing in the large pool of hot water, Yohan closed his eyes and considered his next moves. Luca had jumped in, splashed about, and dragged himself out, announcing that he was off in search of food. Less concerned with food than with their trip into Rome, Yohan worked through a variety of scenarios. They could walk, take the back trails. The city walls were lightly guarded. They could slip through one of the lesser gates.

He settled deeper into the water. *Someone knows too much of our movements. They will watch the gates.* He considered riding a farm wagon. For a gold bezant, any farmer would take the three of them into the city. *Gold always attracts attention.* Besides, he needed something the Weavers and the Apostles wouldn't have considered.

Yohan had almost dozed off when water slopped over his face. Spluttering, he sat up and wiped his eyes. Ruslana had slid into the bath next to him. She grinned. "You looked lonely."

Small breasts, trim, she'd barely changed over the years since he'd last seen her... been with her. *How long since he was with anyone?* This close, the tiny wrinkles at the corners of her eyes showed as did the creases across her forehead. Her hip touched his. He felt her hand on his knee. "I thought people came here to relax," Yohan said...

"Women do... men, no."

They had the bathhouse to themselves. Yohan wondered if Aurissa had arranged it that way—*Weavers.* "You know, this is a bad idea for reasons I don't have to explain."

She slid her hand up his leg. "Why don't I just wash your back? You won't even have to look at me."

Yohan turned and straddled the bench they shared. *Always give your quarry an easy way out, then strike when they take it.* He was too tired to resist. *And maybe I don't want to take the easy way out.* He felt her knee against his back as she turned to face him.

Ruslana started with his shoulders, rubbing the heavy muscles just below his neck, working her way down his back, kneading the ropy cords between his ribs. No longer washing, she ran her hands over his chest. Yohan started to object but she shushed him. "Sometimes you can't control everything, ushkuinik. Here, I'm in charge."

He let it happen. She leaned forward and wrapped her arms around his chest. Head against his neck, she whispered, "If I told you that I missed those times we had together, would you believe me?"

"For the sake of those times, I would let myself believe."

"Then turn around, ushkuinik. We have some catching up to do."

Tiber

Morning light glittered off the placid Tiber River. Yohan pulled on an oar. He ached in places that hadn't ached in a long time. Luca sat on the bench beside him, pulling the same oar. Glancing over, he grinned. "You are very clean this morning."

"I had some help, if that's what you are asking."

"Not ask. She is loud, sè? Entire cazzo house knows. Maybe across the river, they know too."

Yohan smiled at the thought. The person in question sat in the bow, ignoring them both. Ten others sat on benches fore and aft, pulling oars of their own. The idea had come to him in the night, relaxing on a comfortable bed in Ruslana's apartment. She'd called him ushkuinik and asked him to row the boat. In the dark room, lit only by a small candle, he'd complied... once more. But the idea stuck, and in the morning, he located a shipment of oil headed upriver.

As rowers, he and Luca would each receive ten copper *sestertii* on arrival in Rome. Yohan doubted anyone would notice two rowers. Ruslana claimed their kit as her own and paid with two nondescript silver coins for her passage. It being the dry season, the Tiber ran low and sluggish between its banks. Yohan saw nothing of the countryside beyond an endless string of marsh, broken only by the occasional rotting pier.

By midafternoon, he smelled the city, smoke, sewage, and fifty thousand unwashed bodies. It wasn't until early evening that they tied alongside the Tiber docks. Ruslana made a show of hiring them to carry her bags. "Come," she said. "I know another refuge we can use."

Luca slung his kit over one shoulder and hers over another. "Again, it is *paradisu* tonight."

"Paradise for a Sicilian, maybe. Wait and decide for yourself, but it's getting late, and we need to hurry."

Yohan didn't argue. Too many nights he'd fought the gangs that ruled Rome. Once away from the docks, he stopped to belt on his sword. Luca did the same. As he unrolled his kit, Yohan caught sight of another, smaller blade and scabbard. He bent for a second look. "What is that Luca?"

The Sicilian muttered something in response. Yohan asked again. Flipping back his blankets and spare clothing, Luca said, "Is half-sword of cretino diavulu." He made a show of rolling it back in his kit. "Boy maybe needs it."

"Simon is probably a thousand versts the other direction."

The nearby sound of fighting brought Yohan back to their present situation. Skeletal buildings, all columns and broken walls, threw long shadows across the road. Guttering flames licked between a cluster of brick ruins. He counted at least six figures lounging among the shacks and hovels. "Ya, best thing we move on."

Ruslana took them north, up a low valley between the hills. Men shouted in the distance; babies cried. She pointed to a broken silhouette limned against the western sky. "That was once the center of the world. Tonight, we sleep in its shadow."

She led them through a doorway hung with knotted cords, paused to run her hand over a few strands, then pulled them away. Yohan ducked inside. Barrels, black with age, wept droplets of wine almost as black as the barrels that held it. More refuge than paradisu, the shop sold bad wine and old bread. The entire space smelled of yeast and rotting fruit. Luca pressed against the wall, just inside the doorway, and nodded to Yohan. Ruslana pushed past them. "Donetta?"

A small, round woman of indeterminant age stepped from behind a wine tun. Dark hair, clean smock, she said, "Greetings, sister, I heard you were coming."

Donetta showed them through a narrow opening in the back to a small furnished room with a single pallet and two chairs. "I keep this for Travelers"—she gave Luca a sidelong look—"but seldom more than one."

Yohan glanced around the room and nodded. "Ya, Ruslana can take the cot. Luca and I will sleep on the floor. Is there another entrance?"

"Back the way you came in. The other door, it leads outside to a water butt and a latrine. You will have to share."

They ate dried fish from Ostia that night along with some of Donetta's bread and fruit. Yohan set a tallow candle on the only table. "Tomorrow, we visit Banko Grigorio, and after that, you, my factor, will be free of our company."

She tilted her head. "Is that what you want?"

"I thought it was what you wanted. The Weavers have set you to some urgent business here, or has that changed?"

"I can't say, and I won't say. But you will soon find that my business in Rome is critical to our plans, to your plans, and to so many others. Two, three days at most, and we will know."

Yohan sat back and gave her a cold smile. "My Weaver is back, as dark and silent as ever. It was fun, this past week, pretending to be friends again, pretending to share our secrets."

Ruslana jumped to her feet. "That's not fair. I have my vows, as you have yours. We work to the same goals, even if you can't understand that."

Luca rose and headed for the door. "If you two fight, I go visit the latrine. Is more musical I think."

Yohan shook his head. "I'm sorry. One more night, we should be able to maintain the peace for that long."

"Then what? After the bank, what will you do?"

"Luca and I will find a place to hide until the Knights arrive from Palermo. And you... you go to do whatever it is you do."

"What I do may take several days. Can we make the peace last that long?"

"You suggest we stay here?"

"No, we can't. We would kill each other. I can find us a better place, but you have to trust me."

"Like Luca trusts you?"

"He's all bluster, but I don't have to tell you that. One thing I can say"—Ruslana checked the doorway behind her—"Luca has good instincts.

He thinks of things that you haven't—trust him. That's all I can tell you, and it's too much, I fear."

Yohan considered her words as he made up his kit for the night. *She knows this city, better than I ever want to.* Her suggestion made some sense, even though he knew he was being used somehow. *It's a trap, it's another goddam trap.* He wandered out the back to visit the latrine and met Luca returning from a prowl. "Pazzu mafankulos, they try to rob me." He slapped his chest. "Me!"

"Is it safe to stay here?"

Luca nodded. "Sè, four dead bastardos say it is safe."

"We finish our business and leave tomorrow then."

"And your màgaru? What does she do?"

"What if she stays with us for a few more days?"

Luca grinned. "It makes you happy? She stays."

Yohan wasn't sure if it made him happy or not, but it might answer some questions. When he returned to their room, Ruslana had rolled herself in her blankets and turned toward the wall. Luca curled up against the opposite wall. Yohan blew out their candle. Lying awake in the darkness, he tried to plan for the next day. Noises in the night, soft footsteps, perhaps Donetta closing her shop. Drifting off, the barrels of wine almost smelled like lavender.

Daylight painted Rome in colors only slightly less bleak than the night before. Wagons trundled through the streets. Families walked or rode, and dozens of vendors, little more than tables and tents, sprang up throughout the ruins. Banko Grigorio occupied a small marble edifice just behind the next hill.

A hundred paces distant, Yohan stopped the three of them near a fruit seller's stall. "The morning is early still. I want to watch the traffic before we go walking in."

A few patrons entered and left. Four guards loitered around the doorway. A nearby church rang terce and still nothing had happened. Yohan touched Ruslana on the shoulder and passed her the locked letter of credit. "You take this and follow ten paces behind." He turned to Luca. "After she goes in, count to one hundred. If nothing happens, move up and guard the entrance."

Yohan tightened his sword belt, loosened his sword, and walked the short distance to Banko Grigorio. People passed. A dog barked. Ruslana's footsteps pattered behind him. He looked back—no one followed them. Reaching the entrance, the guards ignored him. He climbed three steps and halted. Christián Vendini stood blocking the doorway. "You have something that is ours."

Unholy Alliance

H and on his sword, Yohan backed down the steps. "So, you do speak the vulgate."

Christián's eyes never wavered. "And High Latin, and Greek, and even your dog's degenerate Sicilian when I must."

The guards once loitering about the entrance, now closed on Yohan. From behind, he heard Ruslana. "I'm sorry, ushkuinik, I truly am, but there was no other way."

Yohan didn't look back, didn't want to give her the satisfaction of seeing his face. "Why, Weaver?"

"You will learn soon enough. Just please, take your hand off the sword and don't try anything heroic."

Yohan glanced at the four guards. Mail, swords, bucklers, they held themselves with the confidence of seasoned fighters. "So it was you in Genoa then, ya?"

Christián brandished a slender dagger, spun it Sicilian style, and dropped it into a sheath at his belt. "I will not underestimate you again."

Yohan wiggled his sword loose and let it slide up a finger's width. *Where in holy hell is Luca?* Ruslana had read his thoughts. "You won't see your friend for a while. He has problems of his own."

Damnation, set up, set up again. He returned Christián's steady gaze. "I think I could kill you before your men cut me down. Should I try?"

"You should listen to the woman. She is smarter than you are."

Yohan let his sword slide back into its scabbard and dropped his hands to his sides. *Dead, I'm of no use to anyone.* "So, what comes next, Vendini? Remember, she is also smarter than you."

Pointing toward the river, Ruslana answered for him. "This way, and pray we are not too late."

She took off past the small square, back toward the Tiber. Yohan followed, ignoring the guards, hoping the Vendini kept his knife in its sheath. He opened his stride. Half a pace ahead of the others, Yohan was determined to maintain some show of control.

Hustling past a row of shops and impromptu markets, Ruslana led them to a stone bridge and stopped. Across the Tiber, the massive Castel Sant'Angelo loomed above the water, the ancient fortress now fallen into decay.

A young woman passed. Her hair tucked into an enormous burlet, wearing man's leggings, Yohan almost mistook her for a boy. She smiled and made a brief hand gesture as she went by. Ruslana didn't watch her go but rather scanned the hills behind them.

Christián complained that he hadn't come all this way just for the view. Ruslana poked his chest. "Do you think this ushkuinik is going to simply hand over forty thousand gold bezants because you asked?" She held up the leather portfolio. "I doubt he even carries the key."

"You read me well." Yohan had to smile, despite his anger. "Luca has it, along with the transmittal agreement."

She kept her finger on the man's chest. "Now tell me your people have captured the Sicilian. Where is he?"

Christián spat on the ground at her feet. "You should have said he had the key."

"Give it up," Yohan said. "She didn't know until right now. She guessed when I yielded so easily."

"Then there is no reason I shouldn't just cut both of your throats and maybe make a deal with this Sicilian."

Yohan relaxed his shoulders. "Take your finger off his chest, Weaver, and explain to both of us what we are doing here."

Ruslana backed off and twitched her head to one side. "Across the bridge now. Quickly, if you ever want to see your friend again."

Yohan worried about Luca as he crossed. *What could the Weavers know of my friend?* As he reached the other side, an enormous bell tolled sext, midday. Yohan swiveled that direction. The basilica, St. Peter's Basilica, the center of western Christianity. "You brought us beneath the Pope's very nose, Weaver. This is the Church's ground, no place I want to be caught."

Christián nodded. "Nor I. Enough of these games." He drew his knife. "Either we all return to the bank, or I return alone."

Ruslana tossed her head. "Just wait, damn you..."

Yohan lost track of the conversation at that point. A troop of mounted soldiers had approached the bridge and begun to cross. *Just step into their midst and walk away?* He considered it, but something seemed odd, no banners, no insignia, no glittering processional crosses. Hesitating, he glanced at Ruslana. She was busy exchanging invectives with Christián. Bored, the guards watched them quarrel. Halfway across the bridge, the soldiers rode in an undisciplined string. Four men in cowled robes rode with them. Yohan considered his odds for a moment, then spoke up. "I suggest we move off the roadway, ya?"

Ruslana turned, cursing. She pushed Christián away. Yohan felt her drag him by the arm. "Back, all of you. Get back—they come."

It would be easy, drop over the embankment and dash along the river, but now Yohan was curious. He turned a practiced eye on the soldiers, *Mercenaries, no better than the guards rattling their swords at my back.* That left the hooded figures. Not much to see there. Ruslana put her mouth to his ear. "Watch the tall one," she whispered, "but on fear of your life, do nothing."

The first of the men drew near. On closer study, Yohan's estimation dropped by several degrees. *Hired ruffians.* Ruslana leaned closer. "Those are brigands you would have fought had you crossed from the east. Watch now."

Perhaps a dozen men passed before the cloaked riders approached. A head taller than the others, the central figure rode stiff and upright in the saddle. Drawing alongside, he turned and gazed in their direction. *Simon.* Yohan stiffened and would have shouted if Ruslana hadn't pinched her thumbnail into his earlobe. "Silence, fool."

Riding past as if in a daze, the boy stared off at the basilica behind them— not a shred of recognition crossed his face. Yohan's eyes followed the group as they marched across the Tiber and down Via Cornelia toward St. Peter's.

"What just happened here, Weaver?"

"The Apostles captured your friend Simon. I've known it since before we reached Genoa."

"And you chose to keep this from me?"

"What would you have done?" She paused a moment. "No, I'll answer. You would have dropped everything and gone charging after him, arriving too late at every stop."

"And here I am. Once more too late and now without men or resources."

"You have forty thousand gold bezants and"—she nodded toward Christián—"a very ruthless potential ally."

The man in question stood glaring at them. "Enough whispers, witch. I've seen your parade, and I am not impressed. The gold—now."

Yohan stepped forward, an easy target for the dagger in Christián's hand. "It has just become more complicated." Unblinking, he met the man's eye. "If I am dead or she is dead, then that letter of credit becomes worthless. Your brothers will not appreciate it, but the Templars may thank you for wiping this debt from their books."

"It will be just as worthless to you, dead man."

"But for half the gold, say twenty thousand bezants, would you be interested?"

"You bargain at the point of my knife?"

Yohan shook his head. "No bargain. You get the gold, but you must use some of it to raise an army."

When Christián balked, Yohan repeated his offer, but the man showed no sign of interest in an alliance, profitable or not. Ruslana finally held out the leather portfolio. "Just tell me who wants this. I'm tired of carrying it."

"I'll take it then," Christián said. "It was ours in the first place."

Yohan didn't argue the point. "Give it to him, Weaver. That worthless bundle of paper will be the stone about his neck that he carries to his grave."

"I have a better idea," she said. "I can let the bank hold this in trust for both of you."

"She's your factor," Yohan said. "I would listen to her."

Christián Vendini flicked his eyes between them. "Of course, the bank then while my comrades search for your Sicilian friend."

As factor, Ruslana would make the arrangements. Banko Grigorio would only recognize the Knights of Palermo and deny any connection with the house of Vendini. Yohan didn't comment but let Christián stew on that angle. By the time they finished at the bank, he seemed more inclined to negotiate. Yohan suggested taking a meal together. "I doubt any of us have eaten since yesterday. Perhaps our factor can recommend some food that we won't later leave on a street corner."

"You ask a lot of me... a lot of Rome. This city runs with sewage and foul humors. It is garbage piled on top of garbage. It is rats eating rats." She paused a moment and eyed Christián's men. "I do know of one place nearby, but it may be costly, and our ruffian friends will not be allowed inside."

Yohan smiled. "Ya, that sounds good. I even have a few Venetian bezants left to spend."

Ruslana led them to a clean-looking establishment with polished tables scattered in discreet corners. The proprietor brought them loaves of hot bread and trenchers of roasted lamb.

Christián broached the topic on his second cup of wine. "What is it exactly you want of me, pirate?"

"I want you to raise a band of mercenaries, men like your friends from this morning."

"Rome has been sacked so many times, I doubt you would find an able soldier anywhere but guarding the banks or Vatican Hill."

Yohan rubbed his chin. "I am considering the Vatican."

"On the bridge today, that militia?"

"It was a gang of brigands." Yohan waited for a reaction. When none came, he continued. "And four members of Apostoli Lucis."

Christián didn't blink. He gave Ruslana a questioning look, "Apostolis? They are what?"

"For a man so well educated," she said, "I would have thought you knew."

Yohan explained. "They are conjurers, the dark reflection of the Church. They seek knowledge without faith as the papists seek faith without knowledge."

"So, tell me pirate, which side are you?"

"I would prefer neither, but in this I have no choice. The Apostles took our friend captive. I will have him back."

Christián called for another jug of wine. "I think you are telling tales. Four men enter the Pope's sacred basilica, and I should believe they belong to some secret cabal."

Ruslana poured them each a cup. "Say they do. As your factor, I tell you they do."

"Your pirate here would storm St. Peter's, burn it down, and kill the rats as they come scurrying out."

"Let's hope it doesn't come to that," Yohan said. "I'll need a way to draw them up from their hole."

Ruslana took a sip. "And that is why we are here, gentlemen. We have a situation developing that involves the Papacy and the Apostles."

"I suppose it involves the Weavers as well?" Yohan said.

"We are simple observers, but it certainly involves your Knights of Palermo. We spoke of a certain Jacob ben Reuben—I believe he will be your next Pope."

"A Sephardic polemicist, a Templar renegade, how could he ever become Pope?"

"Jacob passes for a Cistercian monk in these days, but believe me, he is your old foe, ben Reuben."

Yohan poured Christián another cup of wine and sat back. "Drink up. She shares her mind in small pieces. Believe me, you will need some fortification to hear what comes next." He topped off Ruslana's cup. "You too, ya? I want you just as addled as the rest of us."

Nodding, she looked off across the room. "Perhaps Luca can join us."

Yohan followed her gaze. Luca sat not five spans away. He touched his brow in return. Waving him over, Yohan said, "I trust you have secured the key?"

"My mother could not find this thing, and she is very thorough."

Christián jumped up, knocking over his wine cup. "You! I should have you taken now and disemboweled."

"Sit, Vendini. That is not a request. Ya?"

The Venetian turned toward the door, raised one hand, and shook his head.

Luca pulled a stool from another table and straddled it. "We are friends, sè? Like wolf and goat?"

Yohan scowled. "We are becoming allies." He briefed Luca on what Ruslana had revealed. "So, don't spoil it."

Recovering his wine cup, Christián said, "What is it, this next thing I hear?"

Yohan said, "I expect she is about to tell us that Jacob ben Reuben has returned to his brother Apostles."

Ruslana had filled her own wine cup and passed it to Luca. She refilled Christián's and said, "Not yet. He has returned to further his own schemes. There are factions within Apostoli Lucis who would support him. Already he has arranged the Pope's assassination."

"Impossible," Christián said. "Urban III has sequestered himself in the north, away from the poison and knives of Rome."

"You will find poison and knives enough anywhere," Ruslana said. "Against a determined assassin, he has little defense."

Luca asked about Simon. He had missed seeing him at the bridge. Yohan sipped his wine and let them talk. *Ruslana, she isn't telling all she knows.* He wondered what the Weavers' interest was in all of this. *Defend the Pope?* Not likely. *Raise their own candidate for the Papacy?* It seemed even less likely.

While they talked, Christián studied Luca. It wasn't hard for Yohan to imagine the man's thoughts—*kill him now or kill him later?* Yohan tried to work out a scenario where no one died. Even with a small army, they weren't likely to wrest Simon from the Apostles' grasp.

He felt Ruslana kick him under the table. "I said, wake up, ushkuinik."

He sat up—all eyes were on him. Ruslana said, "Your Brother Luca asked why we are paying this Venetian. He had other words as well that aren't worth repeating."

Yohan steepled his fingers and spoke over the top of them. "I suppose it is because it's what you want us to do." He waved off Ruslana's objections. "I am not the idiot you think I am, Weaver. The tumbrel, the attacks, the pursuit, then lo, house Vendini knows of our cargo and wishes to buy it. Now, here he is with his own band of hired swords."

"But the money, it is ours," Luca said.

"It was never ours. I expect if you look back far enough, it never rightly belonged to Simon's master."

Ruslana smiled and crossed her arms. "You have such a creative imagination for a pirate."

"The truth, Weaver. You brought me here, you brought him here, and you have provided us with enough gold to hire an army. What do you want?"

Ruslana exchanged looks with Christián. "Are you surprised, Vendini? The ushkuinik is right. We are all here for a purpose. Summon your men if you don't like it. I doubt any of you will survive the encounter." She spun on Luca. "And you, put that damned knife away. He's not going to try anything if there is still a chance at some of the gold."

Christián placed his own knife on the table, a wicked-looking thing almost sword-length. "I don't like being used, especially not by a woman I have hired for... other duties."

Yohan expected his friend to brandish a dagger as well, but Luca leaned back and grinned. "All are used, especially when there are women, sè? I ask Weaver this too, what is it she wants."

Ruslana's eyes had never left Christián's face. "It is your friend Simon." She flicked a glance at Luca. "The Apostoli Lucis are holding him here in Rome. I expect you to retrieve him unharmed."

"So, you *do* want us to assault St. Peter's," Christián said. "You will have us all condemned to the eternal flames for one idiot boy."

"Not St. Peter's. For what the Apostles have planned, they cannot perform their rites anywhere near such a hallowed place."

"Then why take him there?" Yohan said.

"For the very reason the Vendini fears. None would dare assault the center of Roman Christianity."

"I wait," Luca said. "They come out, and then they die."

"And your idiot boy dies too," Christián said. "We cannot be seen when they leave the basilica. How do you propose we do this, woman?"

Ruslana drained her wine cup. "I expect you to solve that one, gentlemen."

The Unremarkable Man

Morning sun glittered off the waves. The rower didn't notice. He didn't notice the freshening north wind that filled their sail. He didn't notice that he had been pulling the same oar for two days straight. His vision was filled only with the bent back before him and the rhythmic grumble of the oars in their tholepins.

A horn sounded. It meant oars up. Simon complied, as did his neighbor on the bench, as did the other forty-five rowers. Somewhere in the back of his mind, he knew water was coming, a bucket and a ladle. There might be food, there might not. Too well fed, and the men would defecate at their benches. Too little food and they would begin to lose strength. Simon took a moment before the water bucket arrived to piss between his feet. It had always been so.

Water is good, need water, but the oar... my god the oar! Simon waited, wiggling with impatience. Again, the horn. Again, the dip and pull. He bent forward and dragged the wooden bar to his chest. Life had balance again, purpose, even meaning. *The oar.*

Night fell, but the oars continued their dip and rise. Rowers took shifts, resting and pulling. Not Simon—he watched a crescent moon cross the night sky as he bowed to the sacred oar. Morning brought sight of land, a burning faro that marked their destination. Ancona, he had been told, landfall. Simon pulled with renewed fervor. *The Sethiarch awaits.*

He didn't wait in Ancona. Somehow, it seemed to Simon that he should have known that. Marching him off the galley, over the dock, and up a cobbled street, his three minders barked curt orders but otherwise walked in silence. Building fronts passed unnoticed. A few words sent him down a flight of steps, through a low portal, and turned him to face an open door. A minder barked at him to go in. Simon obeyed.

The door shut and latched behind him. Two spans above the floor, a latticed opening supplied the only light and air in his cell. Simon never considered testing the door or climbing to the window. He sat, instead on a wooden bench and watched a gray shadow creep across the opposite wall.

The shadow had moved over half a span before Simon began to wonder what he was doing there. Ancona had been reached. The oar had lost its glamor. He examined the weeping blisters on his hands and for the first time, felt the knots of pain in his back. A row of shallow cuts marched up his left arm. One, perhaps the most recent, still bled down to his wrist.

From above, he heard the distant chime of a church bell ringing sext, midday. A moment of panic. *We should be leaving.* There was someone. A scatter of images pattered across his mind like a rain squall on a pond. *Someone, I have someone.* He tried to concentrate, a nest of orange hair beneath a puffy round burlet. *Amala, my wife.*

Simon jumped to his feet and was at once knocked back. He tried again. The blow, harder this time, slammed him against the wall. Dizzy, his head spun a moment. Simon waited. Nothing moved. His invisible adversary waited as well. *Your own adversary*, someone had once said. Simon tried to remember. Days of travel, swords, horses, Luca, pankration. Bits and raveling pieces of his past, a vast midden heap of memories surrounded him. Eventually, he dug long enough to uncover the Apostoli Lucis.

Putting a hand to his chest, Simon waited for the barbs, the claw. It came, a crushing sensation little worse than the ache in his back. He settled against the cool stone wall. *If I don't fight, I cannot be my own adversary.*

Simon closed his eyes and tried to put the pieces together. The church in Ponteventi, the wooden box—they had used the Nemesis against him. *I should be dead.* But he wasn't, and Simon mulled on that for a while. *And Amala... had she escaped?* He whispered, *"Find her, I'll find her, but not now."*

He kept his eyes closed. *What happens next?* They would return for him—of that, he was certain. A forbidden rite, nonetheless, Simon knew he had been given a Compulsion. The Apostles, his minders, would set another on him when he next saw them. For a moment, he longed for a weapon, a knife hidden, *indraga mano*, behind his arm. It hardly mattered, save for his breechclout and sandals, he was nearly naked. *Besides, Yohan had said my art is my weapon.*

Simon turned that thought over for a while. Not against the adepts of Apostoli Lucis. He would be a kitten defying the wolf. He'd given up his half-sword for that reason, the sword of Jacob ben Reuben. Simon opened his eyes—he knew.

Before they return... he fought down the urge to rush. *Slowly... allay the adversary.* He moved to the bench and felt beneath it until his fingers discovered the rough edge of a badly finished board. He pushed. It gave. Simon pushed harder and tore off a long splinter. Beneath his upper arm, he scratched a row of symbols into the soft skin, the same symbols found on his father's sword. Repeating until the letters bled, until blood dripped from his fingertips, he waited.

They came. He felt them descend the steps before he heard their soft footsteps in the hall. Hooded cloak, bald head, Simon recognized the man who entered first. He held the Nemesis, safely boxed. With the same lizard's smile, he said, "You are rested? That is good. Tonight, we ride for Rome."

Simon nodded but didn't reply. He had played the cretino long enough to give a convincing performance. Two others entered. One, young and heavy, brought out a leaden disk. He grabbed Simon's wrist and wiped his bloody fingertips across the talisman. Like a pitcher of strong wine, Simon felt it sap his will, steal his wit.

He invoked the script hidden beneath his arm. It did little to ease the Compulsion, but it did enough. Simon followed without resistance. He could do no else. Walking, he concentrated on their movements, their voices, their commands. *We ride for Rome?* It had been his destination in any event. At some point, they would make a mistake, underestimate him, leave him unguarded— and if not? *Just give me one chance at them, any of them.*

Leaving Ancona on horseback, the four wound their way down from the city center and passed beneath the outer gate. Behind him, Simon heard the great cathedral bell ring *none*, midafternoon. His mount could have been a plow horse for all he knew—it was certainly no Perun. He didn't care—they said ride and he rode. The countryside passed as a blur of fields and trees. Simon sat unaware in his saddle. He saw only the figure riding before him and heard only the rattle of hooves at his back.

Lurching along, he clung to his spirit, his pneuma, that tiny sense of self that Compulsion could not steal. Simon let the day pass, riding along the sultry coast. He no longer felt fatigue—the Compulsion took that, along with his pain and his volition. He wondered how long his captors could sustain their pace.

Riding late into the evening, he found himself following a darkened silhouette down a narrow trail. *The road?* He had missed where they turned. The trail ended at a villa standing half ruined on a cliff above the sea. Almost in a dream, he drifted inside with his minders, ate half a loaf of bread, and collapsed on a filthy pile of straw.

The sun rode high above the horizon when Simon awoke. Rocking and lurching in the saddle, he had no idea how long they had been riding, but the same cloaked silhouette filled his vision as though they had never paused for the night. Simon let the time flow by, concentrating on what little fragment of self he retained.

It seemed like days later when they turned inland and climbed to the high mountain valleys of the Apennines. Hardly aware of the change, Simon had lost track of time. At one point, a rattling band of armed men accompanied them. *Knights of Palermo?* He couldn't make sense of it. *Not knights, perhaps guards or mercenaries.* Simon rode on in unquestioning silence.

His arm bore three new cuts by the time they descended from the mountains. His horse bumped and jolted down the steep roadway. Simon tasted the blood running from his latest cut. Somewhere in the maze of dreams and images, he recalled the leaden talisman pressed against his arm. His fresh blood, invoking Compulsion with every new day.

One morning dawned with Simon huddled in a bundle of rags, his head against a square marble stone. His fingers had marked it the night before, tracing XII in the darkness. They would reach the gates of Rome before midday. He invoked the charm for protection scratched into his arm and staggered to his feet. Exhausted, few of the travelers had yet risen. Simon ducked between the trees where the horses were tied. He remembered seeing white mare with an ugly scratch down her flank. She was easy to find, even in the gray light of dawn.

He stroked her behind the nose and worked his way back. The scratch still wept. She snorted and shied when he picked beneath the scab and smeared blood on his arm. Retreating to his bed of rags he found the fat little Apostle waiting for him. The man squinted and rubbed the lead talisman across Simon's bloody arm. Turning it over, he spat on the back. "You don't go piss until I tell you to piss. Understand?"

Closing his eyes, Simon hung his head. Docile, obedient for now, he wondered if the mare felt any different. The hooded Apostles gave him a robe to wear and led him to his horse. By the time the morning sun had crested the western hills, he was riding in procession with his captors and their guards.

The morning passed among fields and vineyards, following a well-worn road that led to Rome. Without Compulsion to steal the pain, Simon felt every jolt and sway in his aching back. They rode without stopping until the outer walls hove into view. Above the city, a gray miasma marked ten thousand ovens baking bread. The thought of it made his stomach growl. They had fed him little since leaving Ponteventi.

Like an approaching thunderstorm, the city wall grew higher. Simon began to remember details. Vague thoughts. *I was a street urchin once.* That would have been long before... *the church, dragged kicking and biting into the church.* He remembered the man, tall, arms like tree roots, enormous beard. *My father.* All of Rome came back to him, the shouting between his father and the priests, the near battle that erupted in the sacred nave of St. Peter's. Simon struggled to hold his upright posture and placid face as they entered the city.

Every turn brought back another memory—the slapdash hovels on the outskirts, the brick ruins with their furtive occupants, the rare monument to glory rising above the squalor. As the bell of St. Peter's Basilica rang sext, Simon passed the Great Circus, now but a shallow valley filled with market stalls. Circling the market, they descended toward the Tiber River and crossed the Ponte Sant'Angelo. Simon turned to face the basilica, that monument to Christianity concealing devotees of Apostoli Lucis in its ancient heart.

Via Cornelia had deteriorated into a rubble-strewn track that skirted St. Peter's and ended in the ruins of Nero's circus. Caligula's obelisk remained, but the pens and balconies that once surrounded it had crumbled to piles of brick and broken stone. Simon dared look up at the granite spire. *Fitting that it should be dedicated to Rome's most notorious tyrant.* He pondered a moment on the strange juxtaposition that placed it next Rome's holiest site, the Petronilla dome, erected over Saint Peter's bones.

His captors dismounted, but Simon remained in his saddle as no one had told him to get off. He stared straight ahead, straining to hear what was said. Mumbling, the clink of coins, he sneaked a look at the proceedings.

A small purse had changed hands. Lizard-lips threw his cowl back and pointed toward the bridge. Their escort filed off in that direction. Simon's horse made to follow, and he let it have its head just to see the reaction. He'd passed the obelisk before a string of curses and shouts brought him back.

Dismounting, he stood to watch the chaos as acolytes scrambled to take their horses and gear. Simon's bladder felt ready to burst. Grinning inwardly, he let go, fouling his breechclout, his robe, and dripping on the ground between his feet. More curses, he pretended not to notice. Having been reprimanded by the others, the fat little Apostle vented his ire on Simon. The slapping and pummeling hardly mattered—he'd taken worse in the past few weeks, and the proximity had given him a chance to relieve the man of a small dagger carelessly belted outside his robe.

Simon was eventually given a fresh tunic and undergarment. His boots, trophies of the battle outside Krakow, now reeked of a thousand indignities. They remained, leaving wet footprints where he walked. A few steps took Simon through a small postern door beneath the Petronilla. Followed by his minders, he descended an iron ladder into a narrow stone well.

The ladder ended in a warren of crypts and corridors. Simon remembered every turn. In the whispering darkness, someone produced a candle and lit it. He'd once prowled these deep chambers. With or without light, Simon's feet still knew the way. There were libraries filled with books and sacred objects deemed too dangerous by the church but too valuable to be destroyed. He'd worshiped at that altar of knowledge, once long ago.

Simon trudged after his captors, musing on his own folly and ignorance. *All that knowledge still locked away.* He knew where they headed. The deep sanctum. The seat of the High Sethiarch. He'd only been there twice, once for his initiation and once to receive the brand on his chest. Simon could ignore its pangs for now but still feared the Nemesis it was bound to. Holding his purloined dagger indraga mano, he descended the final staircase. *God grant only that I survive this next encounter.*

Oil lamps threw dancing shadows about the cold chamber. On this third visit, Simon took in features he hadn't noticed before. The stark walls, the columns bare of ornamentation, even placement of the lamps, all designed to intimidate the visitor. Simon stood, his arms hanging, his face slack, and awaited the Sethiarch's arrival. Holding his head still, he allowed his eyes to wander. *There must be another entrance.* He saw none.

His guardian stood fidgeting on Simon's right. The other of his hooded captors took position on his left. Simon shivered knowing that the lizard-lipped man stood right behind him. His neck had started to cramp by the time a rush of air swept through the chamber, flaring the lamps and revealing two files of robed figures entering along the sides.

A grotesque shadow swept the far wall and hung like a pall of smoke in the center of the room. The lamps brightened and the shadow coalesced into the figure of an unremarkable man. Simon heard the command to kneel, and he dropped to his knees. The unremarkable man took one step forward and fixed his eyes on Simon. "The spawn of ben Reuben kneels before me, as he should."

Daring to look only at the floor, Simon wondered if this man, the Sethiarch, was near enough to strike with his little hidden knife. He gauged the likely distance to his target. His eyes flickered upward for a moment. *Yes, two steps only, then jam the blade between his ribs.* He inched one knee forward and thought, *Am I ready to die?*

The Sethiarch hissed and stepped back. "I sense this man is not fully under your control. Did he receive Compulsion this morning?"

Wrenched to his feet, Simon struggled to keep the knife hidden against his side. The man on his right answered. "Yes, my Lord. I invoked it myself."

"Confine him for now." The Sethiarch turned as if to leave, then turned back. "And administer it again in double measure, but you must make sure that he doesn't forget to breathe."

A knifepoint against his back reminded Simon of who stood behind him. Pushing, jostling, a few growled orders, and they hustled him back up the stairs. A passageway to his right led to the Roman crypts buried beneath the apse of St. Peter's. One dark opening had an iron grate hung between upright marble columns. The little Apostle pushed Simon inside and followed. Talisman in one hand, he patted his belt in momentary confusion.

A simple blow to the chest slammed his captor against one wall. Simon flicked his knife to the man's throat. "Are you looking for this?"

Lamps in the corridor shed a faint light within the ancient burial chamber. Simon could see by their glow the initial outrage and then growing terror in the man's eyes. "How? How..."

"It doesn't matter. If you want to live, then you will talk."

His eyes flickered from the empty corridor back to Simon's face. Moments passed, then the man grunted something that could have meant yes. Simon kept the knife pressed against his throat. "What is your name?"

"Esau deFoligno." The little man straightened. "*Baron* Esau deFoligno."

"So, Baron Esau deFoligno, tell me why Apostoli Lucis wants me so badly."

The man's eyes flicked to the corridor. Simon knew he would talk as long as he thought someone might walk by. Esau hesitated, then said, "We don't want you—we want your father, Jacob ben Reuben." He twisted his lips to a smile. "You, Simon deVia, Simon of the road, are his bastard son by a filthy whore... and that is all."

Simon pressed the knife harder. "Then why all of this?"

Esau squirmed and rolled his eyes but said nothing. Simon pressed harder until a rivulet of blood trickled down the man's neck. *He thinks of shouting.* Simon grabbed the man's hair and slammed his head into the wall. He struggled. Simon struck him again and felt his body shake and collapse. The lead token dropped from Esau's fingers and rolled.

Simon released the little Apostle and let him slide down the wall. Snatching the talisman from the stone floor, he studied its markings. Nothing familiar. It didn't surprise him; their vows would normally forbid Compulsion. A high adept, the Sethiarch perhaps, only he could know how to make and bind such a thing.

Esau twitched and vomited on the floor. Simon regretted hitting him that hard. *He got to me.* Kneeling, he checked the man's injuries. The cut on his throat had stopped bleeding. Simon rolled him on his side and touched the back of his head. Swollen, damp with blood, it didn't feel broken or badly gashed.

His talisman for healing, Simon glanced at the red scar on his hand and remembered the bargain he had made to save Amala. *Where is she now?* Once more, he begged the gods, all of them, *Please...have her riding north, riding back to Baba Jezinka.* It crossed his mind that without Amala by his side, the old witch's aegis was lifted, and his Anathema could return at any time.

He pushed the thought aside to concentrate on more immediate problems. *Perhaps this Esau had something.* Simon untied the purse from the man's belt and found that it held a small collection of talismans. Mostly copper or bronze, they would be bound to lesser entities. He held a tiny silver disk up to the lamplight. Nothing like the one he'd used on Yohan and Amala, still he invoked it on Esau. After a few moments, the man lifted his head and blinked.

Simon hadn't considered his next step, but healing Esau reminded him of the Compulsion. He returned the silver disk and examined the lead token. Larger than the others, it had been cast into a golden frame. Lead, sacred to Saturn and the underworld. On its face, a seven-pointed star. On its reverse, a jumble of lines and circles. Simon knew they symbolized the astrological position of various stars and planets. He could see no words, no invocation. Esau had used it, used it with blood from Simon's arm.

He smeared its face with blood from the man's scalp. Nothing. Simon felt no different, and the little Apostle only glared up at him. Stepping back, Simon tried to recall, something to complete the connection. Esau wavered to his feet, eyeing the iron-barred doorway.

It came to him a moment later. Simon flipped the talisman over and spat on its back. "Stand and remain silent."

The man stiffened momentarily. Simon felt him resist. *Is this what the Sethiarch sensed?* He wondered what impression Esau had gotten from the little white mare he'd bound. Leaving him where he stood, Simon checked the iron grate that closed their chamber. It swung open with a gentle push. He peeked out into the corridor. Save for the flickering lamps, nothing moved.

Again, that tickle behind his eyes, he turned to see Esau working his way closer. Simon ordered him back. *Attention, if I turn my attention elsewhere...* He would remain Esau's prisoner, only in a different way. *The Nemesis too. Lizard-lips would have that.* Simon considered searching the corridors but gave up on the idea. In the end, waiting seemed to be the best option. He looked into Esau's eyes and pointed to a spot near the iron grate. "Stand here." He stepped away as the man crossed the chamber. "You will watch the corridor and tell me when someone comes."

Simon edged back and sat against the far wall. Esau resisted, but the Compulsion turned him toward the corridor. Waiting was the hardest part. *They will send someone for me.* He considered what would happen, dreading that he might have to kill again.

Esau jerked and started to turn. Simon watched him fidget. "Tell me, who comes?"

The little man seemed torn in two directions, twitching and shaking. His mouth open, he gagged on his words. Simon stood, his knife hidden, his face expressionless. *All I need is one moment of hesitation, one moment more of deception.* He tensed as footsteps approached the doorway.

The chamber darkened as a shadow filled the passage. Esau collapsed, thrashing on the floor. The iron grate swung open, and in its place, the Sethiarch stood grinning. "You have exceeded our expectations, Simon deVia."

A Matter of Balance

Bells from a nearby church rang *none*, the call to prayer. They were answered by a myriad of others on both sides of the Tiber. Yohan finished his wine and said, "If we are to gather any force at all before the Apostles move, we must do so now." He turned to Ruslana. "Where will they be taking Simon?"

"Apostoli Lucis holds their rites beneath the Capella de Santa Maria on Aventine Hill, but don't expect them to start until after the sun sets."

Christián rubbed his fingers together. "I have seen no gold here."

Ruslana stood. "I will take Luca to the bank and arrange for an advance."

"Go then, get your advance," Yohan said. "Vendini, find us as many swords as you can before sunset. I will go visit this Capella de Santa Maria and see how it is defended. We meet at the Tiber docks."

Ruslana waved the Venetian out ahead of her. "Take your men—you will be paid when I see your army."

She made a point of watching him leave. Yohan put a hand on Luca's shoulder. "Take two hundred bezants, no more... and be careful of that lot." He saw Luca blink in Ruslana's direction. "Ya, all of them."

Staying, after the others had left, Yohan took another cup of wine and mulled over their options. *The Apostles will expect us to attack.* He let that sink in. *Sometimes it is best to give your enemy what they expect.* He thought about confronting them before they reached the hill. He wondered what they might achieve by such a direct strategy. *Too obvious. Apostoli Lucis are not men of force—they are men of stealth.* Yohan tried to think like they did. *I would hustle Simon to the Capella before anyone suspects he has left the Basilica.*

He considered Christián's guards. Not one of them could be trusted nor the men he hired. They would put up a token fight, little more. He and Luca then. If he could free Simon, that would make three of them. *The Weaver?* She would just have to stay out of their way.

Yohan found the proprietor and placed a gold bezant in his hand. "If I did not want to be seen leaving, how would I go?"

The man led him through a narrow storage room into a weedy courtyard. "You would scale that fence and climb out through the ruins beyond." He looked Yohan up and down. "I don't think the squatters will give you much problem."

The ruins turned out to be a roofless brick structure, one of many that littered the flanks of Aventine Hill. Yohan found himself in a neighborhood of shanties and gardens, a short walk from the Pope's Lateran Palace. He turned west toward the river and followed a herd of goats up a grassy hillside. Ruins lined both sides of the path, mostly small foundations, long plundered for their marble building stone. A little farther up, he approached a cenotaph, its iron door firmly in place. For a moment Yohan wondered why it, among all the other structures, remained intact. Drawing closer, he saw the Serpens Crucis incised into its marble capstone. *Reason enough.* He circled to the south.

Near the top, he paused beneath a stand of tall cypress. Yohan settled at the foot of one ancient tree, half hidden behind a thorny bush. The goats had kept grass and weeds from overrunning the hilltop. His objective stood not a hundred paces away, a square marble chapel crowned by a gilded cross. Pigeons flapped and pecked about the open terrazza. They would let him know if anyone approached. He tried to picture the interior.

Ruslana had described it as the Temple of Diana. The golden cross belied that. *Virgin huntress gives way to a virgin saint.* Yohan imagined an altar near the center with a crucifix behind it and a shrine to Mary somewhere to one side. *What else? Not much. It's not big enough for more than a few monks.* He pictured the gathering, a congregation of Apostles. *They would need more space—there had to be catacombs beneath the chapel.* The marble cenotaph and its iron door suddenly made sense.

The pigeons hopped about—a few flapped into the air. Movement he hadn't noticed before. Yohan sat up. A small figure wearing an enormous burlet stood to one side of the terrazza. *Where had he come from?* Gliding toward the church, the pigeons ignored him. A moment later, the figure vanished. Yohan waited, but nothing more happened.

Curious, he stood and circled the building from the back. Weeds grew taller there, and a few goats jangled their bells in the late afternoon shade. Yohan stood among them and studied the marble wall. It once had other openings, doorways and fenestrations now filled with rough-laid stonework. He inspected both sides—it seemed abandoned.

Keeping to the shadows of the northern wall, he crept toward the terrazza. The pigeons chuckled and cooed among themselves. Yohan stopped and drew back. *Pigeons, they wouldn't be here unless someone fed them.* Cursing his own stupidity, he worked his way back along the building. *Whoever waits inside is listening for the beat of wings.*

Descending Aventine Hill on the far side, Yohan thought on what he'd seen. *No one comes or goes unnoticed.* He glanced back at the marble roofline. *Unless they wear a large hat and move like a phantom.* At the foot of the hill, he circled, tracing the remnants of Rome's original wall back toward the Tiber River.

A short distance from the docks, he plunged through a copse of willows and stepped out onto a cobblestone road. Yohan followed a gang of porters back toward the city. The late afternoon sunlight painted Aventine Hill in shades of yellow and red. He looked up at the pockmarked cliff that faced the river. Masonry, bricks, and mortared stones filled some of the cavities. *Why would anyone build on the face of a cliff?*

A tap on his shoulder broke Yohan from his reverie. Ruslana grinned at him. "Lost?"

Luca stood behind her, studying the traffic along the river. Yohan glanced at the satchel he carried. "It is arranged?"

"Vendini is not going to like it."

"Two hundred, it's the money he is owed. If he wants more, he will have to perform."

"So tell me you have a plan."

"Just above us stands a church. It bears a cross, but I doubt it's been consecrated.”

“Capella de Santa Maria,” Ruslana said. “Only the Apostles attend.”

Luca interrupted. “Speak of diavuli.” He twitched his head toward a small group standing across the roadway. “I think those are too interested.”

“We keep walking then,” Yohan said. “If they see us, it doesn’t matter—better in fact.”

“Already, I hate this plan.” Luca had slung his satchel across one shoulder. It bumped his side as he walked. “They know we come. There is no chance.”

“They will already know we are here. The Weavers aren’t the only ones with spies.” Yohan led them past the end of Aventine Hill and crossed the open field where farmers and vendors were dismantling their market stalls. “We need to stop at Donetta’s shop and pick up a few things.”

By that, he meant that he had to don his leather gambeson and mail hauberk. “Time to armor up, Brother Luca. It’s you and me against the world.”

“I do not hear a plan, and still, I hate it.”

Ruslana looked back. “They follow, but not close. Tell me your plan now, ushkuinik. How do we recapture your friend Simon?”

“We don’t. We let Christián’s men attack the Apostles’ procession.”

“And your boy dies. I say it is a bad plan.”

“He won’t die. You will have to take my word for now.”

Donetta let them in. It had seemed like days to Yohan since that morning. He rummaged up his gear and shrugged into his gambeson and chainmail. Luca picked through his selection of knives and buckled one above his boot. Another he strapped to his left arm. “And look, I have sword for our cretino.”

Luca unrolled his gear and grunted. Yohan glanced over his shoulder. “I saw you pack it. Where did you put it?”

“Gone.” He searched under the pallets and glared at Ruslana. “Where is half-sword, witch?”

She shook her head. “I’ll ask Donetta if anyone was in here.”

Yohan checked through his own gear. “Why would anyone steal that relic?”

Ruslana returned. “She was here all day. No one could have stolen it. Besides, why would anyone choose a broken sword over all of your other weapons?”

Yohan repacked his kit. “You dropped it somewhere last night.”

Luca shook his head. "It is stolen by diavuli who make maldicaru on our Simon."

Yohan couldn't quite discount that idea. "He is better with a knife. Give him one of yours when we see him."

Ruslana gave Luca's collection a wary eye. "You don't expect me to use any of those?"

"No, my dear," Yohan said, "I expect you to do what Weavers do best—spy."

"We already have a spy inside. She waits for us."

"No doubt," Yohan said. "But she doesn't report to me. You, on the other hand, have some task you wish us to complete. That makes you *our* spy."

Yohan ignored her sour look. "At this point, the transaction at Banko Grigorio is complete. The gold is under our control. Therefore, you are no longer an agent of the Vendinis, ya?"

"Christián does not know that."

"He should know it. He just might not realize it yet. Are you going to tell him?"

Ruslana glanced at Luca before answering. "It depends on whether I can trust you—both of you."

"In this city of eternal decay, you know we are the only ones you can trust."

"Then you can tell me your plan—all of it."

Yohan checked the narrow hallway before replying. "The Apostles know we are here and expect us to come against them, which we will. Christián and his men will intercept their mercenaries at the foot of Aventine Hill, but Simon won't be there, and neither will we."

"Then boy is where?" Luca said.

"I'm not sure, but he will be close by. I expect Capella de Santa Maria will be filled with more of the Apostles' mercenaries, perhaps some nasty little sorcerers of their own, too."

Ruslana crossed her arms. "My spy would have told me of these things."

"If you can trust this spy. He may have other loyalties."

"*She*. And I rather doubt that."

"For now, I have more faith that the Apostles will anticipate our attack and will prepare for it. They will be defending the chapel, but I have discovered—"

As he spoke, Donetta stepped in from the hall. "You have some visitors." She held up four fingers. "They insist on seeing you."

Yohan and Luca sprang to both sides of the doorway as Ruslana backed against the far wall. Clad in mail hauberk, a large figure shoved Donetta to the floor and burst through the doorway. Yohan severed his hamstrings and pushed him back. Luca followed, catching the next intruder off balance. A knife to the eye dropped him where he stood. Scuffling, a sword stroke Luca barely deflected, and a third man entered the chamber. He ducked Yohan's swing and aimed a thrust at his midriff. Yohan sidestepped, parried the sword, and jammed his own dagger into the man's neck. *That makes three. Damn it, where is the other?* He was answered by the thwack of a crossbow. Cursing, Luca barged out the door. Yohan followed.

The crossbowman lay face down in the hall, three steps away. Luca's knife protruded from his back. Screams and grunts from the chamber, Yohan returned to find Donetta on the floor, struggling with the lamed attacker. A sword stroke ended the fight.

Yohan turned, looking for Ruslana. At the back of the room, she stood silently against the wall, pinned there by a crossbow bolt through her chest.

Yohan wasn't sure why he'd fallen to his knees or what malaise held him there. He clutched his sword, still jammed in the attacker's neck, and shook. *A leader does not weep for his fallen.* Still, his eyes ran with tears and sobs clogged his throat looking for escape. Luca's hand gripped his shoulder. "Peace, friend."

Donetta struggled to her feet, pushing both Yohan and the dead intruder away. She went to Ruslana's lifeless form, closed her eyes, and kissed her on both cheeks. "You were the best of our order. You were our *Stella Maris*, our guiding star. Whatever will we do without you?"

Luca knelt and crossed himself. "*Vade in pace* madonna."

Yohan recovered enough to stand, tears still streaming into his beard. He choked out, "You will not die unavenged, my love."

"Mafankulos all dead."

"Not all. Don't you recognize them?"

Luca rolled one of the intruders on his back. "Merda! They are Vendini bastardos."

"The four guards from the bank, the same four who followed us here."

"Mafankulo Vendini thinks to have gold and leave."

"Or his men got greedy, ya? They wanted the gold for themselves."

"I think it is the Weaver they come to kill."

Yohan shook his head. "I don't know—I can't think right now. Help me..." He gasped and swallowed. "Please, help me take her down."

Between the three of them, they lifted Ruslana from the crossbow bolt and carried her to a pallet. Covered in blood, the bolt remained embedded in the wall. To Yohan, it pointed an accusing finger straight at his heart. "Leave that there until we return. I don't want to forget what happened here today." *Or who it was who brought her here.*

"Now we go kill cazzo bastardo Vendini, sè?"

"No. We still need him and whatever army he has managed to raise. I think these men simply got greedy." Yohan gripped his friend's shoulder and held him at arm's length. "It's just you and me. We must finish. We must disrupt whatever the Apostles plan. We do this for her... and we do this for Simon."

Donetta had been kneeling at Ruslana's side. She looked up. "You don't know?"

Yohan shook his head. "I seem to be the only one in Rome who doesn't."

"This is about power and balance. Pope Urban III desires power. We desire balance. Apostoli Lucis desires both, as long as it favors them."

"Ruslana told us as much, but what of Simon?"

"He is the lever that moves Jacob ben Reuben. His blood will bind ben Reuben to the Apostles. The balance will tip, and I fear that what fragile peace this world knows will collapse into chaos."

The City of Radiance

They had dragged Esau from the chamber and relieved Simon of his stolen talismans. By sleight of hand and pure luck, he managed to keep his small dagger hidden. The iron grate was now bolted from the outside. The Sethiarch remained. Attentive, silent, he dismissed the others once Simon's prison had been secured.

A thin streak of blood marked where Esau had fallen. Simon looked up at those watchful eyes. "Will he live?"

A brief nod. "As will you, for now."

"Then why bring me all the way here? If I am to die, it would have been easier to have me killed in Ponteventi."

"We need you for an important task, Brother Simon. You are for the moment, indispensable."

Brother Simon. He wasn't sure whether to be flattered or insulted. "Did you explain that to your mercenaries at Krakow and Vienna?"

"One of our adepts made a mistake. He has been... *disciplined.*"

"And the Anathema? That was a mistake as well? Because it came very close to killing me—more than once."

The Sethiarch pinched his brows and stared at Simon. "There was no Anathema."

"Fire and flood, rain and pestilence, not Anathema?" Simon spread his arms. "Look at me—I am in a cage. Why do you even bother to lie?"

"I do not need to lie. If Apostoli Lucis had set Anathema on you, I would know."

Simon dropped his arms and slumped. "And yet you set a Nemesis on me.

Or that wasn't you either?"

"I created the Nemesis. It was that or kill you outright. Your father had something to do with it. You may not remember, but it was he who stole you from me. It took us over six years to find you again."

"Why couldn't you just have left me Simon Prostoi, Simon the fool. I was happy following Jacob the fur trader."

"Your happiness is not my concern."

"Then what is this great concern of yours for which I am indispensable?"

The unremarkable man turned to leave. "I will have food brought."

Standing alone, Simon examined his knife. Tip to pommel, it was no longer than his hand. *Esau will awaken and tell.* Simon resolved not to give it up easily. He shoved the stolen knife into his stolen boot. The food arrived, monk's fare, bread, cheese, and a small bit of gristly meat. He gnawed on the meat and brooded on the Sethiarch's words. *Jacob ben Reuben, his father, had helped with the Nemesis.* It made no sense.

And the Anathema? *No Apostle stands higher than the Sethiarch. Who then? Who benefits if I die?* Simon couldn't imagine anyone would care either way. *The Church?* He knew Yohan and Luca had some issue with Rome. *An ambitious cardinal with goetic knowledge?* He'd met cardinals as part of his training at St. Peter's. It didn't seem possible.

Sitting on the stone floor, head between his knees, Simon chewed on the Sethiarch's words. The iron grate rattled, and he looked up to see a cloaked figure unlocking his cell. The man said nothing but gestured toward the empty corridor. Simon thought of his knife. *It would be easy. Too easy.* A few hesitant steps. He eyed the cloaked man. No threat, no talisman of Compulsion. *Is this a test?* He wasn't sure.

Simon did know he was getting answers. *What I came for, after all.* He nodded to the Apostle. "Lead on, *brother.*"

They followed the corridor in a different direction. Simon passed through columned galleries and up a short stairway. At the top, a door led to the papal burial crypts beneath the basilica's south transept. A gathering of monks in brown robes awaited him there. Three of them had been tonsured to look like the other Cistercian brothers who filed through St. Peter's every day. Except they weren't.

Among them, Simon recognized several Apostoli Lucis, including lizard-lips. A moment later, the Unremarkable Man entered, looking every bit the unremarkable monk. "You are not ready?"

Simon noted the loose robes, the open sandals. *Not much chance of hiding my knife.* He ran a hand through his hair. "I didn't know I needed a costume."

Two monks pinned his arms behind him and bent him over a large basket. Lizard-lips produced a thin, straight blade and began hacking at Simon's hair. He felt his scalp sting like it had been invaded by ants. "Hold still," the man said, "or I will make you look like a rabbit flayed for market."

Simon watched the mound of hair grow in the basket, thinking of his small dagger and whether he should use it, or give it up. Someone washed his bare head with vinegar. It burned like fire and he shook himself free, smashing a fist into the nearest tormentor. Two others dragged him down. Pummeling, kicking, they bore in on him. Without a word, the Sethiarch raised one hand. The beating stopped.

Simon resisted a moment longer, then looked up. Brandishing a flat wooden box, the Sethiarch said, "I would threaten you with this, but you are of no use to us dead."

A moment of pressure, the claw in his chest, Simon felt the Nemesis, hidden but so near. He forced a breath. "I am of no use to you alive either, whatever it is you want."

"I had anticipated that—and yet, I need your willing cooperation." Returning the Nemesis to some hidden pouch, the Sethiarch drew out a simple pendant that hung about his neck. "Would the sight of this be more effective?"

In spite of himself, Simon gasped. Rising slowly to his feet, he stared at the little dragon's skull, cunningly drilled and strung on a cord. "Where?"

"She is a winsome young thing, wouldn't you say? A Weaver, she carries messages, runs errands. Sometimes she carries messages for me. Did you know that, Simon deVia? Your friend gave this to me and told me to say, 'It is good.' Do I have it right?"

"That's a lie." Simon made a move to snatch the pendant but was grabbed and held from behind.

"No, not a lie at all. If you come with us now, you may see her for yourself." The Sethiarch tucked the pendant beneath his robes. "One last time."

Lizard-lips held out a coarse brown robe. "Quickly now. You've made us late." He watched as Simon slipped off his tunic and shrugged into the robe. "The boots too."

"I need sandals."

"You can go barefoot. Consider it a penance."

"Penance for what?"

Unremarkable once more, the Sethiarch had faded in with the other brown robes. He stepped forward. "For taking Esau's knife. Leave it in your boot—we need to go."

A flight of worn stone steps led to the basilica above. Shoved to the center of the group, Simon found himself emerging from a narrow slot in the floor. As he stepped from the shadows to the sunlit hall, a nearby bell tolled *none*, afternoon call to prayer.

Simon had forgotten how enormous the echoing nave felt and how empty and decrepit it was. The wooden rafters hung with generations of pigeon's nests. Leaves and feathers formed drifts among the columns below. Lizard-lips took the lead, marching them out through the atrium and portico, past the Castel Sant'Angelo, and across the Tiber River. Seldom without shoes, Simon felt every stone and goat turd on the road.

Evening fell as they trudged through the middle of the city. Heads bowed, muttering prayers, they looked to be five Cistercian monks to anyone they passed. Simon risked a peek at his surroundings. They walked in the shadow of crumbling ruins that once had been the center of all civilization. A ragged band of armed men rushed past—Simon wondered what could be so urgent.

Pacing single file, they crossed a shallow valley filled with market stalls. Simon followed the others up a grassy hill that rose amidst a field of broken marble like his shaved pate rising amidst his remaining curls. He tried to pick the Sethiarch from among the brown robes but failed. *He may disappear at will, but there will come a moment when he makes a mistake.* Every time Simon tried to concentrate, the image of Amala rose in his mind. Filled with wrath and half-mad with worry, he climbed toward the top.

Halfway to the crest, the party halted at a small stone structure. Simon hung back, watching the others. He didn't look at their faces but rather watched their movement. One scanned the market below. Simon concentrated on his hands, his feet, the cut of his robe. *The next opportunity...* He didn't have time to finish his thought. The man caught him watching and smiled a faceless smile before vanishing behind the other brown robes.

The touch of a knife blade between his shoulders brought Simon back from his reverie. He recognized lizard-lips' voice. "Inside, now."

The monks parted ahead of him, revealing an iron door swung away from a dark entrance. The afternoon light slanted across a marble capstone. Inscribed above the door, a crucified serpent watched him with its solitary eye. Simon was handed a lit candle and pushed forward. Ducking through the entrance, he lifted the candle, partly to better light his way and partly to dazzle any who followed.

By the hissing rattle of sandals behind him, he guessed that all had entered the chamber. His feet crunched on what felt like fragments of bone and the air bore the musty scent of rags long decayed. Simon paused a moment to look around, but the knife once more pressed against his back and the voice said, "Continue."

Row after row of niches lined a broad tunnel leading back into the hill, each bearing a desiccated corpse. A hundred paces in, Simon arrived at a large circular chamber. Around the edges and down passages on all sides, bones and skulls rose in great stacks like bread in a bakery.

"This is where the loyal members of our fellowship come when their labors on earth are finally completed." Simon found himself facing the Sethiarch. The man continued. "We stand just below the Temple of Diana, now reborn as the Capella de Santa Maria. One virgin goddess or another—it really doesn't matter. But you do appreciate the symbolism, don't you?"

"Where is Amala?"

"Ah, neither virgin nor goddess, I'm afraid. She is nearby, but that is not why you are here."

"You said I could see her."

"So I did, boy. I just didn't say when. Soon though, I hope."

Much like the crypt beneath St. Peter's, this ossuary of departed Apostles had a stairway up one wall leading to the church above. Simon imagined it led from the alter, a final journey into the underworld. He hadn't waited long before a clatter from the top announced someone descending to their level.

Slender, dressed in tunic and sleeveless open surcoat, the newcomer presented an aristocratic aura. Pausing halfway down the steps, the man held a candle up and scanned the shaven pates. "We prevail. The Knights' rabble has been destroyed, and they are routed."

The Sethiarch approached the stairs. "Have you brought me their heads?"

"My men have not returned."

"And the Weaver?"

"She will be found."

All about, candles flared, then died to a constellation of dim blue dots. Shadows gathered behind the Sethiarch. His figure seemed to grow, towering almost eye level with the man on the stairs. "I sense you hold something back. What more?"

"There is nothing more, Lord. I swear."

"You lie, Vendini. On your belly."

The man collapsed at the Sethiarch's words and tumbled from the stairs. Trembling prostrate on the floor, he kissed the stones at the Sethiarch's feet. "I don't know... I do not know."

"Tell me everything that happened today."

Addressing the floor, he said, "I hired an army of brigands, as agreed, and brought them against your rabble from the basilica. I thought..." He choked as if a noose had been tightened about his neck. "I... saw the Knights—they led my army, but I didn't see them afterward."

The Sethiarch placed one foot on the man's back. "Afterward?"

"After your mercenaries rode down from the Capella and destroyed my brigands... I thought they were dead."

"You thought?" The Sethiarch leaned forward, shifting his weight onto the man's back. "You were not in the battle then? You didn't watch them die?"

Simon couldn't see the newcomer from where he stood but heard him choke and gasp for breath. Simply glad he was no longer the center of attention, he tried to make sense of the exchange. *The Apostles using mercenaries? Against Knights? And Weavers?* He thought of Yohan and the others.

One by one, the candles flickered and relit, driving the shadows back into their recesses. Straightening, the Sethiarch resumed his normal proportions. The prostate man rose to his knees, and Simon edged closer to study the newcomer's reaction. Face tilted down, blood running from a gash in his forehead, the man looked more defiant than abashed. With a quick swipe, the Sethiarch touched a gray disk to the wound. Simon wondered if it was the same token that had been used on him.

Once more resuming his role as the Unremarkable Man, the Sethiarch said, "Vendini will stay to defend this chamber. We can leave."

The shadows, the milling brown robes, Simon considered losing himself among the bones. A dagger against his back dispelled that notion. Lizard-lips whispered, "That would be a bad idea, boy."

Shoved ahead of the others, he made his way down a darkened corridor. It ended in a pit, barely visible in the flickering candle glow. A touch of the blade moved him closer. Beneath his feet, a wooden ladder descended into black emptiness. Simon crouched, set the candle aside, and started down.

By touch, by stone slabs beneath his bare feet, Simon found the ladder's end. He shuffled one way and met a wall. A few steps the other direction and his outstretched foot met only emptiness. He kicked and waved his arms, stumbling back to the ladder. Above, a yellow glow began to descend. It grew to a pale halo along the wall, heralding the arrival of the Sethiarch. "I trust you have not yet fallen into the abyss," he said. "Remain still, and we will have light soon."

Simon pressed his back to the wall and crouched, hugged his knees. In the guttering light of a single candle, he counted two heads bobbing about the foot of the ladder. Muttered words, the candle rose into the void where it sputtered and died. Simon swam in a darkness more profound than anything he had experienced. Darker than the blackest depths of the Smocza Jama, it crushed all memory of light. He felt the cold stone beneath him and heard a muted soughing like the breath of some enormous beast. A cry like that of a stricken bird echoed from the distant walls. From the darkness, a voice...a trumpet of doom called out, "*Fiat lux!*"

Like constellations in a distant heaven, ten thousand tiny sparks glittered in the darkness above. Simon watched a panoply of colored lights creep down the far walls. Frescos and polychrome statues glowed in the intervening space, and as the lights descended, a city of platforms and bridges appeared. Balanced on an impossible brocade of slender columns and arches, no two elements stood at the same level.

Simon's gaze followed the glow. Bell-shaped, the chamber widened beneath him, a maze of wonders, each more beautiful than anything he had ever imagined. As he watched, the descending light shaded from brilliant yellows and reds near the top to deep violet hues in the misty depths. He looked up. The Sethiarch stood before him. "Welcome to the City of Radiance, our most holy sanctum."

Staggering to his feet, Simon stepped to the edge of the stone platform and gazed out at the spectacle below.

"I'll give you a moment. This is a vision seen by few." The Sethiarch waved an arm over the abyss. "Each of these terraces is dedicated to an astral being—a shrine, if you will—to the powerful entities we command."

"Why..." Simon choked in awe. "Why am I here?"

"You are the new Aeneas. On your bones we will build a new Rome. Come, your Sybil awaits, as does the shade of your father."

Before Simon could object, lizard-lips appeared, brandishing his dagger. "Only a little longer, boy. Follow your new master now."

While Simon gaped at the spectacle before him, the other two Apostles descended the ladder and trailed behind their Sethiarch down a narrow ledge that curved along the wall. It didn't take a knife at his back to make Simon follow. *Somewhere down there they have my Amala.* He thought of the dagger, so carelessly held, and followed the two cloaked Apostles. Halfway around the inner wall, their path ended at a bridge. Simon paused a moment before stepping onto the slender span. Open to the measureless glowing depths below, it wavered and vibrated beneath his feet. He was glad to reach the first platform, the roof of an ephemeral tower of polished marble.

Within the tower, stairs spiraled down its filigreed skeleton of orange travertine. Emerging into an open space, Simon found himself once more crossing a slender span to another impossible structure. *Castles in the air—the description seemed apt—but who could imagine such a thing?* He returned his thoughts to Amala and continued.

They had descended into a dark blue twilight before Simon made out their destination. A platform, an island almost, rose from a vast lake of surging black water. At first, it looked like two figures standing about a low table. Simon descended the final stairway and stepped out onto a low bridge. The scenario on the platform resolved itself as two large wooden crosses flanking a weathered stone altar.

The bridge, flat and straight, glowed pale white against the surging black waters. The altar, its four corners crowned with horns, seemed to float above the far platform. The others halted, allowing Simon to approach. Directly before him, a warrior, tall and muscled, lay spread-eagle across the altar. Naked but for his iron-gray beard, his hands and feet had been lashed to the altar's horns. The cross on his left stood empty, nothing more than a post capped by a simple timber beam.

Simon saw none of these things.

It was the pale figure beneath an orange nimbus that stopped him dead. Naked, she looked smaller than he remembered. Amala hung, cruel nails piercing her hands and feet. She didn't cry out, but her eyes pleaded with him. Amala dropped her head and whispered, "It is good."

Simon twisted about in rage, only to face the Sethiarch and his flat wooden box. "I will use this Nemesis if I must." He stepped closer. "But if I do, you will never again speak with your wife."

"Take her down. I will do anything you want, but take her down."

"You will obey my will in any event. Do you have no words for her?"

He faced the Sethiarch a moment longer, then slowly turned and approached Amala. Anger, pain, Simon had no tears. *There will be time enough for mourning in hades.* He stood beneath her feet and looked up. "How...?"

"I must, *Seimon*. It is the only way."

"It is *not* the only way. Why? Why all of this?"

"Our blood binds your father. The Apostles, he will be theirs."

For the first time, Simon turned his eyes to the second figure, bound like Prometheus to the stone alter. "My father? This is Jacob ben Reuben?"

The man opened his eyes and rolled his head. He croaked out a few unintelligible words. Wetting his lips, he tried again. "I feared for this day. I tried to keep you safe. My old friend, Jacob of Tver... If you are here, he must be dead."

Simon dropped his face and nodded. "Then you were the one who stole my wit."

"I stole your Nemesis as well. It cannot be destroyed without destroying you, so I hid you both the best I could."

Simon felt a knife blade against his back. "It is your turn, deVia. The nails will hurt, but it will be over soon."

A simple move, one of the first Luca had taught him, Simon raised an elbow and spun, knocking the knife aside. He continued his turn, bringing a fist to the man's jaw. *The knife will return.* Lizard-lips grunted and swung. Simon grabbed his wrist and spun it behind the man's back, slamming him to the deck. A twist dislocated his shoulder. Simon snatched the knife and drove it between the Apostle's ribs. Amala shrieked, "*Seimon!*"

He jumped to his feet, knife indraga mano, and faced the Sethiarch. "Kill me now before you all die."

"That was quite unnecessary." Wooden box in hand, the Sethiarch removed its lid and brandished an iron disk. The Serpens Crucis, a mirror of the one Simon bore, flashed its glittering eye at him. In that moment, he recalled it glowing hot, pressed against his chest. Choking for air, he tried to resist, to remain standing. Simon revealed the dagger and took one step, then another, pointing it at the Unremarkable Man. The City of Radiance spun and faded around him.

Regaining consciousness, he found himself flat on the floor, stripped to the skin, and lashed to the cross. The Sethiarch, now robed in black, stood over him. "For this to be truly effective, you must be alive. And for killing one of your own brothers, I want you awake when the nails go in."

Simon jerked his arms, wrenching at the bindings. One of the Apostles pried his right hand open and jammed a nail into his palm. The other struck it with an iron hammer. Simon felt it crush bone and tendons, embedding itself in the wood. He cried out at the searing pain while they seized his other hand.

A shout echoed from nearby. "Santo cazzo Madre di Cristo!"

"We have no more time." The Sethiarch himself lifted one arm of the cross. "Stand him up like he is."

Simon felt the wooden beam lurch beneath him, redoubling the pain in his hand. The world spun and suddenly he was looking Amala in the eye. "*Seimon*," she cried. "Do it now, you do it now, or we die for nothing."

"Do what..." Interrupted by the clash of steel, Simon rolled his head to one side. Yohan and Luca stood on the bridge and battled each other, sword against sword.

Frantic, he turned back to Amala. "What can I do?"

"Nothing you can do, boy." The Sethiarch stood at the altar. "You see, I have many ways of discouraging intruders. Eventually one will kill the other, then in his grief, he will kill himself. I would let you stay and watch the show, but the planets align, the moon has not yet risen, and we have wasted too much time."

The Sethiarch knelt, then stood holding a short leather scabbard. From it, he drew Simon's blade and waved it above the bound man. "Recognize this, ben Reuben? With it I will draw the blood of your son and of your grandson. It will make you more powerful than any Apostle in living memory, something I think you have sought for a long time." The Sethiarch leaned back and gazed up at the glittering specks above them. "And it will bind you forever to my will."

Jacob ben Reuben shook his head. "Impossible, I have no grandson."

"Now, don't you?" The Sethiarch pointed his sword at Amala. "Conceived on midsummer's night, it lives in her womb."

Simon screamed as the Sethiarch drove his sword into Amala's abdomen. She didn't cry out. Fixing Simon with her luminous green eyes, she said, "Please, do it now, *Seimon*."

He could barely whisper. "What, my love? What can I do?"

"Die." The Sethiarch held the bloody sword before his face. "You can die now, boy. That is all you can do."

Tied to the altar, Simon's father writhed and thrashed, rocking the heavy stone on its base. The man rolled his massive, bearded face toward Simon. "The Anathema you bear, it was mine, son. Call it now."

The enormity of what he'd seen, what he'd heard, struck Simon to his heart. The void, it came rushing at him, like a tempest overtaking a sparrow. He let it come, he welcomed it, and in that moment, felt the world shake loose from its moorings.

Waves leapt from the dark water and climbed the platform sides. The Sethiarch lost his footing and stumbled to his knees. Straightening, he raised the sword and lunged at Simon. Another sword intervened. Luca, his death-trance broken, leaped from the bridge, and jumped to the altar. Sword in hand, he deflected the Sethiarch's stroke.

Two cloaked Apostles converged on Luca, dragging him down. The Sethiarch made a second lunge, piercing Simon's thigh. He raised his sword and slashed Jacob's right cheek. "It is done!"

Simon hardly felt the wound, hardly saw the enormous shadow rising behind the triumphant Apostle. He faced Amala in her agony. She looked him in the eye and mouthed, "It is done."

As she spoke, the looming shadow writhed among the waves and opened an enormous golden eye. The serpent incarnate arched above them all. The brand on Simon's chest squirmed in response. He turned and met that baleful gaze. For an instant, the world stood frozen. Then, like a descending thunderbolt, the great serpent snatched up the Sethiarch and disappeared beneath the waves.

The world trembled as crumbling bits of marble and travertine peppered down and clattered off the bridge and platform. A large block struck where, but a moment earlier, the Sethiarch had stood. Simon's cross leaned and twisted as the entire platform tilted. The altar slid to one side, ben Reuben screaming in his bonds. It slammed into Amala's wooden cross. Simon held her in his gaze as she fell backward and disappeared, borne away beneath the stone altar.

Hearing Luca curse, Simon looked down to see Yohan and the Sicilian clinging to the platform's upturned edge. Another large fragment struck his cross and splintered its beam. He hung a moment, then his hand ripped free of the nail and he lurched forward, still bound by his legs to the upright. Luca reached over and severed the cords.

Kicking, flailing, Simon fell headlong into the surging water. Half of the heavy timber, still tied to his left arm, pinned him beneath the surface. He kicked and choked but could not raise his head. Thrashing in panic, his right hand useless, Simon tried to work free. He had given up in exhaustion when arms seized him and dragged him naked and bleeding from the water.

Simon raised his head and blinked his eyes. He was stretched across the bridge, its broken end littered with pebbles and debris. A short distance away, one corner of the platform still emerged from the waves. The world shook and beneath him, the bridge swayed and buckled. Yohan yelled something and Luca yanked him by the arm. "Cazzo mafankulo cretino, run. I do not carry you."

Not two spans away, a segment of marble wall hurtled into the water—Simon needed no more encouragement. Limping after Yohan's retreating form, he clenched his teeth and forced his injured leg to move. Luca ran up from behind, grabbed his arm, and dragged Simon the remaining distance. Beneath the shelter of a low overhang, he turned.

Yohan stood, mouth open. Luca, for once, seemed lost for speech. Before Simon's eyes, the vast City of Radiance crumbled and roared into the waves below. A fiery rainbow cascade, it thundered down, only to be quenched in the waters of darkness.

Larger pieces fell, native rock and earth. Yohan wormed his way into a tiny crevice. "Come, we cannot stay here."

Simon followed. Luca backed in slowly. "I see all paradisu destroyed, and now I am dead mafankulo."

"Not yet," Yohan said. "I think I know where this will lead us."

"It leads to hell, and still I follow."

Stunned, half-drowned, and bewildered, Simon didn't care as long as someone else made the decisions. In the darkness, he worked his way into an ever-narrowing passage. Water, displaced from the lake behind them, rose to his knees, then to his waist. He felt each concussion as blocks of stone collapsed into the water. A short distance farther, Yohan stopped. "It is over, ya. The passage ends."

Apostle

"Elysium, Paradisu, Valhalla," Luca said, "I never think she is so beautiful." He raised a cup of wine and downed it in a single swallow. "It is warm here always. Women are bedda and friendly, sè? I stay for eternity and never tire."

Yohan nibbled on a tender chunk of lamb, marinated in pomegranate juice and roasted in a clay pot. "It is a life I may never get used to."

A young woman, clad only in sheer silk, poured Luca another cup. He held it up and grinned. "You are dead, mafankulo. Get used to it."

Simon slumped to one side, head down, arms crossed. "This is not paradise, and we are not dead."

"Three days, you not eat, not drink. You are a worm in the apples of Eden."

Simon considered Luca's analogy. "That is exactly what I am, a serpent in paradise. I should leave."

"No." Yohan stood. "You need to heal, ya? I did not drag you from the doors of hell just to let you wander back in."

"You didn't drag me out. We were blasted out, like a wet fart from the devil's asshole."

"Is good, cretino. Is exactly. And how many mafankulos can brag the same, sè?"

Simon reverted to silence, looking away. The women were as empty wine jars to him—the food, road dirt. *I have lost too much to ever care again.* In the lonely nights that followed, he had wished for death, had prayed to the void. Hearing no answering rush of chaos and destruction, Simon had given up on both life and death. *Why could we not have ended our story there, beneath*

Aventine Hill?

Pulling him from his memories of broken masonry and murky black water, Yohan had tried to explain. "It was the brickwork patches along the cliff that I could not understand. Why would anyone bother to close such small openings?"

Simon had found himself sprawled across the road a few spans from Yohan. By starlight and feel, they searched the riverfront for Luca. Simon's ruined hand hung useless and throbbing at his side. His wounded leg bled into the dirt. He staggered naked and uncaring among the weeds and debris. Yohan finally located their friend, unconscious and bleeding. Another few paces and he would have been blown into the river. Between the two of them, they had dragged him back to Donetta's wineshop.

Matins rang one doleful chime as they slumped against her door. Yohan had hammered with the butt of his dagger until a tiny portal opened and the proprietor herself peeked out. A few brief words passed before Simon heard the bars lifted and the latch pulled. He practically fell inside when it opened.

Simon barely remembered the rest of that night. Donetta had given him something strong. Mixed with honey and herbs, it stunned him like a hammer blow. He had visions of riding in a carriage, of a warm bath and a soft bed. He awoke in the night to find an older woman stitching the wound on his thigh.

He shut his eyes and concentrated. *Had they been there three nights?* Donetta herself had gone with them. She had explained something of the *Templum Veneris.* Simon wasn't sure he understood, wasn't sure he wanted to. The woman who cared for him that night and the next two nights had introduced herself as Aurissa. Simon had read Weaver in her eyes and told her little.

His hand had swelled to the size of a gourd and wept dark humors down his arm. He couldn't move his fingers but still felt their touch. The woman, Aurissa, had said this was good, but little else. Looking at his ruined hand, Simon could only think of Amala, nails through both her hands and her tiny feet, smiling at him. *And she carried our son. She must have known—and still, she let this happen.*

Suppressing more sobs, he sat for a while and listened to Yohan and Luca argue about who was the better swordsman. "I kill bastardo Vendini, and I have you too, mafankulo. You do not know it, but you are dead."

"Why then, were you on your knees, ya?"

"That was after this cazzo big rock fall on us, no? Your memory is bad, old man."

"You were down long before that rock fell. I saw it, so don't lie."

Simon stood and left them to their banter. He expected it would last longer than he cared to listen. *Longer than I need to listen—longer than I need to stay around.* It made sense, his plan. *No one should have to care for a cripple, especially a crippled Apostle.* He stopped by the apartment they shared and rummaged through Luca's kit.

Wearing only his breechclout, he padded over to the bathhouse. A few women lounged in the warm water. They gave him an inviting smile. He ignored them and walked to the far end. Disrobing, Simon folded his breechclout and settled on a submerged bench. A few women strolled by and smiled down at him. He shook his head and crouched lower. They would leave eventually, and he could wait all day.

Simon must have dozed off because, when he looked up, a tall woman sat next to him. Her single long braid trailed off in the water like a knotted black snake. "Greetings, Simon. I'm glad to see you still live."

He pulled away. "Who..." Simon looked again. "Mother Aluná?" He glanced around and behind him. The bathhouse was empty. "What are you doing here?"

"I would ask you the same if I didn't know the answer. I would ask why you don't eat, why you let your bandages get wet, why—even now—you have a dagger hidden behind your arm."

Simon dropped his head. "You wouldn't have to ask if you knew how I feel."

"I cannot possibly know how you feel. You lost a father, a wife, and a son in one night."

"And I am a cripple, of no use to anyone, but why do you care?" He turned and pointed Luca's dagger at her. "You knew, didn't you? Baba Jezinka as much as said so. You sent Amala here to die."

"Kill me now if you must. Or kill yourself as you had planned. I recommend a slash to the inside of your thigh—it is quick and almost painless. But first, believe me when I say, she was not sent to die. Amala chose to die when she could see no other way."

Simon shook his head. "It is the same. They are all dead, and it is Weavers and their schemes that killed them."

"And many more will die, boy. It is the schemes of Knights and Weavers, of Popes and Apostles, of kings and princes in lands you cannot imagine that will kill them." She grabbed him by the arm. "If you are to die now, then Amala's sacrifice will have been for nothing. Is that what you want?"

Weavers talked. He had figured that out. Simon glared at her. "So you are here, and I am here—what is it *you* want?"

Aluná released his arm and settled back. "I want you to eat, to drink some wine, to sleep. Maybe you can help these poor women relieve some tension while you are here."

"Why?"

"Because, in two weeks, I will come and give you a vial of poison that brings a painless death. Use it if you must. Better that than you foul this bath with your blood."

Knowing he was beaten, Simon settled back in the warm water. It meant he would return to the Apostles and finish his training. There would be confusion, new faces—he would have to take another name. It wouldn't be easy, but he had learned something of misdirection and obfuscation.

She waited for his answer.

"Damn you, Weaver. Damn you all."

—End—

If you enjoyed this story, please leave me a review. Reviews and ratings help others find stories they love and help me keep the Tapestry Series alive. Check my website: www.cbmatson.com for a link that will take you directly to the review page. Upcoming books in this series:

ROGUE WIND – *Tapestry Codex II*

IRON TALISMAN – *Tapestry Codex III*

Appendices

In-Story Words

The languages of the twelfth century would not be recognizable by native speakers today. In this story, current words in Slavic, Sicilian, Italian, Latin, and Greek have been used to approximate the protagonists' experience when they encounter foreign terms. My apologies to Sicilianos past and present if I have misused certain terminology. The native speakers I once knew have all passed away, and current texts are not terribly helpful with idiomatic phrases.

Rus/Pol/Slav

These words are lumped together because they have common roots and are almost interchangeable between the languages.

- **Prostoi** – Rus: Simpleton
- **Smok** – Polish: Dragon (of Wawel Hill)
- **Smocza Jama** – Polish: Dragon's Den
- **Ushk** – Slavic: River boat
- **Ushkuinik** – Slavic: River pirate

Sicilian/Italian

In the twelfth century, the Kingdom of Sicily included almost a third of the Italian Peninsula. Sicilian of that period included Greek, Arabic, Libyan, Norman, and Iberian roots, as well as Latin and Italian words. I have grouped them together because present-day Sicily speaks mostly Italian (not all, to be sure). Some colorful holdouts include "Cazzo," and "Sè" instead of "Si."

- **Anziano** – Elder
- **Babbu** – Stupid
- **Bastardo** – Bastard
- **Bedda** – Beautiful
- **Capisci** – Understand (imperative)
- **Capos de merda** – Shit heads
- **Castello** – Castle
- **Cazzo** – Fuck/fucking
- **Collegantia** – Venetian business partnership
- **Cretino** – Idiot
- **D'accordo** – Agreed/I agree
- **Diavulu** – Devil
- **Famiglia** – Family
- **Fatturaone** – Warlock
- **Indraga mano** – Hidden hand knife fighting technique
- **Liccu** – Glutton
- **Locanda** – Inn/guest house
- **Màgaru** – Witch
- **Maldicaru** – Witchcraft (portmanteau word)
- **Mafankulo** – Motherfucker
- **Meràculu** – Miracle/wonderful
- **Merda** – Shit
- **Maschio** – Manhood
- **Minchia** – Cock/penis
- **Monsignore** – My lord

- **Palazzo** – Palace
- **Paradisu** – Paradise
- **Paranza corta** – Sicilian knife fighting
- **Pazzu** – Insane
- **Piazza** – Plaza
- **Pi favuri** – Please
- **Proposta** – Proposal
- **Reghi** – King
- **Santo cazzo Madre di Cristo** – Holy fucking Mother of Christ
- **Sc'chiatta** – Sicilian meat pie
- **Sè** – Yes
- **Terrazza** – Patio

Latin

The hypothetical "lingua franca" of the Tapestry stories is trade-Latin or sometimes "vulgate" or common Latin. Therefore, few actual Latin words appear in the dialog. When they do, it is mostly for emphasis.

- **Apostoli Lucis** – Apostles of Light
- **Cedo** – I yield
- **Oborior** – Appear (imperative)
- **Serpens Crucis** – Crucified serpent
- **Stella Maris** – Star of Mary, Polaris
- **Vade in pace** – Go in peace

Other Words

A few other words are scattered throughout the story that are not tied to one of the in-story languages or, like "Sethiarch," are devised for the occasion.

- **Álfar** – The old people, Amala's people
- **Álfarish** – Language of the Álfar

- **Fólkvangr** – Heavenly fields of Norse mythology
- **Goëtia** – Conjuration
- **Goëtic** – Conjurer
- **Muka** – Flour (Álfarish)
- **Pankration** – Hand-to-hand combat
- **Sethiarch** – Master of a Apostoli Lucis lodge
- **Wærloga** – Literally, oath breaker, apostate, OE source for *warlock.*

Clothing

Our knowledge of early medieval clothing is far more speculative than most scholars of the period are willing to admit. As cloth was hand-woven from available fiber, a wide variety of styles would have been in use. A few of the clothing items mentioned in the story are described here. However, they too are speculative.

- **Bag Hat** – Ring of cloth (burlet) with a shallow bag worn over the head and draped to one side.
- **Breechclout** - A garment belted at the waist and covering the groin area. Generally worn beneath tunic and leggings.
- **Chamise** – Woman's full-length undergarment; a shift.
- **Cotte (M)** – Loose men's garment. It has a cut in front and at the back, long sleeves, the length reaching half-calf, without the lining.
- **Cotte (F)** – Loose medieval dress with sleeves used as a woman's undergarment
- **Gipser** – A purse or bag worn on a girdle.
- **Hose** – Separate leggings laced at the gore. Men's were full length, women's calf length.
- **Kirtle** – A sleeved tunic, worn under an outer garment or alone.
- **Scrip** – Leather satchel
- **Surcot** – The outermost garment of men and women, made in two versions: the sleeveless open surcot or the sleeved closed surcot.
- **Tunic** - A belted, slip-on overshirt reaching near or past the knees, with

or without sleeves.

Church Hours

Hours of the medieval church were mostly subjective, corresponding to the liturgical day rather than solar time. Modern hours shown in parentheses are only approximations.

- **Matins** (2 a.m.) – Perhaps composed of two or three nocturns (Vigil)
- **Lauds** (5 a.m.) – At dawn, earlier in summer, later in winter (Dawn Prayer)
- **Prime** (6 a.m.) – First hour (Early Morning Prayer)
- **Terce** (9 a.m.) – Third hour (Mid-Morning Prayer)
- **Sext** (12 noon) – Sixth hour (Midday Prayer)
- **None** (3 p.m.) – Ninth hour (Mid-Afternoon Prayer)
- **Vespers** (6 p.m.) – Lighting of the lamps (Evening Prayer)
- **Compline** (7 p.m.) – Before retiring (Night Prayer)

Currency

A serious problem in the medieval era was a lack of reliable and exchangeable currency. Many of the city-states struck their own coins of precious metal, but most of them were debased or short-weighted. In the end, the weight of the coin mattered more than its face value.

- **Trachi** – Small Slavic copper coin (plural)
- **Sestertii** – Roman copper coin (plural)
- **Genovino** – CE 1139 to 1339 Gold 3.53 g,
- **Bezant** – CE 1099 to 1291 Gold 2.84 g (0.1oz)
- **Hryvna** – 11th c. to 15th c. Gold (Kievan) 204 g (.44lb) (also silver)
- **4,000 gold bezants** = 11,360 grams = 55.6 gold hryvna = 24.5 lb

Protagonist Characters

Simon Halfsword – Simon's given name was Marco deVia (b. 1170). His father, Jacob ben Reuben was a Spanish Jew who had gained notoriety by publishing several books that challenged the authenticity of the New Testament. Simon's unwed mother was Beatrice, the youngest daughter of an influential Guelph family from Amalfi. Young Beatrice was forced to surrender her child to an orphanage and join a convent. Although he was given the name Marco by his mother, deVia was tagged on in reference to his illegitimate birth. Simon was never baptized, something he kept as a secret source of pride. He wore many names while growing up, finally settling on Simon from the legendary Simon Magus, and Polevoi, a Slavic shape-shifting spirit. Simon's primary driver is his need to know who he is. He is also driven by his nearly bottomless thirst for knowledge. His strength comes from his willingness to change and adapt to almost any situation. His quest for knowledge often has unexpected consequences. Simon thinks he is master of the talismans and conjurations he uses. However, he slowly becomes overwhelmed by them.

Yohan Kozlov – Member of the Knights of Palermo cohort that rescues Simon, later to become their leader. Yohan seems to be northern European. He was once a river pirate, ushkuinik, marauding from the Baltic to the Mediterranean. While still a river pirate, Yohan was in a relationship with Ruslana, a Weaver. When he joined the Knights of Palermo, they went separate ways. Yohan still has feelings for Ruslana, but carries a lot of anger as well. Yohan's primary driver is his loyalty to the Knights of Palermo and his sense of duty to the men he leads. His strength is his courage and his ingenuity. His weakness is his sense of inadequacy and guilt. Yohan thinks the Knights can maintain peace in the world. However, forces of war and chaos are gathering that will overwhelm any small stabilizing influence they might have.

Antagonist Characters

- **Christián Vendini** – One of the four brothers in the famiglia, Christián takes an unhealthy interest in the Knights' transactions in Rome.
- **Esau deFoligno** – Member of the Apostoli Lucis cell that captures Simon. Esau is a recurring character in subsequent books.
- **Lizard Lips** – Leader of the Apostoli Lucis cell that captures Simon. Lizard-lips is Simon's name for the man.
- **Sethiarch** – Leader of the Apostoli Lucis, the Sethiarch, Umberto Tenebrio, is the Unremarkable Man who can infiltrate almost any group without drawing attention.

Supporting Characters

- **Aluná** – A Weaver and local leader, she maintains their network of Travelers and Dwellers. Aluná originally came from the Pacific Islands, crossing most of the known world in her life. Her age is hard to determine, but she is far older than she looks. One secret that Aluná carries is that she is a Cutter, that is, one of the very few Weaver assassins.
- **Amala** – Young woman of the woods, also a Weaver. From an early age, she was sent to follow Simon. She eventually became his wife. Her people are the Álfar, the perhaps the original indigenous inhabitants of Europe. She is wood-crafty and has a way with animals, but limited command of western languages, particularly the vulgate Latin. Named for the goddess Amaltheia.
- **Aurella** – Weaver proprietor of Women's "spa" in Ostia.
- **Baba Jezinka** – Amala's grandmother, she is also Álfar and a Weaver. Jezinka is technically a Dweller, but she has a disconcerting habit of moving frequently and without notice. In many cultures, she would be considered a witch.
- **Carla** – Andalusian, Carla fled the Moorish occupation of Iberia and its strict code for women. She joined Cernak's Knights at an early age and earned her place with them as a fierce fighter and rugged campaigner.

- **Cernak** – Leader of the Knights of Palermo cohort that rescued Simon. Cernak is a pagan from the area around what is now Denmark.
- **Donetta** – Wine shop proprietor and Weaver in Rome.
- **Febris** – Goddess of disease and decay
- **Jacob ben Reuben** – Historically, a Sephardic Spanish Jew who had gained notoriety by publishing several books that challenged the authenticity of the New Testament. In this story, he is Simon's natural father who had once been a Templar and an Apostle until he betrayed both of the groups.
- **Luca** – Sicilian natural son of a Catholic Priest and a Libyan woman. He grew up in the palace of his grandfather, a powerful Sicilian don. Luca ran away from his family to become a thief and brigand. Later, he joined a mercenary legion serving the republics of Pisa and Venice. After the disaster of Cairo and the betrayal of Constantinople, Luca gave up freebooting and joined the Knights of Palermo.
- **Master Jacob** – Jacob Tverskayaski, Jacob of Tver. Mentor character who rescued Simon from the Apostles and looked after him.
- **Ramon** – Corsican by birth, he was the youngest son of a wealthy family. Ramon studied for the priesthood but was expelled when he fathered a child by a neighbor's wife. Fleeing Corsica, he spent time on a merchant ship where he met Luca returning from Cairo. The two joined the Knights of Palermo together.
- **Ruslana Ursupova** – A Weaver from central Europe, once Yohan's lover. Blond hair, medium build. She appears in her mid 30s but may be older. Ruslana has a sharp tongue and a short temper, but she is clever and resourceful.
- **Paolu Niru** – Sicilian galley captain/owner operating out of Genoa that was contracted by Yohan to take his cohort to Palermo.
- **Perun** – Horse, once belonging to Cernak, later Simon.
- **Stephan** – Stephan seems to be from central Europe, perhaps one of the German states. He is older than the others and would be their leader, but prefers to play a supporting role. Stephan is careful and meticulous. In another life he would have been an accountant.
- **Sebastian, Paulo, Adolfo, and Christián Vendini** – A trading famiglia in

Venice.

Key elements

- **Anathema** – A forbidden talismanic rite where a curse of natural disasters is laid on someone.
- **Apostoli Lucis (Apostles of the Light)** – Ostensibly to gather and preserve knowledge in an era of growing clerical censorship, the Apostles has degenerated into a power-hungry group of conjurers and sorcerers.
- **Compulsion** – A forbidden talismanic rite where a person is forced to obey the commands of another against their will.
- **Knights of Palermo** – A fellowship of mixed cultures, nominally western Christian, but including Moslems, Jews, and pagans. They side with Holy Roman Emperor in his conflict with the papacy but generally work to promote peace and order throughout Europe. Known to themselves as the *Eprotrofia Dikaiosýnis*, the Fellowship of Justice.
- **Nemesis** – A forbidden talismanic rite where in a person can be threatened with death if they do not obey certain conditions.
- **Pankration** – Ancient Greek fighting method combining boxing and wrestling, similar to today's Mixed Martial Arts.
- **Paranza Corta** – Sicilian knife fighting technique. It features the indraga mano, the hidden hand stance to mislead the opponent.
- **Serpens Crucis** – The crucified serpent, symbol of hermeticism, knowledge, and talismanic magic. It is Simon's "spirit animal" in more ways than he would wish.
- **Weavers** – The Weavers are an ancient order of women who trade in information in such a way as to further their own designs. In general, the Weavers influence is beneficial and stabilizing to peoples and nations. They work behind the scenes and wield enormous power. There are three primary groups within the Weavers. They are the Travelers who carry information, the Dwellers who maintain safe havens and assist the Travelers, and the highly secretive Cutters who engage in assassination and other direct acts.